Daughters of the Dust

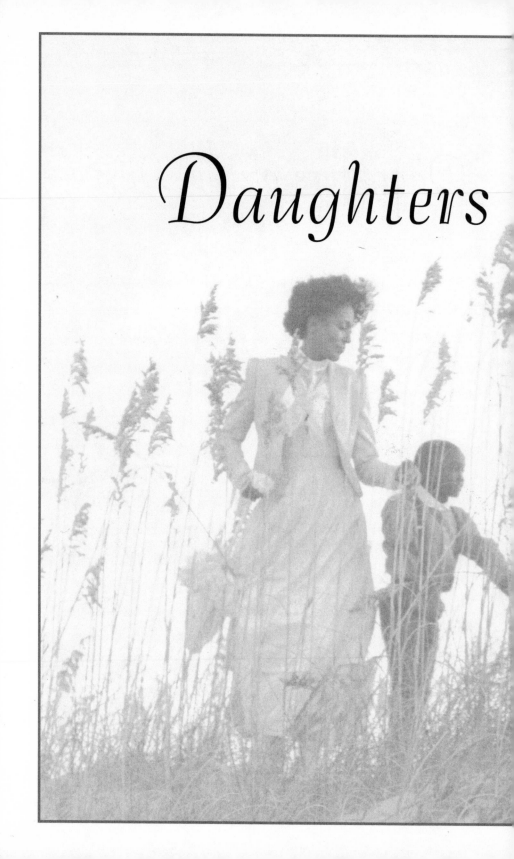

Daughters

of the Dust

JULIE DASH

A DUTTON BOOK

DUTTON
Published by the Penguin Group
Penguin Putnam Inc., 375 Hudson Street, New York, New York 10014, U.S.A.
Penguin Books Ltd, 27 Wrights Lane, London W8 5TZ, England
Penguin Books Australia Ltd, Ringwood, Victoria, Australia
Penguin Books Canada Ltd, 10 Alcorn Avenue, Toronto, Ontario, Canada M4V 3B2
Penguin Books (N.Z.) Ltd, 182–190 Wairau Road, Auckland 10, New Zealand

Penguin Books Ltd, Registered Offices: Harmondsworth, Middlesex, England

First published by Dutton, an imprint of Dutton Signet,
a member of Penguin Putnam Inc.

First Printing, October, 1997
1   3   5   7   9   10   8   6   4   2

LIBRARY OF CONGRESS CATALOGING IN PUBLICATION DATA:
Dash, Julie.
   Daughters of the dust / by Julie Dash.
     p. cm.
   ISBN 0-525-94109-6 (acid-free paper)
     1. Afro-American families—South Carolina—Fiction.
   2. Afro-Americans—South Carolina–History—Fiction.
   I. Title.
   PS3554.A823D3 1997
   813'.54—dc21   97-23597
                                        CIP

Printed in the United States of America
Set in New Baskerville
Designed by Eve L. Kirch

PUBLISHER'S NOTE

This is a work of fiction. Names, characters, places, and incidents either are the products of the author's imagination or are used fictitiously, and any resemblance to actual persons, living or dead, events, or locales is entirely coincidental.

For women of the African Diaspora who dare to dream aloud, and especially those not afraid to see their own reflections inside those dreams.

Acknowledgements

My deepest appreciation goes to Rhonda Scott, a visionary, homegirl, and spirit chaser. Special thanks to Deirdre Mullane, Kim Witherspoon, Vertamae Grosvenor, Angela Smith, and my daughter N'zinga; their support and guidance helped propel all this collective memory into a reality that goes far beyond its original celluloid boundaries.

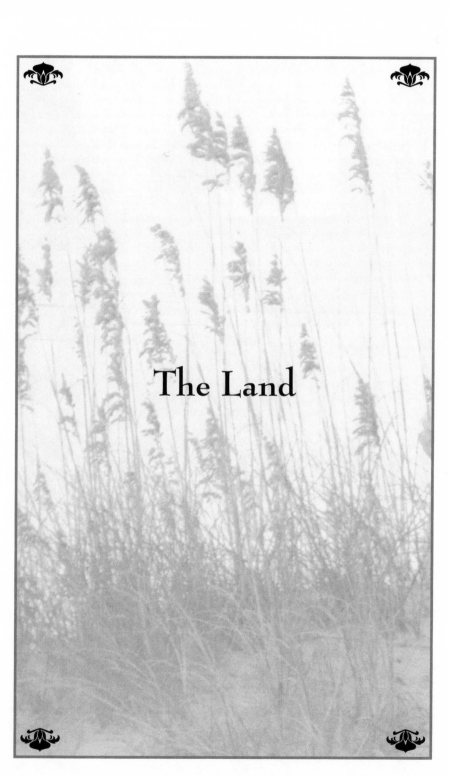

The Land

They appeared along the southeastern coast, a group of shallow islands that rose from the receding waters of the Ice Age. Fragile bits of land anchored by tenacious grasses and pebbles, the islands moved constantly with the roil of the tides and the violent storms that buffeted the coast. Over time the islands began to form themselves as the plants and shrubs took hold. They would continue moving to the west, changing their shape, always searching for a place of permanence.

Dotted with swamps, marshes, and bogs and tempered by the sea breezes and the hot, humid air, the islands were rich with flora and wildlife. Corn, pumpkins, and beans grew in profusion in the peculiar mixture of sand, silt, clay, and natural matter. Wild grapes hung from the boughs of the great oaks, and walnuts and pecans rained down when the warm breezes blew through. Huge herds of white-tailed deer roamed the coastal lands while black bear stalked the swamplands and wild turkeys sounded their warnings from the lush underbrush. The waters, both fresh and salt, abounded with mullet, brim, rock shrimp, spots, oysters, and crab.

Then, as always, following the trail of wildlife came the ancient people. At first they fled the raids of the North; then they sought the warmer climes and the gentler breezes. When they came upon this land of abundance, they gave praise and offered tribute to Mother Earth for her kindness and generosity. Settling along the shores, they called their new home "Chicora."

It was the first of many names that this land would have. Each tribe that settled the land would give the islands other names; San Miguel,

Guadalupe, Gaule, Cheraw, Edisto, John's, St. Helena, Daufuskie, Kiawah, Wadmalaw. By the time the African captives arrived, the land would be known as the Sea Islands.

It would not be the land of refuge for these people, for they had not come willingly. Herded onto the ships that would transport them across the Atlantic Ocean, the peoples of West Africa stolen from Gambia, Angola, Benin, Sierra Leone, Niger, and the Gold Coast would arrive in Charleston, South Carolina, destined for the harsh work on plantations throughout the South. For some the trip would be even longer to the far reaches of Texas; for others it would be a short trip down the coast to the rice and cotton plantations of the Sea Islands.

For most, it would be the last trip of their lives. They would spend their entire lives on the islands, laboring from day clean to day done, clearing the land, dredging the swamps, building the houses, planting the seed, and harvesting the crops. They would rarely see their white masters, who had long since quit to the mainland, escaping the heavy, humid air, the sulphurous swamps, the poisonous snakes, and the black swarms of mosquitoes that brought the plague of malaria. It would be a severe life, but left to their own means they would survive and thrive, raising their families, praying to their gods, holding sacred the ways of the lands from which they had come. They would trade, share, and learn from the ancient people who still walked the islands. And from this blending of old and new came the unique culture and tongue known as Gullah or Geechee.

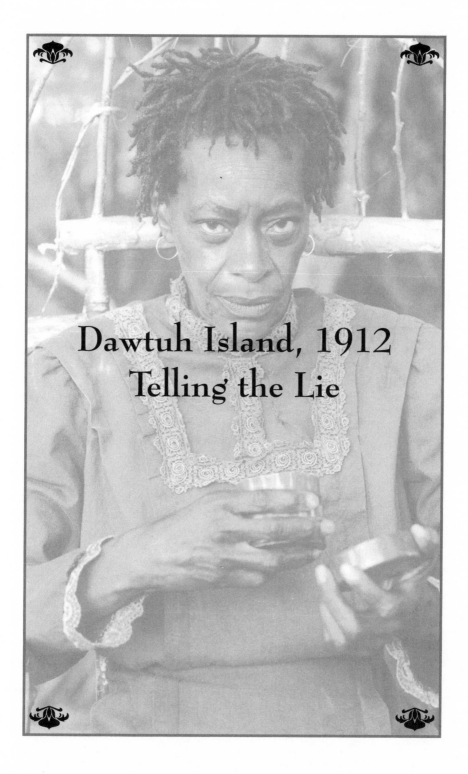

Dawtuh Island, 1912
Telling the Lie

She heard them approach as she sat in the late afternoon cool on her low porch. Their whispers drifted across the dunes through the palmetto fronds, mingling with the sounds of the squirrels chattering and the wren putting her young down for the night. Her eyes closed as she listened to the footsteps padding along the rough trail leading to her yard.

There were four of them, all of them young, for their voices did not strain as they climbed over the huge oak blown down in the big storm last year. One walked with the easy stride of those who knew where they were headed. It was she who carried the baby that chirped and burbled with each step. The other girl struggled to keep up, afraid to be left behind in a place she did not know. The fourth took his time, pausing to tear a low branch from a dogwood tree, whipping the bushes as he made his way along the path. As the sea breeze gently buffed their faces, they broke into the clearing at the edge of the yard. The first one slid the child off her hip and peered into the shadows on the porch. The second one peeped over her shoulder. "This is a lonesome house. Dey dont be dere."

"Her dere."

The boy stepped forward and stared at the house. A pitch-black tom disappeared around the side. "Her somewhere round. Dere she old ugly cat! Her dont go nowhere without dat cat!"

"Where she be then?"

The first girl nodded toward the porch. "She be dere . . . sittin in dat chair by de shutter."

Watching them through half-closed eyes, the old woman stirred as if settling into a comfortable sleep. The second girl jumped as Miz Emma Julia unfolded in the shadows. The boy shook the branch at her. "Laying up dere like some ol black snake just waiting to git ya!"

The girl retreated. "She sleep! You better mind—you know it. It bad luck to wake a old lady when she sleepin!"

The older girl looked at her with a knowing smile and, taking the hand of the baby, strolled across the sandy yard to the porch. The second girl hung back as the boy slid past her with a show of bravado.

"Who dat slippin up on me like a snake in de grass?"

"It be me, Miz Emma Julia, Elizabeth."

"Elizabeth who? Tell me! Who be you people?"

"Elizabeth Peazant, firstborn of Eli and Eula Peazant. You know my family. You was good friends with my Nana."

Miz Emma Julia nodded as she spoke. The girl stood still as Miz Emma Julia noted the deep indigo tones of her skin, the steadiness in her eyes, and the small, wiry frame that marked her as a Peazant. "I know you. You the image of your fadder and all dose who come before you. Dem Peazants spit you out!"

Elizabeth burrowed her toe in the white sand and smiled shyly at Miz Emma Julia. Miz Emma Julia peered around Elizabeth, frowning at the younger girl perched nervously in the high grass at the edge of the yard. The boy looked around the yard, dodging her glance.

"What baby you brung wit you to my place?"

"He be my lil brother Ben."

As Elizabeth explained, Ben pulled free and clambered onto the porch. He toddled to Miz Emma Julia, grabbing the leg of the chair as he frowned up into her aged face.

"Your mama, her jus like the sweet soil I plant my beans and okra in. Everytime I hear bout she, she bringing anudder child into dis world. How many dat now?"

"Three . . ."

"Lord, her aint hardly had time to bring in a crop tween children! How she be gettin on?"

"Her real tired. Dr. Boyd say her need she rest."

"I say! You tell your mama leave dat doctor lone an come see Miz Emma Julia! I give she somptin what let dat body rest. Dem buckra doctors dont take no care with we!"

"Yes, maam."

"Hmmph! Who dat hang back dere like her ready to fly?"

"Her my new cousin, come to see us from Savannah."

"New cousin?"

"Yes, maam. She mama married my daddy cousin, Boot. Him a travel man on de railroad. . . ."

"I know Boot, the color of de sweetest blackberry of de summer! Know how to make a woman shout like her done caught the spirit an cry like tomorrow never come! . . . You gonna stand out dere in dat high grass with dem snakes, girl, or you come in de yard?"

With a squeal, the younger girl darted into the yard and hid behind Elizabeth.

"What dey call you?"

"Clarice."

"What you basket name?"

Clarice looked at Elizabeth, not understanding. Elizabeth explained, "You basket name is the other name they give you when you a baby. Like Ben, we call him 'Babro.' My basket name be 'Lil Bet.' "

"I dont have none," Clarice said.

The older boy shifted restlessly, having studied the yard and seen nothing to tempt him. Miz Emma Julia leaned forward and glared at him. "I know you! You one of dem boys took my Jacob and strung he in dat tree!"

The boy fell back in surprise and fear. "Dat want me! I . . . I!"

"Dont be tellin me dat, boy! I seen you plain as day, runnin with dem others when I come to get my Jacob!"

"Unh-huh! Dat want me!"

She leaned over into the open doorway and called, "Jacob! Come on out here, Jacob!"

The children stared into the dark doorway as two yellow eyes appeared and glided silently to the porch. The large tom stepped onto the porch, stretched, his fur rippling down his spine to his tail, and then hopped onto Miz Emma Julia's lap. Ben reached for him eagerly as Jacob, ignoring him, made a comfortable bed on her thin thighs.

"Jacob, you see anybody out dere bodder you?"

The children held their breath as Jacob slowly turned his head and looked at each one. Elizabeth and Clarice breathed a deep sigh of relief as Jacob dismissively made quick work of them. The boy's eyes widened as Jacob's locked onto him. "It want me! I was just watching!"

Miz Emma Julia chuckled as Jacob, with a yawn, hopped off her lap and disappeared into the house. Ben toddled after him, only to stop at the open doorway and peer into the darkness.

"What you name, boy?"

"Pap!"

"You know what Jacob say to you?"

"Him aint say nuttin. . . ."

She hissed, "Him say next time him come for you in de night!" She smiled as Pap stepped back in alarm. With a sudden laugh, the baby scampered off the porch and threw himself against his sister's legs.

Miz Emma Julia studied the two girls. Elizabeth, thin, dark, and wiry, the image of her father, withstood her gaze with patience. She stroked Ben's head as he babbled and pointed to the darkness that lay beyond the doorway. Clarice kept her head bowed, hiding the topaz eyes that were her treasure. She shifted from foot to foot, quivering as the wood owl sounded his presence.

"So what yall doin back here dis time of de day?"

Elizabeth spoke up quickly. "We come to see if you tell us de lie."

"Why you come to me? You got plenty people tell you de lies!"

"But, Miz Emma Julia, you know you can win any lyin contest. Nobody tell lies as good as you. I been tell Clarice bout dem good lies you tell, an her want to hear for sheself."

Clarice glanced up swiftly and nodded her head. Miz Emma Julia was tickled. The child was so scared she was about to fly away, but still she want to hear the lie. "I dont have a mind to mess wit dat foolishness. I got plenty to do before I rest my head day over."

"Us kin help," Elizabeth declared. Clarice nodded while Pap rolled his eyes at what he thought to be an uneven swap.

"I aint know. I plenty particular bout de ways things be done."

"Us do it right." Elizabeth looked at Clarice and Pap. "You tell we what you want we to do."

Miz Emma Julia reached into her pocket and pulled out her pipe. She drew on it slowly as she thought of all the things she wanted done. "Well, de clothes in de back need to be took in." Elizabeth scooped Ben up and started toward the backyard. Clarice followed her. "It dont take but one to do that." Clarice looked at Elizabeth, who gave her a nod of encouragement while continuing toward the back. "And mind you fold dem so dey not wrinkle. . . . You, new cousin! . . . You know how to snap beans?"

"Yes, maam."

Miz Emma Julia got up slowly. "You wait right here. I got a whole mess a snap beans." She shuffled through the doorway, disappearing into the darkness. Pap slid up beside Clarice, whispering in her ear, "I tole she been de hag!"

"Shh-hh!"

"Mama say she 'fix' people and it las all dey life!"

Miz Emma Julia stepped onto the porch with a half-filled croaker-sack and an old wooden bucket. She dropped them on the edge of the porch and settled back into her chair. Clarice sidled to the porch and dragged the sack and bucket to the far end, away from the doorway.

Pap watched Miz Emma Julia expectantly. When she didn't speak to him for several moments, he turned his attention to a pile of bottles he'd glimpsed on the side of the house. As he reached over to pick up an emerald-green bottle, she said, "De yard could use de rake." With a moan, he snatched the rake from where it lay in the sand and began combing the sandy yard with short, angry strokes.

She leaned back in the chair and listened to the sounds and rhythms of the children working; the crisp snap of the beans, the harsh stab of the rake, and Elizabeth's low humming as she took down the clothes. Her ears searched for the rhythm she knew as sure as she breathed, the wind sweeping across the water as the waves brushed the shore. She drew it into her body, slowing her heart and taking long, deep breaths. As the rhythm took over, she sank deeper into the chair and began to sleep.

She awoke to four pairs of eyes staring at her and Jacob curled in her lap. The sun melted over the piney woods as the sea breeze whipped the moss that hung low from the branches. "Yall finished everything I tell you to do?"

"Yes, maam!" the three replied in unison.

The baby tightened his arms around his sister's neck, sleepily turning his face into her shoulder. Miz Emma Julia sat up and stared at the pile of neatly folded clothes and the wooden bucket filled with beans. She waved them aside and inspected the yard. She hid a smile. As all man-children cannot help but do, Pap had turned it into a game. The yard was carpeted with deep swirling patterns of sand, images that connected and disconnected, disappearing into the high grass that marked the beginning of the woods.

"So yall ready for de lie?"

"Us ready!"

Pap, with a quick look at Clarice, slyly suggested, "Tell us de lie about de devil an how he stole de girl in the woods!" Clarice shivered in the evening breeze. Elizabeth put her arm around her and pulled her closer.

"It get right chilly out here. You, boy, Pap, go in my parlor room and get de kiver offen de trunk!"

"Me! You want me go in dere?"

"De trunk right by de door. Go on an dont be mess with nuttin!"

Pap slowly approached the doorway. He paused and looked back at them, his eyes wide.

"Get on in dere, Pap!" Miz Emma Julia snapped. "Dont nuttin want you, bad as you is!" she grumbled. Pap plunged into the room and reappeared almost instantly, clutching the quilts to his chest. He pushed the quilts at her and withdrew to Elizabeth's side.

She handed the worn, colorful quilts to Elizabeth. The children wrapped themselves and settled on the porch at her feet. She took out her pouch and shook a bit of tobacco into the bowl of her pipe, tamped it, and lit it. As she drew deeply and exhaled over the children, the pungent smoke dispersed the first few mosquitoes that had come for the ready feast.

"Dis lie begin at de beginning of dis world fore we know it. It begin fore de Bible."

Pap, shocked, piped up, "Want nuttin fore de Bible!"

"What I tell you?"

"Want nuttin fore the Bible! Preacher Wilson tole me dat!" Pap insisted.

"Boy, hush up! Dis aint got nuttin to do against de Bible!" Elizabeth scolded him. Pap started to fuss back at her, but remembering all the work he had done in the yard, decided to hold his peace.

"Like I say . . . dis before de Bible. Dis was de time when dere were nuttin but land as far as you could see."

"Where was de big water?"

"What I say, boy? Dere was no river, no creek, no big water, nuttin but de land all over de whole world. Yall hear what I say?"

Elizabeth spoke up. "Us hear you!"

"Only time water come is wit de rain, an den you got to catch it real fast. You got dat?"

"Yes, maam," Elizabeth agreed.

Miz Emma Julia turned to Clarice and Pap. "Yall wit me on de lie? I aint heah yall wit me!"

Elizabeth, urging them to join her, clapped her hands and chanted, "Us wit you! Us wit you!"

Clarice smiled shyly and clapped her hands. "We wit you!" Pap scowled and folded his arms.

"Dere was one old lady live way off in de woods by sheself. She aint hab no people, no husband, no chilren. Her all by sheself."

"Like you!" Pap interjected.

Miz Emma Julia tossed him a dark look and continued. "Her was so lonesome. Her work so hard, just try to get a bit to eat. One day, her discourage an her sit down, begin to holler, 'I so lonely! I so hungry! I so tired! It all I can do to rise from my bed!' An as it happen de elephants was passing, an de big elephant heard she an say, 'Why you cry like dat?' Her say, 'Cause I lonely. Dont have nobody to care bout and nobody to care for!'

"De elephant say, 'What you need is kin. Kin keep you from bein lonely.' 'How I gonna get kin? I aint got no husband. I aint got no chilren. Where I gonna get kin?' De elephant thought about it, an den him went back to de other elephants an dey studied on it, and him come back and him say, 'We hear dat if you take de five nuts from de hickory tree an put dem in a ball of clay and throw dem in de fire and let dem stay for three days, kin will come to you.' The old woman look at he just so and say, 'De hickory tree all de way on de other side. I old. I caint walk dat far.' De elephant say, 'If you want kin, you walk it.' Him start to catch up with he kin, but him come back. Him say, 'One thing to remember, kin is fine, but kin can be trouble.' Den him run off to catch up. . . . Now what de elephant say?"

Clarice whispered, "He say, 'kin is fine, but kin can be trouble.' "

"Dat right." Miz Emma Julia paused to tap her pipe against the side of her chair. She stared into the evening gloom.

"What her do den?"

"Well, she sit dere. Her sit dere coupla days cause de hickory tree was a long ways. But her feel sad, an her make de trip! An a hard trip it be! But her find de hickory tree an gather de nuts to bring dem back. Her made a fire an put dem in de clay ball an let dem cook. Her so tired, her fell asleep an dint wake for three days. When her wake, her pull de balls out of de fire an wait for de kin to come. Her wait two, three days. Nuttin happen. No kin. No nuttin. Her plenty mad!"

Pap declared, "Dat elephant sure fooled she!"

Miz Emma Julia shifted her head wrap forward and scratched her kitchen. "You tink so?"

"Aint no kin come!"

"Mmm . . . Well, her tink de same. Her start up a fuss bout de elephant he fool she. Her work sheself into a regular fit. Her pick up de clay ball an throw it at a tree, an guess what happen?"

"What happen?"

"It broke into so many pieces, and de five hickory nuts, dey fly all over de place. One of dem roll to she feet. Her raise she foot to smash it, an her hear de singing. Her pick up de nut an open it." Miss Emma Julia got up stiffly and walked over to the edge of the porch and brought the lamp that hung from the roof.

Elizabeth asked quietly, "Where de singing come from?"

Miz Emma Julia straightened the wick and shook the base to see how much oil was left. "De nut."

"What in de nut?" demanded Pap.

Miz Emma Julia lit the wick and watched their faces as the light flared. "A girl-child."

"A girl?" all three murmured. Elizabeth and Clarice exchanged pleased looks.

"A girl, sing like you never heard. De ol woman lay dat nut down real careful an run and pick up the others, an you know what?"

"De kin was in de other nuts." Elizabeth spoke with confidence.

"Dat right. Her run here and dere, an pretty soon her hab so much kin she aint know what to do. An dey was some fine kin, too! De boys, dere was one her called Ogun, an him was strapping an fit! De other boy, her call Elegba, an him was as full of mischief as a old raccoon."

"How come her name dem dat . . . Ogu . . . Legba?" pressed Pap.

"Her name dem after de gods . . . Ogun an Elegba."

The children carefully pronounced the names. Clarice, her eyes glittering in the light, asked eagerly, "What about de girls?"

"First dere was Oya, de one who was singing. Den dere was Yemoja, de one with de fractious temperament."

"Dere was five nuts. What happened to de other one?" Elizabeth pointed out.

"I get to dat. Her looked all over for the last nut, an jus when her was bout to give up, her found it . . . an inside was de most beautiful girl was ever seen."

"What her name?" breathed Clarice.

"Her called Osun. An de old lady was so happy. Her got all the kin her could want. From dat day on, it was never de same. Cause each child brought a special gift."

"What did Ogun bring?" asked Pap.

"Him was strong and loved to do de hard work!" As she described Ogun, Pap preened and flexed his muscles. "Oya brought de music to lift people's hearts. Elegba brought laughter. Him could make a dead man laugh."

Elizabeth pointed to the sleeping Ben. She and Clarice giggled. "Osun, her was love and beauty." Miz Emma Julia watched as the blush spread across Clarice's face. "If her was here today, she name be Queen. . . ."

"An Yemo-Yemo?"

"Yemoja. She was de quickness of spirit. De thing dat make all man and woman live and love and fight."

"I bet that old woman was happy." Clarice sighed.

"Dey was happy for a good long while, but you remember what de elephant say?"

Pap intoned, " 'Kin is fine, but kin can be trouble.' "

"Dats right. An after some time, dey begin to fuss and fight among demselves as kin is bound to do. An de old woman, she could barely stand it. It got so bad her run off to de woods, wailin an cryin. An who should happen along but de elephant?"

"What him say?"

"Him say, 'What? . . . You still cryin?' An her tole he, 'De chilren. Dey fight so!' An him look at she, he right disgusted. Him say, 'What I tell you bout kin!' Her start to cry all over again. Him went to de other elephants, an den him come back. 'Us help you one more time, but you got to do what us say. 'De woman promised anything to get de chilren to stop fightin. De elephant say, 'In de morning, you give each child a chore an send each one to a different place, send one to de desert, one to de mountain, one to de woods, one to de grasslands, an one to de hills.' An her did as him say.

"Once de chilren were gone, de elephants come together an begin to stomp de ground. Dey stomp so hard, de land begin to crack an break off. De woman cry, 'What you doin? My chilren!' De elephant say, 'Dis de only way to stop fightin.' Dey stomp an mountains break away, den de desert break away, den de woods, de grasslands, de hills. De chilren come run to de edge an see de others so far away dey start to cry.

"Dat old woman, she cry! Her an she chilren cry so hard dat de waters start to rise and fill where de land broke away. Dey cry a whole world full of tears. An when her cried out, her asked de elephant, 'Will us ever be together again?' An him say, 'Will dey ever stop fightin?' "

Miz Emma Julia shook her head. "It pitiful, it truly pitiful."

"So what her do?"

"Want nuttin she could do. She sit down at de edge of de water and wait for her chilren to stop fightin so dey could come home. And, last I know, she still wait."

"She still wait?"

"Across de big water. She wait . . . she wait for me . . . for you. . . ."

"She wait for me? How come she wait for me?"

"You is her chilren. . . . And you . . . All of us is her chilren. . . ." She leaned back in the chair and examined the children's faces. Elizabeth was thoughtful, her mind sifting through the details of the lie. Clarice's eyes brimmed with tears as she thought of the lonely children.

Pap frowned at her. "How come dey dint just build a boat and go back?"

Miz Emma Julia slowly puffed on her pipe, "How come we still here? It late, get dark. Yall better get on cause I know dey be look for you." The children got up reluctantly. Elizabeth gently laid Ben on the floor as she helped Clarice fold the quilts. Miz Emma Julia handed the lamp to Pap. "Bring it back daytime."

Clarice begged, "Will you tell us another lie tomorrow?"

Miz Emma Julia shrugged and reached down to scratch Jacob's head.

Elizabeth picked up Ben. "Thank you, Miz Emma Julia. Dat was a good lie," she said and followed Pap and Clarice across the yard. Miz Emma Julia watched the light from her lamp flitting through the woods, leading the children home.

Ibo Landing,
Dawtuh Island
September 1926

Elizabeth Peazant awoke to the gentle bickering of the wren couple that lived in the high pines behind the house. Lying in the near darkness before dawn, she listened to the sound of waves brushing the shore the few hundred yards away. As her eyes became accustomed to the dark, she gazed around this room that she had spent so much of her life in and knew so well. The wall next to the bed she lay in was papered with letters from the ceiling to the sloping floor, letters from the Peazants who had left the Island years before. She recognized the looping, florid handwriting of Cousin Viola—"My dearest, darling Nana, it is with the love and joy of Jesus that I write to you . . ."—the cramped difficult script of Daddy Mac—"Mother, trust this find you be well"—and the curt abbreviated style of Yellow Mary—"Nana, things are not as well as I wish or as bad as I believe." She knew these letters by heart for she was the one who had read them to Nana, her great-grandmother, and had helped her paste them to the wall by her bed. Nana had been so proud that her children had kept their promises to write.

"Why for you wan me put dis on de wall, Nana? Dere no pictures in dem."

"I need dese bits of me chilren roun me as I sleep, Lil Bet. Dey hep keep the miseries from crowdin me."

Now Elizabeth rolled on her side and stared at the opposite wall, which was covered with pictures from magazines and her own childhood drawings. Although she could not see them through the dark, her mind's eye traced the dancing stick figures, the flowers stained with the juice of wild strawberries and blackberries, the stiff-legged animals leaping across the yard, and the fish with the human mouth. Elizabeth

remembered the pride with which she and Nana had added each picture to the wall.

Her father, Eli, had been confused by her decision to move into the
old house when she returned to the Island after finishing school. He
could not understand why she would prefer the house that the woods
had taken back over the past ten years. Wisteria vines covered the entire outline of the slanted shack. The tin roof had rusted through in areas, large chunks falling through to the rotting pine floor. The oaks
were shrouded in Spanish moss blocking the natural light that spilled
across the large yard. Debris that had washed up from the big storm of
1911 dotted the yard, and the garden that his grandmother had loved
so much was thick with weeds and young oak saplings.

He had expected her to return to the home where she had been
raised, surely a more comfortable house, with the thick glass windows
and the cast iron stove that he and his cousin, Ezelle, had hauled across
the water from Beaufort. Next year he would put in the new outhouse
and had even thought of adding that parlor that his wife, Eula, had always wanted.

However, Elizabeth had been insistent. She would stay at their home
while she cleared and repaired the old house. She had drafted her
younger brother, Ben, into helping her with the heavy work and finding the scarce wood to begin the repairs. The little ones, the twins and
Rebecca, she had bribed into helping clear the yard and garden with
promises of bedtime stories about kings and queens and dragons that
came from the many books she had brought back. While Eli understood Elizabeth's need to prepare her school lessons in quiet, he worried about the melancholia he glimpsed in unguarded moments.

"I worry bout she out dere by sheself, Eula. Young girl don need to
be alone."

"Lil Bet not alone, Eli. Us not a stone throw from she. Us see she
every day, her pass to go to teach school. Her stop by on way dere an
back. Her take supper wit we every day."

"I don like she living out dere by sheself. Girl need to stay wit family
til her ready to start she own."

"Her not on she own. Nana dere. Dose ol souls, all we people dem
watch over she."

It was this inevitable turn in the conversation, the calling up of the
old ones, that let Eli know his protests were in vain. And as the weeks
passed and he saw the determination that Lil Bet brought to the work,
he, himself, found a quiet joy in seeing the old house come back to life
and joined his sons in scouring the Island for things that could be put

to use. There was still much work to be done on the house before winter set in.

Elizabeth sat up, pushing back the mosquito netting, and carefully placing her feet on the ground. When she had moved in, she had uprooted several wood creatures, including a family of raccoons. While the parents had surrendered rather easily, the young ones were especially curious about the new occupant and all of the strange new things she had brought with her. She had already been rewarded with a yelp and a sharp nip on her ankle as she had stepped from her bed one morning. Although a truce of sorts had been declared after she had chased them from the house with the broom, she was well aware that they had the advantage in the dark.

Stepping quickly, she crossed to the window to look for the morning star. Scanning the deep indigo sky, rich with stars, she caught its distinctive twinkle to the north and knew that day clean would be soon. She shivered in the cold of the morning and wrapped the quilt from her bed around her as she turned the ashes in the fireplace. As the embers glowed and flared, she tossed a few pieces of brushwood onto the live coals and hung the coffeepot to boil. She moved to the table covered with herbs, roots, and flowers and picked among the bottles, tins, cloth bags, and baskets until she found the dandelion root that she was searching for. She dropped a few small pieces into Nana's old coffee grinder and ground it to a fine powder.

When she went across the water to Beaufort this coming Saturday, she would pick up a precious pound of coffee with the other things that she needed; sugar, flour, salt, lamp oil, candles, chalk, and butcher paper for her students to use. She chided herself for her craving. If she would have but one cup of coffee every two days, the coffee might last until she received her first wages. Although coffee made from dandelion root or chicory did not have the rich, full taste that she savored, it would do, and she had often done with less.

She dumped the powdered root into her tin cup and poured the boiling water over it. While it brewed, she poured water from the pitcher into the shallow basin and gave herself a quick sponge bath. Dressing quickly, she sipped the hot brew to take the chill off.

In a few minutes, the light would begin to break and she would head out through the woods to search for the snakeroot and life everlasting she needed for her medicine charms. She would also gather honeysuckle and jasmine to set in sweet oil and check on the wild honey tree to see how the bees were coming along. The making of charms, medicinal and scented, was her passion. Of all Nana's great-grandchildren, it was she who had accompanied Nana on her long forages through the marshes, across the creeks, and beyond the pine forests. It was she that Nana taught to identify and find the roots, herbs, flowers, the porcupine quills, the beak of the wood duck, and the feather from the snipe used to make the charms that would keep evil and bad times from the Peazant family. Elizabeth knew of roots that worked for the good and even roots that were said to bring illness and bad fortune. Ever the practical woman, Nana had little use for conjure, considering the time spent on conjure to be time stolen from a life.

After Nana had crossed over, her old friend, Miz Emma Julia, had taken it upon herself to continue Elizabeth's training. It was from her that Elizabeth learned of the roots that could make a man stay true, cure a child of meanness, or free a woman of carnal restraint. Elizabeth had quietly watched as people from all over the islands and from the mainland had visited Miz Emma Julia's house and left, furtively tucking the vial, bottle, or bag away from curious eyes. She had been amazed at the educated coloreds and the white ladies who sought Miz Emma Julia out under the pretense of getting syrup for a lingering cough or salve for a rash that would not heal. While Elizabeth, herself, was not sure that roots, powders, and potions would stop a man from drinking, she understood very well that it was not her particular belief that brought the true strength to the charm. She had heard the soft sobs and the fervently whispered thanks and knew only that each person searched for their peace. It was what she sought in her root work; her own peace.

She always gathered before day clean as the sun rose and before the dew dried, taking the magic from the previous night with it. She held that the early morning light showed the plants at their best, bringing a soft beauty to the hardiest weed and sharpest thorn. In the early morning, the scents of the herbs and wildflowers swirled through the woods, mingling with the sweet smell of pine, and the salty breeze that blew in from the water. The early morning was Elizabeth's time, and she would make good use of it. In the couple of hours before school began, she could replenish her stock, setting the herbs and roots out to dry on the porch before she left. She took a quick inventory, making careful note of what she would need for her next batch of scents. In a moment of sheer whimsy, she had decided that she would name them after one of her favorite Bible verses, the Fruits of the Spirit from the book of Galatians. She would enjoy the challenge of coming up with just the right mixture of herbs, flowers, and spices that would capture the essence of love, peace, joy, and faith. These are the Fruits of the Spirit.

". . . Dey running dis way. We gots to get back over near the shoal to get de net out."

When she heard the voices floating across the sand, she went out on the low porch and watched the fishermen with the lamps hanging from the stern and the side of the boats. She recognized the voice of Willis George, her mother's cousin. As the light grew, she saw the small figure of his son, Amos, scrambling to help his father prepare the net to catch the blue gill in their run along the shore. She hoped that Willis would bring young Amos in time for school.

As the sun broke from the water, she watched the morning light play among the colored glass that swung from the bottle tree, casting blue, amber, and white light against the wall of the house. Only the neck of a blue bottle had remained from the days when Nana had lived here. When Elizabeth returned, she had led a treasure hunt among her youngest brothers and sister to collect bottles to fill the trees, explaining that the tree provided magic protection for their family. Racing barefoot along the beach, they searched for bottles that had washed ashore. On the day that they placed the new bottles in the tree, Eula brought them a picnic lunch of fried shad, boiled eggs, pickles, cold lemonade, and buttermilk cake. It was a fitting celebration of the renewal of the old ways, and to Eula it was only right that her oldest daughter would be the one to bring them back.

The screeches from the flock of Carolina parakeets that nested in the large magnolia startled Elizabeth from her daydreaming. Clucking at the lost time, she grabbed Nana's large basket and her scissors and headed along the trail that ran back through the marshes.

Home Sweetener

Mix 75 drops of peppermint oil with 35 drops of eucalyptus oil, 10 drops of clove, and 1/2 cup of spring water. Shake the mixture around the four corners of the room to bring the nature inside. As the mixture ages, the scent will become stronger.

Harlem
September 1926

"What you doing there with those eggs? Chile, you better eat them up. They cost too much for you to be playin with!"

Amelia started at her grandmother's sharp words. She looked up to find Haagar watching her intensely, a deep frown sharpening her features.

Reaching over and touching her forehead, Haagar asked, "What ail you, girl? You've been walkin round here like you ain't with us!"

"I was just thinking about all the things I had to do today."

"Well, don't forget to put on that list that you're helping me set up for the wake. So I want you to come home soon as class is over with. No dawdling around talking to them teachers, you hurry up quick an come on back up to Harlem."

Amelia nodded and took a deep breath, trying to quell the excitement and anxiety that had kept her sleepless for the past two nights. She slipped her hand into the pocket of her jacket hanging on the back of the chair and felt the edges of the letter. Since she had received it two days before, she had read the letter over and over again, the words imprinted in her mind. After two harrowing faculty reviews and numerous rewrites, her thesis proposal had finally been accepted by the anthropology department at Brooklyn College. But it was Professor Colby's handwritten note at the bottom of the letter that had caused her to miss her sleep these past two days; "Please come to my office on Wednesday morning, so we can discuss arrangements for your fieldwork."

She sneaked a glance at her grandmother, who was going through the bills as she ate her breakfast. The faculty review had been hard

enough, but the hardest part would be telling her father and grandmother of her plans. Her father had barely tolerated the idea of her going to college, not seeing much use in wasting money on an education
for a girl. He had only agreed when she had received the scholarships
from the Women's Baptist League and the Negro Women's Education
Association. Still, he resented the time she spent studying, away from
his small business.

Her grandmother had her eye set on Miss Rachel Taylor's Finishing
School for Young Colored Women. She knew that the daughters of the
most prominent colored families in Harlem attended the school to re-
fine themselves, learning the basics of comportment and practicing
their rudimentary French so that they could be presented at the big
ball thrown every year by the Monarchs, the colored fraternal order.
Since her arrival in New York more than two decades ago, Haagar
Peazant had been determined to rid herself of all country ties and, having given up on her own children long ago, concentrated all her efforts
on her granddaughter. She was keenly disappointed when informed by
Miss Taylor that the one absolute requirement for acceptance to the
school was that the mother or a close female relative of the applicant
had previously attended the school.

Like her son-in-law, Haagar had resisted the idea of college for
Amelia until she had read in *The Age* that several sons of respected
doctors, well-known ministers, and wealthy businessmen from Harlem
attended Brooklyn College. Never one to miss the opportunity, she surprised Amelia by announcing that she felt that college would be a good
idea, specifically Brooklyn College. She also convinced her son-in-law
that the contacts that Amelia could make would be good for his struggling undertaking business.

Amelia's mother, Myown, was the only person in the family that
knew about her plans and dreams. Myown had encouraged her studies
in anthropology and had conspired with Amelia to keep it a secret from
Haagar and her own husband. Dominated by her mother, ignored by
her husband, Myown had, in her own quiet way, fashioned a relationship with her daughter that was deeply loving and uncritical. Amelia
heard the harsh cough and soft shuffle as Myown came down the narrow hallway leading to the kitchen.

Myown stopped in the doorway and smiled at her daughter.
"Happee Day!"

Haagar snapped, "Aw, don't be coming here with all that ol'
Geechee mess! It give me a swinging in my head to hear it!"

Amelia tilted her head in the old way that her mother had taught her and said, "It be dat." She ignored her grandmother's scowl as she left the table to get the coffee for her mother. As Myown slowly made her way to the table, Amelia moved to help her. Myown waved her away. "I feeling better dis day." She eased down in the chair and sipped the hot coffee. Reaching over and squeezing Amelia's hand, she predicted, "I see dat good tings gonna happen dis day."

Haagar snorted and pulled a bill from the pile. "Oh. Did you see that the flower bill gone up a nickel for each bunch?" She waved it at Myown. "I never trusted those E-talians with their singy-songy talk. Imagine, on Monday, I order flowers for the Haney funeral and he charge me one dollar. Here it is Wednesday, and now they costing one dollar five cents. I got the mind tell him to take them back!"

Amelia and Myown exchanged a glance and concentrated on their breakfast. It was the beginning of the morning tirade that Haagar launched at will. When neither Amelia nor her mother responded to her complaints, Haagar banged on the table with her spoon, her words flavored with the Geechee accent she had striven so hard to lose. "I tired of talking to myself. I work like a slave to hep you husband and you daddy wit his business, and I not feeling de thanks from nobody."

Myown struggled to speak, but began to strangle on a cough. Amelia poured her a glass of water and encouraged her to sip slowly, patting her back gently. As soon as the coughing fit passed, Myown spoke softly, breathlessly. "Well, Mama, if you don like he prices . . . mebbe you look for better prices someplace else."

"Where I gonna go, missy? Up on Fifth Avenue? When I have the time to go look for cheaper flowers? The E-talians, they know the colored people got to take what they bring in here, all the leftovers the buckra don't want!"

As her grandmother plunged into another round of complaints, Amelia cleared the table and washed the dishes quickly. Straightening her suit jacket, she grabbed her satchel of books. Her grandmother stopped her for inspection.

"Stand still. Pull that jacket straight. Let me see the back of them stockings, make sure they running straight!"

She stood stiffly as ordered while her grandmother walked around her. Myown smiled at the neat image her daughter presented. Amelia, who had always been such a neat child, so careful about her appearance, was now a trim young woman with large brown eyes and skin the color of a polished bronze vase. Myown looked down at her own dark, almost blue-black hands and the dark hands of her mother as she pulled and tugged at her grandchild, correcting imaginary flaws. "If nuttin else, I go marry up and give her de granchild she will always prize," Myown mused as Haagar patted Amelia's hair into place.

"Now, you look like the decent sort of young woman I raised."

Amelia dutifully kissed the cheek proffered by her grandmother and then crossed to kiss her mother. Myown pulled her close and hugged her, whispering, "Good luck today! Be smart and brave."

"I will, Mama."

As she slipped out the back door, Haagar reminded her, "Don't you forget that I'm gonna need you to help me with washing the body this afternoon. You come right home after your class."

Amelia scurried down the hall to Professor Colby's office, slipping around the groups of students waiting for the list of grades to be posted. She knocked on his door, heard the distracted "Come in," and entered his office. As she had expected, Professor Colby was submerged in books. She could barely see the top of his balding head over the pile. Peering around the stack, he gestured for her to have a seat. She removed some books from the chair and sat quietly as he flipped pages and, not finding what he wanted, pulled out more books. Finally, he stopped and looked at her, perplexed, "It's in here! I just put my hands on it!"

"What are you looking for, Professor Colby?"

"I had mentioned your thesis proposal to Professor Bryington at Columbia University and he sent over this account written by Northern missionaries sent to the islands during the Civil War. It should be a good place to start."

Amelia nodded and stood up to help him look for it. She sighed at the sight of the piles of books scattered around the room. To his secretary's everlasting chagrin, Professor Colby would never allow anyone to bring order to his office, insisting that he knew where everything was.

Frowning at the mound of books in front of him, he added, "And, Amelia, I've got some good news for you."

She examined a teetering stack of books and magazines, careful not to touch it.

"As expected, the Foundation has provided a small grant for your fieldwork . . . and . . ." He pulled a sheaf of papers from under an assortment of magazine clippings. "My draft for my lecture at the

American Anthropological Society! I wondered where that had gotten off to!"

She stared at him, her heart thudding so loudly she was not sure she had heard what he had said. All along he had assured her that the Foundation would probably provide her with a bit of money, but she had not really taken it seriously. Amelia had learned long ago that wishes rarely came true and that kept promises were even more rare. Although she had so many hopes pinned on her project, she could not quite believe that it was about to become a reality.

"I've found a benefactor for you. He wants to remain anonymous, and he has agreed to provide a monthly stipend of one hundred dollars to you while you're down there."

Amelia stepped back as the blood rushed to her head. She bumped into a pile of books, sending them sliding across the floor. She scrambled to gather them. Professor Colby stood up abruptly and impatiently surveyed his desk.

"So what do you think of that?"

She stared at him, dumbfounded. "I . . . I . . . think . . . it's wonderful! How . . . ?"

He carefully pulled a book from the stack. "Here it is!" Flipping it open, he continued, "It actually contains letters from some of the women sent down there to start the schools for the freed slaves. You were saying?"

She found her way over to the chair and dropped. "I didn't expect it. I thought I would have to . . ."

He waved away her concerns. "It will be money well spent. He's made a killing on land, railroads, and everything he has ever touched. Actually, I suspect he has an interest in the land down there; he's been talking about another summer home. At any rate, he will provide the monies for your board and keep down there. Now, let's talk about when you'll be leaving to start your fieldwork. How long will it take you to get everything together? I think six weeks is more than enough time. You said you had family down there, right? Someone who can provide introductions and show you around?"

Amelia nodded. "I've got quite a few people still living there. I haven't seen them in years, but they write sometimes and when folks go to visit, they send back some word or some kind of gift. My mother's cousin, Eula, wrote that her daughter Elizabeth had come back to teach school."

Professor Colby handed her the book. "A schoolteacher who is a

relative . . . As good if not better than the women who wrote these letters! She will be an excellent resource."

On the trolley ride back home, Amelia watched the other passengers,
wondering if her jubilation was apparent to them. She badly wanted to
share her good fortune with someone, anyone, before she had to face
her grandmother and father.

As the trolley drew closer to her stop, her sense of dread grew. Her
grandmother, Haagar, would never understand or abide with her decision to go to the islands for her fieldwork. She had left Dawtuh Island
twenty-four years ago, determined to wash the Geechee stain from herself and her children. It was to rid herself of "de look of de saltwater
Negro" and "dem old ignorant ways" and to find "de better way of living" that she had taken her daughter and son and moved north to
Harlem. Not for nothing had she borne the ridicule and derision
heaped on these new migrants, not even from the country, but from
some remote islands that nobody, not even people from South Carolina, had ever heard of. With the ferocity that was true to her character,
Haagar had struggled, schemed, worked hard, and fought so that, even
if she was not particularly liked by her neighbors and acquaintances,
she was accorded a certain amount of respect and not a little bit of fear.
Haagar knew that part of that fear stemmed from the belief that
Geechee people practiced hoodoo and could put a spell on someone.
While she, herself, had little time for laying a spell, she was more than
willing to use that fear to her advantage. They had long since stopped
mocking Mrs. Haagar Peazant in her presence.

The only time Haagar had returned to the Island was the summer of
1913, when Amelia turned six. It was a trip planned by Haagar to let
those who had stayed behind see how good life up North was and how
far they had come. Amelia's father, refusing to go anywhere near the
South, complained about the money being spent to present the pros-
perous face to the rest of the Peazant family. "Those old Negroes don't
know nothing from nothing. Long as you wearing shoes, they gonna
think you doing fine."

Haagar ignored him as she packed the new clothes into the new suit-
cases she had bought. Myown stayed in her room, trying to avoid the
turmoil and temper tantrums that the upcoming trip generated.

During their stay on the Island, Amelia remembered being dressed
up every day by her grandmother as if she were going to church. She

was not allowed to play on the beach or climb the trees with the other children who seemed to run wild. During that trip, she saw a part of her mother who laughed and played ring games with her young cousins, chasing them through the woods in hide-and-seek that seemed to last for hours. Up to this visit, she had only known her mother as the quiet woman with gentle hands and a cough that wakened her in the middle of the night. But on the Island, Myown became younger, brighter in manner, and it seemed to Amelia that her cough did not come as quickly or as harshly. She had watched, startled, as her mother had plucked the live crabs from her cousin's net and tossed them into the boiling pot set up on the beach.

And she remembered the arrival of her mother's sister, Iona, who had heard that her mother and sister had returned to the Island. Iona had brought her three children to meet their grandmother and the aunt whom they had never seen. When Iona walked up into the yard, carrying one child and followed by the other two, there had been complete silence as Haagar spotted them, while Myown had run to embrace her sister and her children. Haagar turned away and walked into the house without a word to her eldest daughter. Her relatives shook their heads in bewilderment and sorrow, greeting Iona warmly, admiring her children, and asking about her husband. Everyone on the Island knew that Haagar would never forgive Iona for choosing to stay with St. Julian Last Child, the last Cherokee to live on the Island, rather than move North with her family.

It was not until the food was ready that Haagar emerged from the house. She fixed a plate for herself and Amelia and took a place on the blankets spread in the yard. Amelia had looked longingly at the children who were allowed to eat down near the water's edge, but knew better than to ask to join them. Iona had set her two oldest children down to eat with the other children, while Cousin Gertie insisted on feeding the good-natured baby. When Iona had filled her plate, she walked over and sat on the blanket with her mother. As they ate in silence, Myown and her cousin Eula joined them, reminiscing about the old days. Eula had been plying Myown with questions about New York, her eyes widening in disbelief at Myown's descriptions, when the conversation came to an abrupt halt as Haagar finished her supper and stood up. "Amelia, you eat everyting on that plate and then bring it over for the washing."

As Haagar turned to leave, Iona spoke up. "Mama, I brung my chilren for dem to see dey people."

Haagar stared at the children, who giggled with their cousins as they dug for the fiddler crabs hiding in the sand. She looked back at Iona and said, "Least they got their daddy's hair." Turning her back on them, she strolled back to the house.

Myown reached out and grabbed her sister's hands. "Is you happy?" She repeated it as Iona blinked away her tears. "Is you happy?"

Iona nodded. "I bery happy. Him a good man."

"Den dat all dat matter. De happiness tween a man an woman is all dat matter." Eula nodded in agreement and put her arms around Iona. Amelia stared at the three women as, crying and laughing, they embraced each other.

Amelia stood up when the trolley rolled to a stop, feeling the joy and excitement drain from her. No, having lost one daughter to the Island, Haagar would never agree to let her granddaughter return.

Dawtuh Island
October 1926

Here comes Sally, Sally, Sally!
Here come Sally all night long!

Elizabeth turned the shell over in her hand, examining its shape and color. She walked to the edge of the beach and washed the sand from it in the incoming tide.

"What it called, Miz Lil Bet?"

She looked down at Jacob, one of her three students who was still trying to finish the assignment that she hàd given the class that afternoon before they set out on their field trip. The other boy, Hanley, was in the tall sea grass, looking for an abandoned bird's nest. The girl, her Cousin Gertie's granddaughter, Septima, had waded out a few feet from the beach and was peering into the water. The other boys chased and tackled each other among the dunes while the girls played a line game on the shore, their voices carrying across the gentle ripple of the waves.

So step back, Sally, Sally, Sally!
Step back, Sally, all night long!

"This is a good find, Jacob," she complimented him. "It's called the Wandering Triton."

"De wanna trite!" he announced proudly.

She smiled. "Listen to how I speak . . . the Wan-der-ring Tri-ton!"

"De wannaning trite!" he shouted excitedly.

"That's good, Jacob! Very good for the first time. Do you know what 'wandering' means?"

Jacob hid his face in his hands, shaking his head. As Elizabeth watched, one of the boys, Isaac, broke from the group and ran over to watch the girls playing. Elizabeth kept an eye on him. Isaac was a terrible tease to the girls, just as his father, Pap, had been. She expected him at any moment to kick sand at them or pull their plaits. When he simply stood, watching them, she turned back to Jacob.

Gently pulling his hands from his face, she explained, "Wandering means to go from one place to the next, never staying in one place."

"Like Ol Trent!" he accused.

Elizabeth chuckled. "Yes, like Ol Trent."

"He de walkinest man. Everytime I see he, all he do is walkin talkin. Don need nobody to talk to, eder."

Elizabeth laughed at Jacob's accurate description of Ol Trent. Long before she was born, Trent had started his trek, walking from one end of the Island to the other. As far as Elizabeth knew, he never left the Island, just spent his days trailing through the swamps, marshes, and forests on an endless journey. He was like so much of the Island that had remained unchanged over the years.

Struttin down the alley, alley, alley!
Struttin down the alley all night long!

She looked over at the girls as they began to sashay. Evidently this was the moment Isaac had been waiting for. He jumped in behind the girls and broke into a hucka-buck dance that reduced the girls to giggles. As he rolled his eyes and shook his butt, the girls clapped, egging him on. Elizabeth handed the shell to Jacob and strolled over to the edge of the group. Oblivious to the additional attention he was getting, Isaac closed his eyes, put his hands behind his head, and began to roll his stomach as the girls shrieked with laughter and embarrassment. Grinning, Isaac opened his eyes and stopped abruptly as they met Elizabeth's.

"You want to put a hold on that?" asked Elizabeth dryly. She turned to the snickering girls. "Have yall gotten all the things I told you to gather while we out here?"

They answered in unison, "Yes, maam."

"We'll see about that. I told yall this morning that this was not a play trip. You're gonna be graded on this, just like you are for your reading and writing. Bring your things over so that we all can see." She called to the others, beckoning them to join the group on the beach.

Septima frowned at her from the shallow waters, reached down, and picked up something, dumping the water and sand as she waded toward them. Elizabeth glanced over at Hanley, who had disappeared in the high grass. When the other children had gathered around them, Elizabeth instructed, "Let's see how you did. Come on. Lay it out here so we can see it." The children hesitated, still unsure of Elizabeth's intentions.

"I aint never heard of no schoolin like dis, got to go roun pickin up feathers, shells, and leaves, all that ol trash left behind," complained one of the girls.

Another chimed in, "I likes being outside myself."

"What dis sci-ence expedention is anyhow? It too hot out here!" fussed a third girl.

Elizabeth sighed as the girls bickered and slapped at the sandflies buzzing around them. She had hoped that getting them out of the dilapidated school for an afternoon would stir their natural curiosity. She had been shocked at how little learning the older children had. Some of them could not even recite their alphabets. They were bored easily, and she struggled to keep them interested in the simple basic instruction they needed. Only four, aside from her siblings, could read, two with great difficulty, while the others wrote their names in large, ill-formed letters. She had known that schooling on the Island was desperate, but had not realized how bad it had gotten since the Beaufort School Board had taken it over.

Up until five years ago, the schools had been run by the American Missionary Society with teachers sent from the North. Although they had always been in short supply, the missionary teachers would always write to their congregations asking for help, and invariably the precious boxes of books, chalk, slate, pencils, and paper would come. It was not unusual for them to send clothing and shoes along with the school supplies. But the boxes had stopped five years ago, and the school on the Island had received no supplies since.

Eli had maintained that the missionaries were asked to leave because they were making the colored children smart, and too many were crossing over to go to the colored high school on the mainland. His inquiry to the Colored Elks in Beaufort had gone unaddressed. It was at that point that he vowed to make sure that his children could read and write the way he and Eula had been taught.

Elizabeth agreed with her father. From her first interview with the Deputy Director of the School Board, it had been made very plain to her that she was to teach the children only enough, as he had put to her, "to follow the list that the mistress drew up." That her younger brothers and sisters did as well as they did was the result of the evening lessons her father gave. They complained loudly about the tedium of the lessons, Eli's taste in literature running to either the Bible or tool catalogues, but Elizabeth knew that they would eventually value them.

She had been startled at the number of teachers that had come and gone in the past five years, some staying a few weeks, others leaving with the first weekly boat. The children could not remember a name, but could describe each one in hilarious detail. It was not until the last one, Mr. Asher, had joined Ol Trent on his treks across the Island that the Board had decided that it would be best to send a colored teacher. As soon as Eli heard, he wrote to Elizabeth at school and importuned her to come back home and teach.

It was not a difficult choice for Elizabeth. She believed as her father and mother did in the strength of the Island family and how each of them was expected to bring the best of themselves to serve the people there. The only other job prospects she had were either to teach in a small black town in northern Florida or to return to work for the Bouvier sisters in Charleston as their personal maid. Her parents did not want her going to Florida after the Rosewood Riot in 1921. It seemed that the entire colored world had heard of the burning of the colored town and the slaughter of the men, women, and children. Five years later, folks still shook with fear and revulsion at the mention of the Massacre.

Until the query came from the Beaufort School Board, Elizabeth had been resigned to continuing to work for the Bouvier sisters as she had during her high school years. She had worked for them since she first came across the water to attend Avery Normal School in Charleston. Her teacher, Miss Anna Smiley, had encouraged her to apply to Avery, advising that Avery was much better than the colored high school in Beaufort. When she was accepted, Miss Smiley had found a place for her with the Bouvier sisters, exchanging room and board for maid duties. Elizabeth had no complaints about her years with the Bouviers. Particular and demanding they might have been, but they took a genuine interest in her schoolwork and allowed her the run of their large library.

She had returned to the Island with such high hopes and two boxes of books that she wanted to share with her students, books filled with great stories and ideas that could show them the great world beyond their Island. Remembering the stories from her childhood of the captives whose souls flew away to freedom, she had hoped that the books would do the same for these children. Now she realized how difficult her task would be; teaching someone to read required patience and diligence, but teaching someone to dream required the exploration of a soul. With the introspection and the plainspoken honesty born to the Peazant women, she knew that it was not only her desire to help, but her own fear of that exploration, that had sent her back to the Island. Certainly, her choices had been limited, but she had also been afraid to dream.

Elizabeth looked up as Septima and several girls ran up to her. "What do you have? I want to see it," she entreated the children. Septima thrust a bottle at her.

One of the girls snickered, "Dat aint nuttin!"

"Where did you find this, Septima?" Elizabeth turned the amber bottle over in her hands.

Septima pointed. "In de shallows. It wash up from de water."

Examining the base of the bottle, Elizabeth asked, "Where do you think it came from?"

"De water! She done tole you dat!" was the impatient reply from a boy.

"Where do you think it was made?"

"I don know. How I suppose to know dat?" Septima snapped.

Elizabeth handed her the bottle, tapping its base. "What does that say?"

Septima squinted at the small letters. "B-Bath, E-E-n-n-l-l-un."

Elizabeth asked, "Do you know where that is?"

One of the girls spoke with authority. "It in Bofort! I been dere."

Elizabeth shook her head, and taking the bottle from Septima, she turned it over in her hands. "It came all the way from England. That's a country on the other side of the water."

"Nuh-uh," a boy disagreed. "Aint nuttin but de big water out dere."

"On the mainland they call the big water 'the ocean,' " Elizabeth explained. "It's so big it covers half the world. But on the other side, there are people living there." She stared out across the waves.

Intrigued, Septima tugged on her blouse. "What kinda people?"

"Yall remember the old man lived back up off the Jameson Creek?"

"Dat man who neber cut he hair? It grow down he back like de woman?" a boy asked.

Elizabeth nodded, reminding them. "Paymore. His name was Paymore Muhammat."

A girl blurted out, "Him scare me! He talk in de tongue all de time! I neber cud tell what he talkin bout."

Elizabeth corrected her. "It was the tongue that the people talked in where he came from . . . across the water."

Only a few of the older children remembered Paymore. An ancient when Elizabeth had been a child, Paymore had kept company with Nana, regaling them all with tales of his life in a place he called the bilād as-sudan. Even after the sale of Africans had been banned on the mainland, he and the other captives had been smuggled onto the Island plantations from one of the many slave ships that hid in the shallow inlets off the Charleston shore. Many a time had Elizabeth and her brothers and sisters shivered while listening to the tales about the ships with red flags that waited until darkness to drive their banned cargo ashore. It seemed that for every story about captives walking out onto the water or flying from the fields to begin their long trek back home, another story was told about slavers outrunning the law, and hastily dumped bodies in chains washing up on the shore. It was said among some that on certain nights when the edge of the moon burned red and the fog rolled in from the south, all the dogs would begin to howl and you could hear the wails from the ships as they passed along the rivers. Folks would hide in their houses, barring the doors and securing the wooden shutters, never daring to look out, for it was known that just a glimpse of the ships brought death.

Despite the afternoon heat, Elizabeth shivered. She looked down on Septima's frowning face. "Paymore came from where all our people came from: Afric."

One of the girls piped up, "My daddy say dem ol folks, dey be sal water Negroes, dey do tings de ol ways."

Elizabeth responded, "We come from them, they come from Afric."

"Nuh-uh, I aint come from no place but heah!"

"Before you and I were born here, there were others like my Nana's mother and you great-grandma, Granny Whipple, who was brought here from across the waters."

She scanned their faces for some sign that they understood her. She sighed as she recognized the polite but blank expressions that they assumed whenever a lesson was taking place. She was relieved when Isaac pointed. "Look, Miz Lil Bet. Hanley done foun sumptin."

Hanley stood at the edge of a high dune, waving for them to come. As the children scrambled up the side of the dune, he cautioned them to be careful. Jacob shyly slipped his hand into Elizabeth's as they climbed the dune. Slowly and as quietly as twelve children could slip through the beach grass, he led them to a nest of round, leathery eggs buried in the sand. Carefully, he brushed the sand back from the eggs. The boys pushed forward to look at the eggs. Septima forced her way through while the other girls hung back until Elizabeth urged them forward.

"Dem plover eggs!" Jacob announced as he reached for one.

Hanley grabbed his hand, "No, dey not! Leave dem be, boy!"

"Dey is, too!" insisted Jacob. "Dem plover eggs."

"No, dey not!" answered Isaac. "Dey piper eggs!"

"Who knows what kind of eggs they are?" Elizabeth asked. She put her finger to her lips as she met Hanley's laughing eyes.

Another boy tentatively suggested, "Gull eggs?"

"Well, what creatures lay eggs? Now, you know. You live here!" she prompted.

One of the girls quickly ticked off, "Chickens, ducks, geese, turkeys, guinea hens . . ."

Hanley spoke up, "Girl, everybody knows birds lay eggs! What odder dan birds hab dey babies with eggs?"

She looked at him uncertainly. He leaned forward and hissed in her ear, "They frogs, de alligator hab eggs, and den deres . . . snakes!"

The girl screamed and shouted, "Nakes!" and took off down the dune to the beach. The hysteria spread as the other girls screamed and followed her. Elizabeth turned to scold Hanley, who was rolling in the sand, laughing, and realized that Jacob was clutching her skirt, trembling. She looked down at him.

"Dem snake eggs, Miz Lil Bet?"

Septima, irritated by all the silliness, snapped, "Boy, dem turtle eggs! Turtles come out de water at night and lay de eggs up here!"

Elizabeth looked down the beach at the disappearing girls. "Thank you, Septima. Hanley, cover those eggs back up. Their mama buries them in the sand to keep them warm." She wryly wondered about the tales the girls would tell their parents that night. "Come on, yall. I think this science expedition is over."

Elizabeth pulled her coat closer around her while she sat on the pier in the early morning cold. As she waited for Willis George to arrive with his boat to ferry her across to Beaufort, she heard the voices of others approaching along the trail that led from the woods.

"I gots to get some buttons for dis dress I done made. What you tink, red look good? White? Or should I be downright frisky and get de black ones?" announced a husky voice.

"Why you axtin me? You don listen to me nohow!" was the high-pitched, peevish reply.

"Das why I don listen! You always got sumptin more to say dan what I axt!"

"What I suppose to do? I aint no monkey!"

Elizabeth chuckled as she turned toward the strip of beach that the trail spilled out upon. The two women stepped from the woods, eyes squinting in the bright morning sunlight. Approaching the pier, they both frowned trying to figure out who was waiting there. Elizabeth watched, an expectant smile on her face. Not that she was surprised, but they hadn't changed one bit. Carrie Mae strolled with the casual grace found in tall, fleshy women. As Elizabeth watched her, she remembered trying to capture that same loose, effortless walk that had drawn the attention of boys and men from the moment they turned twelve. To Elizabeth's [twelve-year-old] chagrin, she never quite got it right.

Known for her free and easy manner, Carrie Mae sported one of her elaborate hairdos, into which she had woven the flowers of the wisteria. Toady, as always, limped along beside her, easily matching her long strides. Elizabeth had never been able to look upon Toady's face without remembering her father's comment; "She come into dis worl lookin like she was fifty." She noted from the bulge in Toady's coat pocket that she still carried her gun.

"Who dat up dere?" Carrie Mae demanded.

Elizabeth stepped forward to meet them.

"It me, Carrie Mae. Lil Bet."

"Lawd have mercy! Lil Bet!" Carrie Mae hurried up the trail onto the pier. "Dey tole me you was back!" She hesitated as she drew closer. "You aint too proper to give you friend a hug, is you?"

"I better not be," Elizabeth managed to get out before she was smothered against Carrie Mae's chest. She drew her breath in, enjoying the fragrance of the wisteria, the soap that she had used that morning, and the spicy tang that was Carrie Mae's own essence. Elizabeth made a note that it was a scent that would serve her charms well.

"Look at you! Aint you de lady! Done gone off to school and come back lookin like de mainland!" She held Elizabeth away. "Toady, looka here!"

Toady hung back, grinning shyly at Elizabeth. "Happee Day, Lil Bet."

Elizabeth walked over to her, smiling. "Toady, you lookin all right." She moved to hug her and then stopped, remembering how uneasy Toady was with touching, and waved to her. Toady blushed and awkwardly stuck out her hand. Startled and pleased, Elizabeth gave her hand a quick squeeze.

"So you de teacher now! Spectable woman. I gonna take some of de credit for dat!" Carrie Mae announced with a big grin on her face.

Elizabeth laughed. "Deed you can."

"Yessuh, want for me, you be runnin roun here with five, six, seven head of chilren. Everytime I come across you daddy, I see him with dat shotgun! Chile, I aint neber run so hard in my born days." Carrie Mae shook with laughter as she wiped imaginary sweat from her brow.

They both remembered that night almost nine years ago when their life paths had taken different turns. She and Carrie Mae had been friends since birth and had always played together. However, Carrie Mae had filled out quickly like all the women in her family, and by the time she was twelve was as developed as any eighteen-year-old woman. Elizabeth had watched in dismay as her friend's breasts had grown full and her hips had spread generously, while her own breasts and hips, despite many inspections, had not changed one bit. Her mother's assurances that Peazant women were latecomers did not make Elizabeth feel any better. She was well aware that she would carry the slim, wiry build of Nana Peazant and her aunts all her life.

Carrie Mae accepted these changes as her birthright and the attention they brought as easily as she swam in the creek that ran behind her house. Like most everyone else, she knew what went on between men and women and, in her open way, reveled in it. She had always been amused by Elizabeth's ignorance about such matters, especially coming from a family with six children. At any rate, Carrie Mae was ready to run, and Elizabeth was ready to run with her. They started sneaking out at night after everyone else had gone to bed. At first, Elizabeth had been reluctant, until Carrie Mae had pointed out that it was the best time to gather the flowers of the starfe plant that only bloomed at night. When they stumbled upon Poppa Stoppa and Sugarnun waiting in the woods, Elizabeth realized that gathering flowers was the last thing on Carrie Mae's mind.

It would be the first of several of these late-night adventures. Shy and hesitant at first, it was not long before Elizabeth realized the pleasures of exploring hands and light kisses in the thick pine-scented darkness of the woods. Sugarnun had been a patient teacher and she an eager pupil. Finally, she understood the coded language that men and women shared; the meaning of the blues songs she'd heard all her life changed forever.

She did not realize how much more there was until, one night, she heard labored breathing, frantic movements, and then Poppa Stoppa's shout and Carrie Mae's helpless giggles. Starting toward them, she was held back by Sugarnun with sweet whispers that promised her that she could feel the same pleasures that Carrie Mae was feeling. Startled by the change in his kisses and the boldness of his hands, Elizabeth was overwhelmed by dark and tangled sensations that were far beyond the simple romantic yearnings she had read about in her books. She struggled with the passion that made her gasp, shivering in the cool night air as sweat seemed to flow from every pore in her body.

The angry shout of her father brought her quickly back to the present. "Lil Bet! You better get out here, girl!"

Eli stood in the moonlit clearing near the underbrush where she and the others were hidden. He was, as Carrie Mae clearly remembered, carrying his shotgun. Elizabeth froze as the sounds of the others fumbling with clothes and running through the woods filled the night.

"Eli-za-beth Ayo-de-le Peazant! I aint gonna call you but once!"

She stepped into the clearing, consumed with shame as her father noted the grass and pine needles in her hair and her partially unbuttoned blouse.

He did not speak to her, but pointed the way home. She moved through the woods ahead of him, only to jump as he angrily discharged the shotgun in the air. At the sound of the shot, she took off, running like a white-tailed deer. She ran past Eula sitting by the fire and quickly stripped off her clothes, jumping into the bed she shared with her sister Lucy. Lying in the darkness, she had listened to her parents' low voices, Eli's angry and abrupt and Eula's calming and not without a hint of sympathy.

"I tole you her was smellin herself," Eli accused.

"Her twelve. Don you remember what it like?" Eula soothed.

"I sho'll do, an I don wan that for her right now. Her got enough smarts that her can do sumptin odder dan lay up in de woods wit some ol triflin boy! I don wan dat for her."

"Now, Eli, I member you was always tryin to get me to the woods."

"Dats right. I aint denyin I want trying . . ." Eli hesitated as pleasant memories interrupted his train of thought. "But you wouldnt come into de woods wit me until us was older."

Eula reasoned with him, "She a good girl . . ."

"An her gon stay one! Just like her been raised! Dat Carrie Mae always been too fast!"

"What you gonna do? Lock she up!"

"It aint gonna do no good! . . . I lock she up, I got to lock myself up to keep an eye on her . . . I suppose now is as good a time as any. I been meanin to talk to you bout dis." Elizabeth strained to hear as Eli hesitated, his voice dropping. "Miz Smiley ast me bout sendin Lil Bet to school on de mainland. She say she real quick, can learn anyting!"

"You wan to send my baby away?" Eula cried out.

Elizabeth shivered in the dark as her father tried to calm her mother. She moved closer to Lucy's warmth as chills set in.

"No, I don. But we always knowed she was special, dat she got sumptin else, dem ol ways to see and know how and do."

"Dis punishment aint right!" Eula exclaimed.

"It not punishment, sweetness. It gonna hep her be more dan what her know right now. Her could be de first of us to finish school."

"Eli, you aint sending my baby off!" Eula stood up abruptly and walked out onto the porch.

Eli followed her, cajoling and persuading. As their voices moved farther from the house, Elizabeth got out of the bed and tiptoed to the window. In the moonlight, she saw Eli put his arms around Eula to comfort her. Eula, shaking her head, pushed him away and headed down the beach, her white nightgown shimmering across the sands. Her father gazed after his wife and turned slowly to return to the house. Elizabeth scurried back to bed and held her breath as he entered the house. She listened to her father move around in the dark and then heard the back door slam as he left in the night.

After several days of dense, painful silence between her parents, her father told her of his arrangements for her to go to school on the mainland. Having finally agreed, Eula set about mending her underwear and making two new blouses and skirts for her stay. It seemed to Elizabeth that those were especially miserable days for her and her mother. Normally a patient, understanding woman, Eula had found fault with almost everything Elizabeth had done, from her ironing her school clothes to the way she packed the small trunk. Although Elizabeth knew that her mother's anger was not solely directed at her, for some time afterward she carried the guilt and pain for having caused the anger between her parents.

When Elizabeth looked into Carrie Mae's smiling eyes, she considered the irony of her parents' perspectives. Her mother had welcomed her back from school with all the love and joy that a homecoming could bear. Eula easily accepted the changes in Elizabeth as a part of her being a young woman, a Peazant. Eli, however, was uneasy with this composed young woman who was his daughter. He had sent her away to get an education and was the first to call her back. But he missed the old Lil Bet, whose face had shown her every thought and feeling.

Carrie Mae giggled. "Chile, I neber forget yo daddy comin up in de yard dat next day wit my big ol drawers hanging offa stick and axtin my mama if she knew who all dey was. Lawd, she whip me til okra roped!" She threw her head back and laughed. "But, yall know. Whats done is done! Whats out is gone! And it was out of me!" Winking at Elizabeth, she added, "And I aint missed it one damn bit!"

They laughed together, and Carrie Mae filled Elizabeth in on at least five years' worth of gossip as the others began appearing on the beach and coming out of the woods when the time for Willis George to appear drew near.

Everyone had finally settled; Jacob steadied the boat as the others stepped in and blushed painfully when Elizabeth thanked him. Miz Eunice had found a place for her five baskets of eggs, okras, and the large sugar tomatoes that only she seemed to know how to grow. J.C. Best had packed his three bushels of crabs and packets of salted cod in the bow of the boat. Carrie Mae had good-humoredly taken her place in the stern as gruffly ordered by Willis George. Toady had scrambled to join her, wanting to be as far from the crabs as possible. Miz Pearlie Jane had taken her customary seat in the middle of the boat, primly gathering her skirts around her and tying her hat securely against the brisk wind. After helping to settle her two young cousins in the bottom of the boat next to the bushels of crab, Elizabeth had slipped in next to their mother, Iona.

"I dont know where you find the time to do this with all those children running roun," she said, admiring the sweetgrass baskets that Iona had brought to sell.

"Chile, with six chilren runnin roun always into sumptin, you better find sumptin to do cuz dey be done drove you crazy! Dat's why I looks forward to gettin ober to Boofort every few months." She strained to see what her youngest was doing. "Shadda, don be messin with J.C.'s crabs! An course every lil bit o change can only help." As Elizabeth nodded in agreement, Iona studied her face, her eyes caressing the sharp angular features and the burnished skin with its purplish-blue tints.

"Girl, we so proud of you we bout to bust wide open."

Elizabeth glowed at her cousin's words of praise.

"You done showed up everybody! Gone off to school and come back all pretty and smart!"

Elizabeth laughed. "I wasn't pretty and smart before I left?"

"Now, you know better dan dat! All of us is pretty and smart. But you got sumptin else now. Sumtin dat schooling give you."

"Well, whatever it is, I think it's scarin my daddy."

"Chile, it aint nothin new. Menfolk just wan de lil girls to get older, not grown up. Julian goin through de same ting about Clemmie."

"How old is Clemmie now?"

"Goin on thirteen. You see her soon. Julian say dat now you de teacher, de chilren be goin to reglar school."

"I was wondering if they were going to come."

"Well, you know he pull dem out right after your daddy did. Dat teacher dey sent out dat time was evil, you hear me! He like to beat de skin off Chance's back. It was all I cud do to keep Julian from goin down dere and killin him. So we been doin what we cud at home, but you know, we can only go so far."

They both started as Willis George barked out, "Hold on, everbody. We movin out."

Iona called to her children, "Shadda, Neeny, yall hold on. Stay in de bottom of de boat now, babies."

Everyone held tightly to the seats and the sides of the boat as Willis George pushed away from the pier. Suddenly there was a shout, and they all looked toward shore to see Sugarnun racing for the pier. Willis George shook his head and continued to push away as the others shouted encouragement to him.

"Come on, boy. I see you run faster dan dat!" yelled J.C. as Miz Pearlie Jane looked on disapprovingly.

Carrie Mae and the children giggled at the sight of Sugarnun running with his guitar bobbing behind him. The children clapped as he leaped from the end of the path onto the pier. The planks on the pier shook as he pounded toward the edge. Carrie Mae and Toady turned to see if Willis George was going to push back toward the dock.

Willis George stared at Sugarnun as he slid to the edge of the pier. Once childhood friends, Willis George had had hard feelings against Sugarnun since the time when they had both been courting Sallie Lee Rogers. He had laughed with and admired Sugarnun for his skill with women, but Sallie Lee Rogers was different, and Sugarnun had not seen how that wounded Willis George.

Willis George had been most serious in his pursuit of Sallie. He had loved Sallie since the first time he saw her, strolling down the street with her cousins in Charleston. She was the most beautiful thing he had ever seen, with her little red hat and white lacy gloves that covered her dainty hands. It was her laugh that had drawn him. It seemed to echo through his mind for days after he first saw her.

For Sugarnun, a man known for his loving pleasures and his sense of fun, it was just another of the casual relationships that he thrived upon. He had long since turned those country ways that the mainlanders disdained into the kind of boyish appeal few women could resist.

Sallie, who with her cousins had a reputation for enjoying a good time, preferred Sugarnun's playfulness and sweet mouth to Willis's slow, serious ways. For all of her city sophistication and despite the warnings of her cousins, Sallie had fallen in love with Sugarnun and had been sure they would marry when she told him that she was going to have his baby. Sugarnun had done what he did best. He had run, and when Sallie tried to find him, she came across two other women who had children for Sugarnun. Both loved him as she did, and both were waiting for him to return to them when he stopped his running.

When Sallie's father, a deacon in the Morningstar Baptist Church, ordered her from his house, she stayed with her cousins, refusing to leave the house until Willis George tracked her down, begging her to marry him. He swore to her that he would treat the child as his own. Sick with shame and depression, she agreed to marry him and moved to the Island to live with him. Although he was determined to honor his promise, it had seemed to Willis George that God had stepped in when the perfect baby girl with Sugarnun's high, slanted cheeks had been stillborn.

"Jump! Come on, act like de sheriff after you!" laughed Carrie Mae as Sugarnun stood on the edge of the pier gauging the distance from the pier to the boat.

He stepped back and started to make his run. Willis George stopped pushing and watched him. As Sugarnun closed in on the edge, Willis spoke up, "Man, dont jump in my boat!" Sugarnun teetered on the edge, flapping his arms to regain his balance.

Sugarnun appealed, "Come on back den. You aint dat far out."

Willis George set his oar in the cradle and crossed his arms, gazing at Sugarnun without expression. J.C. stopped rowing and waited to see what Willis George would do.

Sugarnun grinned at him and stepped back, acting as if he were going to run again. "Do I gotta jump?"

"I done tole you, dont be jumpin in de boat." Willis picked up the oar, and with a nod to J.C., they rowed back to the pier. As soon as they got close enough, Sugarnun slid into the boat and made his way to the back behind Carrie Mae and Toady.

"Who you hidin from?" Carrie Mae asked as he maneuvered past her. "Only time you come on back dis way is when somebody chasin you. You can hide the fire but what you gone do with the smoke?"

Sugarnun settled in the back, grinning at her. "Get in odder folk bizness, get de nose cut off."

"Mm-mmph! I spect I hear all bout it when we gets to Boofort," Carrie Mae replied.

Placing his guitar carefully to the side, Sugarnun leaned back in the boat, enjoying the heat from the morning sun. He peered around Carrie Mae's broad back to see who else was in the boat. He recognized everyone but the young woman sitting next to Iona. From her looks, he knew she was a Peazant, but he couldn't quite place her. There were so many Peazants.

Leaning forward, he tapped Carrie Mae on her back. "Who dat up dere with Miz Iona?"

Carrie Mae snorted. "You done had your run at her. Dat you aint gonna get!"

He ran his fingers along Carrie Mae's spine. "Who she be? I know she a Peazant. I jus dont know which one."

Carrie Mae stretched her back as his fingers continued exploring. "You been warned once, man!"

Sugarnun coaxed, his fingers digging into the flesh and massaging. Carrie Mae groaned and looked back at him. "Dat Lil Bet."

Sugarnun stopped caressing her. "Lil Bet? Eli's daughter, Lil Bet?" He leaned around Carrie Mae and stared at her.

Elizabeth glanced up, met his stare, and smiled at him. "Sugarnun."

He nodded to her, tipping his hat respectfully, and sat back carefully, ignoring Carrie Mae's snigger. He, too, remembered that night nine years ago. He had run through the woods taking a little-known route that twisted and turned across the island, leading to the secret place he escaped to when his stepfather's beatings got to be too much. He had heard the shotgun go off and prayed that Lil Bet would not tell her father who had been in the woods with her. Eli was known as a fair and decent man with a temper that would scare the devil himself if he felt that his family was being threatened.

Sugarnun stayed in his hiding place until just before dawn, figuring that he would slip back home before the sun came up. When he stepped from the well-hidden shelter in the copse of juniper bushes, he saw Eli sitting on a fallen log with his shotgun laying across his lap. He had forgotten that Eli was one of the best trackers on the Island.

"I was wonderin when you was gonna come outa dere," Eli said calmly.

He still remembered the terror that threatened to drown him as he stared at Eli, the feel of the warm liquid coursing down his leg as his bladder emptied. To this day, he felt no shame that he had fallen to his knees and begged God and Eli to forgive him for his sinful thoughts. Eli shook his head as Sugarnun cried, prayed, and vowed never to look at another woman.

Hauling him to his feet, Eli shook him by his collar until he stopped sobbing. "Now, Woodrow McKinley Harrison, you know you gonna be doin dis for de rest of your life. Aint no sense in all dis carryin on and lyin to me and de Lord bout you aint gonna be doin dis and dat! Dere ain't but one ting you aint gonna do. You ain't gonna mess wit none of my daughters! You hear me?"

Sugarnun fervently asserted, "Yassuh! I aint even . . ."

Eli hushed him. "Dont make promises with your mouth dat your butt caint keep, boy."

"Yassuh!"

He nodded vigorously as Eli asked, "You understand me?"

He slid to the ground when Eli let him go, his legs quivering. Lying there he watched as Eli disappeared. What he distinctly remembered was that Eli had not made a sound as he headed back through the woods. He had said one of his best "thank you, Jesus" prayers as he lay on the ground, face pressed in the sand. Over the years, he had broken just about every promise he ever made, save that one.

Sugarnun pulled his hat over his eyes. "Yassuh, Miz Lil Bet Peazant always be safe from me," he thought as he dozed off to the steady rocking of the boat.

Elizabeth hurried down the shallow alley lined with carriage houses, clutching her bags and packages. She knew that she was late and that the Bouvier sisters would be impatiently waiting for her. She had gotten the tenpenny nails that Eli wanted, the ten yards of cotton that Eula needed for making new shirts and blouses for her brothers and sisters, the box of snuff for Miz Sara, the tin of chewing tobacco for Mr. Joseph, the bag of hard candy for the little ones, and the few school supplies she could afford. At the last minute, she remembered to stop by the post office and pick up the mail for the Island. It had not been picked up for a couple of months, and Eula had specifically reminded her to get it.

She reached the back gate leading to the Bouvier house and fumbled with the latch. Carefully balancing the packages and bags, she pushed the gate shut with her foot and made her way up the cobblestone path leading to the back porch. As she reached the door, the topmost packages started to slide, and desperately trying to grab them, she let even more packages slip from her grasp onto the steps. The back door opened, and Elizabeth looked up into the face of a young colored girl about fifteen years old.

Dressed in a maid's outfit, the girl took in the spilled packages and Elizabeth's slightly disheveled look. "You E-liz-bet?"

Elizabeth nodded as she picked up the packages.

Placing her hands on her hips, she announced, "Dey been waitin for you all day long! Dey done ast me a hunned times where you is!"

"I had to run some errands. . . ."

"Don make no never mind to dem! You aint got no odder bizness if-fen you work for dem! I jus has time to get a lil sumptin to eat fore dey ring dat bell."

She watched as Elizabeth struggled to pick up the packages, then stepped off the porch and began to pick up others, adding them to the pile in Elizabeth's arms.

"What's your name?" Elizabeth asked.

"My name Katie. I been workin for dem bout two months now. Dey bout to run me to death!" She shoved packages into every open crevice until she had found a place for all of them.

"You better hurry up with all dat!" She turned abruptly, entering the back porch. Elizabeth stopped as the back door slammed in her face. With an impatient cluck, Katie came back and held the door for her. They both heard the bell as they entered the kitchen.

"Dere dey go again! All I hear is, E-liz-bet done it dis way, E-liz-bet done dat!" Katie fussed as she scurried down the hall to the summons.

Elizabeth laid the packages on the floor and looked around the old kitchen. She had spent so much time in this kitchen, shelling peas, washing rice, and chopping onions for Bertha, the Bouviers' cook. She knew this house as well as she knew her own home. Glancing down at the dingy linoleum, she thought of the many hours she had spent on her knees, trying to get it as spotless as the Bouviers required. She noted the curled edges of the linoleum running along the wall, the frayed lace curtains, and the faded wallpaper that the sisters had brought back from one of their trips to Paris. Stepping over to the stove, she lifted the whistling tea kettle and poured the hot water into the pot that sat on the silver tray. She rearranged the silverware and re-folded the napkins in the open-petal design taught to her long ago by the Bouviers. Slipping out of her coat, she made a note that at some point she would have to teach Katie how to set a pretty tray for the afternoon tea. Priming the kitchen pump, she quickly washed her hands, straightened her clothes, and patted her hair into place.

The kitchen seemed so much smaller and the old icebox rattled much louder than she remembered. The lace curtains had turned beige with age and did not look like they could stand up to a good washing. She peered out onto the side of the yard where the vegetable and herb garden had been. It was a thicket of weeds with mint running its length. She heard the sound of quick footsteps in the dark hallway that led to the rest of the house.

Katie rushed into the kitchen and grabbed the tea kettle.

"I've already filled it. Why don't you let me take it in to them?"

"Thank you! I still got to bring in de wash!" Katie grabbed the basket by the door on her way to the clothesline.

Elizabeth reached down into her bag and pulled out the medicinal charms she had made for the Bouviers. Miss Genevieve suffered from deep congestion of the chest, while Miss Evangeline was a prisoner to fierce headaches that made her all but incoherent. Both swore that Elizabeth's charms did more to relieve their discomfort than any medicine Dr. Anderson could provide. Elizabeth would always add a special touch—buttons made from seashells or a small spray of dried flowers—to the charms she made for them because they loved cheerful objects. Only when Elizabeth saw the sisters wearing the charms pinned to their blouses had she realized they could serve another, decorative purpose. She placed the charms on the tea tray and headed down the hall.

When she reached the library door, she stood quietly before entering. The two sisters sat in their chairs, draped in beautiful hand-painted shawls, their laps covered with cashmere throws, and a late afternoon fire burning in the fireplace. Miss Genevieve was squinting at a tapestry that she was working on, while Miss Evangeline read from a book in a quaking voice.

"Bonjour! Bonjour!" Elizabeth called out, stepping into the room.

The sisters started, turning around in their chairs. "Elizabeth, *bonjour! Bonjour!*"

"Comment ça va?"

"Très bien! Très bien! Oh, it's so wonderful to have someone else to speak French with. And you still have such a pretty accent."

Elizabeth set the tray down and poured them each a cup. She added the two lumps of sugar with milk that Miss Genevieve always had and the tablespoon of honey that Miss Evangeline preferred. She handed each their cup of tea and served them the small butter and bread sandwiches that Katie had made. Miss Genevieve clutched Elizabeth's hand as she leaned over her to straighten her shawl. "Our Elizabeth all grown up. You are the picture of accomplishment, isn't she, Sister?"

Miss Evangeline sipped her tea and admitted, "School has smoothed those rough edges." She appraised Elizabeth, taking in the simple cut of the blouse and skirt, the heavy socks, and the sturdy, practical shoes. Pulling her watch from her waistband, she reproved, "However, school has still not taught you to be on time."

"Oh, please, Evangeline, just because we were expecting her this morning doesn't mean that she is late," admonished Miss Genevieve.

Elizabeth walked around the room as the sisters bickered. She looked up at the shelves of books that ran from the ceiling to the floor. When she first came to work for them, she had promised herself that she would read every book in that library. While she had not accomplished that, she had gotten through a goodly portion and was warmed by the sight of some of the old favorites that she had escaped into during long hours spent in the library. The portrait of Miss Genevieve's late husband, Burton Delancey Devries, had darkened over the years, but he still frowned down upon her, disapproving of the young colored girl who dared read his books.

Eli had been dead set against it when Miss Smiley told him that she had found a place for Elizabeth in Burton Devries's home. Long dead, he was still remembered in Charleston for having drafted the harsh Jim Crow laws and having pushed through the high poll taxes that silenced the newborn voice of the colored community. Eli held him accountable for the lynchings that had swept through Forbes County ten years before. Miss Smiley had done her best to assure him that Miss Genevieve and Miss Evangeline were nothing like the man who had ruled their house and Charleston. She pointed out to Eli that their father, Judah Kincaid Bouvier, had been known by both the white and colored communities for his fairness and honesty. Only very reluctantly, and with Eula gently pointing out that his mother's friend, Bertha McCauley, had worked for the Bouviers for over ten years, had Eli agreed to let Elizabeth go to work and live with the sisters.

It had been a difficult time for Elizabeth. She had never been away from her family, and the sisters were so contrary in their ways that Elizabeth lost hope of ever pleasing them. What suited Miss Genevieve fine would never please Miss Evangeline, while Miss Evangeline could care less about things that sent Miss Genevieve into a tizzy. If it had not been for Bertha, she doubted that she would have lasted a month.

Bertha had come upon the broken pieces of the Wedgwood cup wrapped in a tea towel and hidden in the clothes basket, and had stood with Elizabeth as she tearfully confessed to the sisters and had spoken up for her good nature and willingness to learn. Bertha had been twice as demanding as the sisters and right stingy with her praise, but when she believed in something or somebody, she would not back down for anyone. As Elizabeth settled into the rhythms of the house and began to read the moods of its occupants, she would no longer flee to her small room as soon as her chores were done and would linger in the kitchen while Bertha set out the dough for the next morning's bread.

Elizabeth came to realize that Bertha, who had never been to school and could not read, was interested in her lessons. Everyday when Elizabeth returned from school, she would recite as much of the lesson as she could remember for Bertha, who would listen very carefully, but never ask questions. It was Bertha's pointed comments about Elizabeth that had influenced the sisters to take an interest in her as someone other than the colored girl who did the light housekeeping and washed and ironed their clothes. Just as Bertha had predicted, the sisters were startled by Elizabeth's quick mind, and it was not long before they invited her into the library to read aloud to them from one of the many books that lined the walls.

During those long hours in the library, they reminisced about their long stay in Europe from childhood to young womanhood. As the clamor for war with the North had grown, their alarmed mother had insisted on taking the children to Europe. Their father, a successful merchant, would not leave his lumber business, well aware of the demand that war would create. He had put his family on a ship headed for Birmingham, England, stocked with his lumber. His wife carried several Northern bank drafts with explicit instructions for their deposit and use. They had spent eight years abroad, living comfortably in a small chateau on the outskirts of Paris that belonged to a distant cousin. It had been a magical time for them, filled with music, art, books, travel, and concerts. They had only reluctantly returned five years after the War had ended at the insistence of their father, who had tired of the long once-a-year trip to see his family.

"Elizabeth! Come! Come tell us all about what you have been doing," Miss Genevieve entreated.

Elizabeth crossed to them and picked up the charms. "Well, as you know, I am now the schoolteacher on the Island."

Miss Evangeline peered up from the tapestry. "And how many pupils do you have?"

Elizabeth pinned the charm on Miss Genevieve, who exclaimed at its prettiness, holding her head down as she deeply breathed in its aroma. She sighed. "I can feel my chest clearing already."

Wryly, Elizabeth commented, "Well, that depends on what's going on that day. It can range from five on up to twelve. My cousin is going to start sending hers, so that means I'll get two more."

She pinned the charm on Miss Evangeline, who abruptly asked, "Are you a good teacher?"

Ignoring Miss Genevieve's gasp, Elizabeth replied, "I'm not so sure about how good I am, but I know I'm better than what they had."

Miss Evangeline stared at her, then gestured impatiently to Miss Genevieve. "The book, Gennie, give the book to Elizabeth."

Miss Genevieve handed a compact volume to Elizabeth. Elizabeth smiled as she recognized the worn binding. It was one of the sisters' favorites, the French edition of *Madame Bovary*. This was one of the many books that had arrived in shipments from their cousin in Paris. Elizabeth remembered the excitement she felt as she dove into the large wooden crates to find the treasures hidden among the packing straw. While Miss Genevieve had exclaimed over the perfumes, the colorful scarves, and boxes of wonderful hats, Miss Evangeline had glowed as she pulled the books from the bottom of the crate. Elizabeth also remembered the profound disappointment she had felt when she realized that the books were in a language she could not read. At the sight of her crestfallen face, the sisters had taken it upon themselves to teach her French. Because she normally had a difficult time understanding the way white people spoke, Elizabeth was surprised and delighted at how much she enjoyed learning French. To her, French was as musical a language as the Geechee dialect that she spoke at home. Never at a loss for an opportunity, the Bouvier sisters quickly put her aptitude to use.

Pulling the ottoman to a place between the sisters, Elizabeth began reading in a low, clear tone. Miss Evangeline lay back in her chair with a smile and sipped her sweet hot tea while Miss Genevieve peered at her tiny stitches and nodded as Elizabeth read.

Yawning, Elizabeth sank onto the low bed in the smaller bedroom down the hall from the large bedrooms. She had been headed to the tiny attic room where she had spent so much time, but had been stopped by Miss Evangeline and directed to the second floor. Katie had left right after cleaning up the dinner dishes, informing Elizabeth that she would never sleep in the house filled with so many haints. Elizabeth had not been surprised by this because this was a house full of memories, both good and bad. She had often felt a presence in the house, the sharp scent of cigar, a step in the hallway, or the brush of a taffeta skirt as she scrubbed the front steps. Just because she had not been born with a caul over her face did not mean that she could not read a house, could not sense the souls that had passed through, could not feel the emotions trapped within the walls. On this night, however, as she sat tiredly on the bed, all she heard were the creaks and sighs of an old house that had fallen into disrepair along with its occupants.

She glanced at the pile of packages that lay in the corner, looking for the small valise that held her nightclothes. Kicking off her shoes, she crossed to the pile, setting packages aside in her search. As she pulled the valise from the back of the pile, the mail pouch slid to her feet, spilling letters, catalogues, and newspapers across the floor. Kneeling to stuff the mail back into the pouch, Elizabeth casually perused the assortment and noted that her father's tool catalogue and a copy of the *Charleston Free Press*, the colored paper, were included. What looked like a box of prayer cards awaited Preacher Monroe. She turned over a stack of letters tied together and smiled as she recognized her cousin Myown's distinct handwriting. Although her letters did not come regularly, Myown was the one of the Peazants who had moved up North who kept in touch. Eula must have sensed that there would be a letter from Myown because she had twice reminded Elizabeth to pick up the mail. Elizabeth pushed the letter back into the pouch, saving it to be read when the entire family was present. She flipped through the package and then slowly withdrew a letter addressed to her. Although it had the same return address as Myown's, she did not recognize the square, economical handwriting as Myown's or her mother, Haagar's. She tore it open and read:

October 11, 1926

Dear Cousin Elizabeth,
  I hope this letter finds you and yours doing well. By now, you should have received Mama's letter. She is doing a bit better and is very happy that I am coming to Ibo Landing to do my studies. I am writing to you to ask for your assistance in the field project I must complete to get my degree in Anthropology. The purpose of my field project is to gather information about the colored people who live on the islands for my senior thesis, "The Colored People of the Carolina Coast."

Elizabeth stared at the letter, trying to picture the writer in her mind. The only memory she had of Myown's daughter, Amelia, was of a perfectly dressed doll-like little girl who always kept her shoes and socks on, willingly took a bath, and would not leave her grandmother Haagar's side. It had been many summers ago, but Elizabeth remembered the quiet child sitting on the low porch solemnly watching as she and the other children played endless games in the hot afternoon sun. In her few letters to Eula, Myown would mention Amelia's latest accomplishment, a well-delivered poem for the church pageant, an invitation to attend a special party, or a piano recital, but Elizabeth had never given Amelia much thought. She certainly never expected her to come to the Island on her own, particularly "to gather information . . . for my senior thesis." Elizabeth had not even known that Amelia was in college. She had only the vaguest idea of what anthropology was. Shaking her head, she read on, wondering what this girl wanted from her.

  From what I understand, I am related to most of the people on the Island. However, I do not know them and would need your help to make the necessary introductions. I also need to find a place to stay while I conduct my studies and would gladly pay for my room and board. Mama said that you would be the best person to help me. I would be most appreciative.

As she continued to read, Elizabeth tried to sort this out. From what she knew and had heard of Aunt Haagar, she would never have agreed to allow her precious granddaughter to return to the Island, studies or no. And what and who was she going to study?

Like every person from the islands, Elizabeth had felt the ridicule and knew the contempt of the mainland coloreds who sought to distance themselves from their island cousins. Her first few years at Avery Normal had been especially hard, with the teachers and the students making fun of the way she spoke and the home-stitched clothes she wore. She had rarely spoken in class. Everyone knew that Geechees were slow and backward, the hardest people to teach anything. When the teachers saw the results of her schoolwork, they naturally assumed that Elizabeth had copied someone else's lessons. She would never forget the shame she felt when the teacher had moved her from her assigned seat to a desk beside her where Elizabeth's work could be monitored. It was with great reluctance that the teacher noted that Elizabeth's schoolwork was as good as her other students. Regardless, through that first year, she kept Elizabeth at the desk beside her.

As the years passed, Elizabeth had learned to speak like the people on the mainland, but every now and then a simple Geechee phrasing or inflection would slip easily into her speech and she would hold her breath waiting for the quick correction or taunt to come. Elizabeth remembered the airs that Haagar and others would put on when they returned to the Island to visit kinfolk, the fine store-bought clothes they wore, the careful way they spoke, and how they held themselves above those who had stayed. If Amelia thought that she was going to come down here and then go back up to New York and tell funny stories about them, she could think again. Several years before, Eula had mentioned that a white man had come up and wanted to talk with them about the way they lived, but it did not make much sense to them. When no one had anything to say to him, he soon left.

As far as Elizabeth was concerned, you did not study family, you lived with them. She was of the mind to write Amelia immediately and tell her not to waste her time and money, until she read the last sentence.

I will be arriving in Beaufort on November 7. Mama has given me directions for making my way to Dawtuh Island if you cannot meet me. I look forward to seeing you.
Your Cousin Amelia

The letter fluttered to the floor as Elizabeth calculated quickly. Cousin Amelia would be arriving this coming Saturday.

Amelia sat in the colored waiting area at the Beaufort train station. She clutched her bag as she watched white people greet each other while colored porters grabbed their luggage, placing it on carts to be hauled to the wagons and cars that waited out front. She was sunken-eyed with exhaustion and quite hungry, for it had been a long trip and she had found little comfort on the hard wooden benches in the colored car.

She turned as someone cried, "Lanie!" and laughter broke out when a group of colored people rushed over and hugged the young woman with two small children who had gotten on in Baltimore. Amelia had been startled when she was awakened at Baltimore and instructed with several other passengers to move to the back of the train. It was not until she had struggled with her bags and pushed the door open to see a car filled with sleeping colored people that she realized they had crossed into the South. As she found herself a place among the sprawling bodies, she recalled her father's words; "You be back as soon as you get a taste of what it like down there! Your mama go on bout de land and good folks an all, but she ain't tell you bout them evil buckra folk down there. Do all they could to keep a man a slave!"

It had been especially difficult, these last few weeks as she had prepared for her trip. Just as she had expected, her father and her grandmother had initially refused even to consider letting her take the trip South to work on her field project.

"You ain't going nowhere! There ain't nuttin to study down there! Ain't nobody down there but them old ignorant country negroes!" Haagar howled when Amelia explained what she planned to do. She turned on Myown. "This ain't coming from nobody but you! You done filled her head with all that mess about the Island! Well, she ain't going! Ain't that right, Arnold?"

Amelia's father had shaken his head in agreement. "This school stuff was always foolishness. I ain't never liked it! Who gonna help me wit my work? You know I caint afford to bring nobody in to pay."

Everyone had been startled when Myown spoke up firmly. "I help. I take she place. You aint gonna have to hire nobody."

There was a stunned silence, and then both Haagar and Arnold laughed, mocking her. "Woman, you know you ain't got the stomach for this kind of funeral work!" Arnold responded.

"Girl, just the fumes would make you sick. Remember when you first started, it took all you had to hold yo head up," Haagar snapped. "Look at you. You sickly all the time."

"I say I help, I gonna help!" Myown said with conviction.

"That's all good and well, but we ain't got no money to send her down there!" Arnold pointed out.

"I got a little bit saved, and the school is going to give me some money," Amelia said quietly.

Her father was disbelieving. "The school gonna give you money to go down there and mess around with some old country fools?"

Amelia felt herself shrinking into the protective posture she had learned to assume as a child. Hunching her shoulders, she hung her head, preparing for the harsh words that inevitably followed.

"Now, if that ain't some mess! Ain't that some mess! What kind of school this is? I declare I ain't never heard of nothing like this!" her father shouted.

"Have you lost your mind?" demanded Haagar.

As her self-confidence evaporated, Amelia's hands began to shake. She felt weak with anger at her father and grandmother and a deep disappointment in herself. She had never been able to stand up to those two and had always done as they wished. Myown leaped over and stilled her trembling hands.

"It cause she got a good mind dey gonna send her. An she goin! I don care what yall say, she gon do dis! Somebody in dis house gon do sumptin dey want!" Myown spoke in a low, ferocious tone.

Haagar and Arnold stared at Myown and then looked at each other. Arnold had never seen his wife show this type of spirit before. He had married her to seal his agreement with Haagar, who had given him the money to start his business. Arnold had not only acquired an undemanding and meek wife, but also a tough business partner in his mother-in-law, and although he would never admit it, it was only through Haagar's skills and determination that he was still in business.

He had known little of Myown when he married her, and he knew little of her now. She was as quiet and colorless as her mother was noisy and bold. Haagar would drain the life from any man with her constant complaints and demands, while Myown faded into stillness at the sound of a raised voice. After her difficult pregnancy and Amelia's birth, Myown had retreated even further into her silences. When she moved into Amelia's room two years after the birth, to nurse the child through a bout of pneumonia, he had not missed her. She had been of so little interest to him that even Haagar's spiteful observation that Myown was not going to return to their bedroom had failed to rouse him.

He leaned back in his chair, not recognizing this newfound courage his wife displayed. Myown's eyes met his, and he was taken aback by the clarity and determination he saw. Haagar started to speak. Myown raised her hand abruptly. "Enuff! Aint gonna be no more fussin bout dis! You done run everyting! Now, I done decided! She gon finish her studies."

Haagar glared at her daughter, then stood up and stalked from the room. Arnold looked at his wife and then at his daughter. With a grunt, he stood up. "Don't be expecting no money from me!" He made a big show of putting on his topcoat, setting his hat on his head, and then slamming out the door that led to the downstairs parlor.

In the silence that followed, Amelia felt hot tears splash down her cheeks as the anger expelled in the room vibrated around her. Myown wiped them away with her bare hands, whispering, "It all right, baby. Aint nobody gon take dis away." Amelia clutched at her mother's hands, drawing strength from the deep, dark lifelines that marked her mother's palms.

As the time for her to leave drew closer, Amelia developed the shell that would let her deal with her grandmother's disapproval and her father's disregard. Her grandmother had launched a daily assault on her and her mother, reminding them of her sacrifices and even going so far as to take to her bed, claiming that her heart could not stand the strain. Her father had adopted an amused, contemptuous attitude, waiting for his wife to collapse as she struggled with the chemical fumes and cleaned the preparation room. Late at night, as they lay in the bed that they shared, Amelia begged Myown to come with her, fearful of leaving her mother there to face the two of them all alone. But Myown was determined to stand by her promise of taking Amelia's place. She would not give her mother or her husband the satisfaction of seeing her fail.

Now, Amelia shook herself as she began to doze. Glancing up at the clock on the wall, she noted that she had been waiting for two hours. It was dinnertime, and everyone else had headed home. She felt a stab of panic as she wondered if Elizabeth had even received her letter. The old colored man who had swept out the station passed a second time, then hesitated and came over to her. "We bout to close up for de night. De las train done come and gone." Amelia stared at him, not quite knowing what to do. "Who you kin? Dey suppose to come for you?" he asked, staring at her clothes.

She stifled a yawn as she spoke. "My people live out on Dawtuh Island. I thought somebody was going to meet me."

He frowned at her. "Oh, you be one of dem Geechees! You don soun like no Geechee. You got de long way to go, lil gal. All de way cross de water! Where you gonna stay tonight?"

Amelia reached into her bag and pulled out a piece of paper. "Miss Harriet's Boarding House."

He nodded. "It aint dat far from here." He pointed. "Go down to de first road, and it de gray house four doors from de corner. You gonna hab to gettin long cause I got to close up now."

Amelia stretched and stood up stiffly. She picked up her valise and eyed the wooden crate that contained the moving picture camera Professor Colby had loaned her. He had insisted that she use the camera sent to him by an old friend. It was a 16mm, hand-cranked camera.

At first, she had demurred. Accustomed only to her Brownie camera, she had been intimidated by the bulky Akeley camera equipment and how much it would cost to replace it if she damaged it. He had brushed aside her concerns by explaining that in exchange for testing the war-weary camera, her benefactor would pay for all the film and processing. He enthusiastically spent several hours tutoring her on how to operate the camera, maintaining that the images she brought back would add weight to her research. The crate was very heavy, and she did not know how she could get it to the boarding house. She stared at it, trying to figure out what her next step would be.

Amelia carried her valise to the platform leading to the street and then returned to push the crate across the floor. As she struggled with the burden, headlights from an approaching car swept across the room. An old Model E pulled up in the front of the platform, its horn weakly sounding. The car was covered with dust, and rust spots stained the fenders and the roof. When the car slowed, it wheezed and knocked, idling down as if it were about to cut off. She peered into the car, and a young colored woman waved from the driver's seat.

"Cousin Amelia?" Elizabeth leaned out, putting the car in gear. "I don't dare turn it off. It may not start up again!" With that comment, she hopped out of the ancient car and climbed the steps to the platform.

As they appraised each other, Elizabeth noted the steady, solemn gaze that had not changed since the last time she had seen Amelia. She did not see much of her cousin Myown in this young woman who stood before her in a city-smart suit and fashionably bobbed hair. Although she had never met Amelia's father, his mark was clear, from the way she held her head to the reddish tint in her skin and hair.

In response to Elizabeth's pin-neat appearance, Amelia self-consciously straightened her rumpled suit. She took in the sharp, ebony features and the coarse, thick hair that was neatly braided and pinned on top of Elizabeth's head. Amelia shyly extended her hand, not quite sure of herself. "Cousin Elizabeth."

Elizabeth tilted her head and smiled at her as she took her hand. "Cousin Amelia."

They both looked down as their hands touched, Elizabeth's fingers slim, nimble, stained the color of freshly brewed coffee and Amelia's, broad, blunt-edged, the color of red oak. As she clasped Elizabeth's hand, Amelia felt the effects of the long trip, and the anxiety from the wait at the station sweep over her. She shuddered with weariness, blinking back tears as she looked into eyes that gently reflected her. "I wasn't sure that you got my letter. I didn't think anyone would come."

Elizabeth's grasp was strong as she apologized. "I just did get your letter. I had to come over from Charleston." She picked up the valise. "You come on now. Miss Harriet's holding dinner for us."

"Willis George is a good boat man. Can't nobody read the water and the wind like him," Elizabeth said, leaning over to reassure Amelia. When Elizabeth had appeared with the car, Amelia had naturally expected that they would drive out to the Island. After Elizabeth explained that her employers had lent her the car simply to get back and forth from Charleston, Amelia had been a little bit relieved because the old car did not look like it could make it back to Charleston, much less out to the Island. However, she had been thoroughly alarmed when she found out that the only way to get there was by boat. She had thought that, by now, a bridge would have been built to Dawtuh Island. Elizabeth quietly reminded her that little had changed since her last trip as a child.

Amelia's natural caution, her fear of deep water, and the sight of the faded boat that would carry them across to the Island almost sent her back to New York. Several men, women, and small children stood on the pier, laughing and talking among themselves. Watching as the men loaded her box and luggage into the boat, she had not realized that her every doubt showed on her face. One of the men on the boat had looked up at her and nudged the other as she stared into the swift, murky water. "Ah, lil gal, don let Yemoja pull you down into de water," he warned.

She looked at him, not comprehending his thick accent, unable to find the rhythm in his speech. He spoke again. "Yemoja, she don like what she see, she pull you in de water and wash you clean to Fuskie."

She stepped back from the edge of the pier, bumping into Elizabeth, who stood behind her. "What did he say? What does it mean?" she asked.

Elizabeth waved to the men as they took their places by the oars. "Most folks still believe in the old ways they brought from Africa. Yemoja, she's a god from there. She live in the water and folks say she snatch you into the water if you make her angry. He was telling you not to stare too hard at her lest she decide to take you with her way out to Daufuskie Island, that the first island out there in the water." Amelia peered off toward the horizon, but all she could see was water and waves.

Elizabeth stepped around her to the edge of the pier. "They're about ready to leave." A man moved forward to help her into the boat. He steadied her as a wave caused the boat to rise slightly out of the water. He then turned to help Amelia, who hesitated slightly and then moved forward. Amelia grasped his hand, holding on for dear life as she stepped into the boat. Tightly shutting her eyes, she held her breath while the boat rocked, unwilling to let his hand go. When he gently squeezed her hand, she opened her eyes and thanked him, half-embarrassed by her fear. She perched on the seat next to Elizabeth as the others climbed in.

Taking deep breaths of the sharp sea air, Amelia tried to concentrate on the people around her, making mental notes to be written up when she arrived and was settled. They had settled into the boat with the easy camaraderie of family and longtime friends. Greeting Elizabeth, they stared at the young woman who sat stiffly beside her, wary of her city clothes and the reddish cast to her coloring. Even after Elizabeth had introduced her, saying, "This Cousin Amelia. She belong to Myown," they had simply nodded politely and taken their seats for the trip.

Amelia noted that the people had not changed much from her childhood memories. They still wore the rough, sturdy clothes that she remembered, the women favoring the long skirts with burlap aprons and the men in their overalls with the old topcoats. She could tell those who worked on the mainland because their clothing was a solemn mixture of handmade and store-bought pieces, all carefully put together. She studied them as they talked easily among themselves in low voices, using unfamiliar intonations and musical inflections that floated back to her. As she could hear but not understand, she felt the same uneasiness that she had felt as a child on that earlier trip.

At that time Amelia had been frightened by these people, their shabby clothes, the strange words they used, and the wild, uncontrollable energy that seemed to swirl around everything they did. When her grandmother kept her at her side, she took comfort and felt safe. These people were nothing like her neighbors, the parents of her friends, or the people at her church, back in Harlem. The young cousins who ran wild in the woods, the old people who gathered to sit at the edge of the yard, the stories of ghosts and hags who had put a spell on someone, all those things had kept her on that porch next to her grandmother.

She saw what her grandmother and father had meant when they called someone "country" and "backwards"; the rolling gait as they ambled down the street, the slow, almost distracted way of talking punctuated with long pauses and a lot of head scratching, and the gaudy colors they wore that clashed with the darkness of their skin. "She too black to be wearing all that yellow!" Haagar would declare as a young woman would sashay past them on the street. "That girl straight out the country!"

Amelia had also been terrified of their blackness. They had been too black, to her child's eye. Only used to her mother's and grandmother's darkness, she shrank from the sea of black faces that surrounded her, afraid of the secrets held within all the darkness. At an early age, she *knew* that the darkest blacks were rude and loud, more likely to put up a fuss about anything. She had seen the difference between the dark-skinned family that had lived a few doors down with the children racing through the hall and the light-skinned family who lived beside them and kept to themselves. When the light-skinned family had moved out, Haagar had raged for days about "them no-good coal-black negroes driving out the better coloreds." She saw the difference in treatment in her school, readily accepting, as every other child in her class did, that the princess in the school pageant would be the lightest girl with the longest hair. It was only right that in her church the lighter-skinned members sat in the front pews.

Haagar had pointed out to her the advantage of being lighter, the invitations that would come her way, and the opportunities that she would have because she was not as dark as the others. She was well aware that her grandmother had pushed her mother to marry a light-skinned man, to "marry up" so that the family could do better, prospering as their children took advantage of the opportunities that lighter skin brought. But she had not seen any happiness in her father, who cursed the white man who left only his coloring to his three children and seemed to feel only contempt for his own people. Puzzled by his choice of her dark-skinned mother, she would realize years later that it was an act of defiance against two worlds that would never accept him.

Casually practicing the bias herself, Amelia's friends tended to be the brown-skinned girls from her school or the high yellow girls in her ballet class. Her grandmother eagerly noted which family each girl came from and what position they had. It had pleased her to make her grandmother happy until, in the fifth grade, she was teamed with Portia Clarke for an arithmetic contest. Portia was the smartest, funniest, and darkest girl in her class, and they became great friends. She would escape to Portia's house, where there was always laughter, good food, and interesting talk. She enjoyed Portia's older sisters, who were the most stylish and jazziest young women she had ever seen. She was always invited to the family outings that might include a trip to the museum, a day at the beach, or a Saturday-afternoon matinee.

At first Haagar had disapproved of Portia because her family came from Jamaica, but she quickly fell under her charm and good spirits, noting that Portia's father was educated and ran his grocery store like a white man. A special bond formed between Portia's mother, Kathryn, and Myown as they discovered the similarities of growing up on an island and spoke together in sweetly accented tongues. Amelia was happy that her mother had finally found a good friend that she could talk to.

Both Amelia's and Portia's hearts had been broken when the Clarke family moved back to Jamaica for her father to teach at the University. Despite their earnest promises, the stream of letters between them had dwindled and finally stopped over the years as they both moved on to other interests and friends.

Amelia changed after Portia left and no longer cared about the teas and socials that the rest of the girls so enjoyed. At her grandmother's insistence, she did attend them, but she found little comfort in these formal affairs presided over by righteous women who treated others according to the shade of their skin color. Always the quiet child, she watched as they carefully schooled the young girls on being the "better Negro," advising them to stay out of the sun and warning them about the primitives and their blues music.

It was also the time when Myown's illness threatened to get the better of her. Myown had never adjusted to the thick, acrid air of New York and over the years had developed a persistent cough. A deep chest cold had worsened the cough and sent Myown to her room for weeks. Amelia sat by their bed and watched as the rich brown tints in Myown's skin faded to a gray tinge. When the doctor finally came, he said there was little he could do and that it would be best for the family just to wait. Haagar had stomped from the room, and when Amelia awoke much later that night, she had been alarmed to find Haagar and a very old woman named Mother Hill leaning over Myown. Everyone knew that Mother Hill was a conjure woman, and Amelia flung herself across her mother to protect her. Calling for her father, Haagar pulled Amelia away. As her father dragged her from the room screaming, she looked back to see Mother Hill sprinkling herbs over Myown and chanting. That night, fearful that the witch had come to steal her mother's soul, she cried herself to sleep on the settee in the front parlor.

Hours later, waking to a silent house and shaking with dread, she slipped down the hallway to the room she shared with her mother. Myown lay on the bed so still that Amelia was sure she had died. As she watched her mother, she heard the sounds of shallow breathing. A rustle from behind her made Amelia turn, and as the shadows fell away, she saw Mother Hill sitting in the corner watching her. She stepped back as Mother Hill shuffled to the bed and lifted her mother's hand. As Mother Hill held Myown's hand, Amelia could see color saturating her mother's skin. It seemed that with every rise and fall of her chest, color would pulse through her body, washing the ashiness from her hands and flushing the pallor from her cheeks. Mother Hill placed Myown's hand in Amelia's, advising her, "You watch de color. De strent of de color show de strent of de body." And she had stood there for hours, waiting and watching as her mother regained her strength and her color.

Sitting in the boat now, she studied the different hues that marked the blackness of her fellow travelers, from blue to purple to mahogany to jet. Unlike the blemished or ashy complexions familiar in New York, their skin was soft and flawless, like moist, shimmering satin. Scrutinizing their features, she saw in them the same lines that she had seen in the photographs, wooden sculptures, and masks that lined Professor Colby's office, the lines that led directly to Africa. She wondered if they tried to hide the ancestor lines like the colored people in Harlem, or if they lived easily with evidence of their past. Her grandmother would never talk about the past except to say that they were much better off, and her father claimed his past had ended when he left Arkansas at thirteen years old. Myown would share bits and pieces until Haagar interrupted, admonishing Myown about filling her child's head with all that silliness.

Every now and then, one of her fellow travelers glanced back at Amelia and touched their chest. Only the children were bold in their stares, blushing and giggling when she smiled at them. Elizabeth had also noticed the gesture, the touching of the protective charm that everyone wore under their clothes. She chided herself for not remembering how suspicious people were of "red-bone" people. Cousin Amelia with her brown hair and red-brown coloring would have much to overcome.

Willis George shouted as the boat cleared the inner harbor and moved into the open water. The men guiding the boat slipped into their places and picked up their oars. Willis sang out in a strong baritone, *"Oh, when. Oh, when. Oh, when. Oh, when."* The others, including Elizabeth, joined in setting the rhythm for the rowing. *"Oh, when I come to die. Give me Jesus."*

Amelia turned to look back at the shore and, in her mind's eye, saw her mother and grandmother and the other Peazants crossing these same waters to make the big trip up North. Some had come back, stung by the coldness of the weather and the people, but most had stayed up North. Amelia had not been witness to the closeness that had held the Peazant family together since their beginnings on the Island. Once they had reached the North, it seemed that everything that had held them together disappeared as they struggled to provide for themselves and their families. Like Haagar, in the rush to fit in, so many left much of the Island behind. Only Myown spoke wistfully of those bygone days when family would get together to simply celebrate one another.

At the shout from Willis George, the tempo of the song picked up and the boat shot forward through the waters. Amelia turned from the shore and peered through the harsh sunlight at the islands that waited for them, floating in the distance.

It was just before sundown when the boat drew close enough to shore to drop off the first group of people. The trip had been uneventful, and Amelia was relieved that she had been able with Elizabeth's help to quell the seasickness. Elizabeth saw Amelia clutch the side of the boat as the waves rocked them and whispered to her, "It helps if you draw in de air like dis." She demonstrated with long, even breaths of the sea air. Amelia did as she was told, trying to suppress the dizziness and the nausea that swelled in her stomach as the boat surged through the water. It would not do for her to get sick in front of these people who rode the sea so well. She had cringed inwardly as the group passed food and drink around during the trip, happily eating as the boat heaved.

Once she had taken her mind off her sickness, she had actually enjoyed the ride, the cool breeze providing relief from the hot sun rays that reflected off the water. Her excitement matched the children's when a school of dolphin swam beside the boat, racing it through the waves and turning away as they headed for the shore. A brown pelican flew in their wake, swooping down to catch the fish that trailed the boat for the small bits of food being thrown overboard. Elizabeth sat beside her in silence for most of the trip, responding to the few questions or comments made to her and then returning to her book. Amelia had been surprised by Elizabeth. She was not the Lil Bet she remembered who had led the others through the woods to hunt for rabbits, who could beat everyone in a footrace and had taken a cousin's horse on a wild ride through the swamp. Amelia suppressed a giggle as she stole a glance at the "Heathen Child" of Haagar's description who sat next to her sedately reading a book.

Amelia had noticed that several of the people had taken their shoes off and tied them around their necks once they got into the boat. She had assumed that their country feet had tired of city shoes and they had taken the first opportunity to rid themselves of the confinement. However, as they drew closer to the Island she realized there was a practical reason for this. Because there was no dock on this stretch of beach, the boat could only come in so far without getting caught on the low shoals. Two men slipped over the sides of the boat and held it secure as women and children slid out into the waist-high surf and made their way to the shore. She watched fascinated as a woman, with a baby strapped to her chest, balanced a large basket filled with dry goods on her head and settled a toddler on her hip to carry him to the shore.

Once on the shore, a man lit a tar pitch torch, signaling to Willis George that all was well. As he pushed back into the deeper water, she could hear their calls of "Bydee-bye-bye" floating out across the waves and could see the torch moving along the beach, lighting the path back into the woods.

She stared into the gloom that began to shroud the Island as the sun fell. The large oak trees that had beckoned them from across the water blended together to form a thick cover that ran along the shore. As they moved closer to the shore, they could hear the night sounds, the screech of an owl, the chattering of a raccoon, and the bark of a fox. Amelia swatted at a mosquito that brushed her face. Every now and then, she would see a flicker of light from a house that sat back off the beach in the first stand of woods, but for the most part, the Island was completely dark. Used to the sights and the sounds of the city, she felt an odd mixture of fear and excitement. As they moved along the outer shore, she saw, in the distance, a low pier lit by torches.

Elizabeth touched her shoulder. "We'll be getting off there."

Amelia swallowed, looking into the dark water. "Do we have to wade in?"

Elizabeth shook her head as she began to gather her things. "He can pull in real close to the pier." Amelia tightened her grip on the seat as a large wave rocked the boat. "We on the north side, the water is a bit rougher here," Elizabeth explained. In the dim light she pointed to a patch of swift water that ran about a hundred yards out from the pier. "We get past that and everything be right."

Amelia could sense the change in mood as the men fought the current to get the boat close enough to the pier. They stopped singing and listened carefully for Willis George's commands as they pushed and waited, using the strength of the current to move closer. Amelia gasped when a wave slapped the side of the boat, spraying everyone with water. Elizabeth threw her arm around her and held her close as the men heaved together, sending the boat directly into the current. Fear shot through Amelia as she felt the current catch the boat and push it just past the pier. For one moment, she was sure that the men had lost control of the boat. A shout from Willis George and the men heaved again, popping the boat out of the current. As they reached the calmer waters, the men grinned at each other, their white teeth flashing in the dark and at Willis George, nodding in satisfaction. They then rowed for the pier at Ibo Landing.

Though Amelia felt a shudder pass through her, she quickly assured Elizabeth that she was all right as she waited for them to tie the boat to the Ibo Landing pier. Ignoring Elizabeth's outstretched hand, she clambered onto the pier and straightened up unsteadily. Still swaying, she made her way over to the edge and bent double. Elizabeth held her head until she had stopped heaving and then helped her to sit down. Amelia kept her eyes closed in embarrassment, sure that everyone had watched her discomfort. When Elizabeth wiped her face with a damp cloth, she mumbled, "Thanks," and took the cloth, pressing it to her pounding temple. She listened to the teasing of the men as they unloaded the boat.

"I seed yo face, J.C. You aint gon tell me you wasnt callin on de Lord." A man laughed.

"Boy, dat wasnt nuttin. Willis George and I done com in here on worst nights dan dis," J.C. bragged. "You was as close to white as anyone eber seen you!"

Amelia looked up at the sound of approaching footsteps. Willis George stood in front of her, holding out her bag. "How you doin, lil gal?"

She stuttered as she met his direct gaze. "I-I-I'll be all right."

He spoke abruptly. "You right dere wit us."

She stared at him as she took her bag. "I was real scared."

"Aint nothin wrong wit being scared." He turned away and called to the others. "Yall finished? J.C., we got to get movin. It close to Sallie Lee time, an I got to get home! You get somebody to come get dis box, Lil Bet. It too heavy for yall!"

Elizabeth waved to them as they climbed into the boat. "Yall be careful out there. Willis George, I spect to see Amos in school reglar!"

As Elizabeth picked up her valise and walked back to Amelia, she heard his grunt drift across the water. She looked at Amelia, whose face sagged with exhaustion. "We got to get you to bed." She leaned down to pull her to her feet. Grabbing a torch from the pier, she helped her cousin along the path to her parents' house.

It was Amelia's third attempt at waking up. Try as she might, she had not been able to open her eyes; each time she thought she was on the verge of waking, she would slip back into the deep sleep of exhaustion. Lying there in the twilight between sleep and wakefulness, she could hear the sounds of the house around her. She recognized Eula's soft rustle and quick step as she moved around the kitchen and stirred as the smell of frying fish filled the house. Somewhere outside, her younger cousins played, their shouts and laughter filtering through her sleep. From a distance, there was a steady metallic clang, and she wondered idly if the streetcar would stop in the front yard when it came through. As she told herself that she would count to three and then get up, she drifted back into her sleep.

Eula stood on the porch and watched Eli as he washed his hands for dinner at the pump. He splashed the cold water on his face and headed toward the house. She handed him a soft cloth and went back into the house. He wiped his face as he entered, glancing over at Amelia as she lay in the low bed she had shared with Lucy.

Peeping in the pots, he spoke to Eula as she set up the dishes for dinner. "You sure she all right. She aint moved since her lay down. Her sleep like she dead."

Eula sighed and handed him the spoons to set out. "She jus dat bone weary. Dat long trip an de rough crossin. From what Myown wrote, I spect dere was no peace to be had in dat house when her made known what her was gonna do."

Eli nodded. "I still spectin Haagar to come bustin up in here to take she back home." He chuckled. "I hope her dont spect no peace in dis house. Dem chilren aint quiet when dey sleep. You hear Henry snorin, soun like a hunnert-year-ol man!"

Eula looked over at him. "You know where he got it from."

Eli tilted his head at his wife and crossed his arms. "You aint gonna lay dat on me!"

Eula turned from filling the bowls with rice at the stove. "Eli, after twenty-some-odd years of sharin a bed wit you, you gon tell me you dont snore?"

Eli grinned at her. "Not like dat! Aint never heard a Peazant snore like dat!"

"All right, now," she scolded him as she spooned the okra and tomatoes over the rice. "Why dont you call yo chilren for supper?"

He stepped out onto the low porch, picked up the conch shell, and blew three times. The sycamore tree on the edge of the yard rustled and shook as the twins, Henry and James, dropped from its lower branches and raced across the sand. Lucy straightened from the weeding that she had been doing in the backyard garden. And the metallic clanging stopped as Ben dropped his hammer, banked the fire in the forge, and headed for the house.

Eli blocked the door as the boys ran up onto the porch. "Where's Rebecca?" he inquired, looking for the baby of the family.

"Her stay to help Lil Bet at de school. She gon hab dinner wit her."

Eli grabbed Henry as he tried to duck under his arm. "Yall wash up?"

But Henry chose to discuss this with his father. "I wash my hands dis morning."

James sprinted over to the pump. Pushing Lucy aside, he sprinkled water on his face and hands. Dodging her cuff to the back of his head, he ran up onto the porch just as Henry was banished to the pump. Eli shifted back and forth across the doorway, keeping James from entering. "Let me see dem hands!" Eli demanded. James ducked and feinted with his father, and when he saw the opening, scrambled through his legs into the house.

Eula hushed them as they dragged their stools to the table. "Sh-sh! Cousin Amelia sleepin." Henry marched over to where Amelia lay under the mosquito netting and stared at her. He had been excited when he heard that they would be having a visitor from up North, but he had lost interest in this girl who had not risen from the bed since she had arrived two days before. Lifting the netting, he moved in for a closer examination. When Amelia's eyes slowly opened, he fell back.

"Her wake!" he shouted excitedly. James rushed over to get a good look and bumped into him, pushing him against the bed. Amelia turned her head and looked at Henry as James peeked over his shoulder. She stared at this two-headed apparition, then closed her eyes tightly, thinking that she was dreaming again.

Eula appeared and shooed the boys back to the table. She slipped under the netting and sat on the edge of the bed. "Happee-Day! How you feeling?"

Amelia struggled to sit up. Eula moved forward to help her. She reached out and touched the netting tentatively. "I couldn't remember where I was."

"Right where you been for de las two days," Eula informed her.

She looked at Eula in horror. "I've been asleep for two days? Oh, my God, you must think—"

Eula interrupted, "That you needed you sleep." She stayed Amelia as she made a move to get out of the bed. "Where you going? We bout to eat supper. You sit here, and when you feel like eatin, come on over and join us to the table." As Eula comforted her, Amelia became aware of the voices of the others standing outside of the netting. She had only the vaguest memory of her arrival at the house after the crossing. James pulled back the netting, and she saw her other cousins peeping in to get a glimpse of the newly conscious visitor. Embarrassed, she turned her head. Eula turned and fussed at James. "Dint I tell you to git ober to the table? Eli!"

From somewhere beyond the netting, Eli intoned, "James!" James reluctantly dropped the netting as Eula stood up.

"Where can I wash up?" Amelia asked self-consciously.

Eula called out, "Lucy, get one of my shawls and some cloths and show cousin Amelia where she can wash up." With a quick smile, she slipped outside the netting and crossed to the kitchen.

Amelia sat on the edge of the bed and looked for her shoes. When she could not find them, she slid to the floor on her hands and knees and looked under the bed. A pair of broganed feet appeared, and she looked up to find Lucy grinning down at her. "Better be careful under dere! Neber know what cud be layin up under dere waitin for you!"

Amelia sprang to her feet and hopped on the bed. Lucy laughed at her and handed her the shawl. "Yo shoes over dere wit yo odder tings."

Amelia wrapped the shawl around her and followed her out of the netting. She looked over at the kitchen table, where the rest of the family watched her. She said, "Good morning."

The twins frowned at her. "It not mornin," Henry declared.

Eli nodded. "Good mornin, Cousin Amelia."

Henry frowned at his father. "It not mornin!" he insisted. Amelia ducked her head and went out to wash up.

Amelia stepped out on the low porch and looked around the yard. She could see glimmers of light reflecting off the water through the thicket of trees and bushes that faced the house. She could hear the waves breaking on the beach and realized that they could not be as far from the pier as she had thought. It had seemed to her that the last trek of the journey after the crossing had taken hours. She stepped off the porch and walked over to the side of the house, where Lucy primed the pump for her. Lucy pointed to the basin, the soft cloths, and the rough piece of soap that sat on the crude table by the pump.

Picking up the basin and holding it under the pump, Amelia asked Lucy, "Do you think I might be able to take a bath sometime soon?"

Lucy looked at her in shock. "It aint Saturday!"

Almost apologetically, Amelia explained, "I just wanted to get this travel dirt off me."

As the water spilled from the pump, Lucy declared, "It aint Saturday!" She stopped pumping and frowned at her cousin. Shaking her head, she turned and walked back to the house, leaving Amelia to wash up.

There was only the sound of the wood popping in the fireplace as Eli and Ben pried the top of the wooden crate open. From the moment they carried it up from the pier, the wooden crate had stirred the curiosity of everyone but Eula. As soon as the family finished dinner that evening, the twins had demanded that Amelia open the crate. Eli waited until Eula had scolded the twins and then offered his assistance in opening the crate while Ben appeared in the doorway with tools from the forge.

When they pulled the top off, Amelia dug into the crushed newspapers for the gifts that she and Myown had slipped into the crate. Eula was as delighted with the smart hat that Myown had selected as she was with the hatbox that accompanied it. Lucy, after suspiciously accepting the gift, slipped into the thick cardigan sweater, exclaiming at its warmth. Eli and Ben thanked her politely for the Sunday shirts that crackled with starch as she pulled them from the box. The twins were thoroughly unimpressed with the dime novels that she had presented them with. And Rebecca stared bewildered at the yellow-haired doll with the rosy cheeks.

As Amelia pulled more papers from the crate, Rebecca asked, "You got sumptin in dere for Lil Bet?" Nodding, Amelia searched until she pulled out the glass bottle carefully wrapped in paper. She noted with relief that it had not been broken. She had been puzzled by Myown's choice of a gift for Elizabeth. From Haagar's description of Elizabeth and what little she remembered of her, the last thing she would have chosen would have been the bottle of French perfume from the drug-store up on Seventh Avenue. But Myown had insisted that this would suit Elizabeth perfectly.

"Kin I tek it to her?" Rebecca tugged at her arm.

Eula pulled Rebecca into her arms and reminded her little one, "That Amelia gift to her. She give it to her tomorry."

Eli and Ben looked at her expectantly since the box was still half full. She pulled out her Brownie camera. "I wanted to take pictures of everybody."

Eula commented with emphasis, "Man come through few years back, take pictures of folks. I been trying to talk Eli into going to the main-land to get some good pictures of the family." Eli shrugged and turned his attention back to the box.

James leaned over into the crate and tugged at the tripod in the box. He dropped it when Eula slapped his arm. "Boy, I don know whats got-ten into you."

Amelia cautioned him, "This is not for play, James. You're not to touch this." She leaned over to lift the Akeley moving picture camera from the crate.

The camera was small but heavy, and Eli and Ben helped her as she struggled with it. They gasped as she pulled out the metal contraption with the assortment of dials, gauges, and lens turrets. The twins pushed forward to get a look at the suspicious object. When she pulled out the flat boxes of 16mm film, Ben could contain himself no longer and blurted out, "What is dat?"

She looked up from the crate and replied, "It's a moving picture camera."

Astonished, Ben asked, "Like in de picture show in Bofort?"

Slightly embarrassed, she admitted, "Yes. My professor loaned it to me so I could test it."

Eli stared at the machine. "It take de pictures dat move?" At her nod, he asked, "Why you need all dis?"

There was complete silence as they waited for her tentative answer. "I need it for my study . . . to show how folks live down here."

"Why you want to get into folks' bizness?" Lucy immediately chal-lenged her. "It aint none of yo bizness!"

Amelia struggled. "It's what I study, how people live, how they do things."

Lucy interrupted her. "You come down here with all yo fancy tings an yo wantin to take a bath in de middle of de week. You aint up to no good!"

Eula hushed her. "Lucy, dis fambly you talkin to."

Lucy continued to accuse her. "We dont know she. She come down here to make fun of us like de other mainlanders. Ackin like we de fools!"

Eli, looking troubled, spoke quietly to Amelia. "When yo mama asked we to help you with de studies, her dint say you was studyin we."

Amelia gazed at him for several moments, a shock going through her as she realized that the difficult time she went through with the faculty review was insignificant compared to the grilling she was now receiving from her own relatives. She struggled for words. "I want to find out where we came from. It's important to know what makes us different."

Lucy hissed at her, "You de one different! We just de way we are!"

Amelia looked around at them, Lucy angrily patting her foot, Eli's face showing his concern, and Eula rocking Rebecca as the silence deepened. She glanced over at Ben, who was examining the windup camera, fascinated by the gauges and the dials. Amelia tried again, "I don't want to upset anyone. I just want to find out more about where we come from." She appealed to Eli. "I was hoping that you would share some of your stories with me. Mama said you were a grand storyteller."

Eli sighed and stood up. "Well, I don know. Dont nobody like anybody pickin at dem. Most of dis is fambly talk, aint for other people. You best be careful how you do dis." He glanced at Ben, who was leaning over the equipment. "Ben, we got to go put de animals in for de night." He lit a lantern and went outside, reluctantly followed by Ben.

Lucy shook her head, sniffing. "I aint habin nuttin to do wit dis foolishness! Dont be askin me nuttin." She stalked off to sit in front of the fireplace.

Eula got to her feet, nudging a sleepy Rebecca toward the back room, where she and Eli slept. Amelia began to gather up the packing material and put the camera back into the crate. Eula stopped in the doorway, turning to watch her. Amelia glanced up at her. "You got to give folks time to get used to all dis," Eula said.

The shutters flew open as the wind picked up outside. In the flickering light, Elizabeth pushed her lesson papers away, rubbing her eyes from the strain. When a gust swept across the room, blowing the papers from the table, Elizabeth crossed to secure the shutters. Before she pulled the shutters closed, she looked out at the quarter moon, which hung over the water. In the dim light, she could see the storm clouds blowing in from the East. She had smelled rain all day, but had given scarce thought as to how the old house would hold up in a decent storm. Her father and brother had replaced over half of the roof, but with winter coming on, would not be able to start up again until the spring. She knew that Eli was still irritated with her for insisting on seeing through the winter in the old house.

She could see the edge of the storm, the curtain of rain moving inward with spears of lightning flashing in front of it. She grabbed her shawl and stepped out into the yard to watch it advance. When the thunder and winds shook the trees at the edge of the yard, she thought of the many times she and Nana had stood in that yard and watched the storms close in.

Nana had taught her to look for the spirits that rode with the storm; Oya, who brought the fierce winds, Obatala, whose booming voice was masked in the thunderclaps, and Yemoja, whose moods would change quickly, one minute sending the rain down with stinging force and the next minute gently sprinkling the land. Many a time, Elizabeth had glimpsed a fierce face as she stared into the storm.

She whispered the old incantation, calling out the thunder by its name, "*maulin a bumba.*" Even as she shivered in the cold and jumped at the crack of thunder, she loved the excitement and sense of renewal it brought. In the early morning after the storm, the sea would be calm and the animals would come out slowly from their hiding places, seeking the warmth from the morning sun. There would be new finds on the beach, bits and pieces tossed ashore as the struggle between water, wind, and sand continued.

Letting the shawl slip from around her, Elizabeth lifted her arms to the skies and felt the first drops of cold water splatter her face and body. She gasped as the wind sucked her breath away and the thunder shook the ground under her feet. She stood there cleansing for as long as she could, her gown plastered to her body and rivulets of water running down her legs. Yelling at the top of her voice, she challenged the storm, but when the lightning shot across the yard and she smelled the heat from its charge, she quickly retreated to the house with Nana's words ringing in her ears, "You can be so foolish, gal."

She regretted that she had not set a fire earlier that evening as, shivering, she stripped off her wet clothes. Quickly slipping into her flannel nightgown, she spread her shawl and the old cotton nightdress out on the floor to dry. She knelt to light the fire, expertly packing the dry moss in around the kindling, including a bit of wild cherry bark to sweeten the smell. As the fire caught, she threw more wood on and warmed her hands. Sitting back on her heels, she surveyed the room looking for the leaks. There were several places from which the water dripped in relentless streams. She dashed from one place to the other putting pots and cans under the leaks, thinking ruefully about her father's offer. He would have much satisfaction if he could see her now. She also noted the chinks in the walls that would have to be filled to keep out the wind that was sweeping across the room. She pushed her bed in front of the fireplace away from a leak. Wrapping herself in two quilts, she sat on the bed staring into the fire, listening to the storm.

Her finger traced a square on the quilt. She recognized it as having come from Nana's old winter coat. Lifting it to her nose, she breathed deeply, trying to summon Nana's essence and the joy and safety of days past. She wanted to feel like Lil Bet, who had never known more than what was on this Island and had never questioned her rightful place. She was ill at ease with Elizabeth, who had come back in her stead with her dark moods and a mind filled with doubts. It seemed these days that there was such restlessness and longing inside her. She wished she had been like Lucy, who had returned from her year at school on the mainland and refused to go back. As she glimpsed the books lying on the table, she wondered what good her schooling had done her if she could not get her students to learn their alphabets.

She wondered what all of the schooling had prepared her for. It had opened her eyes and mind to things that were simply not a part of her world, this world. What good did it do her to read about places she had never seen and people she would never meet? What difference did her speaking French make if all those around her struggled with English? Then she felt the panic rise as she saw the years of teaching and being helper to the Bouvier sisters stretch ahead of her.

Jumping from the bed, she ran over to the walls lined with letters, searching for words of hope hidden among the mundane family news. She read the names of all those who had left. Some like Daddy Mac and Yellow Mary had come back for visits, while others like Lil Ray had just disappeared into the big cities. Nana had cried for each child who left, lamenting that each would forget their family and the old ways that had held them together. Elizabeth sighed. What was worse, being just another letter on the wall, or one of those eagerly waiting for the letters to come?

For the first time since she had returned, a picture of Dexter came to her mind. Perhaps she should have accepted his proposal. She shook her head. Of that, at least, she was sure. He would have been content with whatever she gave him, but it would not have been enough for her. She had wanted what her parents had, a passion and love that flashed between them like a living flame. What she and Dexter felt for each other was a mutual sense of comfort and gratitude. He had not stirred her in the passionate moments they shared. She could no more see herself as a minister's wife presiding over church teas and attending baptisms any more than she could see herself flying.

She trembled as a thunderclap shook the entire house and then scrambled back into the bed. As the storm moved on, she began to take deep breaths, calming herself. She thought of Cousin Amelia and wondered how she was holding up. When they had returned to school after supper, the twins had reported that she finally awakened. Elizabeth had admired the way Amelia struggled to make her way to the house that night after the crossing. She also felt a certain envy that everything Amelia would see would be new, while Elizabeth struggled for ways to see new things about the old.

When Rebecca pointed out that the day before Lil Bet had eaten a poor dinner of cornbread and molasses, Amelia jumped at the opportunity to take dinner to Elizabeth today. She had not been out of the yard since she had arrived and wanted to explore the Island. Besides, she was eager to start on her fieldwork, and she needed Elizabeth's help to provide the introductions. Eula had offered to send Lucy with her in case she got lost, but Amelia was sure that she could find the way on her own. Lucy had said very little to her, making her disapproval clear. Amelia's tentative gestures of reconciliation, her offers to help in the garden, had been rebuffed. Even though they shared the same bed, Lucy would climb in at night, turn on her side, and fall right to sleep without so much as a "good night."

Amelia followed the path that Eula had pointed out running back through the thick woods. She waved to Eli and Ben as she passed the forge, where they were repairing a cart wheel. Ben grinned at her as he securely held the hot piece of steel down while Eli hammered. She had promised Ben that she would show him how to use her moving picture camera, and in him, at least, she had an ally. Eli called after her, "Make sure you head back before dark." Lucy looked up from her weeding at the far end of the field as she passed and stared at her, hands on her hips. When Amelia waved to her, she nodded, pausing to wipe her face with her apron. Amelia could feel Lucy's eyes on her as she made her way down the path. However, when she ventured a backward glance, Lucy had returned to her gardening.

Amelia picked her way carefully among the worn ruts of the path. She could only see a few feet ahead and, city girl that she was, found herself reacting to every noise around her. The path ahead was mottled with bits of light and dark as the sun found its way through the trees. It reminded her of a drawing from a nursery book she'd had long ago, the top of the trees entwining to form a thick cover. Her heart jumped as a pair of quail flew out from the underbrush in front of her. She hurried down the path, only to be stopped by a mother opossum and her babies, who took their time crossing. She was thankful that Eula had insisted on her applying bug liniment, for even in the cooler weather, there were swarms of gnats and mosquitos along the path. At the sound of soft hooves, she looked over into an open glade and saw two deer, who stopped peeling the bark from a tree and sniffed the wind for the smell of the human. When they sighted her, they took off. She listened to the sound of their flight as they crashed through the woods. Myown had often described the simple pleasures of the walk to Nana's with the other children. She could so easily see her mother and the others walking along this path, picking ripe berries, throwing wild walnuts at each other, and playing games of hide-and-seek in the woods.

As she crossed the low land bridge that led from one side of the creek to the other, Amelia listened to the frogs and peered down into the water looking for minnows, watching as they fled when her shadow fell on them. She stopped and lifted the moving picture camera to her eyes to shoot the slow-moving creek and the tops of the trees that lay just below the surface of the water. She thought it was bothersome having to wind the film through the lens to make it work.

Slipping out of her jacket as she walked, Amelia adopted a looser stride, taking her time, lightening her steps. She had set off as if she were headed to the corner store for her grandmother, but now she slowed down, enjoying her surroundings. She giggled at the thought of her having a country walk, letting her hips roll and her feet sling before her as if she were in no hurry to get anyplace.

In the distance she heard the steady clop and squeak of a cart coming up behind her. She stood to the side and let it pass, waving to the driver who touched his hat and nodding to the solemn woman and child who sat in the back among the baskets. When the path turned, she saw the open sky up ahead and knew that she was coming to the wider road that led to the east side of the Island, where Nana's old house was. She had been intrigued to find that her cousin did not live in the large house with her family, but had moved into the old homestead.

Amelia turned onto the road covered with broken shells. She stopped and caught her breath as the beauty of the grassland marsh stretched before her. She had never seen so much green in her life. Interrupted here and there by silvery strips of water, it seemed as if it went on forever. She desperately tried to position the heavy camera as a flock of geese rose from the marsh and wheeled over her headed south; she pursed her lips with disappointment when the birds flew from her view before she could get them in focus. When she turned back to the marsh, a single cloud blew across, the shadow it cast bringing a dark mystery to the grasslands. She wound the film through the camera as the cloud tracked across the water, its shadow disappearing in the woods.

When she reached the turn for Nana's house, Amelia looked for the chinaberry tree with its carved trunk that Eula had described. She stopped at the tree, wondering what the pattern of crosshatched, straight, and curved lines that reached up into the lower branches meant. Stepping back to get a better view, she noticed a small, faded blue satin bag tied with a pink ribbon that was attached to the base of the tree. Amelia knew enough of Island tradition to know that the bag provided protection against any evil spirits that would enter this way.

Moving briskly past the tree, she followed the grass lane that brought her around to the front of the house, which faced the small cove. She stood in front of the old house, remembering the afternoon that she had spent on the porch next to her grandmother. Nana had already passed on by then, but one of her sons or daughters had still lived there, and it would always be considered the family place. As she walked up into the yard, she realized the house looked much as she re-membered, the indigo blue rimming the windows and the slanted steps leading up to the open front door. She could see the signs of repair that Elizabeth had begun. New wood shutters closed over the windows; the first coat of whitewash covered the front walls.

Calling to Elizabeth, Amelia walked up onto the creaking porch and stood at the open doorway. When there was no answer, she knocked on the doorjamb. "Elizabeth, it's me, Amelia." She stared into the dark-ness. Dark as it was, it was not frightening, and she felt at ease, waiting for her eyes to adjust. She could see that the room had little furniture; a low bed in front of the fireplace, a trunk, a high-back chair, and a table with two crude stools. Several pieces of crockery, pots, pans, and a coffe-pot sat on a sideboard that also served as a dry sink. Elizabeth's clothes hung from several pegs on the walls. Setting the camera in the near cor-ner, she walked over to the table, which had a pile of books on one end and an assortment of roots and herbs laid out to dry on the other end. Bunches of flowers hung from the rafters.

She laid the dinner bucket and her gift for Elizabeth on the table. It struck her that her cousin lived with the simplicity of the old times; she had just what she needed, no more, no less. She opened a shutter to provide more light and exclaimed with surprise as the light spilled on the wall covered with sheets torn from newspapers and catalogues.

Moving closer for examination, she stared at the wall covered with curling brown paper that blared the headlines from Beaufort and advertised everything from iron washtubs to four different types of plow. She was touched by the childish sketches that had been placed among the sheets, wondering which of the children had drawn them. Reaching out to touch a drawing that showed stick figures springing from the earth with much joy and life, she saw the edge of a letter sticking out from under it. She tried to peel the drawing back, but could only uncover the last part of the date at the top; "24, 1902." She stepped back and looked at the lower wall, seeing that much of it was covered with letters, yellowed pictures, and postcards. Finding a box of matches on the table, she struck one and held it close to the wall. She drew back as her eyes met the sharp, suspicious gaze of an old woman sitting in a fan chair. "This could only be Nana Peazant," she thought, as the force of the woman seemed to emanate from the picture. From what she had heard, Nana was a legend, the great-grandmother who had raised the last generation to grow up entirely on the Island. Her word had been absolute, and Amelia had felt her influence in the salt sprinkled in the corners and the broom that stayed by the door in the Harlem apartment. Despite Haagar's determination to rid herself of the old ways, she would not risk the uncertainties of the new life without protection from the old.

Amelia pressed her fingers to the photograph, almost expecting the figure to stir impatiently. "The lamp is over by the fireplace." Elizabeth spoke from the doorway. Amelia gasped and whirled around, dropping the match. "You can see much better with the lamp." Elizabeth entered the house, her arms filled with kindling. For the moment Amelia was speechless, having forgotten why she had come. She stared at Elizabeth as she crossed to the fireplace and stacked the wood in the large basket that sat to the side. Selecting a few pieces, she threw them in the fireplace, packed in some moss, and held out her hand to Amelia. Amelia handed her the box of matches and watched while Elizabeth tended the flame.

"I brought you dinner," she blurted out, pointing to the dinner bucket sitting on the table.

Elizabeth smiled slightly as she put more kindling on and the flame caught. "Becca told."

Amelia stammered, "Y-Your mother was worried about you. I didn't just walk in. I called out and knocked but . . ."

Elizabeth stood up and looked at her. "The door is open. I got to get more wood." She went to get the wood with Amelia trailing her. There was a neat stack of cut wood beside the house, and she selected several dry pieces. Amelia grabbed a few more and followed her back in the house. Elizabeth carefully laid two of the large pieces of wood on the fire and stepped back as the flames shot up. "It's Nana's house. You only knock if the door is closed."

Amelia handed her the gift from the table. "Mama sent this to you." Elizabeth carefully unwrapped the tissue paper. Her eyes widened when she saw the blue curved bottle. She delicately lifted the stopper and sniffed, her face rippling with emotion.

"How did she know?" she asked. Then she thanked her, turned away from Amelia, and placed the bottle on the table and crossed to wash her hands.

While washing her hands, Elizabeth gestured to the wall. "You see how me and Nana decorated the house?" Amelia nodded, staring at the wall. "Nana say she keep her children close to her," Elizabeth explained as she lit the lamp. She carried the lamp over to the wall and held it up so that Amelia could see.

Amelia peered at the other pictures; a group of men standing on the beach, a summer picnic among the dunes, and a laughing, fat baby dressed for christening. Elizabeth handed the lamp to Amelia. Grabbing a fistful of herbs from a jar, she dumped them into the coffeepot. She then set the coffeepot on the fire and crossed to close the front door, noticing the camera that stood near it. Amelia touched one of the letters. "That's my mother's handwriting," she said.

Elizabeth nodded, leaning closer to examine the letter. "From the date, she must have sent it right after they left for New York." She squinted at the neat handwriting, then gave Amelia a brief appraising glance and crossed to see what her mother had included for dinner.

Amelia studied the letter.

My dear Nana,

We are all fin and hope you is the same. We leav at the end of this week for New York. We need your prayers as we travel to the North. Aunt Bessie send you she best. Her been real nice to us and only laugh when Mama fuss bout she cookin. Cousin Ivan talk all the time bout how good things are up in New York. He done foun us a place to stay and he gonna take Daddy Mac and Lil Ray on the job wit he. Mama say for you to mak Iona to come to she. Her verry mad and want you to send she. Her talk about go to the law. Tell Eula, Eli, and Hattie Mae, and my odder kin dat I miss you verry much and I will come back to see you verry soon. I los the charm you give me when we leave. Please mak the blesing to Legba to see us on our way.

Alway your devoted, Myown
PS If you see my blest sister, Iona, tell she her always have my love.

Amelia turned away from the pain that lay behind the words. She looked back at Elizabeth, who sat quietly by the fire, nibbling at the sausage and biscuits that Eula had sent. The coffeepot boiled over on the fire. She crossed and sat on the low stool. Indicating the food on the table, Elizabeth commented, "Mama sent more than enough for two."

Amelia shook her head. "I ate before I set out."

Amelia looked around as the light from the fireplace filled the large room. At the sight of the cans and pots placed around the room, she remembered the rainstorm from the night before. "You're not afraid of being in this house by yourself?"

Elizabeth pointed to a wooden talisman that was attached to the base of the wall. "Nana make sure this is the safest house on the island."

Amelia hesitated and then asked, "What about ghosts?"

Elizabeth hid a smile. "Would only be Nana and her friends come to visit."

They sat in silence, listening to the crackle of the fire. Elizabeth rose and pulled the coffeepot from the fireplace. She filled two cups, handing one to Amelia. Amelia thanked her and then quietly stated, "I need to start my work. I came to ask for your help."

Elizabeth nodded, glancing back at the camera beside the door. She sipped from the cup and fixed a direct gaze on Amelia. "Just what is it you setting out to do?"

Amelia frowned. "It seemed so simple when I was first coming down here, but now I'm not so sure."

There was a long silence as Amelia struggled with her thoughts and feelings. "My professor wanted us to study ourselves so that we could learn to study others. We had to keep a journal about the things we did every day. When I turned it in, he started asking me questions about some of the things I put in it."

Elizabeth looked at her solemnly. "What kind of things?"

Amelia shrugged. "Some words I put in there; he asked me where they came from and I didn't know. It was just something I had heard all my life. When he started asking about them, I was kind of ashamed, because some of it seemed kind of strange, and other stuff I just didn't know what it was. And I started telling him what little bit I knew about where we came from. I told him about that time we came back to visit. He got real excited because he had a friend who had come out here sometime back and said it wasn't much different from slavery times." Elizabeth's eyebrows shot up, but she said nothing. Amelia continued, "He got me to go back and ask Mama some questions, and the more I asked, the more I got interested. So all of this took place over time, and

I decided I wanted to come down here and find out more about my own people, where we came from and why we did what we did."

Elizabeth leaned back and thought for a moment. "So you want me to help you get this infomation about how we not like other people?"

Amelia shook her head. "It's more than that." She pointed to the wooden talisman. "I want to know what all of this means, how it helps people in their everyday lives. I've seen my grandmother throw it away, and I've seen my mother hold it close. I just want to know what it is!"

Elizabeth frowned at her. "You tell this to my mama and daddy? What they say?"

"Your daddy's kind of worried, and Lucy is really mad," Amelia admitted.

Elizabeth nodded understandingly. "Well, you got to understand that living out here you only trust who you know and what you know. Now, Lucy don't go to the mainland if she can help it. She spent a year at the school over there, and even Daddy couldn't get her to go back."

"I didn't know . . . ," Amelia began to apologize.

Elizabeth stopped her, "She's the fighting Peazant. What she brought back with her, she handed out ten times over to those folks on the mainland. You'll get used to Lucy, she wear her anger on the outside. She don't let nothing wear out her insides."

Elizabeth stood up and stretched. She put more pieces of wood on the fire and warmed her hands. "All I know is what come to me from Nana and my mama. You got to talk to the others. Everybody live out here got their own story." Amelia nodded eagerly. "I can take you to them, but you have to get them to tell you. You got to let them tell it their own way. I can tell you right now. It's not going to be easy, because they don't like red-bones around here." When Amelia stared at her, uncomprehending, Elizabeth pointed to her skin. "And you better be careful with that." She pointed to the camera. "Some folks round here liable to think that you trying to steal their souls with that. All of us out here come from folks whose bodies had already been stolen."

Elizabeth slipped into the easy rhythm of Island talk. "You got to learn to listen an hear, gal. Listen to what they say, an hear what they dont say." She pointed to the collage of letters, pictures, and postcards on the wall. "Dont think dat dis be all of us. It not all of us by a long way. Maybe the middle, but not the beginnings or the end."

Amelia walked up and stood beside her. "Then tell me, tell me about the beginnings. What do I need to know?"

Elizabeth walked over to the chimney and removed two bricks. She drew a rusty tin from the space and pried it open. Reaching into it, she took out a piece of a necklace with three stone beads strung together.

"Kona beads. I dont know what dey for." Sliding to the floor, she placed them on the hearth. Amelia came and looked down on them. Her eyes widened as Elizabeth drew a short, thick plait of hair tied with a yellow thread from the tin and placed it beside the stone necklace. She moved forward to examine it, but was stopped by Elizabeth, who held up her hand. She waited patiently as Elizabeth slowly opened her hand. A small piece of faded blue cloth lay in her palm; she smoothed it with gentle fingers.

Beckoning for Amelia to sit beside her on the floor, Elizabeth spoke. "I will tell you the story of Ayodele, the first of us to walk dis lan."

The Story of Ayodele

as told by Elizabeth Peazant

I am Elizabeth Ayodele Peazant. I the first daughter of the first son, an like every first daughter of the oldest son in the Peazant family, I carry the name of Ayodele, the first of us to walk this lan. All I know is that it is African, and it means "Her who brings joy." I give you the words passed down from one Ayodele to the next.

She come into the world hand first! Back den an even these days, that a good sign. Baby coming in hand first mean dey never want for nothing. The whole village happy cause they know she bring prosperity like all those before her. Now, my baby sister Rebecca tell you that Ayodele a princess an her daddy a king. But they was plain folks as far as we know, respected folks where the men could handle any cattle or horse an the women could nurture crops from any type of lan. The village so happy that even the old Head Man broke the custom and visited the birthing hut.

The men in her family traveled far an wide to sell an trade the finest horses an bring back valuable spices an cloth for the village an to pay tribute to the Head Man. Ayodele's granmother an her daughters had they own field to see to. Each of the daughters grew only the crop that she knew best. Im not sure what the others had, maybe okra, cotton, or pumpkins, but Ayodele's mama must have been very quick for she was the one who grew the indigo. Nana say indigo dangerous plant to mess with an very poisonous. So you see, she must been plenty good.

You know all of us are good at raising things. My mother always talk bout how pretty the garden was that your mother an her sister would keep. She say the collards never got bitter an the tomatoes were sweet as sugar cane.

Now, to tell you more about Ayodele. She was raised in the fields with her girl cousins. As soon as they could walk they worked longside their mothers, doing the light weeding, chasing the birds, picking the caterpillars just like I did when I little. The girls would move from field to field learning to grow the different crops from each woman.

When she was a lil girl, bout the size of Rebecca, they give her a special place of her own to start her own crop. Her granmother give her some seeds, an she planted her own garden. An she get up in the morning before she go to the fields, an she weed an water the plants. She look everyday to see which plant sprout. Her mama an her aunts stop by to help an give good advice. Her cousins come over from their gardens an see if her plants as big as theirs.

At the end of the season, all the cousins would bring their plants from the garden for the granmother to see. She would praise them an remind them that it was their gift from the spirits. They would have a big celebration showing their brothers an daddy the fruit of their labor. All the village would take part in the celebration, the potters, the weavers, the basketmakers, an the warriors.

Twelfth year come, Ayodele in the indigo fields with mama, learning all she able bout growing indigo an making it into paste to be sent to de market. It was a long an difficult process, but she patient, an after her first successful batch, they began to call her "My Indigo Girl" as her mother did.

It a good time for the village, much food an no wars or raids from the other villages. Ayodele's daddy an brothers traveled even farther to trade, an on one of those journeys they were robbed of all they goods by tieves who live in the woods. When they returned, they had nothing to pay the high tribute set by the new Head Man.

The greed of the new Head Man was known by everybody, but never spoken of by the villagers. It understood that he trade in those captives caught in raids on other villages. An in his own village there were dose who had displeased him who had vanished, their families never to see them again. When the Arab visited the village, the mothers sent their boy children into hiding to the forest.

When the time came for the tribute to be paid, Ayodele's daddy brought all the grain except what would see them through to the next season. The Head Man demanded full payment an seized Ayodele as part of he tribute. Her father offered to pay three times the tribute if the Head Man would spare his only daughter. The Head Man refused an call for he an his sons to be beaten for trying to free Ayodele. Her granmother offered the Head Man all of the lans that had been in her family before her birth. He not listen. You see, the Arab would offer more for one who could grow indigo than any of the tings they could give. Ayodele was sold to the Arab an dragged away. She swore she heard the cries of her family an the voice of her granmother as she rained curses down on the Head Man every day of her natural life. She knew the betrayal of her family when she saw the horses stolen from her daddy in the caravan that took them west.

Nana told me that the women would never speak of the crossing. You know, those old Africans, they took plenty pride in themselves. The slavers, they did not know or care for the African ways. They throw the women an the men together like so many animals. They do not know about cleansing for women, the ritual washing of the body, the braiding of the hair an the oiling of the skin. For the Africans, it stole their spirit an broke their pride. Paymore, he come over on one of the last ships to reach these Islands, he told Nana the slavers would come down an use the women horribly. He say many women, Ibos an odders, jump from the ships. They tried to starve themselves, they killed their children. Paymore say maybe it was the hardest on the women, so hard they would not speak of it. Nana say one day she asked ol Ruby about coming over, an ol Ruby threw the apron over her head an shed bitter tears.

They did not bring Ayodele here at first. They took her someplace else, an when she come here, they forget all about her being able to grow the indigo. This place used to be owned by the Pinchney family. They come here from Barbados, where they owned a big sugar plantation. Maybe she come with them. Nobody know. Anyhow, the mistress running the place see how good she with getting tings to grow. Now it just so happens that the mistress been trying to raise indigo for a long time, but not having no kinda luck. Indigo a big cash crop back then, bigger than rice or cotton. They didnt have no odder way to dye clothing back then, so the plantation owners made lots of money selling it to England and such. Well, the mistress, Miz Pinchney, she even bring this man from Jamaica who sposed to know everything about growing indigo, an they say he told she to give up. "Dis soil not strong enough to hold up to indigo."

Nobody know how, but some way the mistress found out that Ayodele knew how to grow indigo. Maybe she see this piece of cloth that Ayodele bring with her colored with the indigo. So mistress gave her some seedlings an a small piece of land to work. The mistress told the Boss Man that Ayodele was only to work that bit of land. Oooh, he not like that one bit, but her would not hear nothing else. Well, Ayodele did all right, an the mistress very pleased. All the white men, the master, that planter from Jamaica they brought in, the Boss Man, they fit to be tied. They spent a lot of money bringing that man over here, and he sposed to be the expert, an he was white. Ayodele was just a girl, an she was black.

The mistress took some bottomland her husband save for rice an told Ayodele to plant the indigo. Ayodele bring in a real good crop, an everybody happy except those men. Ayodele did all this while she carry her first child, Nana's grandaddy. The father of her child was Nathan Samuels, a free colored man who come to the plantation to shoe the racehorses the master spent his money on. Maybe Daddy tell you all about Nathan Samuels an his brothers, it a man's story.

Folks real happy that she gonna have the baby because they knew Nathan working to save money so he could buy his child an the mother, Ayodele. Her term for carrying the child hard on she, an the mistress promise she rest. The mistress left to go sell the indigo at the market in Charleston. Now, she told the Boss Man that Ayodele, "Sarah" her called her, not to do any hard work, not to go to the fields. Her stay off her feet an rest easy, waiting for the baby to come. Well, you know right away he put her in the field to help plant the rice. They say everybody tried to help Ayodele, but the Boss Man stop em. She fall in the field, an they carry her back to the shack, where she start labor early.

Her have hard labor, an no one sent for the doctor until the mistress come back. By the time the doctor come, she been in labor close to two days an all wore out. The baby come early an he come strong. The doctor just took the baby an left she all tore up inside. Her had the milk sickness so they had to get another woman to nurse him. The other captives begged they mistress to bring the healer over from the next plantation to see after her. The healer was the only one they trusted to deal with the sickness of the African body an soul. They got word to Nathan Samuels to come at night to get to her!

Nathan took his son outside an held he up for all to see. He threw out the name mistress want, he gave his son proper name, they call the baby Etim. Nathan say to all that his son would be a good man, a just man, an a free man. Ayodele cry with happiness when he told her that he soon have the money to buy their son. They both know that she not see this day as she grow weaker an weaker with the fever.

When he took his leave, he promise that the first daughter of the eldest son would always carry she name so that Ayodele never be forgotten. It a sad time for everybody. They wait for her to cross over to the better world. The mistress sent the Boss Man an he family away. Her stay in she room an not see anyone, not even the master.

When the word went out Ayodele ready to cross over, the odder captives crowded into the small room. They come to sit with she, an those that could not fit in stood in the road outside the cabin. All come to wish she well on she journey. They bring gifts of food an cloth so she not get hungry or cold along the way. Her wave for the healer to come to her an whispered to her to cut the plait from her hair to give to she son.

Taking their places around the bed, the old ones began to sing the funeral songs in the many tongues from the old land. The same songs that Nana an her friends sing when someone passed over, they mourned the loss of the special one an celebrate they release into the new an better life.

A waka mu wone, kambe ya le,
li, le e tombe, kuhama, nog o yao a.

Come to the house in the evening.
She wants to tell you that she is leaving.

A waka mu wone, kambe ya le,
a le e tombe i siha, ye kangaa.

Come to the house in the evening.
For she will soon be gone on her journey.

Ha sa wuli ngo, ndeli li lii ii ya le
a lei i gobe su won, moto a bedo.

Death, please come slow this evening.
She is a good woman, and we do not want to see her go.

Ha sa a wuli tobe, ke se no lii ya te be nor.
Mata a sobo. Mata a fume.
Ke se no lii ya te be nor.

When Death comes, there is no answer.
It stills the heart. It steals the soul.
There is no answer.

Tso te sa mo be dubo ke ii ya nos.
Fume, do sao ke sa a wuli.

We prepare the grave to receive the body.
The soul, it flees with death.

Ndeli lee kujama a gwango,
to te ii bedo so me curo ngo,
haa lo fono a so de da.

To fly among the trees,
to walk along the paths in the woods.
The soul will seek the others along its journey.

As the moaning grew louder, her feel she spirit lift from she body
an reached over to touch she son's face before she leave. There a stillness an then a loud cry from all gathered round that lifted her onto
the breeze that take she on she journey. They say her floated over the
field an past the big house where the mistress stay locked in she room.
Her drift over to Nathan, her scent cause him pause as him fit the
shoe to the horse's hoof. He breathe deeply an feel she kiss on he
face, stirring the passion that they both knew when they first saw each
other.

Her swoop over the street of the next-door plantation as the people
gather for their evening meal. Her shake the trees and laugh as the old
ones wave to her an the young ones run in fear. Her flew up the Ashley
River to Charleston, skimming the waters, almost snatching the net
from a fisherman's hands. Circling the old market, her listened to the
sounds of despair that lay in the wall. Gathering up those cries, her
swept into the home of the slave trader an let them go, wreaking havoc
in the house, overturning chairs, knocking food from the table, shatter-
ing glasses, an slamming doors an windows as he an his family scurried
for safety. Gal, them ol spirits tore that house up!

Her then fly back to the Pinchney plantation to watch the preparations for she crossing over. Her watched the carpenter as he work to
piece together the rough slabs of pine that be her coffin. Her cry with
the women as they gently wash she bruised an torn body, dressing she
in the white nightgown sent down by the mistress, carefully tying the
bows dat secured the sleeves.

Her wait in the street with the children for the mule wagon that would take she to she final resting place. An when the people gather with their torches to lead the procession, her warmed by their words of tribute. Her followed the procession on it way through the woods to the captive graveyard.

When they reached the graveside, her joined in the singing of the old an the new as the captives bade she farewell. She baby's cry tear at she heart as they passed him over the coffin, one, two, three times to make sure that he mama love guide him.

When they lower the coffin in the ground, each person pass an threw a handful of dirt on the grave, an the young men set about to quickly fill it. Her catch the strong breeze that lift she to the winds that would sweep she home across the big water. Flying with arms stretched out, her soar across the waves to where the spirits of she family wait to rejoice in she return.

Amelia was mesmerized by Elizabeth, who had been transformed by the storytelling. Gone was the taciturn and proper young woman, and in her place was this sorceress with flashing eyes and soaring words, punctuating the story with dramatic gestures. Her face flushed with feelings, Elizabeth stood up abruptly to get more wood for the fire. Amelia sat in silence as Elizabeth knelt to lay the wood onto the fire. Noticing the spell she had cast, Elizabeth leaned back and looked at her. "It called telling the lie."

Amelia looked at her. "What?"

"Everybody love a good story. When you tell a good story, folks out here call it telling the lie."

Amelia reached over and picked up the necklace. She looked at the stone beads with the intricate carving, the same lines and crosshatch marks that were on the tree at the edge of the yard. She put it down and picked up the plait of hair, turning it over in her hand. She looked up at Elizabeth, who explained, "When we were little, Nana made charms for all of us. She put a bit of that hair in each charm, and you could not tell us we were not protected."

"Do you still have yours?"

Elizabeth pulled a string necklace from inside her blouse, the green charm covered with painted seeds. "Every time it starts to wear, I just cover it with a new piece of cloth."

Shivering, Amelia laid the plait on the hearth and placed her fingers on the edge of the blue-tinged cloth. A wave of warmth rolled over her as she lifted the cloth to her face and breathed deeply from it. She drew back as a log shifted in the fire, sending embers spiraling up the chimney. She handed the cloth to Elizabeth, who gathered up the necklace and the plait, returning them to the tin. As Elizabeth stood to slide the tin back into its secure place, Amelia touched her arm. "Would you make a charm for my mother to replace the one she lost?" She hesitated. "And if it's not asking too much, would you make a charm for me?"

Amelia listened to the sound of the ocean as she walked along on the edge of the high dune. She watched Ben down on the beach gracefully turning with the camera, winding the motor with one hand and sweeping the beach from one end to the other. She heard his whoop of excitement as a flock of seagulls dove into the waters before him. A family of sandpipers ran along the edge of the shore, pecking at the tiny silver fish that washed up with every wave. She watched as Ben angled the camera and fiddled with the lens to get them in focus. Ben had been fascinated by her cameras from the very first, and after a couple of quick lessons, showed a natural ability for seeing the unusual that might make an interesting picture. His eagerness to learn, coupled with his understanding of the natural life around him, made him a valuable helper when he could get away from his work at the forge.

Oddly enough, when she was using the motion picture camera she would run out of film and have to reload right in the middle of whatever she was shooting. But Ben never seemed to run out of film. He knew how to wait, he knew how to see through the camera. She enjoyed his questions and the sly wit behind his observations. Because Amelia's information gathering was going rather slowly, she encouraged him to use both cameras whenever he could.

Frustrated, she sighed and slid down the dune to join Ben on the beach. She had been on the Island for almost a month, and everything that Elizabeth had warned her about was bearing out. As she had promised, Elizabeth had taken her around and introduced her to residents, explaining what Amelia was trying to do. They had greeted her politely, listened to her requests for information, and continued with the work at hand. When she asked questions about family histories, tales, or customs, they would look at her blankly, shrug, and then suggest she talk with someone else who might know more about what she was seeking. As they moved away from her, they would touch the charm under their shirt or blouse to ward off any bad spirits that followed a "red-boned" person.

She had also been startled to find traces of Haagar in her own reactions to some of the people and their ways. When Amelia had first recognized the charm-touching gesture for what it was, she had been slightly amused. But now, it irritated her, for she saw it as an ignorant habit that emphasized the difference between her and the others. It hurt her, and for the first time in her life, her color was not an advantage among her own people.

True, she had gotten some information after plying Eula and Elizabeth with questions, but they were quick to point out that such and such a person knew more about certain things than they did. Yes, she could now walk into a yard and recognize the signs that people had laid, the grassless yard that was carefully raked each morning to provide the good spirit a place to rest, the frizzled chicken that scratched up any evil buried in the yard, the sprig of wild sage that hung over the door, purifying the house; but these bits and pieces of information did not tell her much more about the people who lived there.

Whenever she tried to set out to find that person to talk with them, they would either have "jes lef" or "be back in a lil bit." Other folks would stare at her notebook and camera, then drift away. She had learned, after waiting for hours, that out here, time simply passed; it was not to be measured.

Eli maintained his polite distance. She had not managed to get him to sit down and tell her the stories about the Samuels brothers that Elizabeth had mentioned because he was either too busy down at the forge or preparing the fields for colder weather or just "plumb wore out" in the evenings. As she reviewed her notes each day from the night before, she knew that Dr. Colby would be as disappointed in her as she was in her own efforts.

Only one person had sought her out to tell her a story. Ol Trent had appeared one day at the edge of the yard and called for the "red gal" to come on out and talk to him, for he had stories to tell. Amelia had seen him from a distance walking back and forth across the Island, but he had never strayed from his path to anyone's yard. Eula's children would run up to him and fall in beside him, imitating his long strides. He would talk to them as they walked along, gesturing wildly, talking a mile a minute, with his long coat flapping behind him. The children would stay with him until they were winded by the effort of keeping up, and then they would come running back.

When she asked them what he was talking about, Henry and James looked at each other, shrugged, and burst into laughter, chasing each other across the yard. Rebecca had informed her with a child's wisdom, "He ast a lot of questions. I dont know what him talkin bout."

When Ol Trent had yelled the first time for her to come out, Amelia had looked to Eula, who was as bewildered as she by his request. When his second shout brought Eli and Ben from the back and Lucy from the field, she grabbed her notebook and hurried down to talk with him. Amelia approached him cautiously as he paced at the edge of the yard. When she drew closer to him, he stopped her by pointing directly at her, though keeping his head turned away from her.

"You de red gal want de stories?"

Amelia hesitated. "I'm . . . I'm . . ."

"Dey tole me ober at de store dat de red stayin with Eli an Eulie want to heah some stories? Ol Trent got plenny stories for you."

Taking a deep breath, Amelia carefully said, "All right, Mr. Trent. Can you tell me a little bit about yourself?"

He began speaking at such a fast pace that Amelia could just barely make out a few of the words he was saying. As she strained to listen and scribble notes, Eula walked up behind her, wiping her hands on her apron.

"I Trent Wilkerson. Dereis waysan dereis ways ander isodderways. De good book say, " 'Myson, attento mywords, inclinethine earsunto mysayings.' "

He stopped abruptly and looked at her directly for the first time. Startled by the black depth of his stare, she swallowed and nodded. With a cunning look, he continued, "I ha been young and now am old, yet I hav not seen de righteous forsaken nor his seed beggin for bread. He is ever merciful and lendeth and his seed is blessed. Depart from evil and do good and dwell forevermore." He threw his head back and pointed to the skies, his arms outstretched. Amelia stole a nervous glance at Eula, who simply watched him with her arms folded. "And de man dat committeth adultery with another mans wife, even he dat committeth adultery with his . . ."

Amelia was puzzled when Eula leaned forward and said deliberately,

"Trent, why dont you tell Amelia bout when you work for Mr. Burton Devries?"

Trent continued, his voice rising, ". . . Neighbors wife, de adulterer and . . ."

Amelia still could not completely understand what he was saying, but she could see that Eula was becoming upset with him.

Eula spoke forcefully, "Trent, dont come talking all dat mess roun here!"

Trent began chanting, "De adulteress shall surely—"

Eula lifted her apron and shooed him. "Dats enough now, Trent! Go on home, Trent!"

Trent stumbled back as Eula advanced on him. "Be put to death!"

Eula shook her finger at him. "You better get!"

Trent took his hat off and tipped it to her and then turned and struck out on his journey. Eula sighed and shook her head.

"What was he talking about?" Amelia asked.

"The same ting him talks about all the time, men and women and all dat under de skirt stuff him tink him know," Eula replied shortly as she watched him disappear into the far woods. She shook her head and turned to head back to the house. Amelia trailed her. "Him been talkin dat stuff for years. One of dese days him gonna run up on de wrong person and somebody gonna get hurt behind all dat foolishness."

Lucy stood at the bottom step, and as her mother came up, she asked with an expectant smile, "So what did Ol Trent have to share wit our cuzzin here?"

Eula looked at her briefly. "Same ol ting he been talkin bout since him come back from de mainland."

"Seem like Trent done found somebody to listen to him, take down de notes. Dat de kin of stories you lookin for?" she asked as Amelia passed her to enter the house. She laughed out loud and turned, swinging her hoe, and headed back for the field.

Eula had started working on the bread when Amelia came back into the house. Amelia watched as Eula kneaded the bread, shaped it into loaves, and dusted them with flour. Amelia waited until she had laid the loaves out to rise again, and then she asked, "Who is that old man?"

Eula stepped up on a low stool to get two jars of speckled beans down from the cabinet. She crossed to the table and placed both in front of Amelia for opening as she went to the pantry to get ham. As she began to slice the ham, she explained, "Trent used to work for Burton Devries as a gentleman's man. Devries was de husband of de lady dat Lil Bet work for. But dis long before Lil Bet time. Him took care of he clothes and drove de car for he. You can tell he a gentleman's man by de way he carry hisself, he dress."

Amelia nodded in agreement. She had noticed as he spoke that although his clothes were a bit dated, they were kept in good condition. Trent was carefully groomed, with his neat bow tie and his trimmed fingernails. Amelia asked, "Does he have family?"

Eula shook her head. "All he family eider dead or move on. Him de only Wilkerson lef on the Island. Well, Mr. Devries die, Trent come back and begin to spen all his time walkin de land. Him aint lef de Island since him come back. Jus walkin back and forth and talkin all dat stuff him be talkin."

Amelia was baffled. "How does he live? He just spends his whole day walking."

"When him need sumptim, him give whoeber cross over de list and dey go to de store and brung it to him."

Amelia was even more curious. "Who pays the bill?"

Eula shrugged. "I spect de sisters, Mr. Devries's wife and she sister. I got an ol friend who used to be dey cook. Dey pay for all her tings. Folks say Trent got it good!"

Amelia thought of Ol Trent on his endless journey around the Island as she watched Ben turn the camera on a pair of lone footprints that headed down the beach. "Do you think those belong to Ol Trent?" she inquired idly.

Ben followed the footprints along the shore until they faded in the incoming surf. "Dose prints long to a woman." He glanced at Amelia's large feet and added mischievously, "A lil woman."

"Why aren't you with your daddy today?" she asked.

Ben smiled at her. "Him take de day to go do a lil huntin fore de real cold weather set in. I aint much for huntin." At her silence, he defended himself, "Now, I can track! I almos as good as my daddy, an anybody tell you him de best out here! An I a fair shot! I jus aint got much stomach for shootin and cleanin an all dat odder stuff you got to do."

Flippantly, she asked, "So what if you were lost out here and you were starving and all you had was a gun. What would you do for food then?"

He looked at her incredulously and burst out laughing. He laughed so hard that even she had to smile at the silliness of the question. When he could talk, he said, "Yall people from up North. I swear yall say some of de funniest ting!"

She helped him place the camera on his back. "You think you ever come up North?"

He stopped walking and looked at her. "You always astin sumptin! Why you do dis? Why you do dat?"

She turned away, embarrassed. They walked along the beach in an uncomfortable silence.

"Lord, I dont want you to tink I like Lucy, now," he said by way of apology. "You know, Lucy aint usual like dis. Her jus worried."

"It seems like everything I do just gets on her nerves."

Ben agreed, "For some reason, you do rub she. Fore you come, James and Henry rub she reglarly. Her be better when Charles come back."

"Who is Charles?" Amelia could not help herself.

Ben laughed. "Him her man! Dey be gettin married next year!"

"I've never heard anyone talk about Charles."

"Well, him aint here! Him down in Tampa working at de phosphate plant. He an Lucy tryin to save enough money so dat dey can buy de ol Wilkerson place an den work dat. Daddy done give she a piece of lan, an she workin de other bit of lan for Daddy. De money she get from dat an what Charles bring home from workin down dere be enough to start dem off real nice." He looked at her, surprised that she had not known. "Lucy love working de lan, and she a good farmer."

Amelia was bewildered. She and Lucy shared the same bed, but had little to say to each other. Every time she had tried to approach Lucy, she had been rebuffed, so she knew little of Lucy other than her moods. Whenever she had seen Lucy working in the field, she had simply thought of it as one of Lucy's chores, not realizing that this was Lucy's chosen work. Remembering what Elizabeth had said about the Peazant women, she felt a twinge of shame that she had not noticed Lucy's love for the land. She winced when she saw how Lucy could think that her offers to "help in the garden" would be mocking.

Shivering, she pulled her coat tightly around her as the cold wind skipped across the water. Ben smiled at her; his eyes stung by the cold were bright with tears. She looked at the simple jacket he wore and said, "We better get back."

Ben nodded in agreement. "Feel like de first real cold coming in."

She looked out past the edge of the land spit that lay south and saw irregular bits of wood sticking out of the water. As the waves fell and the light changed, she could see that the wood had been worn away by water and wind, carving crude features that reminded her of the pictures of African masks in Professor Colby's office. From the right angle and with a simple twist of the imagination, one could imagine the masks headed out to sea.

Tugging at Ben's arm, she exclaimed, "Look, there's a great picture right there. You see, right there where that old wood is sticking out of the water. Doesn't it look like a line of men walking into the water?" She started to move toward the edge to get a better view and was surprised when Ben caught her arm, holding her back.

He shook his head, his face troubled. "Dat Ibo Landing." He turned away quickly and headed back.

She ran behind him, struggling to keep up. "Why can't we take pictures?" He kept walking, his head down. She caught his elbow and tugged, "Why is it called Ibo Landing?"

He stopped and looked back at the wood. "Most de time you caint see it. De storm must have moved de spit."

She stopped him before he could move on. "Ben, please. Tell me about Ibo Landing."

The Story of Ibo Landing

as told by Ben Peazant

When I was a lil boy, dere was an ol man live on de beach. Him name Paymore. Him one of de elders, good friend wit Nana. Folks say de elders use to sit in Nana yard an talk bout de ol days, use some of dem ol words, have a good time wit each other. You know, I never see Nana. Her pass on fore I come. But I know she. Everybody come from she, know she.

Paymore, him come over on one of de las ships bring de captives cross de big water. Him a funny ol man. Him got heself a lil shack on de beach and live dere all de days. Big storm come and knock down dat shack plenty times, him build it right back. Daddy say to he, "Paymore, why don you build dat house back in de woods where you got some cover from de big storm? Him laugh, say, "Dat my place, right dere! I know my fambly right cross de water!" And him go right on, build dat house in de same spot. Daddy shake he head an jus keep on helpin he build dat house in de same spot.

What I member was dat him can read. Wasnt none of dem elders could read. Dint need to. But Paymore can read. All day long him walk roun carryin de book him have from when him come over. I remember dere was some pictures in it. Him have a fair han at picture makin. Sometime him make picture in de sand for we; tree, strange houses, big boats, plenty women. Him tell we to run through dem real fast fore de waves wash dem away. Course we like dat!

Often times him stop by de house, him stand at de edge of de yard an watch all we chilren runnin roun, screamin an playin, raisin all kinds of noise. Him laugh jus to see us play. Mama always bring he a plate of food, an him always say someting make she blush.

You know how bold Lucy is. One day him standin dere, laughing at we, an she go over to he an say, "Why you always laughing at we?" Mama mad cause Lucy so bold! But ol Paymore, him dont mind none. Him jus laugh an say, "I see de faces of Africa! When I see yall runnin roun like dat, I see all de faces of Africa!" Course Lucy took a whippin behin dat.

I dint know what him mean when him say dat. It wasnt till I come up on my time an Daddy sen me to Paymore to learn de ways of bein a man dat I see what him mean. For long time, ever boy-child get send to Paymore to learn de ol ways, de secret ways been passed down from one to de next. Paymore, him know all de ways. Like I say, him come straight from dere to here. So him de one teach we. Now dat him gone, I don know who gonna teach de ol ways. Dont nobody know all of it like Paymore. Gal, I aint tellin dem secrets! Him tell de secrets, struck dead in de middle of de night!

Well, him build a big fire on de beach, an us all sit roun an listen to what him got to say. Him point at we and say, "Fida, Ewe, Kisse, Mende, Gola, Ibo . . . All de faces of Africa right here cross de Big Water! Fida known for de cunning; Akan de fightin spirit; Ewe de hard worker, can grow jus bout everting; Kisse comely, sweet-nature women, learn fast, good in de house; Gola tall, strong, dark like de bark of de walla tree, not run off, not sickly like de po sad Ibo. Ibo, lil, de color of dark honey, melancholy run all through de Ibo." Him know we, him know where us ol people come from back in Africa. Him look at de face, an him can tell where de family stolen from. I ask he how him come to know all dis, an for de first time him not smile. "I put dem on de boats."

Paymore come from long line of captives. Dey been captives from de beginning. It all him people know. De work of de gatherin de captives dey pass on from one to de other. Him learn when him a lil one running in he daddy footsteps. Him say dey live in de place where many captives come to be put on de boats dat cross de big water. It a big place, bigger dan Charleston, him say, get big off de money come from gatherin de captives. Him know how to look at de turn of de head, de bend in de back, de flash in de eye, an him could tell whether a body is good for de field or de house. Him know how dey is, which one gonna run, which one gonna fight, which one gonna steal he soul back. Men come through offer plenty money for Paymore, but him master say, "No!"

Paymore plenty proud of de work him do. Now, he master, him no trust de captain on de boat. Him sen Paymore an him own son on de boat to see to he business. An you know, de master right! Paymore say dat boat get out on de big water, an de captain kill de son an throw Paymore down dere wit de other captives. It like to drove Paymore out of he min! In de ol land, him a captive, but long as him do de good work for he master, him almos free. Could come an go like him please. Him eat de same food as he master. Him take de same lesson as he master chilren when dey lil. Dat how he learn to read an cipher like him do. Now him down in de hole, praying to he God to save he!

Him say it a terrible ting. Caint nobody magine de sickness of it, treat like dey aint got no souls whatsoever! De captain make Paymore an de others take out de ones who pass over an throw dem in de big water. Paymore say de big shark follow de boat all de way cross, jus waitin on dem bodies to fall. Sometime dey not pass over an dey jump in de big water, trying to get back to dey family, dey home, to Africa! It misery all over! Paymore never know de misery til he in it heself.

De boat finally land in de place him call Brazil. Paymore say dey many captives dere. Seem like every tongue heard dere! Plenty Akan dere, too! De Akan always takin off to de woods, an de buckra caint find dem. One day Paymore workin in de fiel, an dis woman come up on him. Her carryin de water. Her look at he an den throw dat water an come after he. Her try to fight he! Rain curses down on he an he family cause he de one put she an she baby on de boat! Baby die. Woman fix it so her can have no more chilren be sold to de buckra. Paymore, he shame. Him see what all he work come to.

Den de sickness come. Folks fallin sick an dyin like flies. Buckra an captives. Now, you know what him say? Him say de captives call up an old conjure man from Africa. Dat ol man take the water from de sores from the sickness, an him scratch folks an put dat water on dem, an dose folks dont get de sickness. Dat what him say!

Paymore catch de sickness, an him glad. Him ready to pass over cause dis worl too bad for he. Him send de conjure man away. Him lay dere too weak to eat, caint hardly draw breath, feelin he spirit bout to fly. But who come dere but dat woman. Her say he aint goin no place so easy. Her gonna see dat him live wit de misery him cause.

Oh, yea, her brought he back. Him almos gone, but her pull he back. You got to know wasnt a lick of kindness in what her do for Paymore. It hate drive she to it.

De next ting him know dey back on de boat. Seem dat de captain hear dey more money to be made up dis way, so him head on out. Sick as dey still was, it dint make no difference to de captain. Him bring dem up to Charleston. Take dem off at night. Put dem in de pens out back so folks not see how bad dey is.

Dey fill dem with flour water to make dem not look so poorly. It one of de worse tings dey can do, dey die all the quicker. De captain man he mad cause he not gonna get de money he want from dem. Paymore watch he dicker wit de man in de money house. Paymore laugh when he tell dis part. It a funny laugh like he hurt in de body. De captain sell dem for lil or nuttin, and Paymore say him shame cause him know dey worth more dan de captain get. Den him shame cause him still tinkin de way like did fore him cross de big water.

Dey brung dem out here. Paymore say him never see place where de lan float on de water like dis an de water everywhere. De place him come from dry as de bone, wind blow all de time. De water come everyday, him tink dey gonna float back over de big water. But him say it remin him of home cause him dont hardly see no buckra out here. Aint nothin but captives live out here. Caint hardly no buckra cept maybe de Boss Man live out here cause de sickness in de water run dem out. Only de captive can stan de sickness out here. He see captive from everywhere living out here, Fida, Ewe, Kisse, Mende, Gola, and Mandingo! Dey out dere turnin de land, build de house, drain de field for de rice. Everting dey learn back in dey own place, dey do here. Fida known for raising de rice, dey raise de rice. Gola make de basket. Kisse build de boat, make de net, an fish de waters, can catch anyting! Paymore shame cause all him know to gather an sell de captive, an aint nobody out dere got use for dat. It a shame him carry all he days.

Him work de fields, clear de land. It hard work, but dat all right wit he. Him too tired to tink bout how he come to dis. But one day him come in from de field, an dey new captives dere, just come in. He look at dem an see dey Ibo. He shake he head. De Ibo, dont nobody who know bout sellin de captive want de Ibo. Dey lil people, hard to make to work, given to de sickness of de min. Him never see an Ibo laugh, only cry an wail, lookin back over de water to dey place. Soon as dey snatch away from dey place, de Ibo sen dey spirit to go home. Him look in dey eyes an see dey spirit done gone back home.

Dey put de Ibo men to work in de fields, but it no good. Dey lay down an not get up even when dey beat half to death. It like dey want to die, an dey help demselves to it. Dey put dem to all kinds of work, but dey no good for nuttin. Dey set de Ibo women to work in de yard, an it not much better. De other captives mad wit dem cause when de Boss Man mad wit dey, it bad for everbody. Paymore him tell de Boss Man dey fair builders, an de Boss Man put dem to work carryin de wood for de new landing. De ol landing blow way wit de big storm. Even Paymore hisself surprise at how dey help wit de landing. Him say dey want to work through de night, but de Boss Man stop dem. It not long dat dey hear de Ibo say dey buildin de landing to take dem back home. It gonna go cross de big water an everbody gonna be back home. Paymore know it foolishness, but it aint in he heart to say no different. If dat what dey need to keep dey minds strong, him not say nuttin.

When de Boss Man say dey finished, de Ibo start wailin an carryin on. Cryin so dat de birds in de trees stop de callin, de animals in de woods run for cover, all de work stop cause de cryin hurt so bad. De Ibo women come from de garden an walk on de landing to be wit de men. When dey start de wailin, even de Boss Man scared, de cryin so fierce. Him tell dem to get off de landing, but dey dont hear he! Him call to de other captives to get de Ibo off de landing, but dey too scared cause dey hear another sound, bigger dan de one de Ibo makin. Paymore swear it come from cross de big water! It coming for de Ibo! It cuttin through de other captives like an evil spirit, take dey strength away, weak dey minds. Dey know it carry de hex from all de Ibo! De Boss Man havin a fit cause nobody want to mess wit de Ibo!

Dey stop dey crying all de sudden. Everting stay quiet! All de Ibo start to walk to down de landing headed to dey home. De Boss Man try to stop dey, but dey walk right through he! Das what Paymore say! Dey go through he like dey a summer breeze. Him holler for de others to come help he, but de other captives can see de Ibo walk right in he front an come out he back. Dey aint messin wit dat! Oh, no! Dey step off de landing an start to walk cross de water, head for home. De other captives run to see the Ibo walk de water. Dey walkin all right! Caint nobody say dey aint walkin de water. De Boss Man hair turn white as cotton when him see dem walk de water. Now dey get aways out, an de other captives dey run to follow dem, but when dey step off de landin dey fall in de water. Dey pull some of de captives from de water, but some just gone like dat! Everbody watch dem Ibos cross de water til dey couldnt see dem no more.

Folks look to where the Ibo go an see the sky turn black an start to boil like a stew pot. It seem like de sky an de water come together an is comin for dem! Dey run to dey house an hide from de madness to come! De Boss Man hide wit dey, an Paymore say he worse dan a lil one cryin to he Lord to save he! De madness tear de roof off de house an reach down to snatch de weak ones! De water wash all de way back to de creek an take everting back to de water. De madness las seem like one two days. Folks wet, cold, dont have no food or fresh water. Dey wish dey dead, an den . . . de madness go way!

When dey come out, dey see everting tore up. A lil boy come runnin up an say come see de landin. Well, de landin still standin dere like the madness never come! Strong jus like de Ibo build it. Den it start to break up, bit by bit, like somebody takin it apart. Dey watch as de wooden planks lift in de air an fall in de water. De nails fly out, lan on de beach. It sway an make a noise like a sick ol man, den it tremble an fall into de water cept for de poles holdin it up. Dat what Paymore clare to be de absolute truth! Dat why it call Ibo Landin.

Ben shifted the camera on his back. "Everybody have a different story. Some folks say dey walk across de water to Ibo land, some folks say dey fly back, odders say dey walk into de water and drown." He lowered his head and murmured, "I like to tink dey walk back." He looked up at Amelia self-consciously.

They were walking along, each in their own silence, when she heard a steady, rhythmic thump like the beating of a drum. She turned to Ben, eyes wide. Ben chuckled and pointed his finger toward the water.

She saw a lone fisherman standing in his boat, striking the side of the boat with an oar.

"What is he doing?" Amelia asked.

Ben reached for the camera. "He call de fishes." At her skeptical look, he said, "You watch. He call de fishes. He make de noise an look for de dolphin to come. De dolphin a nosey fish, come to find out what all de noise about. De odder fishes dey run ahead of de dolphin, an you catch dem. You watch. He trow de net an get plenty fish."

The fisherman continued his rhythmic strokes. Ben squinted in the camera and then stepped back and looked at the water. They waited for quite a while, and just when Amelia was about to suggest that the dolphins did not seem to be interested, he pointed to a distinctive ripple in the water. "Here dey come." She got only the briefest glimpse of a silvery back as the dolphins raced toward the boat. The fisherman had picked up his net and stood ready as the waters around the boat began to bubble with fish. Just as Ben had predicted, the man gracefully swung the net above his head. The circular net almost seemed to be moving in slow motion when he flung it onto the water. As the fisherman pulled the net into the boat, she could see from her distance that it was full of fish and that he struggled with the weight of it.

At her gasp of amazement, Ben laughed. "You see? I tole you him call de fish. De ol folks, dey call de dolpin de horseman cause him run de fish ahead of him. Gal, you mighty suspicious about stuff you don know!" He grinned at her, and she laughed with him. A breeze caught their laughter and carried it across the water to the fisherman. He looked up from sorting the fish and waved to the two on shore. Amelia waved as Ben put the camera away and they headed home for dinner.

When Amelia sighed deeply for the third time while she poured the sweet oil into the small scent bottles, Elizabeth glanced up from the piles of scent that she had just mixed. Amelia had come over to spend the night and had insisted on helping Elizabeth put together the herbs, roots, and dried flowers that would perfume the oils. She had listened patiently and had written down everything that Elizabeth had to say and now knew all about the healing qualities of marigold and that a touch of lemon balm would cut the bitter taste of almost anything. She had paid special attention when Elizabeth explained how herbs used for medicine and perfume were different from the herbs used for root making. She glanced down at the recipe she had scribbled for what Elizabeth called her "Faith" balm.

Soak the spices in hot oil until the spices break apart and the oil absorbs the scent of the spice. Mix 5 drops of allspice oil, 4 drops of lemon oil, 3 drops of chamomile oil, 3 drops of geranium, and one teaspoon of sweet oil together. Swirl gently and pour into bottle.

As Elizabeth filled the small bottles to halfway with the blend, she asked Amelia, "Somethin botherin you?"

Amelia stopped pouring the oil. "I just feel out of sorts."

Elizabeth glanced at her. "Are you sick?"

Amelia shook her head. "I just feel kind of . . . bored."

Elizabeth nodded sympathetically. "You got the miseries."

Amelia glanced at her, skeptically. "The miseries. I had my miseries last week. Remember, you gave me the catnip tea for the pain."

"Those aint the only type of miseries," Elizabeth chided her, "I'm talkin bout those miseries that come from the soul, that restless feeling, make you want to do somptin, just about anytin to get rid of that feeling!"

Elizabeth stuffed the small corks into the bottles. She stepped back and looked at her handiwork, then spoke abruptly. "Go get your coat. We gonna go see some folks."

"Now? Out there . . . in that dark?"

Elizabeth picked up the lantern, "We got light, gal. Get that coat. We got to get rid of dese miseries." She threw on her coat and opened the door.

Amelia's miseries lessened considerably as she looked out into the black night. They almost disappeared when Elizabeth handed her a stout stick to carry, "just in case, we run up on somptin." By the time Elizabeth secured the front door, Amelia was quite sure that her miseries were under control and was more than ready to learn more about herbs and flowers. She sidled up to Elizabeth, who stood on the front step gazing up at the few stars. "Where we going?" she asked gently.

"To see my friend Carrie Mae." Elizabeth stepped down, but stopped as Amelia caught her arm. "Isn't she going to think it's kind of odd that we're visiting her at night?"

Elizabeth grinned. "All Carrie Mae's visitors come at night."

As they embarked on the trip in the dark through the back woods to Carrie Mae's, Amelia gained a new respect for her cousin's knowledge of the woods. It seemed to Amelia, stumbling behind, that they had twisted and turned across the entire Island before she heard the sound of music and people talking and laughing. The strong smell of hot fish grease drifted through the woods on the crisp night air as they came to a clearing, ringed by tar pitch torches. A group of men talked around a fire, passing a bottle. At another fire, several couples sat in the sand while a couple behind them danced to the music that came from the small shanty. Elizabeth and Amelia almost stepped on a couple that lay in the short grass at the edge of the clearing. The man sat up angrily, and Amelia apologized several times as the woman pulled him back down into the grass. She glanced back as the couple rolled over into the deeper woods.

The small shanty leaned wearily to the side and was propped up by two poles. Smoke poured from a lean-to kitchen that sat a few feet from the side of the shanty. A tiny wizened man waved at the greasy smoke that billowed under the lean-to. When they walked up on the porch to the half-open door, a slight figure rose from a rocking chair in the shadows and met them at the door.

"Is dat Lil Bet?" the figure asked. "I dint spect to see you back up in here."

Elizabeth laughed. "Well, Toady, my cousin Amelia feeling de miseries, an de only two places I know to get rid of de miseries is in church an at Carrie Mae's. Right now, only one of dem open!"

Amelia looked at this slight person, not sure if it was a man or woman. The person wore a man's suit and had close-cropped, curly hair, but also had the tiny features and the low voice of a young woman. Toady's light gray eyes swept Amelia. "Dis your cuzzin wan to hear de stories?" Amelia looked at her in surprise. "Aint nuttin goin on on dis Island we don hear bout!" Toady explained. She pushed the door open. "Why don yall get in outa de cold?"

Toady stopped Amelia as they started past her. "You aint carryin no razor or gun, is you?" Without a word, Amelia handed Toady the stick that Elizabeth had given her at the house. She tossed it into a barrel that sat by the door, and Amelia knew by the metallic clang that the barrel was not empty. Amelia slid around her into the room, deciding that Toady's gender was the least of her concerns.

From the outside, the shanty looked like it could not hold more than ten people, but when she and Elizabeth stepped inside, the place was packed with more than she could even begin to count. They squeezed by a couple who hugged near the doorway as Elizabeth made her way to one of the few tables in the room. A man called out, "Hey, Lil Bet. What you doin up in here? Aint you de teacher?"

Elizabeth retorted easily, "Teacher caint get out some, Johnnie?"

Johnnie sputtered, "No, I, I just thought dat—"

"Man, leave dese purty gals alone!" a man said, cutting him off. He grinned at them as they slid past, his four top teeth missing. "Hey, sweetning! Why dont yall lemme buy you a drink!"

Elizabeth smiled. "Thank you, Delroy, but we just gettin here. We gonna wait a bit."

He fixed his eyes on Amelia. "Let me know when yall ready!"

Elizabeth kept moving. "Hey, Queen Esther . . . Mozell." Amelia noticed that Elizabeth was very careful to speak to a table of rough-looking women. She followed her lead and nodded to them, but the women stared at her and then whispered among themselves.

On the far side a stout, pretty woman played cards with several men. As they drew closer, she leaned over and looked boldly at the hand of the man sitting next to her. He pressed his cards protectively against his chest. "Go on, now! Don be cheatin!"

Giggling, she waved him away. "You lost this game two rounds ago. Boy, you still holdin that ace, an you aint got nuttin!"

He fussed at her as the others laughed. "Dont be tellin folks my bizness."

Delighted surprise swept across her face when she saw Elizabeth approaching the table. "Lil Bet!" She stood up, knocking some of the cards from the table.

The men moaned, "Aw, Carrie Mae, look at dis."

She hushed them quickly. "Yall shut up! Lil Bet aint been back here in ober five years." She pushed at the two men sitting on either side of her. "Get up an let dese ladies have a seat."

One of the men argued, "We aint finish with de game."

Carrie Mae tilted the table, sending all the cards to the floor. "You is now." She waved Elizabeth and Amelia to the chairs. "Pidgen," she called to the man who stood behind the short counter that served as a bar, "bring us some . . . What yall want?"

Elizabeth sat down. "What you got?"

Carrie Mae thought. "I got some Black Bear Beer, some of dat Savannah Mint Tonic, some High Country Rye, and whole barrel of sumptin Dawkins just run in for me."

Elizabeth chose. "I take a Black Bear Beer."

Carrie Mae turned to Amelia. "How bout you, baby?"

"Do you have any sasparilla soda?"

Carrie Mae frowned at Amelia, but yelled back to Pidgen, "Need a beer and sodey water, a sasparilla sodey water!"

Elizabeth made the introductions. "Carrie Mae, this my cousin, Amelia. You remember Myown. This her daughter, Amelia. Carrie Mae and I was raised together."

Carrie Mae took Amelia in. "You must be de spittin image of you daddy cause you sholl don look like you mama!"

She let Amelia struggle with that while she turned her attention to Elizabeth. "How de schoolteacher doing? I keep sayin, one of dese days I gonna stop in an see how you teach."

Elizabeth shot back, "You do that, I'll be glad to help you with your figures."

Carrie Mae burst out laughing. She confided to Amelia, "All de while I was in school, Lil Bet did my figures for me. So dis de cuzzin tryin to get some stories? Folks got lots of stories round here, folks live for de stories dey could tell."

The music started to slow down. Carrie Mae jumped to her feet and yelled across the room, "Crank, baby, crank!" to the sleepy little boy who was standing next to the piccolo, keeping it going. The little boy shook himself awake and quickened his cranking. She giggled and spoke with pride. "Dat my nephew, young Tom. My sister, Jane's lil boy. I wonder where dat Sugarnun is! Him supposed to be here ober a hour ago! Worthless rascal! Lemme see if I caint fin someone to crank dis ting for me! I got to put dis baby to bed."

People made a way for Carrie Mae as she waded into the crowd. Amelia looked around the room; these were night life people. With few exceptions, they looked like the people she might see on the corner of any Harlem street, even down to the odd bits and pieces of flashy clothing. "Who are these people?" she asked.

Elizabeth perused the room and considered. "I only know some of them. Some of them come from back up there in the swamp. See that big man right there?" Amelia peered at a huge man with a long burn scar that ran from the top of his head to his neck who stood a few feet in front of them. "He's a rum runner, come from the Cooder family. They an old pirate family still live down on the south side."

Amelia stared at him and his flailing arms that looked to be the size of logs. "There were pirates here? Pirates like Blackbeard?"

Elizabeth smiled wryly. "Africans were not the only treasure brought to these islands. Pirates were in an out of these islands all de time. Every now and then, somebody from the mainland show up wanting to look for some of that treasure they say is buried somewhere around here.

Dawkins there alway willing to take these mainlanders in to the swamp to look for treasure."

Amelia eyed the man who threw his head back and roared with laughter. "I wouldn't go anyplace with him."

Elizabeth shrugged. "Folks got that treasure on they mind. They not thinking right."

A slim, caramel-colored man with two slanted scars on each cheek placed the drinks on the table in front of them. "Thank you, Pidgen." Elizabeth took a drink from the bottle of beer.

"Good to see you, Lil Bet." He looked around the room. "Bring some respectability here."

Elizabeth laughed as he looked at Amelia with interest. "That ain't possible! This my cousin Amelia."

His eyes smiling, Pidgen wiped his hands on his apron and extended one hand to Amelia. "My pleasure, Miss."

Amelia tried to place the accent. "Nice to meet you."

He held her hand. The music began to slow down again and Carrie Mae yelled, "Pidgen!" He nodded to her and slipped back through the crowd.

"He's not from here. Where is he from?" Amelia asked.

Elizabeth thought hard, "He come from South America. Um-m-m . . . Brazil, I think it is."

"What are those markings on his face?"

Elizabeth remembered. "He told Carrie Mae that down there the old Africans keep some of the old ways, and they mark they cheeks. I hear that some folks livin on the islands down Georgia way do the same thing."

A woman came over, stood squarely in front of the table, and fixed a cross-eyed glare on Amelia. "Who dis?" she demanded.

Elizabeth took a long sip of her beer. "Dis my cousin." Amelia smiled at her, which caused the woman to look at her even more suspiciously.

"What her doin here?"

Elizabeth calmly responded, "We just come out to have a good time."

The woman pointed to Amelia. "Red-bone, don be lookin at none of my mens!"

Amelia agreed immediately, moving closer to Elizabeth. The woman stomped off, pushing her way across the room. Having noticed the numerous scars that marked her face, Amelia asked, "Is she one of those people from Georgia?"

Elizabeth half-laughed. "Gal, them razor cuts from fighting!"

Amelia looked at Elizabeth to see if she was teasing. Not sure, she turned her attention back to the room. It looked like the walls were glistening in the light. She reached over and gingerly touched the back wall, and her fingers came away wet. "Dem walls sweatin, gal!" Carrie Mae boasted. "It hot in here!"

At the sound of a commotion at the door, Carrie Mae strained to see what was going on. An ordinary-looking man dressed in a rough wool jacket and collarless shirt was trying to get further into the room, clutching his guitar case. Carrie Mae stood up and ordered, "Yall move! Let de man through! Sugarnun! Where de hell you been? Folks been waiting for you!" He made his way across the room. As a couple of women called to him, he waved to them, almost shyly, and kept on moving to where Carrie Mae, Elizabeth, and Amelia sat.

When he reached the table, he tipped his hat respectfully to all three women, letting his eyes rest gently on Amelia. Carrie Mae fussed, "You was suppose to been here long time ago."

"I here now, woman. What you fussin bout? Is that Lil Bet?" he asked.

Elizabeth smiled up at him. "How you doin, Sugarnun?"

He reached out and took her hand. "I didnt know who you was de first time I seed you goin to Bofort. You is a handsome young woman. I know Eli Peazant proud of you." He turned to Amelia. "An who might you be?"

He took her hand and, to Amelia's consternation, stroked her palm with his thumb. "She anudder Peazant," Carrie Mae interjected. She winked at Elizabeth. "Eli and Eula dopted she an sent she up North to live." Sugarnun's smile wavered just a bit as Elizabeth and Carrie Mae burst out laughing.

Pulling her hand away, Amelia looked at them, confused. "I'm Amelia Varnes, Lil Bet's cousin."

Sugarnun cast them a triumphant glance. "Glad to meet you, cuzzin to de Peazants. My name Woodrow McKinley Harrison. Folks roun here call me Sugarnun."

Carrie Mae thumped the guitar case. "Get on up dere, man, an do what you got to do. Get dese folks on deir feet so dey can start dancin an drinkin de way folks spose to! Dawkins want his money." As he headed over to the corner near the bar, Carrie Mae excused herself, "I got to handle the bar while Pidgen play. I send anodder beer for you." She looked at Amelia's drink skeptically. "You want some more sodey water?" At Amelia's nod, she rolled her eyes and slid across the floor to the bar, fussing at people, ordering them to drink up.

Pidgen went to the corner and pulled back a sheet that covered a worn set of drums. As Sugarnun tuned his guitar, Amelia was alarmed to see people from the outside squeeze into the small room, waiting for

Sugarnun to start. Sugarnun took his time, placed his hat on the end of the bar, pulled up a stool, and sat down.

Yo can come to my house, baby

At the first quavery note, the crowd stirred, the women leaning back while the men stood up straight. When Sugarnun sang, the shanty began to shake as bodies started to sway, feet began to move, and hands clapped to the beat.

An I do eberyting I can for yo

The women laughed and shouted while Sugarnun shook his head.

> *Yo can come to my house, baby*
> *An I cook de meal for you*
> *Yo can come to my house, baby*
> *An I let you lay up in de sun*
> *Cuz I got sumptin for you, lil dahlin*
> *Dat could make a dead woman come.*

Amelia jumped as the women screamed in ecstasy and a man behind her shouted, "Das me! Dat boy talkin bout me!" She peered over at Elizabeth, who swigged her beer and swayed to the music. She looked around at the other faces, greasy and sweating, who howled with laughter each time Sugarnun described what he was going to do to this woman. It was just what her grandmother had always warned her against—loud, backward, all kinds of ignorant. Amelia watched these people, some laughing, some shaking their heads in another kind of misery, all trying to enjoy themselves after a long, hard week of work, and God help her, she loved it.

Amelia breathed a sigh of relief when Sugarnun and Pidgen took a break. She had been pulled to her feet during the second song and had not been able to get back to the table since she left it. Every time she would head back to get away from the press of bodies, another man would grab her, and she would be back out on the bouncing floor. There were so many people on the floor that she simply stood in one place and swayed to the rhythm with everybody else. She was sure that the walls were being held up by the crush of people, and as soon as everyone left, the shanty would collapse. She looked for Elizabeth and saw her at the bar helping a bustling Carrie Mae serve up drinks and fish sandwiches. At one point, they had been next to each other on the dance floor, and Amelia had noted that Elizabeth's jing-a-ling was one of the best ones out there.

Carrie Mae grinned at Amelia as she slipped around the bar to stand next to her while Elizabeth stepped to the back to get more fish sandwiches. "Dem men sholl like you. I tinkin I gon dye my hair de color yours, see if I get all dat tention."

"Be careful," Amelia warned her, accepting another soda. "They might think you're the devil."

"Dey tink I de debil anyhow," Carrie Mae retorted.

Carrie Mae appraised Amelia. "Gal, you still drinkin dat sasparilla sodey? Lemme put some in dere so you know what a real drink taste like!" She grabbed the bottle from Amelia and reached under the bar, pulling out a Savannah Mint Tonic bottle. She poured a bit of the soda out and then filled the soda with the tonic. She shook it up and handed it to Amelia. "Taste dat, gal!"

Carrie Mae turned back to the bar. Handing a beer to a man, she took his money, then handed him a second beer. "You gonna have to drink two, cause I aint got no change."

The man protested, "Aw-w, Carrie Mae, you charge too much, an you aint neber got no change! Dat aint right!"

Carrie Mae shrugged. "You don like it, take it up wit Toady, or don eben come out here." The man glanced over at Toady, leaning against the wall, and walked away muttering.

Carrie Mae reached over and touched Amelia's hair. "I serious, gal. I have hair that color, I make plenty money like you cuzzin, Yellow Mary."

Amelia had read the letter from Yellow Mary on the wall with its cryptic message.

Dear Nana,

Thank you for getting the money to me. Now that I out, I thinking about movin up to Atlanta. If I stay here, they fraid of what I know and who I tell. I let you know when I get to where I headed.

Your loving grandaughter,
Yellow Mary

Amelia remembered the picture on the wall of Yellow Mary and another fancy woman standing on the beach, elegantly dressed with large hats and billowing veils. Although the veil had partially covered Yellow Mary's face in the photo, Amelia could sense the defiance in her as she faced the camera, straight on, feet planted firmly in the sand. According to Haagar, her grandmother, Yellow Mary was the one Peazant woman that was "ruint," and it was the taint from Yellow Mary that threatened every Peazant woman.

"What do you know about Yellow Mary?" Amelia asked Carrie Mae quickly. Carrie Mae's reply was interrupted by a shout and the sound of a scuffle. They both looked up to see Sugarnun backing away, a slow grin on his face and his hands up, as a young woman held back an angry man. The crowd fell away.

"Aw, hell!" Carrie Mae muttered as Toady limped across the room. She stepped between Sugarnun and the couple, her arms crossing her chest. People began scrambling away from the area, pressing against the walls, bumping into others coming in from the outside to see what was going on. She stared at the man as the woman frantically whispered into his ear, stroking his arm.

"Now, I aint got no dealing wit you, Toady. Dis nigger gonna come up here an try to get my woman to go wit he . . . ," the man complained.

"You know de rules, Lil John," Toady warned him. "Anyting going on roun here is my dealing. You better take dis someplace else." Lil John's lip quivered with anger. He took a deep breath as Toady put her hand in her pocket.

The woman tugged at his arm. "Let go, Johnnie. You dont want make Toady mad."

Lil John trembled, clenching his fists. He looked past Toady to Sugarnun. "You lucky you here, boy! I better not catch you sniffin roun Viola!"

The woman pulled at him. "Come on, Papa. I got sumptin for you at my house."

He looked down at her as she ran her hand across his chest. He put his arm around her and pulled her close." All right, baby. I ready for it. Lets get you home." They walked out with their arms around each other.

The other people began to stir and laugh with relief and some disappointment. Toady scowled at Sugarnun. "You got to pick de woman of de worst nigger in de place?"

Sugarnun gave her a sheepish grin. "Dat girl sweet as molasses." Toady turned from him and walked out the front door. A light flickered briefly on her face as she lit a cigarette and stepped out into the yard. Sugarnun sidled up to a table with two women who looked like sisters and were ripe for offering him sympathy.

Carrie Mae heaved a sigh of relief. "Dat de only problem bout having Sugarnun around. Him always sniffin roun de wrong thang!"

"That man was twice Toady's size!" Amelia exclaimed. "She's so little!" Her eyes widened as Carrie Mae grunted. "Lil woman got big gun."

When Elizabeth returned with the pile of fish sandwiches, she offered one to Amelia, who shook her head at the sight of the grease-soaked bread. "Your cuzzin askin me bout Yellow Mary," Carrie Mae told Elizabeth.

Elizabeth looked at Amelia quizzically and shrugged. She put her hand on Carrie Mae's shoulder. "You know more bout her than I do. You tell her."

"Let me get dis piccolo goin for I start talkin. Pidgen, crank dat piccolo! I want dese folks dancing!"

Yellow Mary's Tale

as told by Carrie Mae Johnston

Now, Yellow Mary, her an my oldest sister come along together. Dat my sister Agnes by my daddy first wife. He have three wives, each one real young. I come from his third wife, her have five chilren for he. I de knee baby. Dat lil boy you seen cranking dat piccolo, he my baby sister boy. I don know how many odder sisters and brothers I got, cause dey was some big families back den, ten, fifteen head of chilren.

So I was tellin you bout your cuzzin Yellow Mary. Her a purty girl. Her tall for a Peazant, got dat skin de color of coffee wit two spoon of sweet cream, and dat thick hair. Her had that bit of Cherokee in her from her mama's side, and you know how colored men like dem women wit thick hair. I understan her was a nice girl, a lil mouthy, but her a good girl. She and Buddy, he her second? Third? Lil Bet, what kin was Buddy to Yellow Mary? You dont know? How come you dont know? Anyhow, Yellow Mary and Buddy dey been sweet on each odder since dey was lil. My sister say dey talk bout gettin marry when dey chilren, eight, nine years. Everybody know dey gonna get married. Buddy, he a good boy, too. He daddy hire he out to work de fields, an he give he daddy all he make. You aint gonna fin nobody do dat today. Chilren dont listen like dey used to.

As dey got up in age bout fifteen, sixteen, Yellow Mary and Buddy start makin de plans to get married. But dey different now. Dey dont wanna do like de parents do. You know, jus get up an get married an den live wit de family till you get your own. Dey wanna start out on dey own together, so dey lookin for ways to make some money. Dat where my sister come in. She been stayin ober on de mainland workin in de kitchen for one of de big buckra in Bofort, own de sugar plantation ober on Edisto Island. Got plenty money, lots of people workin in dat house. Dey looking for somebody to take care of de young master's chilren. My sister tell Yellow Mary bout de job, and her come ober an her get it.

Bout dat same time dey open up de DeSota Mining Company, an dem country boys was gettin hired dere reglar. And hear tell, dey was makin good money! My sister tol me bout frien of hers went to work at de mine, bought he some new clothes, and den went home to visit he mama. He walk up in dat yard, de dog set on him. Chase he out de yard. Dint know who he was. His mama come out on de front porch an ast he who he was. He was dat clean! Everybody was goin. All want dat long money, and so Buddy, him gonna go too. Him and Yellow Mary both workin, dey figger dey get married all de sooner. Now, dat where your granma Haagar come in.

I don know if you should be hearin all dis cause dis bout your granma. If you dont know it, it aint someting her want you to know. See, I dont know. I dont wanna be tellin you nuttin that gonna hurt your feelin. Dis your granma, now. Well, all right, but if it get too much for you, you just tell me to hush up.

Haagar work in de house wit Agnes and Yellow Mary. Her do de scut work, you know, scrubbin de floors, washin de pots. You know Haagar come from Hog Alley in de east part of Bofort. Well, I aint surprised her dint tell you bout Hog Alley.

Whoo! It a poor place, misery all over. It de poorest part of de colored part of town! Dey use to run de hogs up dat street on dey way to the market. An smell! Chile, my sister said when de wind was right, you could smell down in Clifford, an dat a good five mile away. Haagar, her bout fifteen and so poor, her didnt even have no shoes when her first come dere. Dey didnt let her in de house to work till her got some shoes. You got to excuse me for laughin, but her was so poor, when dey took her to show her how clean de toilets, dey flush de toilet and her run screamin from de house, thought it was de debil!

Anyhow, her got to likin Agnes and, specially, Yellow Mary, and her follow dem all ober. Now my sister say her aint never care for Haagar, but Yellow Mary never had a mean bone in her body, an her let her come roun like her want to. Her even brung Haagar to de Island wit her when her come back to see her family.

Well, one day Haagar see Buddy comin to pick Yellow Mary up, an her take a likin to him. You see, he a nice man, easy smile, an workin hard at de mine. Haagar see her want dat for herself, an her set out for him. My sister said her told Yellow Mary dat Haagar was up to no good, always hangin roun and tryin to fix it so her could go wit dem. But Yellow Mary not worry. Her and Buddy been together all dey lives. Her say ol conjure woman say dey gon be together forever.

Now you got to understan. Buddy a good man, but Buddy a country man. He not use to city women, and Haagar, poor as her was, was a city woman. So her went after him. My cousin told me one time, Yellow Mary had come back to de Island cause her mama sick—you know her mama part Indian and dat why her got that hair. Anyway, Yellow Mary come up on Haagar and Buddy down dere at de wharf eating oyster sandwiches. My cousin say her ask Buddy, "Dis your woman now?" and he just laughed and say, "Haagar? Gal, you crazy!"

Now some say after dat Haagar went to a root doctor herself and had sumptin put on Buddy. Whatever, in a couple of months, Haagar looking bigged, an her tellin everybody dat Buddy bigged her. Yellow Mary come up on her tellin dat story and run out de big house, run all de way down to de mine where Buddy work to ast he. Wasnt nuttin him could say. She say dat was de last time her ever say a word to he. He get off from work dat night, come up to de big house, my sister tell him Yellow Mary don want to have nuttin to do wit him. My sister say he cryin like a baby, he beggin her to come out an let he talk wit her. He took dat girl's heart, you hear me, an jus tore it to pieces. My sister say Haagar hide behin de window while he cry in de backyard. Her say her felt like knocking Haagar silly bringing all dat misery to dem two.

Next day, Yellow Mary quit her job an go back to de Island. Now, I know Buddy go back dere an try to talk wit her, but her had nuttin to say. You see, her done save herself for he all dose years, and he just throw it all away. He come back to work, but he don wanna have nuttin to do wit Haagar.

So Haagar go over to talk wit Nana Peazant and de odder old ones. In dose days, de old ones tell you what to do an you do it. Her tell Nana her having a Peazant dat dont have a Peazant name. So dey send for

Buddy, an him come out an him say it he baby, and dey tell him he got to give de baby a name. He marry Haagar cause dey tell he, an dey move back to de Island to live. I tell you right now. Haagar dint know bout respectable til her marry into de Peazants.

Well, dis place not big enough for Yellow Mary, Buddy, and Haagar. So Yellow Mary, her get her job back at de big house. Agnes say dem white folks crazy bout Yellow Mary! De mistress happy her back, de young master he happy too.

Yellow Mary, her a young, purty woman, an her want her fun too. Her and Agnes, one day dey go on up to Charleston, an dey meet Eddie Cobb. Him a charmin man, but him aint no good. Didnt do nuttin but run de games for de numbers man. Wouldnt work to hit a lick at nuttin! I seen Eddie Cobb bout five years ago! Him jus come back from Memphis, runnin some kind of game, chasin everyting young enough to be his daughter! Well, him took after Yellow Mary, and some folks say him did all right by her cause he married her. But odder folks say him marry her cause him know her a hardworking woman.

Agnes say it not long Yellow Mary and Eddie Cobb fallin out an gettin back together, fallin out an gettin back together. Her say when Yellow Mary find out her gonna have a baby, her pray dat Eddie will come to, but him was no kind of real man. De night her had dat baby, dey went down dere to get Eddie out de dance place, and him wouldnt come. Dat baby come here dead, an Yellow Mary bout to lose her mind. Her heavy wit milk an her baby dead. Poor girl so fill wit hurt and rage.

De family her work for, de mistress her have baby right long wit Yellow Mary, but her don have enough milk. Baby sickly. So Yellow Mary go back an nurse dat baby like we do ever since we come here. De young master, him tell her him takin de family to . . . What dat place, Lil Bet? You know . . . way down dere where dey, after Florida, where dey don't even speak de same tongue as we. Cuba! He family got a big sugar plantation down dere, and him want Yellow Mary to come wit dem an see after de chilren.

Her come home to see Nana. See if her read de signs for her, tell her what her gonna do. Her run into Buddy. Buddy weak wit love for her. Mebbe he found out dat every edge of Haagar tongue sharp like de knife. You laugh, gal. You know you granma, huh! He beg Yellow Mary not to go to Cuba. Him beg her to leave wit he, go someplace. Now, you got to understand. Buddy de only man her love. Dey come together agin an dey makin de plans.

Haagar smell sumptin, an dat Sunday, her call Yellow Mary out in de church. Stood up dere, holdin she baby girl Iona, an call she out in front of everybody. Chile, dey was talkin bout dat when we was lil, wasnt

dey, Lil Bet? Yellow Mary run from de church in shame. Buddy, him
dont care! Him want Yellow Mary, an him ready to leave wit she. But
her caint go wit him. Her leave wit him, her never come back. Her love
her family, dey would turn away from she if her run off wit Buddy.

Yellow Mary have no choice. Her gotta leave an go to Cuba wit de
white family. Her not down dere long til de young master, he come up
on she in de night. What her gon do? Her tell Agnes, her nurse he baby,
her look after de odder chilren, her sit wit he wife when her sick, an
now her got to do for him! Whew! Her ast him to send she back. Him
not gonna let she go! Yellow Mary don know what her gonna do.

Dis when her tink hard, an dis when her start to change. Agnes said
before her go to Cuba, her got a giving heart, give de clothes off she
back an her do anyting to help somebody. But after her come back, her
heart like de ice in de bucket on a January morning!

First ting her do? Dry up she milk. Her say her not suckling the baby
and de daddy in de same house. Somebody might tell you dat den her
get wit some ol conjure woman down dere, and dat woman give her a lil
sumptin for de young master. I dont know, cause her pretty powerful
on she own. You know what I sayin? Well, him start to follow she like he
a lil puppy. De mistress her don like this. Her tell Yellow Mary to go,
put her out in de street wit nuttin! De young master him go get she an
brung she back. An Yellow Mary ruled dat house, you hear me!

I don know how long dis went on, but one day de mistress come to
Yellow Mary an say her give her money to go away. Dis jus what Yellow
Mary been waitin for. Yellow Mary smart, her don take de first one. Mistress figger her give her a little bit an her run wit it. Her don take de
second one. Her don tell de mistress how much her want. Mistress all
upset. Yellow Mary take de third one. Now, her aint never tole what de
mistress give she, but her come back an her doin all right.

Oh, de young master look all ober for she. Her don come back
straight away. Her take boat an it go all around, stoppin lots of place.
And her don come back to Bofort. Oh, no, her buy a house in Savannah, a nice house from what dey say. Her brung womens into de house,
and dey work for she. An her live dere for quite a while, an den
sumptin happen. She move up to Atlanta, get a bigger house, and dats
where I went to work for she.

Every now an den, she come home. Not reglar, jus every now an den!
She visit her mama, Nana, an get dat root stuff an anyting else she
needed from Miz Emma Julia. You know Miz Emma Julia could fix
sumptin to take care of anyting! You aint gonna tell me dese white folk
comin to see Miz Emma Julia jus want somptin cause dey head hurt! I
work in dat house goin on two years, an every morning dem girls had to

take dat medicine. Only two girls got bigged while I was dere, and dey didn't have no baby!

Her was out here visitin one time an come up on me in de woods wit somebody. I cant member who dat was! I was jus having a lil fun, an he was carrying on like he bout to die. Anyhow, her come roun later an ast me how come I givin all dat away. To tell you de truth, I didnt know what her talkin bout. Sometime dey bring me a soda, a fish sandwich, or sumptin. Her laugh. Her say I could get hard cash for what I was doin, back in de city. Now, I got kinda mad at that! Den I ast somebody to bring me sumptin from de store, an he rared up at me! I said well, wait a minute now, I do for you. Him went on bout women takin his money an all dat ol stuff. An I seen de way. I knowed what her was talkin bout. So next time her come, I say I ready to go wit her, an I do. My sister Agnes mad wit her to dis day bout dat.

Me? I stay two years, an den I come back. First, I work as de maid, an den after her tink you ready, you go upstairs wit de odders. Now, Yellow Mary, her a businesswoman. Her know how to run dat house. Dat where I met Toady. Aint dat right, baby? Everybody made good money, an she take care of you good. My heart wasnt in it, though. I aint never liked buckra mens! An her didnt have no colored men comin dere. Hell, I likes to be served, too.

Amelia tried to fit all that Carrie Mae had said with what she actually knew about her grandmother. She knew so little of Haagar. Haagar had always discouraged talk about her coming to the Island, and what My-own knew, she never spoke of, preferring the stories of boisterous play with cousins and the natural beauty of the Island. The Haagar Amelia had seen every day of her life seemed to be made of equal parts rage and censure. Before Carrie Mae's story, she could not have imagined her grandmother young, in love, and needy. She did not know how much of Carrie Mae's story had been true. She had watched Elizabeth's reaction while Carrie Mae had been telling the story, but Elizabeth was content to let her friend tell the story the way she knew it. If half of what Carrie Mae said was true, Amelia understood both her mother's desire to recall only the things that brought her peace and Haagar's determination to leave stories untold.

Her eyes ringed with exhaustion, Amelia leaned against the counter as Carrie Mae woke a man sleeping in the corner and pushed him out the door. She had no idea what time it was. Elizabeth and Pidgen pushed the table and chairs back against the wall. Amelia bent to pick up the bottles that were stacked in the corners.

A second fight had broken out, but had not taken long once Toady stepped in. Amelia admired Toady's efficient methods. Toady didn't ask one question, he shot first. That shot stopped all the fighting and cleared the room. The only people standing when the smoke from the shot cleared were Toady and Amelia, who had a death grip on her bottle of soda water and mint tonic.

Carrie Mae inspected the damage. "Pidgen, we need to get dat patched fore de next rain come through." Amelia glanced at the ceiling, which had so many patches from gun shots that it looked like a quilt. "Come on, yall. Leave dat alone. Lets go sit outside fore de sun come up." Carrie Mae dragged herself to the door. Amelia and Elizabeth followed her, pulling their coats tight against the morning chill.

Carrie Mae grabbed a few pieces of wood from beside the door and laid them on the one fire that still burned in the sand. The tar pitch torches had burned out quite a while back.

Toady came out of the outhouse sitting back in the woods. "Toady, grab some of dem quilts out de back and bring dem ober here." Carrie Mae sunk into the sand near the burning fire. Elizabeth flopped down beside her. Amelia slipped to her knees. Pleasantly surprised by the warm sand, she breathed a sigh of relief and took off her shoes, holding her feet to the fire. Toady dropped a quilt on her, then on Elizabeth, and stared at Carrie Mae expectantly. "Come on, baby." Carrie Mae held out her arms, and Toady slid down in front of her and settled into her arms, her head nestled against her chest. Carrie Mae wrapped the quilt around both of them. She looked up at the twinkling stars. "Dat de morning star," she pointed out to Amelia. "Day clean come soon."

Amelia lay on her back, staring up at the brightening sky and thinking about Carrie Mae's story. So, her grandmother Haagar was just as high-spirited in her youth as the wild women who shook Carrie Mae's shanty last night. Amelia was as captivated by the stories of the women who raised her as by the women lying there with her at sunrise on the sandy shores of Dawtuh Island. She could hear the murmurs of conversation between Carrie Mae and Elizabeth. As she felt herself drifting off, she heard the low thump of a drum. When it grew louder, she sat up, frowning. Toady lay on her side, wrapped in the quilt and sound asleep. Carrie Mae and Elizabeth laughed at her puzzled expression. "That's Pidgen." Elizabeth pointed. "He bringin in de day."

Pidgen sat at the edge of the clearing, facing the sunrise, beating on an old skin drum. Despite the chill of the morning air, he had stripped off his shirt, and she could see the other scars that marked his back. As the light spread across the sky, the intensity of the drumming increased and the rhythms changed. Try as she might, she could not keep her eyes open and lay back down. She heard the whisp of the sand as feet moved through it and watched through half-open eyes as Elizabeth and Carrie Mae danced to the drum in the morning light.

"Amelia, wake up! Wake up." Elizabeth leaned over her. Amelia rolled to her side and moaned as the sun shone directly in her eyes, her head rocking.

"Get up, gal! We got to get home!"

Amelia sat up, looked at Elizabeth and shook her head "No," and lay back down, pulling the quilt closer.

Elizabeth leaned down and pulled her into a sitting position. "We got to get home so we can get ready for church!"

Amelia looked over at Toady and Carrie Mae, who were bundled together and sound asleep. There was no sign of Pidgen. Amelia argued, "We haven't even been to bed yet!"

Elizabeth looked for her shoes in the sand. She pounced on one, partially buried. "We got just enough time to get back home and get ready for church." She found the other one. "Get up, gal!"

Amelia threw the covers back and frowned. "I've been to church every Sunday since I've been here and . . ."

Elizabeth stood over her, extending her hand to help her to her feet. "If we not there this morning, my mama will come looking for us." Amelia wobbily scrambled to her feet. She had learned during her stay at the house that Eula, being the mother of six children, was not the kind of person who held close to rules. However, she was serious about her church. The last thing she wanted to do was to face Eula after a raucous night in Carrie Mae's juke joint.

Elizabeth started out at a fast clip, but had to slow to wait for Amelia. Every few steps her cousin would step off the path and bring up more sarsaparilla soda and mint tonic than she remembered drinking the night before. Amelia could not ever recall being this sick, even when she'd had the flu and thought she was dying. Elizabeth pushed the damp hair back from her face and helped her along the path. When they finally reached the house, Amelia fell on the pallet of quilts and covers on the floor and moaned. As she dozed off, Elizabeth went out into the yard to pump the water for a quick sponge bath.

Amelia awoke to Elizabeth sponging her face with a cool cloth and helping her out of her sand-filled clothes. She stumbled over to the pitcher and basin and slowly began to wash. Elizabeth put a cup of steamy liquid beside the basin as Amelia slipped into fresh underclothes. "This will help some." Amelia picked up the cup and peered into its dark depths. "Dont ask, just drink," Elizabeth instructed as she briskly brushed Amelia's hair.

Sipping the bitter and pungent brew, Amelia wondered how she would make it through the three-hour church service that was the weekly highlight of so many of her neighbors' lives.

Brother Martin Butler rose to lead the song, his soft tenor spiraling to the rafters of the praise house.

> *You can run to the rock*

Everyone joined in. Some clapped their hands, others shook their heads in affirmation, several jumped to their feet.

> *But you can't hide!*
> *But you can't hide!*
> *But you can't hide!*

Brother Martin began to sway in rhythm with the clapping.

> *You can look for a hidin place*

Already on their feet, Eli and Eula stepped from side to side, moving away from the bench into the aisle.

> *But you can't hide!*
> *But you can't hide!*
> *But you can't hide!*

Women, children, and men moved to take their place in the ring shout, clapping and stepping side to side. Amelia, her eyes closed, let the raised voices wash over her, pushing her exhaustion aside for the moment. She had to admit that Elizabeth's bitter-tasting remedy did make her feel better; her stomach had stopped heaving, and the pounding headache had been reduced to a persistent throbbing.

> *An' the rock cry out*
> *But you can't hide*
> *You can't hide, sinner, you can't hide.*

In the weeks since she had been here, she had gotten used to the simplicity of the service. It could not have been any more different from the large spectacles that her church in Harlem specialized in. While her Mt. Calvary Baptist could not compete with the prominence and the wealth of the larger, older churches, it was known for giving a good service with its one-hundred-voice choir and twenty-five ushers, dressed from head to toe in white. As she heard the scrape of the simple wooden benches against the rough floor, Amelia thought of how members of Mt. Calvary Baptist scrambled for the good seats in the cushioned pews. Opening her eyes, she watched Rebecca clap her hands and move forward, singing with the same fervor as the adults around her.

> *You can run to the sea*
> *But you can't hide*
> *But you can't hide*
> *But you can't hide*

She recognized Lucy's rich, mellow voice lacing around and through the other voices as she moved around the room. Amelia had never joined in the ring shout, at first uneasy with its country roots, and then unsure of herself. Oh, she believed and she prayed, but the serene faith that glowed on these people's faces eluded her. She envied the way they took everything to Jesus and didn't trouble it anymore.

You can look for a hidin place
But you can't hide
But you can't hide
But you can't hide

Elizabeth slipped past her and joined the group as they turned to go in the opposite direction, making sure that their feet did not cross. Amelia glanced around her at the others still seated. There were not many; a young woman holding a newborn, Ben and his friends. Although Ben and the other young men looked bored, she noticed that several pairs of heavy boots tapped to the rhythm. Even the oldest of the church members had managed to get to their feet and were shuffling forward either by leaning on their canes or holding tightly to someone's arm. Amelia wryly noted that none of the people who had been at Carrie Mae's last night were sitting in the church today—except, of course, Elizabeth and herself.

And the sea cry out
But you can't hide
But you can't hide
But you can't hide

She knew this song. She had heard it throughout her childhood, softly hummed by Myown when she was trying to get her to go to sleep and sung out loud when Myown had retreated to her room, hurt by a careless remark from Haagar or ignored by Arnold.

You can run to the Church
But you can't hide
But you can't hide
But you can't hide

She stood up slowly, hesitantly, and stepped into the aisle. A woman stepped back, making a space for her as she began to sing and clap.

An' the Church cry out
But you can't hide

"Hear me, Jesus, cause I wanna testify."

Amelia caught herself as she nodded off. They had been testifying for quite a while, and as she felt the exhaustion close over her, she feared that once she fell asleep, they would not be able to awaken her. The woman testifying stomped her foot as she talked about the most recent trials in her life. Tears streamed down her face as the others answered her call.

"My mama was sick an I asked de Lord."

"Yeah."

"Please dont take my mama from me."

"Oh, yeah."

"But he say, Bessie Joe Deans . . ."

"Well."

"Come on, home!"

"Home."

"Not ten days later, I was sittin on my porch."

"Uh-huh."

"My baby brother, live up in New York. Walk up on dat porch an into my house."

"Oh, Jesus."

"He smile at me, but he dint say a word."

"No word!"

"I gets up to follow him, an he aint nowhere in de house."

"Oh, no!"

"I knew right den, my baby brother gone!"

"Gone!"

"I said, Lord, why you visitin all dis on me?"

"Me!"

"He said, I dont give you more dan you can take!"

"Oh-oh."

"I was questionin my faith."

"Yes!"

"But he had faith in me."

"All right!"

"I say, he had faith in me."

"Amen!"

"Amen!"

They moaned and hummed as she slid down on the bench. There was a brief pause, and a man stood up. Amelia recognized him as Willis George, Eula's cousin who ran the ferry.

"I want to send a prayer an a thanks up to God."

"Yes."

"For my wife an dese chilren her done give me."

"Well."

"Us jus had my third child, an her de purtiest ting I ever seen."

Folks chuckled as he talked.

"Mm-hmm."

He nodded to the woman, who rocked the newborn and looked up at him with tired eyes. Two small boys who were the image of their father sat beside her, solemnly watching as their father spoke.

"I want to thank my wife, and I want to thank the Lord for bein so good to me and my family."

"Yes, sir."

He sat down and touched his wife's arm.

"And I got something to say!" Amelia woke up completely as Ol Trent stood up and shouted. The other people looked at each other warily, but politely waited for Ol Trent to testify.

"Our father, who art in Heaven. Hallowed be thy name."

"Yes, Jesus."

"Thy kingdom come, thy will be done on earth, as it is in Heaven."

"As it is in Heaven."

"Forever and ever, Amen."

"Amen!"

"Jesus met the woman at the well!"

"Well."

"He told her, 'Go call thy husband and come hither.' And she said, 'I have no husband.' And he said unto her, 'For thou hast had five husbands; And he whom thou now hast is not thy husband.' "

There was a stir as people shifted uneasily. The baby fretted at the sound of Ol Trent's raised voice. Her mother comforted her.

"Sinners! Repent! Eve! The first sinner! Potiphar's harlot! The whore Jezebel!"

Eula leaned over and whispered to Eli, who jumped to his feet and started to sing "Wade in the Water." The others quickly joined, singing loudly.

It was a lovely custom, Amelia thought, when she awoke in the late afternoon. After the big dinner on Sunday, Eula would insist that everyone take some quiet time for themselves. Making a quilt pallet for Rebecca in the front room, she would put the young ones down for a nap while Ben and Lucy often went to visit friends. Despite their protests, the children would drop off rather quickly, and Eli and Eula would close their bedroom door to get the little bit of privacy they would have until the next Sunday.

Amelia lay in the bed and listened to the faint sounds of loving that escaped from behind that closed door. Amelia could not remember the time when her parents had shared a bedroom or exchanged a simple caress, and she saw how Eli could hardly pass Eula without touching her in some way. At first, she had been shocked and a bit embarrassed, but even the young ones seemed to understand that their parents needed that time together and left them alone. Ben and Lucy would go off on their own business; Elizabeth would either head home or out to the woods to gather plants. It was as natural to them as the large Sunday dinner they shared. Envying the easy intimacy that Eli and Eula had with each other and their children, Amelia quickly got over her discomfort. She could not help but wonder how her mother would have bloomed if such a love had come her way.

She lay there for a while listening to the children play outside, then vaguely recalled Ben trying to cajole her into an afternoon stroll to use the movie camera. No telling where he was now. She sat up and searched for her shoes. Once she got them on, she wandered over to the kitchen and grabbed a biscuit from the bread safe and went out onto the front porch.

"Yall know where Ben is?" The boys raced by engaged in a fierce nut-throwing war. They disappeared around the side of the house. She looked at Rebecca, who played on the steps with her dolls. The blond doll that Amelia brought her sat on the top step, while Rebecca held her two corn shuck dolls in either hand.

As Amelia walked up behind her, Rebecca chided the two dolls, "You got to do what her say cause her de boss of you!" Speaking for the two dolls, she went on, "How come her de boss?" "Cause her purtier dan you. Her got good hair. Her not nappy head like we," Rebecca solemnly explained.

Amelia recoiled at Rebecca's words. She had expected Rebecca to treasure the store-bought doll because of her looks, but now Rebecca's words made her wish that she had never brought the doll. She leaned down. "Rebecca, I like your hair. It's thick and pretty."

Rebecca shook her head. "It nappy."

Amelia touched her hair. "It's pretty hair, Rebecca. I wish I had hair like that." Rebecca looked at Amelia, her eyes accusing her of the most ridiculous type of lying.

Amelia felt helpless. Her heart hurt as Rebecca tossed the corn shuck dolls aside and grabbed the store-bought doll. "I'm going to see Lil Bet. You want to come with me?" she encouraged. Rebecca shook her head and began to comb the store-bought doll's golden hair.

Amelia recognized the woman from church that morning, Willis George's wife. Without intending to, she had followed the footprints that led along the edge of the water. When she came around the edge, she saw the woman sitting on the low bluff, staring at her hands. The woman was so deep in her solitude that Amelia decided not to approach. But as she came closer to her, the woman looked up. Amelia nodded, and then not knowing quite what to do, she walked toward her.

"Evening." The woman's gaze swept her from head to toe. "I'm Eula and Eli Peazant's cousin, Amelia."

She waited a few uncomfortable seconds before the woman spoke. "Sallie Lee, Willis George's wife."

Amelia said brightly, "The woman with the pretty little baby." Sallie Lee stared at her vacantly.

Amelia could see that Sallie Lee had been a pretty woman at one time. Her sallow skin was without blemish and stretched tightly across her strong features. There was a trace of dimple when she spoke, and her dull eyes were the same brown color as her skin. She noted that with the exception of her full breasts, Sallie Lee carried little of the weight of a woman who had recently given birth.

Amelia tried again. "What's your baby's name?"

"She dont have a name yet. We call her Sugar. I give her a proper name when she baptized."

Amelia nodded. Sally clenched her hands and then slowly opened them. Amelia backed away. "Well, it was nice talking to you."

Sally looked down at her hands, calloused hands with small scars from nicks and cuts. "I got a story for you." Amelia blinked at her. "They say you come to gather folks' stories?" Amelia drew a deep breath as she sat down awkwardly beside the woman, who stared into her palms.

How I Come to This

as told by Sallie Lee

They dont even look like they belong to me. There was a time, if you had told me that Id let my hands go like this, Id a told you you was crazy. These hands were my vanity, an I used to have ten, twelve pair of white gloves that I would wear all the time. Look at this. I mashed this finger trying to pull a piece of cane out the mill. I put this cut on there the first time I learned to skin a bonneta. This here nail aint never gonna be right.

I used to spend every Saturday afternoon, after I finish work at the mill, fixing my hair, my nails, and my toes. Wouldnt go no place until everything was looking just right. Folks use to tell me all the time, I look just like that colored actress Fredi Washington or could go for her sister. You know Fredi Washington? I seen her in *Farewell, Traveler* down at the Montrose Theatre in Bofort. I used to go the movies all the time. Me and my cousins would step out for a Saturday, and folks would move off the sidewalks as we come through. You couldnt tell us nothing! We was that well put out!

I come from a good family over there in Bofort. We always lived in the city, wasnt nothing country about us! My daddy is a deacon in the Episcopal Church. He a respectable man, a hard man, but a good man. He raised me and my sisters and brothers right. My mama died when I was born. My daddy shut himself away in that room with my mama and wouldn't let nobody in. His mama come all the way from Memphis and brought him out so that they could bury my mama. My daddy took real good care of me. He always said out of all his children, I was her image.

I had plenty boyfriends. All the men, they wanted to talk to me, take me out, but I had one rule. I wasnt going no place without my cousins, Hettie and Magnolia. If they wanted to be with me, they had to bring someone for them! We used to have a good time. Yes, indeed! I wasnt wild, mind you. Daddy say I have to be home at a certain time, and I be there, cept when I stayed over at my cousins' house. I was a good girl.

I was so good at playing that game, had men in love with me every week, tryin to buy me earrings, scarves, all that stuff. But I dint take nothin from nobody. I had my little bit of money from my job, an Daddy would get me anything I wanted. You couldnt tell me nothing.

One day I was standing in front of Monte's Soda Shop with my cousins, and these two country negroes come strolling up the street. They was country coming an going! The tall one, he was kind of simple-looking and had all these gaps in his mouth, an the short one had a chest like a flour barrel an didnt say much of nothing. We started laughing at them. You could always tell them that just come over off the Islands. Their clothes hang funny, the hair look rough.

They was trying to talk to us an we was just laughing! That tall one he claim he a singer. But you know, everybody a singer. His friend say he a fisherman. We just laughing. We ask him if it easier to catch a shark or a drum. He so tongue-tied he cant say nothing. The tall one he tell us to come the Red Rooster an hear him sing. We almost didnt go. My cousin had a friend who was gonna take us up to Charleston, but he didnt show up. So we went on over there not expecting much of anything.

We got there and everybody was having a good time! Dat boy came out there, and he tore that place up. And all the time he was singing to me. You hear me? Looking in my eyes telling me what he could do for me! My cousins start messin with me. Dont let him put those country roots on you! Im from the city! I know how to handle a man! Specially a country man!

I aint gonna say he put roots on me, but it was so good I start runnin behind him. Couldnt think of nothing but being with him all the time. He left a burning inside me that was like the fire in the wilderness. When he was loving you, he could make you cry with weakness and scream with joy. Wasnt no part of my body his mouth dint touch, wasnt no part of my being that he didnt rock. I shaming you? I just tellin the truth. He got these fingers. Lord have mercy, those fingers would make you just open up an let him do whatever with you and you be lovin every minute of it. I got up one time in the middle of the night, sneaked out my daddy's house, and found him down at some club. Couldnt wait to go no place. We was in the alley, an I dont know who was howling more, me or them cats. You couldnt tell me nothing!

You look at him and you dont see much of nothing, but chile, he do you right. I was crazy foolish for him, and I come up pregnant. Lord, my daddy find out, hell kill me, an it likely to kill him! I figured it wouldnt take much to get him to come round. Men always did what I wanted. I went lookin for him, couldnt find him nowhere. Even went out with his little friend, figuring he knew where to find him. He wasnt nowhere. He a travelin man. Then my cousins start tellin me bout who he been with and what he done. Somebody told them he was living over there in Hog Alley with this woman and her children. I aint never step foot in Hog Alley, but that day I went. He wasnt there. She been waitin on him for long while, since they have they last baby. She told me about another woman claiming she got two children for him out in Collinswood and gonna have another baby for him.

I didnt know what to do. I was gettin bigger and bigger. All them little pretty dresses I had, couldnt fit into them. Didnt know what was worse, gettin sick every morning or tryin to hide from my daddy. An I could see him worrying bout me. Then I passed out on the job, an they sent me home. Daddy want to take me to the doctor, an then I had to tell him. It broke his heart. He listen to what I said, an I swear I could hear his heart breaking. He walked out that room, an he never spoke to me again. You see, I was his baby, the special one. Couldnt do nothing wrong. That hurt sit on his shoulders weighing him down to an old man. Well, I went over to my cousins' house cause the silence in that house was too much to bear.

It was all right at my cousins' house, but I got tired of their talk. They say my sisters was telling folks that I had come to no good cause of all that spoiling Daddy did to me. They always was jealous of me, and it didnt surprise that they would be so spiteful. What surprised me was that I was hurt by it. I thought nothing could hurt me worse than I was feeling. My cousins, you know, they had to say what they wanted to say, too.

I was sitting out there on the back porch thinking bout what I could do, an who come around in the backyard but his little friend, Willis George. He say he been looking for me an he want to talk. I got all hopeful cause I thought he knew where Woodrow was. But he come to talk with me an how he was feeling for me. He want to take care of me, want me to marry him. He didnt care nothing bout who the baby's daddy was. He jus wanted me. I look at that little man with them rough hands, an I jus about bust out laughing. How I come to this!

He telling me bout how hard he work an how much he love me, an I start laughing. I laugh so hard I make like I cryin. He say he give me everything he can an take care of me like my daddy did. I laugh hard, chile. Nobody take care of me like my daddy!

He kept coming round. Sometime he jus sit there an dont say nothin. An all the time I gettin bigger and bigger. Then I got word that

my daddy was sick, an I went to see him. He been sick since I left, an nobody, not my sisters, not my brothers, not my cousins had said a word to
me! I got there, an they said he just passed. I was fit to be tied! They
didnt come get me! They didnt say nothing! I dont care what my sisters
said, my daddy didnt die without asking for me! I could have tore them
apart with my bare hands! I was carryin on an tearing up that house, an
they was tryin to hold me down, an here he come. Dont know to this
day how he found me. But he make them let me go, an I leave that
house with him an I aint never been back.

I married him figuring I could do right by him. I told him that I
could never love him, an he say he gonna spend every day tryin to
change my mind. Wasnt my mind I was talkin bout! I come out here
cause I figure out here with all these backwards country people, this
hot sun, and the bugs that drive you out of your mind is punishment
enough for what I did to Daddy. This place aint nothin but hell floating
on water. An its right where I need to be.

Did I tell you I lost that baby? She come here, perfect as she can be,
without a breath of life in her. I made Willis George go in to Bofort and
get the picture-taking man to come out and take her picture fore we
buried her, cause nobody would believe how perfect she was. She look
jus like her daddy. I still got them pictures if you ever want to see them.
She look so pretty layin there in her christening gown.

Willis George a decent man. I aint never heard a harsh word from
him. After we buried her, I couldnt stay busy. The more I work, the
tireder I got. The more pain I felt, the better the punishment. I clean
house, wash clothes, cook the food, work in garden. Mule get tired, I
pull the plow! Thats where I got this. At first, he didnt say nothing. Just
come home, smellin like fish, an look at me with sad eyes. Then he
tried to stop me, said I was wasting away. I didnt want to hear anything
he had to say. He couldnt tell me nothing!

He woke up one night an found me out in the garden, pullin weeds
in the moonlight, an he come to get me. I cussed him! I cussed him
with words I never knew! Wasnt one name I didnt call him! An he just
stand there an look at me. I tell him to leave me alone! He go back in
the house. I work out there until it started raining so hard I had to
come in. I standing there wet as a dog, an I hear him crying. He crying
like a baby! You ever hear a decent man cry! An he a decent man. If I
cant love him, I can do right by him.

I look deep in me to see what little bit I got to give to this man!
There aint much there, but I give it to him. I give him his children, give
him that lil gal he been wantin so bad, I make sure his house clean, his

food is cooked, an his clothes mended, and whatever little bit left, I save it up so I can give it to him when he need it.

This here, this my reward, this my punishment. I swear I cant tell the difference. If you had told me way back then that I would spend my days out here in the country, strugglin to face every new day, I would have laughed at you. Because back then, you couldnt tell me nothing!

Sallie Lee's words tumbled over and over again in Amelia's mind as she walked across the yard to Nana's house. She hesitated for a moment when she saw that the door was closed. There was smoke coming from the chimney, and as she got closer, she heard voices, laughing. She knocked on the door and was surprised when Elizabeth said, "Come on in, Amelia!"

Opening the door, she hesitated when she saw Lucy sitting next to Elizabeth, helping her patch Nana's old quilt. She closed the door behind her and moved farther into the room. She was curious. "How did you know it was me?"

Elizabeth smiled. "Anybody else would call from the yard without coming up on the porch."

Amelia nodded and took a seat, watching them at their handiwork. It was the first time that Amelia had seen Lucy and Elizabeth together, just themselves. They were so different in personality that if it were not for the family resemblance, she would have never thought them to be sisters. Where Elizabeth tended to take her time before saying something, Lucy would blurt out whatever she felt like saying. Elizabeth dressed simply and neatly, her hair always tidy, whereas Lucy would throw on anything that was clean and would fit, her hair more likely to be scattered all over her head.

"How are you feeling?" Elizabeth asked. Lucy snorted.

Embarrassed, Amelia stole a glance at Lucy and answered defensively, "Much better."

Lucy leaned forward to pull a bit of cloth from the pile that lay on the table. "When I left after dinner, you was callin dem hogs, gal!" She and Elizabeth looked at each other and laughed. "Lil Bet tol me what yall was up to last night an dis morning, an I seen you in church. Look like you half-dead!" She giggled as she imitated Amelia's careful movements in church. Amelia shifted uncomfortably when Elizabeth giggled. Lucy chuckled. "I been out dere to Carrie Mae's, it too fast for me! She give you some of dat mint tonic she like to put in everyting?" Amelia nodded. "Yeah, it taste good going down, but coming up, Lord have mercy!"

Amelia looked at Lucy warily. She saw none of the anger and impatience that Lucy usually directed toward her. "Charlie coming home," Elizabeth said with a wink.

Lucy pushed her sister. "Go on, gal. Dont be tellin all my bizness."

Elizabeth responded, "Thats your problem, you aint got no business!"

Lucy protested. "All right now!"

Elizabeth continued, "All you do is work that field, go to church, an wait for Charlie to come home."

Lucy countered, "An whats wrong wit dat?"

"Cause when he aint here, you givin everybody a fit! Aint that right, Amelia?" Caught, Amelia looked at Lucy. Lucy glared at her. Amelia defiantly nodded in agreement. There was a pause, and both Lucy and Elizabeth burst out laughing. Amelia smiled shyly.

Lucy admitted, "I guess you did get de brunt of it, but you come up here wit your city ways talkin bout studyin somebody! Dis you family! How you study you family?" She thought about it for a minute, then grinned. "Maybe thas what I do to Charlie when him get here. How you put it? Study? Maybe I study Charlie some!"

Amelia reached over and began to sort the pieces of cloth that lay on the table. Elizabeth pointed to a pair of sharp scissors on the table. "Can you start cuttin some strips for us, bout long as my finger an bout this wide?"

Amelia spotted a piece of red cloth in the middle of the pile. She pulled it out and flattened it on the table. It was a deep red satin that had faded in spots. "This is pretty," she commented, holding it up. "Do you know where this came from?" Elizabeth and Lucy were both startled to see it.

Amelia looked from sister to sister, waiting for an explanation. Shaking her head in mock disgust, Elizabeth glanced up at her. "That Lucy's doing. She got to tell you bout dat!"

Lucy hemmed and hawed. "Aw, Lil Bet. Her already tink I de meanest ting her ever seen!" Elizabeth shrugged. "I gotta get one ting straight. Dis aint for no study, dis family bizness!"

The Red Satin Patch

as told by Lucy Peazant

It happen dat time Yellow Mary come out here hiding from de Sheriff for some kinda mess her was into, an her brung her friend, Baby Dell, out here wit she. Mama had jus had de twins, an her wasnt doin too well. Folks was talkin all that ol African hoodoo mess bout twins bein a bad sign, an folks bringin all dem ol bits an pieces to fight off de evil spirits. Not dat I aint gonna say dem boys aint bad, but dey aint de debil! An her had de baby born blues. You know how some women get all sad after dey baby born an stay tired an cryin an all dat. Dat de baby born blues.

Lil Bet, you see Sallie Lee in church today? Her got dem same blues. Oh-h-h, her lookin bad! All thin an dried out. Lil Bet, you should take some of you medicine over to she. Well, Mama had two babies, an her have two kinds of baby born blues. An we was tryin to help, but wit Lil Bet bein off at school, it was hard.

An Daddy! I dont know what was going on wit Daddy! Mama real busy an her so tired, an I declare he actin like him one of de babies! Couldnt nothin please he! Dey couldnt come two feet apart witout dem goin at each other, jus fussin! I figure him blame her an her blame he. Anyway, it was misery all around.

Den Yellow Mary show up! You know, her may be kin, but I swear if I never seen she agin I aint gonna miss she! I know! I know! Lil Bet! Her didnt do nuttin . . . but brung that ol hanckty woman wit her! Ol tired heffer call sheself Baby Dell, wit all dat paint on she face and dat ol smell of she. Her wear that ol smell all over her. To dis day, I wont wear, what you call dat stuff you be making up, Lil Bet? Pur-fume. To dis day, I dont wear no pur-fume! Dont make no sense to me! Put dat sweet-smellin stuff on you, an den you might as well call dem skeeters out for dinner! You could walk through de woods an tell where her been. Ast the bird, bird say her went dat way! Ast de rabbit, rabbit say her went dat way! Ast the gator, gator say her went dat way!

Well, her run into Daddy. Now dat gonna happen out here. Aint dat many folks out here! But her make sure her keep runnin into Daddy. An him in he misery cause him an Mama fightin like cats an dogs, an him aint gettin he tention de way him want. An her one of dem city women an her work for Yellow Mary, so her know bout men an dey weaknesses.

So Daddy, he de best tracker on de Island. Oh, yeah, white folks come out here all de time, an Daddy track for dem. Take dem out in de early morning for deer an bear an such. Well, Daddy start gettin up at night an going out to hunt. Now, aint nothing too odd bout that, us needs de meat! But him was doin a lot of huntin an him a good shot, but him wasnt bringin home dat much meat. So I ast Ben bout it cause sometime him take Ben to learn he. An you know, mens stick together, dont dey? Lil as him was, him wasnt gonna tell me nuttin bout Daddy.

So one night Daddy go out to hunt, an I follow he! I could tell from the way him wash up he hands and face dat him wasnt huntin no bear! So I follow he, an sho nuff, he head on back to de ol Wilkerson place. Wasnt nobody livin dere. Dey all had gone to de mainland. An I see he slip in dere, and den in de next coupla minutes, I smell she comin down de path! Den I see she, her carrying ol kerosene lamp an wearin a coat. Now it hot. Dis de middle of de summer an her wearin a coat! Her get up to de door an take dat coat off, an her aint got nuttin on but a red slip! Lord have mercy!

So I come on back. Aint nuttin I could do bout him slippin out witout tellin my mama. I feels bad, but you know, I know dat heffer comin my way one time! Dey keep on carrying on! Dis a small place, an folks find out an get into you business real fast. I hear chilren at school talkin, get real quiet when I come by. Ben gettin into fights almos every day! De twins real fretful, an Mama plumb wore out. Folks talkin out loud now bout Eli an Baby Dell. I fraid Mama gonna hear an lose her mind! Her crazy worryin over de twins anyhow.

I go see Yellow Mary an tell her what I know is goin on. An her listen an her shake she head. Her knew all along. Her knew fore I knew! Her say her talk to Baby Dell, but Baby Dell and Daddy grown up. Dey aint gonna listen to her! I say well, den I gonna have to do sumptin myself! Her say, "Baby, you do what you got to do." An her knew what I was talkin bout!

I tink Yellow Mary talk to ol Baby Dell, an I tink it made that ol cow bold, cause next ting I hear, her tellin folks her an my Daddy leavin together. Daddy done got real quiet now. He and Mama dont say much of nuttin to each other. I at school, an Ernestine Palmer run up to me an say, "Dat lady goin to you house! Her goin to tell you mama dat you daddy leavin wit her!" I call Ben, an us struck out for home. I tell Ben us got to stop dat woman from comin up on Mama.

We run through de woods cause we know her got to come de long way. We cut through dere, an sho nuff, we could see her comin from some ways back. I told Ben to get some rocks an go around her an chase her down where I was waitin. Ben can throw some rocks. An him did, cause her come runnin up dat trail in dem high shoes, breathin hard. Him musta hit her hat, cause it was sittin on de side of her face jus like dat. Yall laughing! I know it sound funny now, but it wasnt funny when it was goin on!

Her come up dat lil bump, an I waitin for her. Her see me an her stop an drew herself up, straighten up dat hat. Her see me, her see lil gal! Us Peazant women lil, but us strong! Her not a big woman like Carrie Mae, but her lot bigger dan me. I ast her what her doin. Her got right nasty! "None of you business!" I ast her where her goin. "None of you business!"

Her gonna push past me to get to my mama. I grabs her. Bout that time Ben let loose a rock, an it hit her in de back, an her fell on me! An I was ready! Her could have grabbed a mad dog an come out better cause I was on her like white on rice! An I was wearin her out! I learned long time ago, you gonna fight, you jump in dere an you hold on an you dont let go til you done what you come to do. I held her down an plucked every hairpin out her hair, pullin out fistfuls of hair! I slapped her so many times my hands were covered with all dat paint her was wearing. Her was hollering an tryin to get away, crawlin, grabbin at trees, tryin to get away. I catch my breath, an I haul her right back out dere an put some more on her! Gonna talk to my mama? De las ting I did to her was I held her down, lifted dat dress, an snatched dat red slip off her! Indeed I did! Dats where dat come from. An I tol her right dere, "I aint gonna be round all de time to keep you from gettin to my Mama. But you tink of dis. Dis whuppin I put on you, aint gonna be nuttin like de one you gonna wear if you talk to my mama!" I didn't care what her do wit Daddy, but her wasnt going to hurt my mama!

Coupla days later, Yellow Mary come by an let drop dat her friend had left de day before cause her needed to get some rest. I was all right wit dat!

Mama and Daddy dey work dey way back together. It took a while, but dey always been together. You thought dey had a perfect love? Gal, love caint be perfect! Mens gonna do what dey gotta do. Women, too, sometimes.

Elizabeth listened carefully for the change in the engine's knocking that would let her know that the old Model E might be on the verge of sputtering to a halt. So far they had only stopped once on their way to Charleston, and after a few minutes she had managed to get the car running again with a quick adjustment to the engine. Amelia had been startled when Elizabeth steered the flagging car to the edge of the road, hopped out, pulled a screwdriver from under the seat, and flung open the engine hatch. Amelia had slid from the passenger's seat and cautiously walked around to the front to look over Elizabeth's shoulder as she leaned into the engine. When Elizabeth had requested a wrench, Amelia stared at her blankly, then wisely brought back all of the tools under the front seat, allowing Elizabeth to choose the wrench she needed.

"I been doing this for years," Elizabeth explained good-naturedly. "Miss Genevieve and Miss Evangeline couldn't find nobody to drive them the way they like so they got Isaac next door to teach me to drive. Now, he had the patience of Job, cause I was so scared when I first got in the car, I forgot to open my eyes, ran all across the backyards and through the gardens. Killed plenty tomatoes and cabbages!" She chuckled. "And then as I figured out what I was supposed to be doing, I got interested in what was going on under here and talked Isaac into showing me what to do. The car was pretty old then and not too many people wanted to bother with it or the sisters."

Although Amelia had watched skeptically as Elizabeth adjusted screws and turned valves, she did carefully crank the engine when Elizabeth asked. After a sixth attempt, the engine caught, and Amelia flung her arms around Elizabeth, the both of them dancing on the side of the road like children. When the engine threatened to idle down, they scrambled in and continued on their way to Charleston.

It was Amelia's first trip to the mainland in the two months since she had first arrived, and she was a bit excited, caught up in that "crossin ober" spirit. Aware that about once a month Elizabeth would cross over and stay for a couple of days, she did not know until Elizabeth told her that she had a second job. When Elizabeth had matter-of-factly explained how little she received for teaching and that she needed every bit of extra money to buy supplies for the school, Amelia had quickly offered to share her stipend.

The stipend had proved to be an embarrassment to Amelia from the start. When she had first offered to pay for her room and board, Eli and Eula had been shocked into silence. Eli, the first to recover, had tersely asked her how he was going to accept money from a relative living under his hospitality? Eula had suggested that she keep the money for the things that she would need. Elizabeth had also turned her down, allowing that the job also gave her the opportunity to get away for a couple of days. Amelia was still searching for a way to use the money to show her appreciation without insulting anyone.

Amelia ran over the list of things that she had to do while she was on the mainland. She had to mail several cans of film and a copy of her journal pages to Dr. Colby. She was a bit nervous because getting the information was a much slower and more difficult process than she had imagined. People were gradually getting used to her, but they were still cautious. She had to acknowledge that the realities of gathering information did not fit into the academic calendar. Eula had asked her to get the mail, and she was looking forward to finding a letter from her mother. She had sent a letter after her first month, but had not yet received a reply.

She worried about Myown and how she was holding up. Over the past few weeks, she had experienced unsettling moments when her senses had stirred to an odd note on the wind, the scent of someone close, an almost imperceptible touch. She had spun around, searching for the person who had come upon her unawares, and found herself alone. When it first happened, she felt a rush of cold fear, terrified that something had happened to her mother. But one night, as she listened to Eula explain to Rebecca that a spirit walking had brushed against her on her way to the kitchen, she remembered from years before when Myown told her that you could send your spirit walking to visit a loved one. She had taken a special comfort in knowing that with all the angry and mean ghosts the folks insisted lived on the Island, her mother's good-hearted spirit had found a way to visit.

Amelia had another purpose for this trip, one that she had not mentioned to Elizabeth. She wanted to visit Hog Alley and see if she could find any of her grandmother's family. It would have been difficult, for she had not known her grandmother's family name. Although she knew that Haagar had married into the Peazant family, she could not recall a time when her grandmother had referred to herself as anything other than a Peazant. If it had not been for the family tree in the old Bible that Eula had so diligently preserved, she would never have known that the family name was Devries.

Elizabeth sighed when she saw the shiny new Chevrolet sitting in front of the Bouvier house. Their niece by marriage, Martha Bingham, was visiting. Elizabeth did not relish the idea of running into Martha, and when she had lived in the house had learned to quickly disappear when Martha came for her obligatory visits.

About the same age as Elizabeth, Martha at first had treated Elizabeth like all the other servants around the house except Bertha—as if she were her personal servant. It seemed to Elizabeth that Martha had gotten a distinct pleasure out of having Elizabeth run back and forth as she changed her mind about whether she wanted the blue gingham, the yellow check, or the pink voile dress ironed. Bertha had declared her suspicions outright one day when Martha had rung the bell in her room a fourth time. "Dat girl change dem clothes three times a day when she stay here an ack like she dont like what I cookin! Now, I know deir cook! She all right, but when dey havin a party, dey always after de Missus for me to come over dere an cook! She aint tryin to do nuttin but run you in de groun! Let me go up dere!" And sure enough, when Bertha appeared, Martha sputtered that she had rung the bell before she found the shoes under her bed.

Martha's attitude had taken a truly spiteful turn when she realized that the Bouvier sisters had given the run of the library to Elizabeth, and she had simmered with resentment as Elizabeth read to the sisters in the evening. Quite often Miss Evangeline would discuss some point from the book and would turn to Martha and Elizabeth for their thoughts. Elizabeth had seen the outrage in Martha's eyes when Miss Evangeline had briskly disagreed with her answer and had turned to Elizabeth for verification. The more Elizabeth tried to temper her response, the angrier Martha had gotten. Later that evening she spat at Elizabeth in the kitchen, "You better watch yourself, black gal! You are lucky my uncle is dead, cause he wouldn't put up with this silliness going on in his house around you! He knew what to do with yall!"

After that incident, Elizabeth would escape from the library as soon as she had finished reading. When she was around the sisters, Martha ignored Elizabeth, treating her as if she were a piece of furniture. It all came to a head when Martha, under the guise of perfecting her French, began to engage the sisters in French-only conversations during the evenings. It had never occurred to Elizabeth to enter any private conversation with them in English or French, but when Miss Genevieve absentmindedly asked Elizabeth about the last shipment of goods they had received and Elizabeth answered in French, Martha exploded, "You taught her French? What good is that going to do her? That's like teaching a dog to drive a car! I swear, I tell my mama some of the things that go on in this house, and she declares her brother would come out of his grave to put a stop to this!"

Elizabeth slipped from the room as the tirade continued. Neither Miss Genevieve nor Miss Evangeline ever mentioned Martha's blowup, and although it was never discussed, they accepted Elizabeth's decision not to join them in the evenings when Martha was visiting. It was not long afterward that Martha left for the traditional European tour that all the socially prominent young women from Charleston enjoyed as their rite of passage, and Elizabeth left to study at Fort Valley State College.

Now Elizabeth carefully edged around the Chevrolet and drove the car to the carriage house in back. "I can't believe we got here!" Amelia teased. "I kept expecting it to putt-putt-putt to a stop!"

Elizabeth patted the dashboard. "She run hard, but she don't give up." She slid from the car, the tingling in her fingers reminding her that she, too, had been worried about the car stopping. "I'll see if I can't get Isaac to look at it before we leave."

Amelia stood in the backyard and looked up at the tired old house. "You lived here for how long?"

Elizabeth pulled packages from the car. "Little over four years. It wasn't as worn down as it is now. Folks get older, they can't see after things like they used to!" She led the way to the back door. Amelia followed her, stepping carefully among the cracked flagstones that dotted the path.

Elizabeth took a deep breath before she knocked on the parlor door. She and Amelia had taken a few minutes to freshen themselves after they had placed their things in the room. Katie had been very relieved to see them, warning them that the "she-cat" was visiting the sisters. She also relayed Miss Evangeline's request that Elizabeth come to the parlor as soon as she arrived.

"*Entrez-vous,*" came the reply to the knock. Elizabeth entered, followed by Amelia.

"Ah, here she is. Elizabeth, you remember Martha?" Miss Evangeline waved toward her niece.

Elizabeth nodded briefly as Martha's gaze swept her from head to toe, taking in her demure appearance. Miss Evangeline stopped in surprise as she saw Amelia behind Elizabeth. "And this is?"

Elizabeth spoke up. "This is my cousin, Amelia Varnes. She came down from New York to stay with us for a while." Amelia nodded to the sisters as Elizabeth finished the introductions. She noted that Martha had been startled to find herself appraised in the same way that she had appraised Elizabeth. There was a slight movement, and everyone looked at a young well-dressed woman sitting on the settee.

Miss Evangeline turned to the woman. "Elizabeth, I wanted you to meet Natalie Duvalier, the daughter of our oldest friends in Paris." Miss Genevieve interjected helpfully, "She was the one who always put those exquisite scarves and blouses in the boxes."

"Martha ran into her on her last trip, and she decided to come for that visit that we have been begging from her!" Miss Evangeline continued.

Natalie smiled at Elizabeth and Amelia, speaking in heavily accented English. "It is my pleasure." When Elizabeth responded in French, Natalie clapped her hands and began to speak rapidly in French. Miss Genevieve and Miss Evangeline beamed at each other, proud of their student's skill. As Elizabeth apologized for the rustiness of her French, Natalie shook her head. "Oh, no! It is quite wonderful, very clear with a touch of yourself. That is the best way to enjoy a language. Who taught you? Have you ever been to Paris?" Martha snorted at the questions.

Elizabeth turned to the sisters. "It was the books you sent. They wanted me to read them aloud."

"And you?" Natalie turned to Amelia.

"Oh, no, just a bit of Latin, I'm afraid."

Miss Genevieve touched the goldenrod and chinaberry charm that was pinned to her blouse. "And Elizabeth made this charm that you liked so much."

Natalie smiled at Elizabeth. "They are really quite exquisite. They set off the blouse just so."

Miss Evangeline added, "She also does a creditable job with scents."

"Scents, also?" Natalie exclaimed. "This is wonderful! You must show them to me!"

Martha quickly spoke with emphasis. "Well, we're going to have to be getting back because we have that dinner party tonight!" She stood and began to gather her things.

Miss Genevieve asked, "Natalie, couldn't you come and stay a few days with us?"

Martha admonished her. "Now, Aunt Gennie, I've got her whole trip planned to the last minute! She showed me such a good time in Paris that I am determined to give her the grand tour of Charleston, then we're going down to Savannah, and then up to Atlanta! I wanted to make sure she got a chance to see you before we took off." She strolled over and opened the parlor door.

Miss Evangeline pointed out, "I'm sure that you can visit us again before you leave."

Natalie reluctantly stood up. "Of course, I will see you again." She spoke to Martha. "We will work something out." She crossed and hugged the sisters. She turned and extended her hand to Elizabeth. "I need to find out more about these charms." After a slight hesitation, Elizabeth took her hand. Martha frowned at the visitor. Natalie then extended her hand to Amelia. "My pleasure." Amelia shook her hand firmly.

Martha stirred impatiently, "We have to go. Bye, Aunt Gennie. Bye, Aunt Evangeline!" She blew them a kiss from the door and turned down the hallway. Natalie shrugged and followed, her *"Au revoir"* floating back into the room.

For some reason, the sisters had decided that it was time to go through all of the trunks and crates stored in the attic, clear out the old things that were of no use, and bring down the others for inspection. Katie had flatly declared that she wasn't going up there "wit all dat dust, dem haints, an dem ol spiders hanging all over," so Elizabeth and Amelia had been directed to begin the housecleaning. Amelia could not believe the number of trunks and crates that were crammed into the attic. Several crates held men's clothes, either belonging to the sisters' father or Miss Genevieve's husband. Amelia marveled at the crisply ironed clothes that lay neatly among the tissue paper in the trunks. Both Elizabeth and Amelia exclaimed with dismay when they discovered that many of the clothes had dry rotted and fell apart even with the most careful handling. It was not until quite a bit later that Amelia could appreciate the beauty and utility of the old steamer trunks that had enchanted Elizabeth from the beginning of their task.

Natalie appeared in the attic during the middle of the cleanup. Somehow she had cajoled Martha into making another visit to her aunts and had managed to slip away to look for Elizabeth. When she appeared in the doorway like an apparition, both Elizabeth and Amelia jumped.

"Oh, I am so sorry," Natalie apologized as she stepped into the dimly lit attic. "The young girl in the kitchen said that you were up here, and

I so desperately wanted to talk with you!" Elizabeth and Amelia exchanged quizzical glances.

"You wanted to talk with me?" Elizabeth asked hesitantly.

"Yes, yes!" Natalie was excited. "About the charms you make . . . and Miss Evangeline mentioned scents, too?"

"I just make them for the sisters because they like them," Elizabeth explained. "Miss Genevieve is real partial to them, an I don't dare make anything for Miss Genevieve without making anything for Miss Evangeline."

Eagerly, Natalie crossed to Elizabeth. "Do you have any others with you?" Elizabeth stared at her, a little put off by her eagerness. She looked over at Amelia for help.

Amelia shrugged. "You might as well. It's not like this stuff is going anywhere."

Elizabeth led Natalie down to the bedroom on the second floor and laid out the few charms and scents that she had brought with her. Natalie examined the charms, exclaiming over Elizabeth's exquisite handiwork. She questioned Elizabeth carefully about her choices for putting together scents, and when Elizabeth explained with some embarrassment that she mixed the scents by matching the person's own scent with herbs and flowers that seemed to add to that personal aroma, she clapped her hands and laughed. "But this is the best way! To find that which is of the person and make it their own!"

"It just sounds kind of funny when you try to tell that to someone," Elizabeth acknowledged.

"Excuse me. I do not mean to be forward, but how much do you charge to make these?"

Elizabeth was shocked. "You mean, ask money for this?"

Natalie was nonplussed. "But, of course." She stared at Elizabeth, then asked quietly, "You do this as gifts?" Elizabeth nodded. There were several moments of silence. "Well, then how much would you charge to make some for me?" Natalie ventured.

When Elizabeth did not reply, Natalie spoke up quickly. "Let me explain. In Paris, I am an assistant in a shop where they design and make fine clothes. I have been talking to the owner about adding things that women can wear to accent the clothes. She is very good at what she does and a very proud woman. She does not believe that anything can add to her clothes without taking away from them. And I have been telling her for two, three years that something simple and elegant like this would be perfect. But she insists that women should buy things like your charms and scents in shops that only sell charms and scents. I would like to show her that women would be willing to buy the whole look in one shop! I could sell these! I know I could sell these!" She waited for Elizabeth's response.

"I . . . I just never thought about selling them!" Elizabeth muttered.

"Well, you won't have to sell them. I will sell them! I will give you the money to make them and send them to me, and I will sell them! We will split the sale. So how much will it cost?"

From downstairs, they heard Martha calling, "Natalie, Natalie, where are you? We have to be getting along! Where are you?"

Natalie frantically dug into her purse, searching, and triumphantly pulled out a small white card. "This is my address." She thrust money into Elizabeth's hand. "Make as many as you can, and then send them to me!" Martha had started up the steps still calling her name. Natalie closed Elizabeth's hand around the bills and whispered, "Please, give it a chance!" Elizabeth stared at the money in her hand as Natalie rushed from the room to intercept Martha.

The twelve dollars lay in her purse like a stone. Elizabeth swore that she could feel the additional weight of the money as she shifted the purse from one hand to the next. It was almost a month's salary for Elizabeth. Despite herself, she had already begun to think of the blue velvet and the satin ribbons that she had seen in the general store. She had stared longingly at them as she waited for the clerk to wrap the rough muslin and gingham that Eula wanted. It would be perfect for setting off the rosemary and summer savory flowers that she had been saving to use.

There was a stir as the front doors to the Beaufort Book Depository were thrown open. It was the fourth Thursday, the only time of the month that the colored teachers could come to the Depository and pick up the supplies needed for their students. As Elizabeth checked her list, Amelia scrutinized the small group of teachers, noting to herself that this was part of the colored elite of Beaufort. A middle-aged white woman wearing a black mourning dress stepped out and looked down on the crowd. "I want yall to line up an have your supply chits ready so we dont have to waste any time this morning!" she briskly instructed. Amelia glanced down at her watch, which showed that the Depository was forty-five minutes late in opening. A thin, young blond woman in a flowered dress appeared in the doorway with a clipboard and papers. "Now, yall have to sign in with Miss Chambers. She'll check to see if yall name is on this list."

Noting Elizabeth's place in the line, Amelia whispered, "What are you going to do if they don't have anything left?" Elizabeth looked at the long line of teachers patiently waiting to get into the Depository and replied, "I'm just going to have to make do, like I been doing, with what little I got."

Amelia sat on the running board waiting for Elizabeth to come out with her supplies. When Elizabeth exited the building with only one box, Amelia could see the disappointment in her face. Amelia opened the boot of the car. "There wasn't much of anything left," Elizabeth said as she placed the box in the boot. She reached down and pulled a tattered book with a broken spine from the box. "This was the best I could find." She slumped as she went through the odds and ends in the box. She held up a tablet that had three sheets of paper left. "How am I supposed to keep them going when I don't even have paper for them to write their lessons?" Amelia glanced over at one group who had loaded several boxes of books and supplies into a car and were giggling as they tried to fit the last box in. Elizabeth shut the boot hastily, not bothering to hide her frustration. Amelia climbed into the car to start it while Elizabeth cranked. She slid over as Elizabeth slipped behind the wheel.

They rode in silence for the next few minutes, then turned to each other determined to speak. They spoke at the same time, stopped, and then started again. "I got an idea," Amelia said at the same time that Elizabeth announced, "I know what I can do."

Elizabeth plunged ahead. "This money I got for the charms. I can use some of it to get some more paper and books."

Amelia shook her head. "No, you use that money to get that nice stuff you were looking at in the store for those charms. I think that's going to pay off a little bit faster." Elizabeth was hesitant, but Amelia insisted. "Look, I get money every month for my keep, and Aunt Eula and Uncle Eli won't let me give them nothing! Just won't hear of it! So the way I see it, I can use some of that money to get those school supplies."

Elizabeth protested, "That money's for your schooling."

But Amelia corrected her. "That money is for anything I want to spend it on, and I can't think of a better use for it."

Elizabeth hummed as the car rumbled down the street. They had gotten the paper and pencils for the school and the blue velvet and satin ribbons for the charms. The store also had a few old textbooks in the back, which the storeowner was more than glad to sell. They were not the same textbooks that the School Board distributed, but Elizabeth knew she could make good use of them.

Amelia had remembered to get the mail and had eagerly opened the package from her mother once they were settled in the car. Inside the box was a pretty cotton blouse and a colorful scarf. Wrapped inside the clothes were letters for Amelia and Eula and a packet with Iona's name on it. Amelia opened her mother's letter at once.

My darling girl,
    We receive the letter you send after you get there. I know Cousin Eli and Cousin Eula happy to see you. We doing as well as can be espected. Folks still taking bout how you daddy put Essie Carmichael away, an we get other people coming to us want the same for they own. I miss you, my girl. An I think this good for both of us. You get your schooling done an you enjoy the rest of Peazants, that what important now. They dont worry me so much as before, they too busy. Please ask Cousin Eli if he could see that Iona get these letters I send her. I been writing to her since you gone in hopes that these letters will get to her. Well, I must close. We have two coming in today. Write soon, my darling girl, an remeber that your mother always thinking of you and missing you.

                                                                                    Mama

Amelia stared out the window, summoning her mother's image. Since she had come to the Island, she had seen so much of her mother in everything, from the flowers that grew along the path in the woods, to the light breaking through the clouds, and the dolphins that played offshore. She had wondered how her mother, who she now knew had to be a creature of perpetual light, had survived the darkness of her life. Surely, Haagar was the stronger when it came to will, but Myown drew her life directly from her soul.

Glancing over at Elizabeth, Amelia sought to frame her request. "How much time do we have before Willis George heads back?"

Elizabeth shrugged. "A couple of hours." She waited for Amelia to explain.

"I was wondering if we could go over to Hog Alley before we head back. I wanted to see if I can find any of my granma's kin. I know the name is Devries."

"That's Miss Genevieve's married name," Elizabeth pointed out.

Amelia nodded. "I figured at some point they owned my granma's kin." She looked over at Elizabeth. "Do you know how to get there?"

Elizabeth half-laughed. "Oh, yeah. Everybody know how to get to Hog Alley. Not that far from the railroad station. Colored part of town always close to the railroad station." Sensing Amelia's disquiet, she assured her, "We got time if you want to head on over there." For a moment, she saw a shadow move across Amelia's face before she nodded in agreement.

Elizabeth and Amelia picked their way around the puddles and the stinking mud that filled the narrow street. Aware of the reputation of Hog Alley and its residents, Elizabeth had left the car at the railroad station. On their way, they had passed the neat houses and yards with flower gardens that made up the rest of Shermanville, the colored section of town. When they drew closer to Hog Alley, they could see that the houses were not well-kept and that the yards disappeared under weeds. They turned the corner and stood at the beginning of Hog Alley. Despite what she had heard, Amelia was not ready for Hog Alley.

The first thing to hit her was the smell of the place. She turned to Elizabeth. "They still run the hogs through here?"

Elizabeth shook her head. "That the smell of people live here. The toilets sit on the water line from the river back there. When it rains, it washes into the street. Every now and then, folks will get real sick back here, and they close the place off. Can't nobody come and can't nobody leave til it passes."

Amelia took a deep breath. "You don't have to come with me."

Elizabeth looked at her in astonishment. "Girl, I'd be crazy to let you go in there by yourself!" Amelia peered down the street lined with shacks and the few pieces of lumber laid down to help people across the muddiest spots. As she hung back at the end of the road, Elizabeth stepped past her and said, "If we gonna go, we better go now." Elizabeth carefully stepped on a piece of lumber and turned back to her cousin, extending her hand. Amelia grasped her hand and they edged their way into the Alley.

There were few people on the street, and the rough shacks were closed against the chill in the air. An old woman dressed in layers of shabby clothes carrying a bucket of water shuffled toward them. "Who you looking for?" Elizabeth asked Amelia.

"Her daddy's name was Jackson Devries. He may still be alive."

When they drew closer to the old woman, Elizabeth asked, "Excuse me, ma'am. We looking for somebody named Jackson Devries. Could you tell us where he lives?"

The woman glared at both of them, spat out "No!," and then pushed her way past, almost sloshing them with the water.

They continued down the street. They came to a quick stop as two men flew out the door of one place and landed in the middle of the muddy street. A big, burly man smoking a cigar stood in the doorway and watched the two men struggle and slip, holding on to each other and trying to work their way out of the mud. He shouted at them, "Dont yall be comin in here unless yall got my money!" As he turned to head back in, he saw Elizabeth and Amelia. He looked at them and grinned, showing several missing teeth and much gum. "Hey, what yall gals doing out here?"

Elizabeth spoke warily, "We come to visit somebody."

"Well, I needs somebody to visit me, specially some pretty womans like yall. Come on in here!" he invited.

Elizabeth was polite. "We got to get along."

She and Amelia moved carefully past the door. They could hear a mournful blues song coming off the piccolo and people fussing and laughing. The dark door that led to an even darker room bore no resemblance to Carrie Mae's. The man smirked at Amelia. "Who yall going to see?" With a quick shake of her head, Elizabeth cautioned Amelia. He shouted after them, "Yall got to come back dis way! I be waitin for you!" Amelia trembled and held on to Elizabeth's hand, as Elizabeth muttered, "My daddy know I come back here, he have a fit!"

Amelia offered, "We can always go back!"

"No," Elizabeth said, "we already here! Sides, we need to give him some time to forget we come through!" She stopped to free her heel from the sucking mud.

Amelia looked around at the sad houses that leaned against each other. There was nothing that could be considered a yard, only a few patches of grass here and there. She could see the efforts made by a few industrious residents to keep their little space neat with crude, uneven fences that ran around the edges of the yard. There were several dormant running vines that twined up the poles holding some houses up. Bits and pieces of refuse from a better world littered the yards waiting to be put to some practical use. Elizabeth pointed to a house whose roof was a patchwork of old product signs advertising everything from sarsaparilla drinks to hair pomade. "Somebody put a whole lot of work on that!"

A door swung open and a young woman about their age stepped out, carrying a baby. She stopped, as surprised to see them as they were to see her. She stared at them, taking in their neat appearance. Amelia smiled encouragingly at her. "Excuse me. I was wondering if you could help us. We're looking for a man named Jackson Devries. Do you know if he still lives here?"

The woman stared at her without speaking. She clutched the baby closer as it whimpered in the cold. Amelia looked at Elizabeth, not sure if the woman heard or understood her. Elizabeth started to speak, but was interrupted by the woman. "What you want wit ol Jack?" she asked suspiciously.

"He kin to us!" Elizabeth stated.

The woman looked at them in scorn. "He kin to everbody. He got some fifty hundred chilren from all kinds of women!"

Amelia asked with concern, "Is he still alive?"

The woman sputtered, "Yeah, he still roun here spreadin dat evil! De Lord aint gonna see no sign of he, an de debil gonna take he time callin dat one!"

Amelia asked, "Could you tell us where he lives?"

The woman hesitated and then spoke with rising anger, "Why yall goin to see him? Yall outa let him rot down dere in dat house!" The baby began crying, jolted by the woman's angry outburst. She hushed the baby. "I got to go feed my baby." She turned from them and walked away. She turned back suddenly and pointed. "He live down dere in de house wit all de dogs in de yard!" When they turned to move on, she shouted after them, "You tell dat ol man, he stop tellin de lies bout me to my man! I come down dere, pizzen dem dogs an cut he heart out while he sleepin!"

Elizabeth pushed Amelia ahead of her, "Come on. Let's get this over with."

It was a large yard and, as the young woman had described, filled with dogs. They began their racket as soon as Elizabeth and Amelia drew close. Elizabeth reached down and picked up a stout stick. Amelia looked around, but only saw a piece of rotted wood that would be of no use. She eyed the fence that ran around the yard. It was made of everything from old mattress springs to the hood from a car. Along the top and the bottom of the fence ran wire with jagged pieces sticking from it. The dogs' barking and snarling was so loud that Amelia could not hear what Elizabeth was saying. As she leaned closer to her, the front door to the house opened and an old man almost bent in half stood there with a shotgun. He stared from the darkness. "Yall brung my supper?" he shouted. Elizabeth and Amelia looked at each other. The dogs were jumping against the gate, trying to snap at them. The man lay the shotgun against the wall and grabbed a wash pan that sat by the door and banged on it with a spoon. The dogs stopped barking and slunk to the other side of the yard.

"Yall brung my supper? Where my supper?" he bawled.

Amelia stepped forward. "I'm looking for Jackson Devries? You Jackson Devries?"

He grabbed the shotgun. "Who astin?"

Elizabeth pulled at Amelia. "We better go!"

Amelia shook her head. "Amelia Varnes! I am the grandchild of your daughter Haagar!" she shouted back at him. They could see him hesitate, thinking.

"I got plenty daughters. I don't remember none name Haagar!"

Elizabeth was insistent. "Amelia, Amelia, ain't nothing good coming from this!"

Amelia turned to her. "I got to know! I got to know what was in this house that made her turn the way she did!" She turned back to him. "Her mother was Mattie Baker."

"Oh, dat my third wife!" he remembered. "Pretty ol black gal. Give me five, six chilren fore she run off!" His manner changed completely. "Come on in. It always good to see kin!"

Amelia looked for the latch to the gate. He hobbled down the stairs and across the yard, the dogs following him. He reached the gate and peered at them. "Yall some pretty girls, look jus like yall belong to me!" Elizabeth and Amelia watched him carefully as he pulled out a key and opened the ancient lock that held the thick chain through the latch. When he pulled open the gate, several dogs rushed forward, and he kicked at them. Yelping, they ran off and hid under a pile of debris. Amelia and Elizabeth stepped forward cautiously.

"Dey aint gonna bother you! Come on." He waved them in and then shut the gate, wrapping the chain around the latch. Amelia and Elizabeth stood perfectly still as a couple of dogs sniffed at them. Elizabeth held the stick, ready to defend herself and Amelia from the dogs and the old man. The dogs skulked behind them, keeping a safe distance from Ol Jack. Ol Jack headed back to the house. Amelia stopped at the doorway, Elizabeth right behind her. The room was filled with junk that he had picked up from all over. He waved them over to a filthy settee that teetered on three legs as he settled into a large, beat-up leather chair.

"Close dat door. It cold out dere!" he ordered. Elizabeth stood by the door, but Amelia moved farther into the room. He chuckled when he saw Elizabeth's stick. "What you gonna do wit dat stick, gal? What dis ol man can do to two stroppin gals like yall? Sit down, gal!" Amelia perched on the edge of the settee. Elizabeth refused to move from the door. He took off his hat and scratched his head. "So where dat ol gal, you mama?"

Amelia looked at him. "You don't know my mother. You never met my mother."

He frowned at her. "I thought you say you mama was my daughter!"

Amelia coolly responded, "My granma is your daughter Haagar."

He snorted, "Well, I gots least thirty chilren, some by wives, mine an other men's!" He cackled, running his hands through his hair.

Elizabeth held her breath as his features became clearer in the dim light of the room. She had seen that face before, the same brow, the dark, accusing eyes, and the thin, cruel lips. She stepped farther into the room to study him. She noted the thin hair that curled at the edges and the bladed jaw. Although he was the color of a tanned piece of leather, she could tell that he had darkened with age. When she realized where she had seen him, it was all she could do to keep from grabbing Amelia and running from the shack.

He was the colored image of Burton Devries. She knew this like she knew that the sun would rise every day. She could not count the number of times she had cleaned or read in that library under the stern visage of his portrait. The picture had also darkened with age, and it could easily have been painted from this man who sat in front of her, baiting her cousin. She exhaled slowly and listened as Amelia tried to make conversation with him.

"So, what she send me?" he demanded. Amelia stared at him. "I done raised all dem chilren, put food in dey mouths, an dey run off an leave me here all alone. Every now an den, one of dem come back lookin for somebody. But dey dont stay an set me down like dey spose to."

Amelia asked quietly, "Set you down?"

"Yeah, gal! Aint you mama learn you nuttin? Chilren suppose to set dey daddy down. Take care all he needs cause he brung you here!"

"She didn't send you anything," Amelia stated flatly. "She doesn't even know I've come to visit you."

He glared at her. "Den why you here?"

She matched his tone. "I just wanted to know about my grandmother's people."

He eyed her. "What you gonna give me?" Elizabeth stepped forward, alarmed.

Amelia held up her hand. "What do you want?"

He looked from her to Elizabeth and smirked. "You aint seen no miss-meal cramps. Both yall got dem nice clothes an dat fancy talk. It been hard on me. Aint got nobody lookin after me!" She stared at him. He crossed his arms and pretended to think.

Elizabeth appealed to her. "Amelia, let's go! Leave this old man to himself."

He grinned. "You want to hear bout de family, you got to have de money!"

Amelia leaned back and scrutinized him. She slowly reached inside her jacket and pulled out a few bills. She carefully selected a five-dollar bill and held it up for him to see.

"Gal got big nigger money!"

He shot a glance at Elizabeth, who spoke up quickly. "I'm not interested in your story!"

He waved her away. "Den go on out dere wit dem dogs!"

Amelia put the bill in her pocket and stood up. "She stays, or you don't get a cent!"

He looked up at her with grudging admiration. "Mmph, you sound like you belong to me! What all you wants to know?"

What Devries Got, Devries Hold

as told by Jackson Devries

I dont rightly remember you mama. I done have so many chilren, I cant remember all dey names an where dey got to. You granma? Dat my daughter? What her name again? Haagar. Dat got to be one of Mattie gals. She give dem all names from de Bible. She run off! Mattie, she pretty ol black gal! Keep a good house, too! I come home one day, an she done run off. Took de baby wit her an lit out. I caint recall if dat was a girl or boy. But she left de other twelve behind, even her own. I didnt go after her. If she want me to come get her, she wait forever! I aint never had no problem gettin a woman. I get dem black gals, dey love demselves light men wit good hair, an I keep dem in dis house doin as I will. I tole dat boy down dere, he better keep dat gal an dat baby in dat house. She wont stay, you put sumptin on her an she wont stray! Dese young mens dont know how to handle dese women!

Was your mama, your granma, de one wit de cross eyes? What she look like? Was she de one wit de bad leg? Dey was one wasnt right in her head. Aw, hell, she could have been any of dem gals! I caint recall her!

Me? What you want to know bout me? Jackson Devries. Yeah, I know de white Devries. We all come from de same ol man. De white Devries, dey like to tell folks dey use to own us, an all dat mess bout how we tooks dey name after de slave free. We dint take no name but was ours. Every Devries since dey first come here have a white family an a nigger family. Dem Devries was de one brought us here. Dey went over to Africa an brung de people back to sell. Dey slavers from way back. Dey always keep two families. An some of dem chilren from de niggers come up lookin more like Devries dan de white ones.

Dey say every now an den one of de niggers cross over into de white. Marry up an move on! Ol man even get chilren from he nigger daughters, give nigger daughters to dey white sons to get more chilren. Dey want to own everybody. What Devries got, dey hold, and all us Devries got a taste for dey own.

Now de colored always know bout de white ones, but de white ones ack like dey dont know bout us. Dey get in trouble, den dey come to us to take care of it. Dat how I see Burton Devries. Now I seen him lots of times when we was chilren. Ridin down the street wit ol man Devries on dem blooded horses. I sholl want to sit on one of dem horses. Dey ride past me splatterin dat mud all over me like I any other nigger! But he dint come back here den. He dont have no need den.

One day I sittin in de joint playing tonk, an dis proper nigger wit nice clothes come in an tell me somebody want to see me. I ast who it is, an he wont say. An I aint goin! Den he show me his money. It more money dan laying on dat table! I gone!

Burton Devries waitin in de car at de end of Hog Alley. I knowed de car. I seen it plenty time, it pass me in my ol wagon. I climb in de front of de car an he in de back. He tell de proper nigger to drive, an den he stay real quiet. He don say nuttin. Now I likes to ride like everbody else, but dat proper nigger was talkin money, an nobody say nuttin bout money.

We rides along, an I say, "Pull ober. I gots to get out!" Well, dat start him talkin. He say how dere been talk dat the niggers is try to vote like dey did after de War. Him talk bout how dat aint gonna happen, an how he wanna know who do de talkin an what dey say. Now, I got to tell him dat I aint heard nuttin like dat in Hog Alley, an he say he aint talkin bout down here in Bofort. Niggers down here in Bofort know what all dey got to do. It dem muckety-mucks up dere in Charleston he talkin bout. Dey done gone off to dem schools an been up North talking to dem niggers dont know how it be down here. So he want me to go up to Charleston, find out what I can, an let him know who sayin what an what dey gonna do. Dont be lookin at me like dat, girl. He was gonna pay good money!

Well, I dint say much of nuttin. I tole him I had to think on it. I just want to keep ridin in dat car! When dey come back to Hog Alley, I tell him I want to see you face. I dont work for nobody I dont see he face. An I turn round, an him pull dat curtain back, an I lookin on myself. I dont know who more surprise, him or me, cause we like twins, de dark one an de light one.

So I work for him. I go to de meetings up dere in Charleston. I tell dem I tryin to do the same down here in Bofort. An I tell him what go on an who doin what an when dey gonna do it. An some folks got hurt, some run out of town, an some go missin. What dey couldnt catch, dey chase way from here. Dat what happen when you play in de white man garden.

I made a lil bit of money, not a lot, but some money to get me through de hard times cause dem chilren not takin care of me. Not one come back to see how I is! Dont care how I is!

I have four wives, two die, one run off, an de other go home to her mother. Dat one, I glad to see go. See that scar right dere! She try to cut my throat! Mean woman! Fight you like a man! Now dat I look back, I dint need dat las wife. I had all dem daughters comin up! Could use dem like I want.

"Dere dem dogs go again! Dat must be dat ol girl wit my supper! Yall wait right here!"

Amelia put trembling hands up to her face after Ol Jack went out to calm the dogs. Elizabeth said, "Let's go. It's getting late and it's cold." Amelia looked at her trembling hands and said, "I'm not cold."

Ol Jack came in, followed by a thin young girl about thirteen. She carried a lunch pail, and he pointed to the lean-to kitchen in the back. "You take yourself back dere an heat dat food up! I know it wasnt cold when you left wit it!" She stole a quick glance at Amelia as she scurried behind the sack that hung over the doorway leading to the lean-to. He sank in the chair and looked at Amelia. "What else you want to hear?"

Amelia asked, "What ever happened to Mattie Baker?"

He gestured impatiently. "I tole you she run off. An dem chilren bout to drive me crazy wit all cryin an hollerin. I put a stop to dat! I must have whupped til I couldnt hardly stand, but dey didnt cry no more! One of dem boys stopped by a while back, sat right dere where you sittin, wit dat pitiful look on he face, an ast if I hear from he brothers an sisters. I dont hear nuttin witout no money!" He pulled a blanket close around him. "Hey, you over dere!" He commanded Elizabeth, "Put some wood on dat fire, it gettin cold in here!" Elizabeth stared at him without moving.

He turned to Amelia. "I want my money!" Amelia reached in her pocket and handed the bill to him. He snatched it and stuffed it in his shirt. There was a crash of pots from the kitchen. For a feeble old man, he got to his feet quickly, yelling, "Girl, you tearin up my house back there. I aint givin you one cent if you break anything back there!" He disappeared into the lean-to.

Elizabeth said firmly, "We got to go now!" Amelia nodded, standing up. She crossed to Elizabeth, her head bent. Elizabeth opened the door, and the light caught the eyes of the dogs that waited on the porch. She stepped back with the stick raised. "Get that ol man!" she said to Amelia.

Amelia walked quickly to the back and pulled the sack aside. She froze when she saw the young girl silently struggling with the old man as he grabbed at her clothes. The girl looked at her in mute appeal. Ol Jack saw Amelia and let the girl go.

She spoke to the girl. "You better come with us." The girl slipped around Ol Jack and hid behind Amelia. Amelia ordered him, "Get your dogs. We're leaving."

"She got to fix my supper!" he argued. Amelia turned and gently guided the girl in front of her. He followed them. "She dont get nuttin less she fix my supper!"

Amelia walked back to him and leaned over him, speaking deliberately. "Call your dogs!"

He disappeared into the kitchen and came back with several large, rancid bones. The dogs began to mewl and wag their tails. He tossed the bones into the side yard, and the dogs took off after them. Amelia, the young girl, and Elizabeth hurried across the yard.

Once they got down the street, Amelia caught the young girl by the shoulders. "You don't go back there! You tell your mother what he does to you, and you don't go back!"

The girl whimpered, "We need de money! My mama got a new baby!"

Amelia reached into her coat and pulled out several bills and stuffed them in the girl's hand. "You tell your mother! She'll figure out something else that you can do! Tell her to send your brother. You hear me?"

The girl stared at the money in her hand. "Yes, ma'am!"

Amelia let her go. "Go on home." The girl took off across the muddy street.

Amelia led the way out of Hog Alley. She did not say a word as they navigated the mud and the slippery boards. She did not even glance at the men who lingered outside the door of the joint they passed. When the men saw Elizabeth still carrying the stick, they fell silent. Amelia quickened her pace when they emerged from Hog Alley. Elizabeth had to skip to catch up with her.

When they reached the car, Amelia climbed in and stared straight ahead while Elizabeth cranked and got it started. As they drove from the railway station to the pier to catch Willis George, Amelia slumped in the front seat. During the short drive to the pier, Elizabeth could hear the sound of short gasps as Amelia tried to control her crying. The tears rolled down her face, and her shoulders heaved with the effort to stifle her sobs. Elizabeth drew a ragged breath and pulled the car over to the side of the road. When Elizabeth put her arms around Amelia, Amelia burst into tears and let the hurt and anger flow.

Amelia jumped as Elizabeth touched her arm. She looked bewildered when Elizabeth leaned past her to clear the table. Everyone had sensed the change in Amelia as they sat down to dinner that night, even Rebecca. While she did not usually join in the bantering around the table, she did seem to enjoy Ben's quick tongue and Lucy's blunt opinions about anything. Tonight she had sat quietly, responding only when someone would request that she pass a plate of food. Eli watched her, then shot an inquiring glance at Eula, who simply shook her head. Elizabeth had said very little, only that they went to Hog Alley looking for Haagar's family. Eula could see that it had left them both shaken. Rebecca had gotten up from the table and brought her doll back and solemnly handed it to Amelia. "Her wanna eat with you." Amelia had smiled slightly and patted Rebecca's arm.

Amelia got up to help clear the table, but was stopped by Lucy, who enlisted Ben's help. Usually this would draw a protest from Ben, but Lucy's meaningful look cut short his protest. Elizabeth settled the young ones in front of the fire so that she could read from the new books she had bought. Eula brought out a coverlet she had started, and

Eli read the latest edition of the *Charleston Free Press*. Amelia pulled a stool close to the fireplace and sat staring into the fire.

Her mind flooded with the visions of what it must have been like to live in that shack with the old man. She shuddered as she saw the filthy, cluttered room and the old man with the watery eyes and the grasping hands. She recalled how Haagar had always proclaimed that she had come North just to get away from the Island and the backwardnesss of the people, but now Amelia knew that Haagar had run from that hell house in Hog Alley. Amelia wondered how many others had made that trip back there in search of a lost sister or brother and come away sullied by their brush with Ol Jackson Devries. She sent up a thankful prayer that her mother had never met him.

Having finished the dishes, Lucy sat on the floor next to Amelia and dove into the seed catalogue that they had brought back for her. She poured over the pages showing the different corn seeds. Each year she set aside a small piece of land to try something new. It was her treat for all the hard work that she had done. When she turned to the next page, she saw that a letter had slipped into the catalogue. She glanced at it and handed it to Amelia.

Amelia stared at Haagar's handwriting, almost believing it had been summoned by her own thoughts. She turned it over in her hand and then slowly opened it. A return train ticket fell into her lap.

Dear Amelia,

We doing five funeral every week after we put away Essie. We very busy and need you to come home to help. I trust by now that you know what a bad mistake you make. Nothin there for you on that land. I send you ticket to come home. I know your mother hope you see her sister Iona. If you see her sister, do not speak to her. She brung misery to me. Do not speak to her. I forbid it. I spect to see you soon.

Your Granma,
Haagar Peazant

Amelia grew enraged as she read Haagar's words. She held the letter up, clasped in her shaking hand. "She forbids me to see my mother's sister!" she choked out. "She's sitting up there in New York, and she still wants to rule me!" She stood up and handed the letter to Eula, who quickly read it and handed it to Eli. Amelia paced back and forth. The others stared at Amelia, having never seen her display a temper. "She just has to hold her own! She's just like that old man!" She looked over at them. "She doesn't own me! I'm a free woman!" She grabbed her coat and rushed out the door. Elizabeth jumped up to go after her.

Eli held up his hand. "Lil Bet, leave her be. Like she say, she a free woman."

"We gonna turn up here an follow dis runnin creek back up under dem trees," Ben called out to Amelia from the back of the canoe. "You need to watch an make sure we dont run into that stand of cypress layin up under dere! When I say 'turn,' you paddle on the left as hard as you can!" Amelia nodded as they came to the turn. She tried to remember everything Ben had taught her about paddling the canoe. They had set out at late morning for their trip back into Black Water Swamp, and so far, it had gone fairly well. Ben had figured that they would get to the turn where the creek beyond the cypress stand ran around midday. She squinted up at the sun, which she could just barely see through the tops of the trees. From what she could tell, it was almost overhead. It should not be long now.

"Turn! Paddle to the left!" She jumped when Ben yelled as the canoe swung around, just barely missing one of the cypress knees that protruded from the water. She paddled frantically, at first skimming the top of the water and then digging in, pushing through, and finally stroking smoothly as she caught the flow of the current. They carefully made their way around the roots of a tree that had toppled into the water. She drew a deep breath as she peered into the thick brush that ran along the creek. She could easily imagine a thousand pairs of animal eyes watching them as they moved farther back into the denseness that sheltered the swamp. Amelia looked down at the rough pants, the heavy jacket, and the thick cotton shirt that she had borrowed from Ben. Eula had insisted that she wear heavy, protective clothing for her first trip back into the swamp. She was grateful, for the running bramble that seemed to spring from nowhere held thorns that would have torn her jacket as easily as paper.

It had seemed to be a great adventure to her when she asked Ben to take her back into the swamps where her Aunt Iona lived to deliver the letters from her mother. He had eagerly agreed and had described the swamp as a place of unusual beauty and mystery, insisting that they bring the camera. But the farther they moved into the closeness of the swamp, the more Amelia longed for the wide open spaces of the marshes they had left. The sounds of the swamp were far different from that of the marsh, the trill of a bird's cry drowned by the shriek of some animal that moved quickly through the low brush that lay on the black water. Even the vines seemed to have taken on a sinister look, draping down across the water as if they were trying to snare someone. She could not imagine how her Aunt Iona lived back here.

"Ho! Dere go de gator!" Ben pointed at a medium-sized alligator that lay on the far bank. It lay still as a log, its long snout half in the water.

Amelia's voice quavered with fear. "Do you think it might attack?"

Ben shook his head. "Dey pretty shy! Dey dont bodder nobody. Anyhow, it too cold for he to move around too much. Him just layin dere to get warm up from what lil sun dey is."

All the same, she kept her eye on the alligator until they were well past where he lay on the far bank. She heard the flap of wings overhead and watched as a crane soft-landed in a treetop nest. She could hear the cries of the babies as they fought for the food she held in her beak. Ben pointed ahead, and she could see where the sun broke through the trees magically lighting the narrow waterway ahead of them. They slid along smoothly. She glanced back at Ben, who sat tall in the stern of the canoe, strongly stroking, pushing them forward.

There was a wild call, birdlike but with resonance, and Ben stopped stroking. The wild call came again, and Ben threw his head back and answered it. She started to speak, but he held up his hand as she heard a third call. Ben burst out laughing and shouted, "Hey, boy, you been followin us for de las ten minutes! Why you gonna call out now?" As Amelia surveyed the shore, she could see no one in the tangled dark around them. Ben signaled for her to be still.

As they sat there, something whirled from the trees up ahead and whistled past Amelia to smack Ben squarely in the chest. Ben caught it before it fell to the bottom of the canoe. He held the tree pod up for Amelia to see. He tossed it onto the water. "Dat de best you can do?" he shouted. Just as he finished, a shower of wild walnuts rained down on them from a tree that shook directly over them. Amelia covered her head protectively and tried to look up into the tree. Just when she thought she could see a human form, the darkness seemed to swallow it. "You aint got no biscuits to throw, us gettin hungry down here!" There was a burst of wild laughter, and this time Amelia could make out the form of a young man sitting on one of the tree branches.

"Boy, you still crazy! Crazy as a loony bird!"

The young man accused Ben with a wide grin on his face. "What you doin back up in here?"

As Ben paddled the canoe under the tree where the young man sat, he said, "I bring you cousin back to see yall, an you ackin like an ol wild Indian up dere in de trees!"

The young man had the strong features that marked him as a Peazant and was burned to a rich mahogany. His long, straight hair was held back with a string. He stared at Amelia and then stood up on the branch. "You losin you touch, Ben. I been on you since you turn at de creek."

Ben shouted back at him, "I seed you, Chance. I figured I set you five minutes."

Chance stepped over to the next tree. "Boy, I close enough to touch you, an you not see me!"

Ben began stroking strongly, swiftly, "Oh, yeah! You cant touch me now, boy!" he shouted, "Come on, Amelia, let's go!"

She started at his instructions and began to stroke quickly. Chance jumped to the next tree and ran along the limb as they began to pull away from him. Amelia caught the rhythm of the stroke, and soon she and Ben were moving together easily like a piece of machinery.

Her arms stung with the strain as they pushed through the water, smoothly steering around floating logs and cypress patches while Chance moved among the trees, jumping from one to the other. Amelia looked back to see him grab a vine and swing over them into a group of trees in front of them. She shouted to Ben, "Come on! We can beat him!" as Chance disappeared in the top of the trees.

Ben let out a wild yell and picked up speed. "We coming to de las curve. It on de right! When I say 'Go!' let it go, gal!" Ben cautioned.

Amelia did just as Ben ordered as the canoe slid around the corner and they stroked strongly for home. The trees had separated as the water widened. At the far end, she could see a cove, and at the edge sat several houses on stilts. Amelia almost forgot to paddle as she stared in fascination at the houses. "Come on, gal! He gonna beat us!" Ben pointed to Chance, who scrambled easily from tree to tree along the creek. They made their final push. She could hear the dogs barking and the children shouting as they closed in on the houses. She saw Chance swing from a tree and then drop lightly on the landing of one of the houses as they slid to the base of the stilts.

Two small children ran up to Chance, jumping and grabbing his arms. He stepped around them and strode to the edge of the verandah. He leaned over and taunted Ben, "Boy, how you gonna come back here try to beat me? You dont know dese backwoods like I do!" Ben shook his head and steered the boat to the rope ladder that hung over the edge.

Amelia stared at the rope uncertainly as Chance looked down on her. "Take hold of de ladder and stand up real easy now! I hold it steady for you!" She grabbed the ladder and pulled herself up. She cautiously stepped on the bottom rung, the ladder swung out away from the landing, and she gripped it tightly with her eyes closed. "Come on, now!" Chance encouraged. She shook her head. "De lil ones dont have no problem gettin up here! Take my hand." She opened one eye cautiously and peered up at his extended hand. "Come on, gal! Dem gators see you hanging out dere, dey tink you dinner!" With that, she grabbed his hand and scurried up the ladder. He pulled her onto the verandah. She got to her feet slowly and looked up at him, catching a hidden smile.

She put him at eighteen or nineteen, a couple of years older than Ben. He had height; not a short woman herself, she had to tilt her head to meet his eyes. He was broad-chested and had sturdy legs. She was dressed in Ben's old clothes. She nodded acknowledgment to him. "I'm your cousin Amelia. Your mama and my mama are sisters." He shook his head and stepped around her to help Ben tie the canoe to the landing. She turned to the two small children that stared up at her. To the boy who was a smaller version of Chance she said, "You must be Shadda!" She looked at the little girl who was light brown and had thick, coarse hair like her mother, Myown. "Are you Neeny?" The little girl smiled shyly, showing two missing front teeth.

Ben climbed onto the landing and threw himself at Chance. The children ran around them, shouting as they rolled on the floor. A dog ran up and barked, then grabbed at the heel of Ben's shoe as he and Chance rolled over and over, each trying to pin the other to the floor. The dog yelped, running off when Ben kicked himself free and sprang to his feet. Chance jumped up and took a stance as he and Ben began to move in the slow, ritualized movement of the com pe.

Amelia had first seen the ritual fighting when she had wandered up on Eli and Ben playing at "knocking and kicking" in the dusk light after dinner. They practiced in the clearing behind the forge, and she had stood fascinated as they threw signs and signals and then kicked at each other in wide arches, dropping to their knees and feigning arm jabs and punches. Their sharp cries had filled the air as they circled one another and locked arms and legs.

It had been obvious that Eli was the master. He expended half as much energy as Ben, and his moves had a stateliness and precision that were dancelike. But Ben had quickness, and although Eli remained expressionless through the ritual, Amelia could sense the challenge he felt from his son. Ben had backed his father across the clearing and then swept his leg to knock him off his feet. Eli jumped, catching Ben by the shoulders, and neatly flipped him over. By the time Ben hit the ground, Eli had his foot on his chest and was tapping him on the shoulder with his hand, signaling him to surrender. As Eli held him firmly to the ground, Ben signaled his father, and when he got to his feet saluted him with a series of hand signals.

Eli returned the salute and then grinned at his son. "You plenty quick, boy! You learn to see wit de mind fore de eye!"

Ben nodded in agreement as he wiped the sweat from his eyes. "Once you feel de rhythm, you mind tell you how to see!"

Amelia had come upon them unexpectedly and then backed away, embarrassed by the intrusion. But Eli had called to her, "Aint nuttin wrong wit you come back here. It a free land." Then he added with a glimmering of Ben's humor, "You a free woman." He crossed to sit on one of the stumps that sat at the edge of the clearing. As Ben practiced his moves, Amelia made her way over to Eli. She noticed that where the sweat poured off Ben in streams, it lay like a fine mist over Eli. Once he stopped Ben and demonstrated a motion, quietly explaining the meaning of the set of the hands. They then did the motion together in slow, precise movements until perfected to Eli's satisfaction.

Amelia was still hesitant about asking questions of Eli, but she had to ask, "What is that?"

"We call this knockin 'n kickin," Eli answered, signaling with his hands. "It make de mind an de body work together to bring peace an strength of spirit. It come wit de Africans. It one of de ways de captives use to get through de trials." Rocking back on his heels, balancing easily, he explained, "De white folk tink it dancin, some foolishness de captives doing. Dey dont know, it keep we strong, it tie we together as brothers from all of Africa!" Eli swept the sand with his foot, drawing an arc with his toe. "I learn it from my daddy an he brothers, who learn from deir daddy an de other Africans who be around. When I a boy, ol Paymore take we off to learn us de secrets of knockin 'n kickin an show us de trace of Kojo."

He smiled as Amelia waited several seconds before she ventured the question. ". . . The trace of Kojo?"

He teased her. "De path he follow. Nobody tell you bout Kojo? What kind of story collector you be an nobody tell you bout Kojo?"

The Legend of Kojo's Trace

as told by Eli Peazant

Dey call he de captive wit many names. Him have many names from de time when him first stole from he village. Everybody own he give he a new name. Nobody care what he name is an nobody ast. Dey tink he nuttin, he nobody till he belong to dem. An him no tell he name cause he no want he name fouled by dey mouths.

Him de first one of we Africans to walk dis land. De Spain soldiers brung him here on de first ships to come cross de water looking for de treasure. You know all dem people, de Spain, de England, de France, come to look for de gold all de time, an at de same time dey snatching de ancient people to take off to work de land someplace from here. Him come wit dem. Dey call he "Esteban" an dey work he like de dog.

Now dis not de first place he been. Dey come from dem islands way down south. Yellow Mary been down dere. Her could tell some stories bout dem islands down dere. Some story say him come here after de captives try to kill all de Spain soldiers on de island. When dem Africans rise up, dey strike real quick; dey dont want to leave nobody to come after dem, and den dey head for de woods. Folks always scare of de African rising. Folks same today. Scare of de African rising. De Spain soldiers, dey a hard bunch. Dey take all de men an put dem on de boats an send dem all over, wherever dey have villages. Dey say him heart break when him leave wife an baby back dere. Him on de boat dat come here.

De ancient people, dey mostly a good people, a humble people. Dey live deir lives, dey grow de crops, hunt in de woods, share everyting among demselves. De man you aunt marry, St. Julien Last Child, he one of de las of dem ancient people. Dey help you wit anyting. It a part of dem. De Spain soldiers come here, an dey sick cause dey been on boat long time. De ancient people help dem, give dem food an let dem sleep in dey houses, show dem how to track de deer, take care of dem when dey sick. But it not enough for de Spain soldiers. They want to find de treasure, de gold. To dis day, we got white folk comin back up in here lookin for dat treasure of de ancient people.

Now, Esteban, him take to dese ancient people. Maybe dey remind him of how him live back in Africa in de village, folks carin bout each other, takin care of each other, everybody a we. An dey take to he. Dey show he deir ways an him show dem de ways of Africa. But he frighten for dem cause he know de way of de Spain soldiers. Him see dem steal people, kill for de gold, an bring de sickness on dem. He see dem ruin de women, use dem like dey have no worth. To dis day, dem buckras come on our women in de night to ruin dem, to steal dey souls! You take dat from a woman witout her say so, you stealin her soul!

De Spain soldiers ask for de gold an de ancient people say dey dont have none. But de Spain soldiers dey dont believe dem, dey done seen bits an pieces of dat gold. Dey figure lots more where dat come from. An dey steal de elders. Dey not gonna let dem go til dey show dem where dey hide dat gold. De ancient people, dey cry an pray to deir gods to help dem. De elders is de well-being an de wealth of de village. Gold dont mean dat much to dem. De Spain soldiers dont understand dat. Got to be de gold! But only de elders know where de gold is, an dey never gonna say. De Spain soldiers dey start killin de elders, one by one, til a woman tell dem her take dem to de gold on de next full moon. Can only go on de full moon cause dat de only time dey can see de shells that lay out de trace to de gold.

When de full moon come, dey gettin ready to go look for de gold, an de woman come to Esteban an de other captives an give dem a salve. Her tell dem to put de salve all over dem to keep de night bugs from biting. Her say put all over! Dey start out as soon as dark fall, an dey walk long into de night. Her take dem way back up in de woods. Well, her bring dem to a hill. Now, you been roun here. How many hills you see? Dere only one, two hill back here. De hill made by the ancient people to bury deir dead.

Her point to de hill an tell dem dat de gold is in dere. De Spain soldiers cut loose an run for de hill. Dey gonna get all de treasure. Her stop Esteban an de captives an tell dem not to follow de Spain soldiers. All of de sudden, dey hear de worse cries an screams, an de other captives dey light out. Dem ol spirits come at dem like a swarm of bees, cuttin dem down like corn. Didnt even know where dey was goin. Now, some of dem Spain soldiers, when dey hear dat noise dey turn back, an dey mad cause dey figure her send de others to dey death. Dey see she an Esteban standin on the trace, an dey gonna kill she for sure.

Esteban, him see dem kill too many, an him gonna stop dem. Him don have no knife, no gun, all him got is com pe dat him brung from Africa. Him push she back an run to stop de Spain soldiers. De first man slash at he wit de sword, an him feel nuttin. It like de sword pass right through he, an him feel nuttin. Him not cut, no blood, no hurt, nuttin. Him look back at de woman, her fade into de plants. Him become one wit de darkness. De salve protect he. All de Spain soldier can see is he figure, but dey nuttin dere. De soldier slash at he an cut vine behind him. You can imagine de Spain soldier think he lost he mind. Him drop de sword an run back to tell de others. An Esteban, he follow, cause he got plenty work to do dis night.

Dey can see him coming up de trace to de hill, an dey start shootin at him. De bullets pass through he, an him keep coming. Dey try to cut he down between dem, an him use de com pe to move among dem. Dey slash each other tryin to slash at he. See dat move Ben make! Dat what you use when two come up on you. Him move among dem like de wind! Him grab dem, an each one him kill, him whisper in dey ear fore dey die, "My name Kojo!" Dey screamin an cryin, an him cuttin dem down like de sugar cane. Him let one get away. So him can tell de others back at de village.

Him look back at de hill. It goin back to de swamp, taking everytin wit it, what treasure dere was, the dead Spain soldiers, the hill sink into de swamp, takin it all wit it.

Well, the Spain soldier come back in de village screaming dat Kojo coming. De others dey wake up an find all de ancient people gone. Just up an disappear like dey never was. De elders who dey keep in de same room wit dem gone! De village quiet, not even a dog runnin roun. Dey jump up an run for de boat! Dey get out dere in dat water an dey look back. Dey him is, Kojo standin on de beach, him covered wit de blood of de soldiers! Him call out to dem, "My name is . . . Kojo!" Dose words haunt dem de rest of deir lives. Dey wake in de night an hear dat cry no matter where dey be!

Him stay here. Maybe him live on today. Plenty stories from de first days of slavery bout a man who move through de woods wit de animal, who help de ancient people an de captives in dey time of need. My grandaddy tol me dat dere was an overseer who was known by all to be vicious man! Him tink nuttin of killin a captive! Say one day him use a woman so bad, her lay right down an die. Not three days pass, an him go missing. Dey find him hangin from de top of de tree in de backwoods. Dont nobody know how him got back dere. It a tall tree! No way him could get up dat tree to hang heself! Dey say it was Kojo!

An him still look after we. When dem white men set out here lookin to lynch Ira Fielder cause he say all de lynchin dey was doing over dere on de mainland was wrong, it was Kojo who save he. It was Kojo who set de landin on fire so dey got to go roun to de rough side. Kojo took Ira out de back way an den take he up de coast to de train up North. Kojo set dem dogs on dem what wouldnt let dem come up in de yards. White folks think twice bout killin dogs fore dey kill colored folk!

Kojo sent word to St. Julien Last Child to come lead de women and chilren to de safe houses back in de swamps. And it was Kojo dat still de tongue an heal de pain from the beatin dey give dose who would not say where Ira was. An I swear, Kojo held my hand steady on dat shotgun when dem white men kick open de door to my own home! Kojo a part of we, an we a part of he! As long as us here an pullin breath, he live on.

Now, dat move dere! I didnt know dat move til Pidgen come. Pidgen tell me de Africans in he country, dey fight de same way. You know Pidgen. Dont tell me yall aint been back dere to Carrie Mae's! I know Lil Bet, an after all, you is a free woman. Pidgen show me dis, an he tell me he been all over de world lookin for other Africans, an he say everywhere he find dem dere is some kind of fighting like dis. It just go to show dat dem ol African ways, dey stay wit you!

Between Ben's quickness and Chance's size, they were evenly matched. Just when it seemed that Chance would pin Ben into surrender, Ben would, with a twist of the shoulders and a shift in balance, throw Chance off. They were thoroughly enjoying this contest, good-humoredly taunting each other and showing off their skills. Shadda hovered around them, imitating the kicks and punches with childish ferocity. He kicked and just missed the dog, who had skulked back to watch the contest.

Amelia turned away from them and looked at her surroundings. There were four houses in the clearing that, while roughly constructed, appeared to be sturdy and safe. A walkway constructed of planks of wood ran among the houses, and as her eye traced it, Amelia saw that it ran from the houses back through the woods as far as she could see. She felt a tug on her pant leg and looked down at Neeny, who pointed. "Dere my mama."

Iona stepped from the doorway. They gazed at each other, neither moving forward. Amelia's heart pounded when she looked at the woman her grandmother had banned her from contacting, this woman whose presence had haunted her family for as long as she could remember. For every time that Amelia had sought to go her own way, she would hear Haagar's scornful declaration, "You ain't gonna do like Iona! You will not disobey me!" She felt the rise of the old resentment and the pain that Iona's abandonment had visited on her mother. Her mother had needed her sister, and Amelia could not help but feel that if Iona had been there, her mother would have been spared some of the misery that came with the move from the Island.

As she struggled to find the right words, she saw the wariness in Iona's eyes. When her aunt brushed her forehead with the same nervous gesture that her mother used, Amelia's eyes flooded with tears. She reached into her bag and brought out the packet of letters and gave them to Neeny. "Take these to your mama." Neeny ran across the landing to her mother, eager to deliver the gift. Iona took the packet and slowly went through the letters. She looked at Amelia for an explanation.

"My mama sent these to you. She's been writing to you every day because she knew that I'd make sure you got them."

Iona nodded. They both turned as shouts of laughter and boyish giggles brought the contest between Ben and Chance to a halt. Shadda, eager to join in with the older boys, had jumped in between Ben and Chance and was challenging both of them. Ben had grabbed Shadda and lifted him over his head. He easily tossed him to Chance, who caught him and tickled him. Shadda kicked and screamed in delight as the boys held him down. Iona called to them, "Yall dont be so rough with him. He just a baby!"

Shadda shouted in happy defiance, "No, I not."

Chance answered him, "If you not a baby, how come you do dis when I do dis?" Neeny ran over to get her share of attention and was pulled into the mass of bodies by Ben.

Iona turned back to Amelia, who wiped her eyes. Amelia saw everything in Iona's face that she would have wished for her mother, a warmth tempered with love, strength and humor. Iona walked over to her and wiped her face with the edge of her apron. Amelia stood quietly, her eyes lowered to hide the pain that shone there. Iona lifted her chin with gentle fingers and looked into her eyes. "It is good to have you here, child of my sister."

She put her arms around Amelia in a close hug. At first, Amelia stood rigidly, but as Iona pulled back to look at her, Amelia grabbed and held on for dear life.

It had all been so awkward, those first attempts to talk. No matter what question she or Iona asked the other, it seemed that it could always be answered with the fewest of words. Finally Iona crossed to an old chest and, after pulling out assorted quilts, returned with a packet tied with a ribbon. She handed the bundle to Amelia and sat down beside her.

Amelia carefully opened the packet and found a pile of photographs. She had seen copies of some of the photographs either on Nana's wall or at Eula's house. They were from that last picnic on the beach the day before everyone went their separate ways. She pointed to the group of women sitting among the dunes eating. "That's Nana. Look at Aunt Eula. She hasn't changed a bit."

Iona nodded and identified a few. "Dats Clarabelle. Her had nineteen chilren tween two husbands, an every one of dem chilren crazy bout dey mama! Cousin Viola, her preachin now. Her marry de man who took dese pictures, Mr. Snead, dey go all over de place deliverin de Word of de Lord."

Iona stopped speaking when Amelia came to the next image. Amelia remembered that this photo of her family had sat on the mantle for years, but had long since been put away. Myown and Iona were dressed in white cotton dresses. Iona leaned protectively toward her younger sister and Amelia could sense in their secretive smiles the separate world that they had built for themselves. Haagar sat, her eyes fixed firmly on the camera and her arms wrapped tightly around Ninny Jugs, preventing her son from moving. Despite her efforts, he leaned away, straining to get down.

"I haven't seen this since Ninny Jugs was killed," Amelia whispered.

Iona's eyes clouded as she thought of her younger brother. "Him was everything to my mama. Real bold. Us was more like my daddy. I figure her just about lost her mind when Jugs died."

Amelia recounted, "I just remember that he could get her to laugh with him. He'd come in the next morning from being out all night, and Granma would be sitting there waiting for him. Mad! The next thing you know, he'd start telling her about who did what to who and who was wearing what and what this one said about all of that. And she would be in that kitchen fixing him the biggest breakfast and laughing outright!"

Iona understood. "Him was pure charm, even when him was a baby. Him come down here when things was too hot up dere in New York, an folks just loved to see he coming, had dem New York clothes, dem New York ways. Him leave, all de lil boys be struttin, actin like dey Ninny Jugs! De las time I saw he, he say he come back in de spring. Next thing I hear he dead."

Amelia shivered, shaken by an old memory. She turned to Iona and then spoke slowly. "The night he was killed, Granma knew the moment he was stabbed. I remember. I woke up because she screamed. She screamed, and then she ran out of the house in her night clothes. She ran all the way to where he lay dying on the street. They told my mother that the people were still standing around him, and she pushed her way through to him. It had happened so quickly, and the next thing they knew my grandmother was there. She kept screaming at the man who had stabbed Ninny Jugs that she had given Ninny Jugs the money to pay him. There was no need to kill him. And then I don't remember her for a while after that."

Iona nodded. "Dey had to put Mama away for a while. It was like her saved all of she love for he. I aint sayin her didnt care bout we, but it was love her had for he. Emmett." Iona smiled. "We called him Ninny Jugs because he was still trying to get milk at Mama's breast when he was a walkin, talkin, fully grown boy." She looked out at her two youngest ones, who were playing together on the verandah. "I always told myself that whatever love I had I was gonna spread cross all my chilren." She smiled at Amelia and added, "An my kin's chilren."

"She didn't want me to know you," Amelia said. "Matter-of-fact, I just got a letter from her, she forbade me to try to see you. But I had to." She took a deep breath. "I went to Hog Alley."

Iona understood immediately and took her hand. "You see ol Jackson Devries?" Amelia nodded.

"He a miserable ting, aint he?" Iona declared flatly. "After my third was born, I wanted my chilren to know more bout de family from de mainland, so I goes over to see he." She shuddered. "You got to give my mama dis, her got out of dere fas as her could, an her aint never look back. An her didnt let he come nowhere near we!" She put her arm around Amelia, assuring her, "Dat blood runnin through us, too, but you is more Peazant dan you ever be Devries!"

Amelia continued to hold Iona's hand as she went through the rest of the photographs. She stopped at a photo of Iona's family taken some years later. Iona laughed. "Dere dey all are. Oh, dat photography man earn he money dat day. No sooner do him get dem to sit down, an somebody tired, somebody hungry, somebody got to go to de outhouse. You see Chance an dere Shadda an Neeny. Now dis here is Daniel, my second boy. Dis here my oldest girl, Clemmie, an de next one, Margaret Anne. Dey gone to gather sweetgrass and palmetto for my baskets. Dey be back in a lil while." Iona swelled with pride as she looked at the photograph. Amelia was struck by the family traits. The boys were long and broad, dark with the sharp Peazant features and long, straight black hair; the girls were light-skinned with softly rounded features and the clouds of thick, coarse Peazant hair. Iona reached over and caressed the image of her husband, who stood at her shoulder in the photograph. "Dat dere, dats my Julien." Her words carried so much love that Amelia held her breath as she met the intense gaze of the man who had caused so much distress to her family.

Dat Julien, He Hold My Heart So Close

as told by Iona Peazant—Last Child

It only natural. Dat me an Julien be together. It de way de ancien people an de captive live with each other from de very first. De old stories tell bout how de buckra come cross de water wit captives, gonna make de ancien people captives. How de anciens an de captives share what lil dey got, learn each odder ways, take de good from both. How de buckra rain down so much misery an sickness dat de captive took to run an de ancien show dem de way. Dey look for de safe place an fight til dey dead to keep de buckra from stealin dem back. De ancien an de captive build dey life together, clear de land, plant de crop, raise de chilren to be strong. An when de buckra send de army to chase de ancien from dey land, de ancien an de captive run to Florida, some scape to Mexico, an some wind up out dere in Oklahoma. But Julien family never quit de lan. De old spirits show dem de sacred place where de army caint go. An dey was tired, sickness, bad water, no food, an de babies dyin like leaves fallin from de tree. But dat where dey stay till de army go off to fight each odder in de Big War. De ancien an de captive, dey been here all along.

Mama knowed bout Julien an me. Her ack like her dont, but her fraid, an her right to be fraid. I dont know what possess me. I always did everyting my mama say. But dat day us spose to leave for New York, I climb into dat boat an see dat man lookin for me, searchin me out, waitin for me. An I jump outa dat boat an start runnin. Eula say her thought I forget sumptin until her see he sittin dere on dat horse waitin for me. Her say I sprouted wings an flew up on dat horse's back. All I remember is holdin on for my life.

An you know it was hard for me. De first few months all I did was cry. Evertime I think about my family, my mama, my sister, an my baby brother, I cry rivers, I miss dem so much. An Julien, I think bout Julien in dose days an how him comfort me but him never say nuttin. In all de years I been wit dis man, I aint never heard a harsh word from he, not me or none of de chilren. But him got a temper now. Ask Eli bout he temper. Dey both got tempers. Eli got dat hot rage, an Julien him got dat quiet rage. Dont know which one worse. But dey dont turn it on dose dey love. An from de very beginnin when us was lil chilren playin together, I know him love me.

I stay back in dese woods wit him. Afraid an shamed to come out. I fraid dey try to send me up to New York. I know my mama. If her could have, her would have moved heaven an earth to get me up dere. An I don know how to face Nana. I figure I shame de whole family. I always de obedient one, do whatever I told. Your mama, her de playful one. Oh, her was de debil! Always doin someting! Getting into all kinds of scrapes an messes! I took more beatings for she! An I miss Eula cause I know she dont have nothin but love in she heart for everbody.

You see dis. It don look like much, just a lil bit of wood been worn down by de wind and water. Him leave dis for me. Julien. From de first time I wit him, him leave sumptin for me, a shell, a bird feather, sometime a letter. Though my Julien got a pretty hand an a way wit words, him dont say dat much. An him always leave it somewhere dat I will find it. Jus a sign from he to me.

One day Julien leave. Him have to go get supplies. Him ask me if I want to go wit he. I say, "No, I stay back here." Fraid to stay here, fraid to leave. An him gone. Gone all de day. It start gettin long roun dark, an I wonder if he comin back. I can hear de gators roar an all kinds of noise back here. Den I hear he comin up, an him not by heself. He brung Nana back wit he! An I like to died, caught between fear an de need to see my Nana.

He get out dat boat, an her callin an fussin, "Iona Peazant, you better show you face to you Nana! Come right out here! Hidin back up in dese woods like you a old runaway!" An I come out all shame, an her say, "What wrong wit you, gal! Why you hide back up in here witout comin to see you folks?" I start to cry. Lord have mercy, Julien must have thought I was nuttin but salt water!

Nana say, "What you cryin bout? You got a good man! Him come to my house dis day an say him gonna marry you an him want my blessin! Him gonna marry you our way an he people way! Him say you missin you family, an it only right dat we stand wit you. I struck! I know dat boy fore him born an never hear him say dat much! An where my great grandchild, hidin back here fraid to come see her family. Dont you know Eula want you to see her new baby, Lil Bet? De spittin image of her daddy!"

An Nana stay. Her stay two, three days, an us talk! Her tell me my mama sent letters tellin she to come back here an get me an send me up to New York. Her so mad, her gonna pay a man to come steal me back! An how Eli send word back dat anybody come down here stealin somebody gonna get hurt! Her ast me if I love Julien. An I have to tell she dat I dont love him like de gal I was when I run off wit he but de woman I is now dat I been wit he.

Den Nana tell me why her come. Her come to take me back so I can get ready for my wedding! Her say dey all waitin for me to come back, Eula, Yellow Mary, Clarabelle, Daisy, so dey can make me ready to marry.

You know de time dat frighten me de most was dem two days fore I got married. I fraid Julien not gonna come for me! Aint dat silly! Him come for me at Nana's house, an we all walk to de church together. De only one not dere dat I wanted was your mama, who was way up dere in New York! Yellow Mary loan me a fancy dress, but not fore her tell me dat her was sick wit jealousy.

After de church wedding, us come back here, an Julien people waitin for we. Julien people come for de wedding. It last five days! I never seen so much food in my life. De men leave in de morning for de hunt, an de women cook all day. Dey dance into de morning from de night before! We got de blessins of everyone.

Den I was fraid cause it took so long for me to get my first baby. I thought my mama had put some roots down on me, but Julien would not hear dat. Him say it was a time for we to learn each other, an dat what us do. I help he build de extra houses for de others when dey come. Him show me how he mama make de basket. I show he how to raise the sugar tomatoes an de good sweet corn! When de chilren come, dey come so fast dat I glad we have dat time to learn each other.

It not been easy. De Lord tested us in many a way. De Big Storm wash out everyting us had, like it did de same to everybody. When dat rheumatic fever swept through here, it left Margaret Anne weak and sickly, us thought us was going to lose she. But her a happy chile. Everyting all right. I got nuttin to go on about. Long as I got my Julien, I cant want for much more.

He came upon them just as they were about to sit down for supper. His children knew the moment he arrived and turned to the doorway, waiting for him to appear. The half-light threw shadows across Julien Last Child's face as he surveyed his family. It was what Eli called "counting heads," seeing if everyone who was supposed to be there was there. When he stepped into the full light in the room, his eyes sought his wife, who turned from her cooking at the stove and greeted him with a smile. Shadda and Neeny ran across the room and threw themselves at their father, who caught them and swung them both over his shoulders.

As he advanced across the room, Amelia saw the same sturdy, deep-chested build that had been passed on to his sons. Ben jumped to his feet, drawing himself up to his full height, and made a hand signal in salute to him. Julien Last Child solemnly returned the salute and did not flinch when Neeny started to slide from his shoulder and grabbed his hair to steady herself. He let both children down gently and then turned to Amelia. They studied each other. He was not a handsome man, but an interesting one, with rounded features and deep-set, black eyes. Although his hair was streaked with gray, it did not age him.

Amelia could see nothing in his gaze, neither approval nor disapproval; he was simply waiting.

Her grandmother had had little to say about this man. Myown had simply described him as someone they grew up with who, unlike the rest of the boys, had not teased them by stealing their dolls or running through their games. Except for Iona, he had paid little attention to them, spending most of his time hunting, fishing, doing chores, and playing with the other boys. Although they had treated their love as a great secret, no one had been surprised when he had written to Iona the day they were to leave the Island and asked her to remain. Though shocked by Iona's boldness, Myown had never imagined her sister with anyone other than Julien. Haagar would torment Myown for years, angrily demanding to know why she had never said anything to her mother.

Iona moved from the stove to her husband and touched his arm. "Dis Amelia, Myown's daughter. Her come to see us after all dis time." He slowly saluted Amelia with a hand signal. Amelia was bewildered, not knowing what to do. She awkwardly stuck out her hand, only to pull it back quickly when Shadda spoke up.

"Dat aint what you do!" He stepped forward, pulling Neeny behind him. "De man do dis!" He demonstrated. "An den de woman do dis!" He waited as Neeny looked up at Amelia. "Neeny!" he commanded. She returned his salute so quickly that Amelia did not see it. Pleased with themselves, they moved off to take their places at the table. Iona's oldest girl, Clemmie, took them aside, scolding them as she washed their faces and hands.

Amelia stuttered, "It's . . . It's good to finally meet you. Your wife, my aunt . . ." She stopped, embarrassed by her nervousness.

He glanced at his wife. "We are one in this house." Amelia nodded, turning to watch him as he moved past her to where Margaret Anne sat by the fire. He stroked his daughter's hair and kneeled beside her as she split the palmetto fronds for baskets. She gave her father a reassuring smile when she looked up from her work.

Heartstruck, Amelia turned to Iona. "Can I help?"

Iona crossed to the stove. "You just sit. Right now you de guest, but it wont take long for dat to wear off in dis house."

Amelia sat and watched Julien help Margaret Anne split the palm fronds and listened to Ben try to explain to Chance the idea of a moving picture camera. Amidst many questions from Chance, Ben had set the camera on the tripod. There was much argument and skepticism from Chance as Ben described the way it worked. Even when Amelia was called on to second Ben's description, Chance refused to believe it.

Amelia turned from Iona and studied the circular house that was so different from the Peazant homes. Consisting of one large room, its only concession to modern times was the large cast-iron stove that marked the kitchen area. Amelia wondered how they had transported the stove so far back into the swamp. It appeared to Amelia that the areas of the room took on whatever function was needed at the moment simply by moving the furniture. The table was the only piece that had a definite place. The fire was contained in a barrel-shaped form that looked like it was made from clay and stood on short legs. There were handles with holes for easy moving, and slits had been cut into its sides so that the heat would circulate. The top was open for the smoke to escape.

The walls of the house were made of closely fitted slats of wood that ran from the wooden floor to the thick thatched roof. Baskets of every shape and size sat against the walls, and a pile of sweetgrass lay in a corner. The kitchen had low shelves that held an assortment of wooden and pottery bowls and plates, and iron pots and pans. Wooden pantry bins for flour, sugar, cornmeal, and salt sat next to the stove. In a far corner, neatly folded and rolled up, were sleeping pallets and quilts. Clothes hung from pegs that dotted the wall, and a couple of large trunks were off to the side.

Amelia felt Clemmie's gaze from the edge of the room and looked over at her. Her other cousins had been friendly enough, the youngest ones not knowing about the family conflict, the boys not caring, and Margaret Anne simply pleased to have a visitor. However, Amelia saw all of herself when she caught the glimmer of resentment in Clemmie's eyes and recognized her wariness every time Iona and Amelia spoke to each other. Clemmie was Iona's protector, and if Amelia, herself, was any judge, a most fierce defender. Of all Iona's children, Clemmie most likely knew her mother's secrets, being Iona's first daughter and the only female company back here in the woods. Amelia felt Clemmie's appraisal of every move she made, and even now as they gazed at each other, Clemmie neither smiled nor shifted her glance. She had the look of her father, waiting for the other person to reveal themselves. Although she was preoccupied with her younger brother and sister, she was aware of all that went on in that room, her attention gliding from one situation to the next. When Iona removed the meat from the oven, Clemmie immediately crossed to help her mother put the food on the table. She took the meat from her mother and whispered, perhaps a word of encouragement, for Iona tilted her head and smiled at her daughter before she turned to spoon up the other food.

Amelia envied the comfortable way they moved around the kitchen, so used to each other that one anticipated the other's moves. No sooner would Iona look for a utensil or a bowl than Clemmie would hand it to her. Amelia would have offered to help again, but she did not want to disturb the quiet pleasure of that moment. Aside from washing the dishes, Amelia had never spent much time in her family's kitchen. She could not remember her mother cooking, Myown having been banished from the kitchen by Haagar years before. She felt a small jolt of pain each time she thought of what her mother had missed when she had left the Island. Perhaps there would have been more children, the sisters and brothers that Amelia had not known to miss. Now she was growing used to the noises and movements of others and found comfort in the knowledge that she had a place among them.

"Yall come on, now. Dinner ready," Clemmie called to the others. They all stood around the table and linked hands. Neeny and Shadda sang together:

> *Koiya Te He Och Cha De Ma Tekwani*
> *Mata U Soi Ke Ha Be Lito Fey Aka Manani*
> *To San De Do Kata He Ho Upa Paro*

Amelia did not need to understand the words to know their meaning. She suppressed a smile as the two made faces at each other when they had completed their blessing.

Margaret Anne then spoke with a quavery voice. "Lord, thank you for dis food dat we bout to receive for de nourishment of our bodies." They ended the blessing with "Amen" and sat down at the table. Clemmie took care of Neeny and Shadda as the bowls were passed.

"Huckleberries an banga root!" Ben exclaimed as he spooned a healthy portion into his bowl. "De only time I get dis is when I come here!" He handed the bowl to Amelia, who looked at the bright red stew and took a small portion.

Iona nodded. "It a dish Julien sister taught me. De foxberries only good for eatin dis time of year. Any other time, dey can make you sick. Dey kinda bitter, but de sweetness of de banga root cut de harsh taste." Amelia tasted a bit. It would take some getting used to. As she reached for another dish, Iona explained, "Dat dere hominy. Sometime I grind it up for grits, other time I cook it like dis, boil it in de stock."

They ate quietly. Ben and Chance seemed to be racing to see who could put the most food away. Amelia asked for a second helping of a boiled vegetable dish. She recognized only the wild onion, but the taste was wonderful. "Mmm, this is so tasty!" She was surprised when her aunt blushed with pleasure.

Ben interjected, "Dat was one of de reasons I was glad to come! Not dat I dont like my mama's cookin and dat I didnt want to see my kin, but dis ancient people food real tasty!"

Iona demurred. "Julien sister teach me to cook de way dey do. I didnt know dat much, an den I start puttin a lil bit of what Nana teach me wit it. Dat all." She glanced over at her husband, who gazed at her.

He spoke to Amelia. "From the very beginning, our people have shared their ways. It is what we know."

Margaret Anne teased her mother. "Aunt Cecily say her not gonna teach you no more cause at de las gathering, everybody eat all you pan bread. Dey only touch hers when yours gone."

Iona laughed. "I tell you what. I wont make no pan bread for de next one!" The children moaned in protest. "Aint no cause for nobody feelings to get hurt!"

Shadda corrected her indignantly, "Her feelin wasnt hurt! She have more of you pan bread dan we!" Even Julien laughed at this declaration by his youngest son.

The meal over, the dishes finished and put away, they moved into the large area, where the boys talked and Julien repaired a saddle.

"You have horses back here?" Amelia asked. Julien looked up from cutting strips of leather. "We keep de horses on other side of Island. Let them run loose during de cold weather an den get them for de spring."

Iona made room for Neeny, who ran to sit in her mother's lap. "We have another house on de south side near de water. Dat where I keep my garden. We come back here for de winter gathering. It start in a coupla days when Julien folk get here."

Margaret Anne spoke up dreamily. "Dey come from all over for de gathering. Woods filled with folks singing an dancin. You should see it." Amelia's interest showed on her face.

"I would love it if you could stay for more than just one night," Iona said.

Amelia turned to Ben, who said, "I got to get back, but my daddy say tell you stay long as you like, cause Cousin Julien or Chance can bring you back."

Amelia looked to Iona and Margaret Anne, who nodded her head, encouraging her. "Yes, if you don't mind, I'd love to stay."

Iona spoke softly to Neeny, "I want to get de hair done tonight cause de next coupla days I wont have de time to do it." Neeny whimpered and buried her head in her mother's chest. "You want to look nice when you cousins get here," Iona cajoled her. Neeny nodded reluctantly. "We get you in de bath, wash you hair, and den you can tell me a story," her mother soothed her. "Chance, you get the washtub for me?" He nodded and disappeared through the back door. Clemmie went over to the trunk and pulled a pile of soft, clean cloths from it.

Iona turned to Shadda, who watched her anxiously as he moved closer to his father. "You can look like you ready to run all you want to, Shadda. Tonight we fix de girls' hair, tomorrow your turn for de bath."

"Dat right, boy!" Ben teased him. "You need a haircut, too. If I didnt know you, I tink you a girl!" Shadda threw himself on Ben, who wrestled him to the floor.

Iona stood up and spoke to Amelia. "You help me draw the water from de tank?"

Amelia followed her out the back door. Iona lit a torch, then picked up a bucket and walked along the plank walkway to a large tank set on stilts. The top of the tank was covered with a piece of muslin. Amelia grabbed a second bucket and followed her. "Dis what Julien an Eli set up to catch de rainwater." Iona pulled a wooden plug from the side of the tank, and the water flowed into the bucket. "Water back here too brackish for drinkin. Chilren get sick if dey drink de water. Closest spring water too far by much. Eli see dis in one of dem catalogues, an he an Julien set out to make one." When the bucket filled, she chuckled as she handed it to Amelia, who exchanged it for the other. "Dey so proud de day dey set it up. Couldnt tell dem nuttin."

Clemmie had the fire in the stove blazing by the time they returned with the water. Chance had placed the washtub in front of the stove. Iona took the buckets and began to heat the water in the large pots. Iona opened a small wooden chest that sat on the floor and took out several bottles. Amelia immediately recognized her cousin's handiwork. "Elizabeth made those for you," she stated.

"Oh, Lil Bet got dat touch. Her learn plenty from Nana an Miz Emma Julia. I ast she to put sumptin together for de girls' hair, de lye soap so hard. An her put together dis, an it take all de tangles out dey hair an keep it soft." She picked up a bottle filled with a golden substance, removed the cork, and sniffed the delicately scented liquid. "Dis I put on de scalp to keep dey hair from drying an breakin off. It de best thing I have." Iona continued wistfully, "It smell like Nana. I dont know how Lil Bet do it, but I smell it, an I think Nana passing by."

Iona poured a couple of drops of the oil into Amelia's hands. Amelia rubbed the oil into her palms and then put her hands up to her face and inhaled deeply.

Nana's Hair Wash

Mix 10 drops of ginger, 10 drops of rose oil, 5 drops of lavender, and 2 tablespoons of sesame oil together. Let it settle, then shake it up real good. Part the hair and rub into the scalp. Slowly but firmly work up from the roots into the hair. It will soften the hair and soothe the head.

"Come on, baby," Iona called to Neeny, who had wandered over to where Ben, Chance, and Shadda sat. Despite the earlier negotiations, Neeny shook her head when her mother called her.

"Go on, gal!" Shadda, always helpful, jumped to his feet and tried to pull his sister over to the washtub.

"Leave me lone! Leave me lone, ol stinky boy!" Neeny struggled with him, slapping at his hands. She stopped struggling when her father looked up from the saddle and watched her. Pouting, she dragged herself across the floor to her mother. Shadda followed behind her, triumphant.

"Shadda." Julien spoke quietly. "I need your help with this." Shadda eagerly dashed over to his father's side. He picked up one of the tools and stood at the ready as he listened to his father's instructions.

It took some doing to get Neeny finally settled in the washtub. Clemmie filled the washtub with water, allowing Neeny to test it for the right temperature. Only after Neeny had declared for the third time that it was too hot or too cold did Amelia catch the glint of impatient amusement in Clemmie's eyes. Clemmie and her mother exchanged knowing glances. Sticking her hand into the water, Iona pronounced the bath quite ready and helped the complaining Neeny out of her clothes. Momentarily defeated, Neeny sat quietly while Iona massaged the potion into her hair.

When Neeny was bathed and shampooed, Iona sat her down in front of the fire to comb her hair out and plait it, using the special colored strings worn at the gatherings. Amelia watched as Iona toweled Neeny's thick hair and oiled and massaged her scalp. Under her soothing hands, Neeny's eyes began to droop, and Iona finally laid her across her lap so that she could sleep while her mother finished her hair. Iona looked up at Margaret Anne, who had just worked the base of a basket, and said, "You should get started before it gets too late." With a sigh, Margaret Anne put aside her work and crossed to the stove to check the water. "What about you, miss?" Iona asked Clemmie.

"I do it tomorrow night," Clemmie murmured.

"Just so you get it done before dey get here."

Margaret Anne took one of the washbasins down from the shelf and began undoing her hair. She cried out as her fingers snagged on a tangle. Amelia moved over to help her, and Margaret Anne stood patiently as Amelia worked the tangle free. Margaret Anne smiled up at her, "Would you help me wash my hair? It get so heavy dat I need help." Amelia nodded and went to get water while Margaret Anne undid the rest of her hair.

Margaret Anne bent over the basin, and Amelia poured the warm water over her. When her hair was thoroughly wet, Amelia worked the shampoo into it, marveling at the way it richly lathered. Amelia's fingers gently massaged her scalp, causing Margaret Anne to sigh with pleasure. Amelia leaned around and peered at Margaret Anne, whose eyes were closed. She glanced up at Clemmie, who had a slight smile on her face.

It had been a long time since Amelia had helped anyone with her hair. She had forgotten the restorative and soothing powers of working with hair. Amelia's own hair was fine, crinkly, and tangled just as easily as Neeny's. It was what Haagar called "good hair." She remembered how her grandmother had bought every one of Madame Walker's products to put on her own hair to encourage its growth. Aside from the hair-growing powers of her products, Haagar was a great admirer of Madame Walker herself, the self-made colored woman. Haagar would have given her right arm to visit Villa Lewaro, her grand mansion on the Hudson outside New York. Haagar would often cite Madame Walker's story the way others would quote a parable from the Bible. Amelia could only imagine the disappointment that Haagar felt when none of her social contacts led to the sophisticated circle that surrounded Madame Walker.

Despite her investment in hair products, Haagar had never taken much time with her granddaughter's hair. A quick comb through and two pigtails would suffice. Myown was the one who lingered and tenderly brushed Amelia's hair every night. Amelia remembered leaning back into the warmth of her mother's body and dropping off to sleep. When she had gotten older, she had sometimes helped Myown with her hair, but somewhere along the way that had stopped. Amelia realized how much she missed that personal touch as Margaret Anne gave herself over to her hands. Massaging around the edges of her hair, Amelia glanced up as Clemmie came back with the rinse water. Amelia gently leaned Margaret Anne back over the basin, and Clemmie poured the water over her. She smoothed the water through Margaret Anne's hair and spoke quietly to Clemmie. "You can get your hair done tonight. I'd be glad to help you." Clemmie gave a quick nod and turned without looking at her to get more water.

The ancient people began to arrive two days later. To Amelia, it seemed that they had simply appeared. She awoke that morning and the swamp sounds had given way to the low hum of conversation. She sat up and looked around the room. The others were not there: Their pallets lay neatly stacked by the wall. Quickly dressing, she stepped out into the early morning sunlight and stopped at the sight of so many people milling around the houses and on the walkways.

The cove that the houses sat in was filled with canoes. Amelia scanned the crowd, amazed at the mixture of the people who made up Julien's family. She could see where the bloodlines of the ancient people, the African captives, and the whites had melded together. She searched through the crowd looking for a familiar face.

Chance stood with a group of young men by the landing. As they listened to a pale young man with sandy brown hair and light eyes, Amelia noted the different body types, the skin hues ranging from white to jet black, and the hair textures from straight to kinky. The group turned as they were hailed by more people approaching in two canoes. The new arrivals pulled up to the dock, as Chance stepped forward to hold the ladder steady. A woman exclaimed, "The Tallmans! They aint come to de gathering for years!"

The family resemblance was especially strong among this new group. The mother and father were both dark-skinned with sharp features and easily stood over six feet. Amelia struggled to remember the name of the nomadic African tribe she had heard about, for surely these people were their reincarnation. She admired their easy grace and strength as the two sons and daughter climbed onto the landing.

Chance and the others greeted the father and mother with a sign of obeisance. The hand salutes exchanged among the young men bespoke their respectful rivalry. When the young woman drew herself up to her full height and swept the young men with a challenging and provocative glance, Amelia was amused to see that they all became slightly flustered and gave her a hand signal that showed deference and respect for the commanding young woman that she was. She boldly stared at Chance as she followed her parents. He recovered enough to return her stare, but was clearly chastened by her presence. He turned away as the others leaned forward to watch her move among the crowd.

Amelia saw Iona step from one of the houses followed by a woman that could only be Julien's sister. She was sturdy and broad with the same softly rounded features marked by a wide mouth and laughing eyes. As they made their way through the crowd greeting people and helping them get settled, they were greeted by the other women.

Amelia felt someone's gaze and turned to meet Clemmie's eyes. Over the past two days, she and Clemmie had formed a bond of silent communication between them. Amelia had never thought of herself as a person with any particular skill in reading people. But with Clemmie, she could not rely on spoken words but had to interpret the slight gestures, the seemingly innocuous glance, and the subtle body language. She had not recognized the ease with which she had accepted this, but after two days of preparing for the gathering with Clemmie, she felt an odd kinship with this quiet woman-child.

Amelia edged her way through the crowd to Clemmie and her friend, a young woman who could easily have been her sister, so much did they favor each other. When she arrived, Clemmie took her hand and the girl's hand and put them together. The girl nodded to Amelia and said, "Maria." Amelia clasped her hand in her own, and the girl broke into a smile. Maria spoke. "Clemmie has told me of her cousin that comes from way up North. We live over off in Yamassee. One day I will get Clemmie to leave this swamp and her mother to come stay with me. You must come with her." Amelia looked at her, intrigued by her accent and unfamiliar with the location.

"It has been a long time since we have come to the winter gathering," Maria told Amelia, "but my great-grandfather over there"—she indicated an elderly man who leaned heavily on his cane as he indulged in a lively conversation with another elderly man—"Ol Paw Domingues says this will be his last season, and he has come to tell everyone 'good-bye.' "

Clemmie leaned over to Amelia and pointed out, "Does he not look like Cousin Eli many years from now?" The old man laughed, his eyes twinkling.

"He certainly does," Amelia replied.

It was sunset, and the festivities were about to begin. Amelia had walked with the others to the burial ground, a large mound that at first glimpse to an outsider would be mistaken for a hill. They had climbed the earthen walls that led to the large, flat area for dancing, and Amelia now sat among the women at the edge where the sun would rise.

Amelia felt plain, sitting among these women dressed in their finest. Several of the women wore either dresses of buckskin and delicate beadwork or long, black skirts edged with bands of bright color and crisp, white, full blouses. Their hair was elaborately woven with string of almost every color. Amelia glanced over at the Tallmans. The mother and daughter wore swirling robes of deep purple, their heads elaborately wrapped in silk scarves.

By contrast Iona, Clemmie, and Margaret Anne were resplendent in their simplicity, straight frocks covered with long feathered vests and the whitetail deer moccasins that Julien had made for them. Iona had loaned Amelia an old-fashioned long gown made of white cotton and trimmed in lace. It had browned slightly over the years and the lace had unraveled in spots, but it still held its beauty. When she slipped the gown over her head and smoothed it down, she had felt like one of the women in the pictures from that long-ago farewell picnic, and she had guessed that it was the dress Iona had been married in.

The men sat at the opposite end where the sun would set. They also were dressed in their best, their variety of style easily equal to that of the women, everything from elaborate conch and bone breastplates to buckskin breeches lined with beaded fringes to both straw and Fedora hats. As they waited for the last rays of sun to fade, Amelia found herself looking for one of the latecomers.

Earlier, Amelia had been helping set out the food when she heard the sound of a drum, and a ripple of excitement swept through the crowd. The children ran to the edge of the landing, waving and calling to a group that had just arrived. She had stepped back into the cooking hut and emerged with a steaming bowl of fish stew just as a man was passing, followed by the group of chattering children. They both sensed rather than saw the other and stopped to avoid the collision. The man took in the jacket, shirt, and pants that Ben had loaned her that day. He lifted his eyebrow quizzically and commented, "You are not a boy."

Her eyes scanned the smooth nut-brown skin, the clean features, and the lines of wry humor that marked his mouth. "No, I'm not."

He nodded to her. "I am glad," he said, so softly that she was not sure that she heard him.

A small boy tugged at his hand, and he reached down and swung him up onto his shoulders. He strode off with children running behind him, all trying to beat the drum slung across his back. As Clemmie stepped out of the hut with another dish, Amelia could not help herself. "Who is that?"

Clemmie tilted her head and looked at Amelia with interest. "Dat Boaz."

The pitch torches and the herb pots had been lit. The children sat in front, leaning forward with excitement. A group of elders, three men and two women, stepped into the space between the two groups to begin the ceremonies. One woman spoke as the others chanted in low tones.

"We are the Last Childs. The last free children of the Cherokee nation. We Last Childs a strong people, a stubborn people who turn our back on the white man's march and follow the way shown by our ancestors who hid from the Spanish and the white soldiers who came after them. We come from five generations and call places name Edisto, John's Island, Dafusky, Tybee, Warsaw, Ossabaw, Sapelo, and Okefenokee home. We travel by the ancient waterways, Ogeechee, Canoochee, Ocmulgee, Oconee, and the mighty Altamaha River.

"We have gone in many directions to seek our own way, but always we must return to this land for our renewal. Once again we are together in this season of cold to send prayer and thanks to our ancestors who brought us to this land. Let us join together to tell the story of our people, and may you draw strength and courage from this land we call 'Chicora.' "

The Lifesong of Chicora

All:

> They come to me
> > While I sleep.
> The Voices
> > From the Ring of Fire.
> They speak of days

> *In my Fathers' time*
> *Of how we came*
> > *To the land*
> *We call "Chicora."*

Voice of Dark: *There was a time*
> > *In the land*
> *Where the sky rolled*
> > *With waves of fire.*
> *And our elders called us*
> > *Together*
> *To seek our counsel.*
> > *For we could no longer*
> *Pay tribute to those*
> > *Who would raid us*
> *In the night.*
> > *And the young men shouted*
> *With rage and joy.*
> > *For they had dreamt of*
> *Songs filled with glory*
> > *And triumph.*
> *And the old women cried*
> > *For they had sung*
> *The songs of death and despair.*

Voice of Light: *But then a single voice*
> > *Spoke out*
> *And rent the sky*
> > *With clarity.*
> *"What will be gained*
> > *That we must fight?"*

Voice of Dark: *The young men stirred*
> > *In anger and impatience*
> > *That a woman*
> > *Should speak so free.*
> *"Who is this person that*
> > *Shows no shame*
> *And would question what we know*
> > *Must be?"*

Voice of Light:

"I am but one
    Who wonders why
We seek the endless time.
    For they are many,
Fierce and cruel who war
    Just as they breathe.
And we, the people of the serpentine hills,
    Would coax a seed in fallow earth."

Voice of Dark:

The young men shouted in rage
    "What would you have us do?
We live as one with Mother Earth
    To bring forth her fruits
That fill their bellies on cold winter nights
    And hush their children's cries
And still they show us no honor!"

Voice of Light:

"This Honor, who will it save
    As you go off to war?
What will we do with this Honor
    When you are no longer here?
Tell your mothers, your wives, and our young
What is to be done with this Honor?"

All:

The young men rushed to silence her
    But they were stayed!
By the woman who came forth
    For she spoke with the voice of many.
The elders declared, "We must leave
    this place where our ancestors began.
To stay would see the end of our days!"
    There was greater fear among the people
For this was all they could remember.

Voice of Light:

"Our Mother Earth, has she not provided
    For us in all the days that have gone?
Will she not provide for the days to come
    Wherever we may journey?"

Voice of Dark:

"But this is ours!
    It is as we've made it!

> *Why should we run from that*
> > *Which comes from our Life's Spirit?"*

Voice of Light: *"Then it is truly time to move on*
> > *For what She has given us*
> *We would keep only for ourselves*
> > *When She has shown that it is*
> *To be shared by all."*

Voice of Dark: *"It is not us that will not share!*
> > *It is they that take*
> *And demand more!*
> > *It is they that wait*
> *As the corn unfolds from within*
> > *And reaches to the sky!*
> *It is they that watch*
> > *As we gather the fruits and save*
> *The seeds that will bring another year of Life.*
> > *Only then to demand*
> *A tribute they have not earned!"*

Voice of Light: *"Then we will leave*
> > *And take that which is most precious*
> *to All*
> > *And that is our Life's Spirit,*
> > *The wisdom we hold for living as one*
> > *With our Mother Earth.*
> > *For we know She will provide."*

All: *So it was said.*
> > *Then it was done.*
> *Our people prepared for the long walk*
> > *From darkness into light.*
> *Yet it was not without pain.*
> > *Many a night was pierced with the cries*
> *Of the women who lost children along the way*
> > *To those who would stop us.*
> *Still our Mother provided and sent an early*
> > *Storm that chased those who pursued*
> *Back to the lands that we had fled.*
> > *Then she sent a sweet-scented breeze*

That led us south to the land
We now call "Chicora."

It was the fourth sunset of the winter gathering. Everyone walked to the dancing place for the final coming together, the women leading the men. Amelia had noticed the rising tension in the air as the days passed and the various rituals took place. Separated into their own huts for sleeping, the women had performed their purification rites while the men and boys had disappeared into the woods to hunt and to carry out their rites of passage. Amelia had not expected them to find much in this season where most of the animals were burrowed against the cold, but each day they had returned with enough meat to feed the entire group.

There was a rhythm to this family gathering, maybe to all family gatherings. Amelia could not look on this and not think of the last family reunion she had attended as a child. It seemed that the first day was set aside for welcome, renewing the relationships. Everyone was happy to see those that they had not seen in a long while, the joy of reunion setting the mood. The second day was for remembrance, tracing the old stories and fond memories, recalling the good times and the happiness. The third day, however, was for settling of old accounts. The memories of the good times faded as the recall of old hurts sharpened. Looking back on her only trip to the Island as a child, though Amelia could not remember exactly what Haagar had said when she heard that Yellow Mary was on her way, she could easily summon the harshness of the accusations that Haagar had flung at Eula, Clarabelle, and the others. She had scant memories of the hasty trip back to New York with a furious Haagar and a weeping Myown. But these memories flooded back when on the third day of Last Child gathering, an old argument was renewed.

She had been sitting with the older women, listening and trying to understand as best she could, for the older ones spoke a language that was an odd mix of Cherokee, Geechee, and snatches of English. By letting her sit with them, they had shown much patience, and one old woman whose command of English was a bit stronger had tried to explain to her. She had learned from Clemmie that understanding would follow if she could only be patient.

Suddenly there were shouts and the sounds of scuffling from the men's area. The older women rushed outside to join the others as two men circled warily, shouting and throwing angry hand signals at each other. Julien pushed his way through the crowd and stepped between the two, fiercely countering their signs. As the two men exchanged hate-filled glances and backed away from each other, Julien spoke to them in a low, fierce voice.

The old woman clutched Amelia's arm and said, "Julien want to know why dey bring de bitterness wit dem to dis place." One man shouted his response and threw another angry hand sign. The other started forward and was caught and held by Boaz, who had slipped behind him. He was about to struggle when he saw who held him. Boaz whispered into his ear, and the man slowly began to calm. Julien spoke again. "He tell dem to take dat back wit dem an to settle it dere. He say de land not belong to either one of dem but to Mother Earth." At Julien's words, the man stepped back and turned. His shoulders still heavy with rage, he made his way through the crowd, followed by two young boys. Boaz clapped the other man on his shoulder and let him go. The man lowered his head from Julien's gaze and gave a sign of repentance. When they walked back to the hut, the old woman shook her head in sorrow. "Dey fight over dat land dat the rich white folks wan to buy. It done tore dat family apart."

Amelia was not sure if it was anger from the argument that still lingered after the man and his sons left early, or the anxiety of separation that filled the air as the men and women took their places at opposite ends of the place. She looked for Boaz and found him, just as she had every time she had sought him out, looking for her. They had not exchanged a word since the first conversation, but each had sensed the other across the wide space that separated men and women. She had been thankful for that separation. She needed that space and time to watch him and see him for what he was.

Boaz was a drummer of great skill and held a place of respect and trust among the ancient people. He moved easily among the ages and families, each beckoning him to join them, and it was his laughter that Amelia could single out from the swell of voices.

This last evening the drums began as the sun sank, and Boaz and three other men walked around the mound and settled in front of the open space between the men and women. As the drums pounded slowly, the older men got to their feet and began the Circle of Dark, moving in half-steps and jumps, forward, then back. The women rocked back and forth to the beat as the men flung their heads back and called to the moon. After watching them circle several times, the younger men and boys joined them. The men continued, their dancing becoming more energetic and joyous, with the drumming increasing the rhythm until Amelia thought they would collapse from exertion. When the drumming slowed, the dancers gradually fell away, returning to their places, until only Ol Paw Domingues was left. Despite his great age, he had much vigor, and everyone shouted at the high jumps he managed. He slowed again and made his way back to the group with much approval.

As he took his seat, the older women stood up and began to move in the circle. Where the men had leapt to the sky and appealed to the moon, the women lowered themselves to the ground with much hip swaying and foot stomping in praise of the earth. While the men's dance had been aggressive, the women's was enticing. Amelia saw a different type of challenge in the boldness of the younger women who joined their elders. She watched as the Tallman woman, Clemmie, and Maria moved forward to claim their place among the older women. Their steps had all the energy of the men's and the sensuous control of the women's. She could sense a passionate independence as they changed steps at will and the older women stepped back to let them display. Several of the older women, including Iona, began to adapt the steps into their own movements.

Amelia looked over at Boaz, bent over his drum, his eyes tightly shut as he changed the rhythms and the dancers changed their steps. The range of expressions on the other men's faces was especially telling, and several of the older men frowned. Ol Paw Domingues clapped his hands and yelled encouragement to Maria as she dipped and swayed, sweeping the ground with her skirt. Julien watched his wife, his eyes darkening as they took in the roll of her hips and her fluttering hands. Chance could not take his eyes off the tall young woman who danced for herself and no one else.

Amelia sat next to Margaret Anne, who had explained that she did not dance because it wore her out so much. Even so, Margaret Anne moved with the changing rhythm, shaking her head and clapping her hands. Amelia felt Clemmie's summons and, at first, shook her head. She was just a visitor, an observer to this family ritual. When Margaret Anne leaned forward and whispered in her ear, "It for all women," Amelia got to her feet, awkwardly looking for a place to join the circle. Iona danced in place and beckoned Amelia to the space that she had opened in front of her.

It was time for the men and women to come together. They had eaten, prayed, and danced apart, and now as the full moon floated above the trees, they would come together as a people. Clemmie, Margaret Anne, and several of the other young girls had collected the children and taken them off to bed. Iona had told Amelia about this part of the gathering where the men and women mingled and those who wished could select a partner to be with until the new day. Iona had made it very clear that it was the woman's choice to stay and the woman's choice to determine what would happen.

Amelia had thought to leave with Clemmie and the others as they rose to go, but had been stayed by the directness in Boaz's gaze. As the drums began and the men and women rose to face each other, she averted her eyes, afraid to send any sign. Closing her eyes, she swayed back and forth to the drum. The women moved forward, and then the men advanced. Julien and Iona came quickly together. Several more couples joined, while others mixed, separated, and then regrouped. Amelia stayed to the back, avoiding the first contact. As the men and women moved around her, she could see others pairing and slipping away from the mound into the privacy of the woods or the houses. Chance and the Tallman woman stood before each other, each testing the other's will until they both reached out and touched the other's face.

Amelia looked at Boaz, who pounded the drums, his eyes never leaving her. She slowly walked over to stand in front of him. He stepped from behind the drum and took her hand, and they left the mound together.

He led the way because she did not know the woods. As they walked away from the mound, he turned and looked back up the path. Amelia turned and saw the line of shells that in the moonlight marked the way to the mound. "Kojo's trace," she whispered and saw the faint glimmer of his smile in the darkness. They walked in silence. Night sounds that would ordinarily have sent Amelia's heart pounding were somehow reassuring. She did not know what she wanted from this man, and she did not know what she was going to do when they got to wherever they were headed.

Amelia knew about the way men and women wanted each other, and how a person could get lost in it. She had even experimented, curious to find out what folks were preaching against, but not talking about. She had never discussed passion with her mother, and her grandmother had only mentioned it in self-satisfied tones when she announced the fall of some heretofore respectable young woman in the neighborhood. Haagar, for all her sense of righteousness, had an earthy, realistic attitude about men and women.

Now, confronted with this sensuous man, Amelia knew that he was not some inexperienced youth who would be satisfied with only what she wanted to give. She stopped suddenly and pulled her hand from his. She peered through the darkness trying to read his expression. He waited patiently, then spoke. "We can go back if you want." When she did not respond, he moved past her to head back.

"I just want to know where we're going . . ." She could sense his smile.

"I taking you to a safe place."

She stopped. It was the last thing she expected to hear. "Taking me to a safe place?" She was startled to recognize Haagar's sharp tone come out of her.

Boaz spoke quietly. "You look like you could use a safe place." Reaching out, he took her hand. "Aint nothing wrong with needing a safe place."

She walked beside him, gripping his hand as they stepped over a fallen tree. Just when she was about to question him again, he stopped at the base of a huge oak. Pointing to its low, broad branches, he said, "When I use to get in trouble at de gatherings, an I did, I use to light out for dis place." As she looked up at the branch in disbelief, he bent over and linked his fingers. Awkwardly she stepped into his hands and grabbed at the branch as he lifted her. She pulled herself up and tried to balance herself on the thick limb. He stood under her, waiting to catch her if she fell, and once she had righted herself, he jumped, grabbed the limb, and pulled himself up.

"You call this safe?" she asked.

He grinned at her as she hung onto the branch, afraid to look down. He stood up and extended a hand to her. "You safe with me." She drew a deep breath and shakily grasped his hand. He pulled her to her feet, and holding her steady with gentle hands, he turned her and pointed. "Look at that moon." She stared at the largest moon she had ever seen. "Every place I been, and I been many places, folks got a story bout that moon." They stood in silence, and then he led her back to the broad trunk. He sat with his back against the tree and patted the space in front of him. She hesitated and then sat down, careful to maintain a few inches between them. "You got your back to that moon," he pointed out. She turned with much difficulty, noting that he held his arms out to keep her from falling.

They stared at the moon in silence, and when she realized that she was not going to fall from the branch, she began to relax. Amelia reached out in wonder. "You can almost touch it." She turned slightly, searching his face in the moonlight. When he said nothing, she turned back, flushed with embarrassment. He pulled her to him. She resisted for a moment, then calmed, and slid back into his arms. She felt the warmth of his body as he pulled her back against his chest and held her firmly, soothing her with non-words. They listened to the sounds of the woods, a racoon's chatter and flap of the owl's wings as it hunted overhead. "Tell me your story," she whispered and then listened to the tale of his life through his strong heartbeats.

The Quiet Blessings

as told by Boaz Samuelson

They took me in. My folks died with the sickness when I was but three years old. They took me in, gave me their name, didn't show no difference between me and their own children. Raised us rough. Raised us hard. You fight one, you got to fight all the Samuelsons, and there plenty in line to take you on.

I was born in the Piedmont region. It a harsh life out there in those Carolina hills, breaking horses, swallowing dust, walking behind that plow trying to get that seed to just take hold. Wild! We run wild like wolves! Sometime I think of the things we did. Chase them wild horses up through the pass and jump down on their backs and ride till we fall off! I can't hardly figure out how we here to talk about it. Just barely managed to stay on this side of the law. Wasn't much law out there in them hills but Deputy Big Jim Booker. And you didn't want him looking for you cause he didn't stop till you was caught. Biggest colored man I ever seen! I used to pretend he was my natural daddy. Can't say Big Jim was always right, but he tried to be just.

Folks always coming together to help each other, raise a barn, bring in a crop, cause everybody had a piece in it. And gatherings. Folks would come from all over. When I got married, it ran for five days, singing and dancing and having a good time. Where you goin? Gal, you gonna fall out this tree. I just talkin to you.

I married a lil gal named Mary Rose. Her daddy pure African and her mama mix of Cherokee and African. I told you I come along rough. Didn't have but one sister and didn't know how to be with a woman cept those saloon gals. Them first couple years was hard on her cause I was gonna do like I want. She was real quiet. Didn't hardly talk at all, just look at you real quiet like. So I run with my brothers. Leave her all by herself to go to town and stay a couple of days. Fuss if she ask anything of me. It was all I knew. I didn't know nothing bout kindness.

Then a horse fell on me, and I broke my leg. It was a bad break, broke in two places, right here on my thigh, and down here halfway down my leg. Doctor wanted to take it off, but she wouldn't let him. She and her mama went to work on that leg, pack them roots and potients, and it begun to heal. You'd think I start paying mind to what was going on in my own house, but no, I just wanted to get drunk and stay drunk. And my baby brother, Billy, was too happy to help me. He go into town and come back with a bottle, and we sit up in that house and drank all day into the night. She didn't say nothing.

One day Billy come up there. I just waking up. And I hear her get up and go to the door fore Billy could get there. Then I hear him calling me. I look up, and she standing there with my rifle pointed right at Billy. That rifle almost taller than her! I tell Billy to come on in. "She ain't gonna do nothing with that rifle!" But Billy have more sense than I ever had. He wasn't coming no place close. He know her daddy teach all them girls to shoot. I start to cussing her, and her turn that rifle on me, and them words stuck in my throat. All the while she got that quiet look on her face, but now I know there's something else behind all that. Well, Billy got on his horse and ride, and he didn't come back.

So all I could do was lay up there all day long and watch her work round that house. I seen how she take care with everything. Keep that house clean, cook the food, wash the clothes, work in the garden, change the bandages, kept me clean and fed. I seen how she fix up that house, little things here and there to make it right. I never thought of doing anything like that. She get me out of that bed, give me a stout stick and make me start working that leg. I didn't want to, the pain was so bad. But she left that food on the table, wouldn't bring it to me, so I have to get up and get it.

I seen her. I seen all of her, when she scrubbing the floor, making the bread, picking beans, standing out in the noon sun taking a sip of cold water. This sound foolish, but I never seen her before. I started feeling this hunger for her. It was different from before, but I didn't know how to tell her that. So I come up on her and it wasn't like before. She push me away. Didn't say nothing. Just push me away. I mad! Whoa! Wife don't deny her husband! She run out the house! I can't catch her with that bad leg! I cussed her! Call her every name her mama didn't know!

I don't know where she went, but she didn't come back until it was way late. I laying up there, and I hear her come in. I pretend I sleep.

She stand in the moonlight, moon just like that moon up there, and start to wash up. I watch her, she take off her skirt and blouse, and wash with that cloth real slow. I see the way she let her hands soothe her body. There a gentleness in the way she treat herself. I shamed. Cause I ain't never touched her like that.

I must have made some kind of noise cause she sensed that I was wake and started to run again, but I told her she didn't have to run. I wasn't gonna bother her. And then, I swear before God, I don't know where it come from, but I asked her to teach me to touch her the way she like to be touched. She so still I didn't think she heard me. Then she hold out that cloth to me. I almost broke that leg again getting out of that bed and across that floor. She teach me. She show me how to bring her comfort by just laying on my hands. Now, I didn't push nothing on her. I let her say when she was ready. And she made me wait a good while. A few days! Mmph! Seem like it was a month! But when she was ready, so was I, cause I knew it was gonna be the same for both of us.

Things was so good between us. I didn't think I had much to learn, and she showed me wrong. Taught me to care about a whole different side to a woman. Couldn't get me away from that farm. If I left to work in the morning, I made sure I was home that night. My brothers all sick of me cause if I going to town, she coming with me. Even started going to church.

She died when our first baby come. Wasn't nothing they could do. I heartsick. I can't even look at that baby. Her mama put that baby in my arms, and I tell to take her cause I don't want her! I starts drinking again, but it make me sick! Sick as a dog! I used to be able to drink with the best, but I can hardly stand to look at it now. Billy say Mary Rose put a root on me. It don't make no difference! I ain't got the taste for it!

I couldn't stay there on that farm. She was everywhere I turned, in everything I saw. I struck out, jumped a train headed anywhere. Joined up with these fellas working for the railroad. Been everywhere, all over the country. I come back bout four years ago, just happen to be stopping through with the train crew. I bout to ride out to see my folks, and I see Mary Rose's mama coming down the street with our baby, Mary Rose's image, holding her hand. I lost my heart right there. I come over, pick her up, and she look at me, face all frowning. "Who this man holding me and crying?" She wouldn't let me hold her long, though. I seen myself in that. She wanted her granma. I pledged right there that I was gonna take care of that baby, work my fingers to the nub for that child.

I knew I had to stay with the railroad. I went back and talked with

Mary Rose's mama, and you can ask her, every first of the month, that money waiting for my baby. I got some put away for her, too. I stop, though, every time I get within a hundred miles, and I always make it home for Christmas. My Chloe a big girl now. Started school last year. She a smart girl. Got my first letter a while back. They raising her right. Just like they did her mama.

I miss Mary Rose. I miss her every day. But I ain't looking for nobody to take her place. Cain't nobody take her place. Sides it ain't right to hold a woman to another woman's image. Mary Rose taught me, taught me bout patience, bout being gentle, bout quiet blessings, bout love.

Amelia turned in his arms and searched his face in the moonlight. She could feel his eyes flitting over the angles of her face, sharpened by the darkness. Reaching out, she traced his lips and felt the pleasure and need ripple across his features. She inhaled, drawing in his scent. There was the salty blend of sweat and sea air, an earthy aroma like fresh-turned dirt, and his own essence, surely something Elizabeth would have used for one of her scents. Her skin prickled with anticipation and she leaned forward and pressed her lips to his. He responded tenderly, allowing her to lead him. She pressed closer, cupping his face and holding him to her as she explored his mouth. He tasted of coffee, molasses, and the sweet mint that the folks chewed like gum. She let her hunger and need take over as her hands stroked his head. His heartbeat was so loud that she felt as if she had climbed into his chest. She broke away and looked up at the moon. "It's moon madness, isn't it?"

He shook his head. "Not for me."

She pulled away from him and stood up, his hands steadying her. She began to unbutton the back of her dress. As her fingers fumbled, she heard him stand and his strong hands took over. He stroked her neck and back as he freed the buttons. He helped her pull the dress over her head and chuckled as she flung it into the air and let it float to the bushes down below. As she stood shivering in the cool night, he opened his rough shirt and pulled her to his chest, wrapping the ends around her. She felt his body stir, and a rush of heat enveloped them. He turned with her in his arms and walked her backward to the broad trunk. When she spread her hands against his chest, he cupped her hips and pulled her to him. As he began to unbutton her camisole, she unlaced his pants and eased them down his legs, each stroke causing him to breathe more deeply. She helped him lift one foot, then the other. Pulling her up into his arms, he pressed her against the trunk and she felt the heat from his body. When he came to her, she hungrily sought all of him, his mouth, his arms, his manhood. As he breathed into her mouth and raised her hips, she knew that she had found her safe place.

"Gal, what happen to your cousin?" Carrie Mae poured a drink and nodded to Amelia, who was cutting a mean rug with Dawkins Cooder in the middle of the small room. "Last time her was here, her stayed over here by de bar. Half-fraid to talk to anybody."

Elizabeth sipped her beer and watched as Amelia lost herself in the dance, tossing her head and shaking her hips. Elizabeth smiled and shrugged. "It just de Geechee coming outa she!"

Carrie Mae looked skeptically. "Mm-huh! Well, Dawkins dont know bout none of dat. All dat ol pirate see is dat young gal dancing for he!" Elizabeth glanced at Dawkins, who clumsily tried to keep up with Amelia, his mouth hanging open as she danced just out of his reach.

Elizabeth had noticed a change in Amelia when she had returned from visiting Iona. Eula and Eli had put it down to her being happy at meeting her aunt, but Elizabeth suspected something else. Amelia had mentioned a man she had met at the gathering, but she had not dwelt on it and had not brought him up again. She had surprised Elizabeth by approaching her about moving into Nana's home with her. It was not the offer to pay rent, which Elizabeth immediately refused, but the offer to help fix up the house that decided her. Elizabeth had asked no questions at the time; she was glad for the company. Eula immediately accepted whatever drove Amelia's request. She assumed that Amelia, an only child, was seeking quiet and peace away from her rowdy household. Eli had to admit that he was relieved that Lil Bet would no longer be alone in that old house.

Where Amelia had been hesitant before, she was now more outgoing, pursuing her stories without relying on Elizabeth's help. Even Lucy had commented, "Gal found she backbone!" Amelia was coming into her own.

At the sound of a commotion, Elizabeth looked up to see that Carrie Mae had been right. "Toady!" Carrie Mae shouted. "Dawkins on de loose!" Toady stepped into the room from outside just as Dawkins reached the doorway with Amelia.

"Aww, lil she-man, what you gonna do?" Dawkins grinned.

In one quick motion, Toady had her gun resting on Dawkins's bottom lip. "What you think I gonna do, man?" He stepped back, immediately loosening his grip on Amelia, who bolted to the bar, where Elizabeth and Carrie Mae stood.

"You big wit dat gun, lil she-man. Put down dat gun, an we see what you all about," Dawkins taunted Toady.

She cocked her eyebrow at him. "You want to fight me?"

He sneered at her, "Naw, lil she-man, I gonna give you a tanning just like my brother's chilren, keep dem in line. Somebody got to keep you in line."

"You think you can, I gonna let you try!"

Dawkins was ready. "Put dat gun down, lil she-man. And dont be giving it to Carrie Mae, cause she shoot me for sure!" He laughed loudly.

Toady walked over and placed the gun on the bar. Amelia backed away from it just as Dawkins rushed up behind Toady. As he closed in on her, she grabbed the bat that Carrie Mae had slipped onto the bar and thrust backward with it. There was a high whine as the end of the bat caught Dawkins right below the belt. He bent over, grabbing himself and gasping for air. Toady swung around and aimed at his head. Dawkins grabbed his many-times-broken nose and teetered, not sure which injury hurt the most. He finally sank to his knees.

Toady stepped forward and grabbed him by the little bit of hair on the top of his head. "I dont play, Dawkins. I aint one of your brother's chilren." Dawkins nodded in stunned and painful agreement. Toady turned to a couple of the men who stood by. "Yall get him outside an get him cleaned up," she said as they helped him to his feet. "Put him out dere in dat lil shed wit de quilts an let him sleep it off."

There was silence as Toady crossed to the bar to reclaim her gun. "Put on a fast song an crank dat piccolo!" Carrie Mae shouted. "Yall get on wit de dancing! I got to sell dese drinks!" People slowly began to resume their movement as they realized that all the trouble was over.

Amelia gingerly pushed the gun to Toady, who took it and slipped it into her coat pocket. Toady bowed her head to Amelia and headed out the door.

"She's not worried bout him coming back?"

Carrie Mae shook her head. "Naw, she got all Dawkins's respect now."

"I didn't know what to do when he grabbed me," Amelia exclaimed.

"It wasnt like he wasnt getting no encouragement," Elizabeth commented dryly.

Amelia was defensive. "I was just dancing."

Elizabeth looked at her meaningfully, while Carrie Mae weighed in with her advice. "Dont be couraging ugly mens if you dont wanna have to deal wit dem. Ugly mens aint used to dat kind of tention. Dey dont know what to do!" Amelia frowned and turned away, not before catching Elizabeth's smirk.

Amelia didn't quite know what had gotten into her. Out on that dance floor she had gotten lost in the feeling, the music, and the movement. She wondered where Boaz was traveling. Even now, weeks after they had met and made love, she would catch herself in a memory and feel the passion sweep over her body. Her breasts would swell as she remembered the tenderness of his touch and the heat of his body. She often caught herself blushing when she remembered her boldness and the demands they made upon each other. She knew that Elizabeth had guessed what had happened and was only slightly embarrassed when her cousin had handed her a salve to ease her soreness and to smooth over the abrasions on her back. She leaned against the bar and watched the dancers slow drag to the music.

"Lawd, have mercy! I aint never spected to see she back here!" Carrie Mae exclaimed, and Amelia turned to see who could cause that much consternation. Sallie Lee and Willis George stood in the doorway. Sallie Lee looked at the others haughtily, inspecting everyone in the room. Ill at ease, Willis George nodded abruptly to a few acquaintances who hailed him.

Sallie Lee made her way through the crowd to the bar, followed by Willis George. She smiled saucily at Carrie Mae. "Hey, Carrie Mae!"

Carrie Mae, startled, spoke carefully to her. "Sallie Lee. Willis George. You aint been back here since I open de place."

Sallie Lee scolded Willis George, "I been telling Willis George that since Sugar was born, I needed to get out some! Be with people! Have some fun! He dont need that, but I sholl do!" Willis George stirred uneasily at his wife's pointed comments.

He spoke hesitantly. "How yall doing?"

Elizabeth smiled at him. "We all right."

Sallie Lee continued, "Folks got to have fun sometime! Aint that right, Carrie Mae?"

Carrie Mae glanced at Willis George and spoke too heartily. "And you come to de right place! What yall gonna have? Put dat money away, Willis George. Yall my guests dis night!" Amelia's mouth almost dropped open at the unaccustomed generosity.

As Carrie Mae started to pour a drink, Sallie Mae stopped her. "Dont be mixing it now. I like my liquor straight up."

Carrie Mae handed her the drink and turned to Willis George, who mumbled, "Black Bear."

When Sallie Mae began to sway to the music, there were significant glances all around. "I ever tell you how many dance contests me and my cousins won in Bofort?" Sallie Mae exclaimed.

Carrie Mae responded carefully, "Oh, no! I didnt even know you danced, Sallie Lee."

Sallie Lee sipped her drink. "Yes, indeed, I could shing-a-ling with the best!" As she shook her hips, Willis George turned away, embarrassed.

"Look! Dere a coupla seats!" Carrie Mae pointed.

"Why dont yall go over dere an sit for a while? You want some more, you just come back and get it." Sallie Lee started dancing across the floor to the empty seats with Willis George in tow.

Elizabeth was the first to speak. "She in a mood, aint she?"

Carrie Mae shook her head. "Gal, you coulda knock me out when her come through dat door. Her have look me plenty times in de face, an if her knew me, you couldnt tell it! Her aint never spoke a damn word to me fore." Amelia looked over to where Sallie Lee flirted with Willis, leaning over to whisper in his ear. She turned from the hungry love in Willis George's eyes as he stared at his wife mesmerized. Carrie Mae clucked, "Lawd, Lawd, Lawd!"

They were interrupted by a shout from outside, and several people ran to the door to see what was going on. "What now?" Carrie Mae came from behind the bar and strode over to the door, pushing her way through the crowd standing there. Elizabeth and Amelia followed her onto the low porch. Ol Trent stood in the center of the ring of torches, waving his hands at the couples sitting in the sand. Toady leaned against the outside wall and watched him, expressionless.

"I have come to the Devil's Den!" Ol Trent proudly announced. Carrie Mae moaned. "I come to seek out the sinners, the fornicators, the adulterers and lead to the way of the righteous."

As he finished speaking, there was a cry of ecstasy from the nearby woods, "Lord, have mercy!"

"Sound like somebody already found de way of de righteous!" a woman taunted Ol Trent. The crowd burst out laughing. "Sound real good to me!" "An she havin fun, too!" "Like we all tryin to." They congratulated each other with back slaps.

Undaunted, Ol Trent continued, "I seen you! I seen all of you dancing like the spawn of the Devil, drinking, carrying on, cutting the fool when you should be on your knees asking for God's forgiveness! Cursed be he that lieth with his neighbor's wife!" He pointed to a man who stepped back, self-consciously. "Cursed be he that bringeth the wine that steal the soul!" He snarled at another man, who frowned at him. He turned to Toady. "Cursed be she that lie with her own."

Toady stared at him and then spoke deliberately. "Cursed be he dat forget his own sins to call out de sins of others!"

Ol Trent drew back like a cat. The crowd yelled, "Yessuh! Tell he bout it, Toady!"

Ol Trent shouted, "I praying for all yall sinners. Praying to keep you out of the hell you going straight to."

Toady continued, "When thou prayest, pray not as the hypocrites, for they love to pray standing on the corners of the street that they may be seen by men."

Ol Trent turned away from Toady to the others. An older woman laughed. "Her got he on de run now!"

Ol Trent retreated across the sand to a group of men standing by a fire. "The fires of hell will consume you. Only I, the messenger of God, can show you the way!"

"And when you pray, use not vain repetitions, as the heathen do; for they think they shall be heard for their much speaking!" Toady's voice cut through his exhortations as she stepped from the darkness of the porch into the moonlight, her light eyes glittering.

Ol Trent started to back up, waving her away. Abruptly turning, he stumbled across the sand, heading for the deep woods. "Take ye heed, watch and pray, for ye know not when the time is come!" His words floated back on the night breeze.

Carrie Mae sighed and went back into the joint. "Caint him kill de fun? Him aint been back here in a long time! I dont know why him had to come here tonight." Amelia and some of the others followed her. Those outside resumed drinking and talking.

"Toady handled that old man real well," Amelia commented, surprised.

"Dont nobody come tween Toady an de Lord," Carrie replied.

Elizabeth stared into the darkness where Trent had disappeared. She wondered where his wanderings would lead him tonight. "It time us go home, Sallie," she heard Willis George say to his wife, whose own eyes followed the darkness that had closed after Ol Trent.

Miss Varnes,

Received your latest notes and must say they are much improved. You have finally added voice to your observations. You have identified several characteristics that I did not see during my fieldwork among tenant farmers in Mississippi. I find them quite insightful and am intrigued by some of the terms you have recorded. Have sent them to a colleague who has done quite a bit of fieldwork in Sierra Leone and Gambia. We know from ship's logs that the departure ports for the slave ships were in West Africa. It is well documented that Charleston was the port of destination for these ships.

The film you sent has been developed. I reviewed it and was pleased to find that you possess a strong pictorial sense. The island is quite beautiful and the photo technicians are pleased with how the film responds to low light conditions. I see now why your benefactor has such an interest in the land. Am looking forward to your next set of notes.

Professor Colby

Amelia was thoughtful as she refolded the letter and put it back in its envelope with a sense of relief. She looked down at the two other letters in her lap, one from her mother and the other from Haagar. Deciding to deal with the difficult one first, she opened the letter from her grandmother, letting the return ticket slip to the floor. She reached down and waved it for Elizabeth to see.

"How many tickets is she gonna send?" Elizabeth asked.

"I guess her plan is to send one a month," Amelia mused.

"What you gonna do with all them tickets?"

"More book money." Amelia shrugged.

Despite their jokes, Elizabeth was well aware of the war of wills being waged between Amelia, Haagar, and Myown. She knew that behind Amelia's deliberately nonchalant air were real worries about her mother and her fragile health. In frustration, Amelia had shown Elizabeth the letters from her mother and her grandmother, each telling a different story.

My dear Amelia,

Things are goin as well as can be expect. The business has picked up some wit those show folks comin here when one of they freinds pass on. They a lively bunch. Some of they funerals almos like parties. I work most days now an it not bad. I get to talk to the people an offer comfort to the grieved. Even your granma surprise at how I take to it. She fuss forever bout you bein gone.

Folks always asking bout you. Want to know how you are. That young man stop by to see when you come back. I tell he you come back when you
finish the study. I tell he the study verry important work. You stay till you finish.

That it, this time. Give my love to Eula, Eli, an all they chilren. Give my love an a big hug to Iona on her flock. For you, you got my special love. Wrap it round you cause it will alway keep you safe.

Your loving mother,
Myown

Her grandmother's letter spoke to her in an altogether different tone.

Amelia,

Here another ticket to come home. You needed here not down there. What you do with the other tickets I send? Money don't grow on trees. I write this to let you know you mother is not doing so good. She think she doing fine, but she look poor. She don't want to say cause she afraid to worry you, but I speak the truth. The fixing fumes was too much for her and I sent her upstairs to help with the famlies. Folks seem to like her. Maybe they feel sorry for her cause her look so poor. We need you here. Come home now.

Your Granma,
Haagar Peazant

Amelia knew that her grandmother would use any excuse to bring her back to New York just as she knew her mother would hide the truth of her condition if she thought Amelia would drop her studies. She had decided to ask Eula's advice and had been shaken by her response.

Picking up the packet of Myown's letters, Eula had stated, "You mama say her wish her woulda sent you here long time back. Her sorry her could not make a better life for you up dere in New York."

Amelia was confused. "What do you mean? I didn't want for anything."

Eula soothed her. "A loving life is what her want for you. I dont know what all went on in you house, but you mama say her should have give you de family round you like her had growing up. Her say her read in you letters, an her can see you blossom in de family. Her want you to stay till you ready to come back."

Painful as it was, Amelia could see her mother's reasoning. Myown had sent her daughter to reclaim her family, entrusting to her a priceless gift.

Elizabeth watched as Amelia carefully put the letters and the ticket away. Amelia glanced at the envelope that sat in Elizabeth's own lap, raising her eyebrows encouragingly. Elizabeth slowly turned the letter over, half-afraid to open it.

Miss Genevieve had been so excited she could hardly wait for them to get into the house. For the first time in years, a shipment had arrived from France. For her own reasons, Miss Evangeline had insisted that they wait until Elizabeth came to unpack it. Even Katie, the young maid, who took little interest in what was going on in the house, was intrigued by the large crate. She hung by the doorway to the study, hoping to get a glimpse of the contents.

"Are you coming in here, Katie? Or are you going to hide out there in that hallway?" Miss Evangeline's sharp words sent Katie flying into the room to peer over Elizabeth's shoulders. When Elizabeth opened the crate and started pulling out hats, gloves, and fine lace collars, Amelia thought Katie's eyes would pop right out. Natalie wanted to thank everyone for her marvelous visit to America.

Katie stepped back when Miss Evangeline grabbed a small, prettily wrapped package and read "Katie." Katie stared at the package and then at Miss Evangeline, who impatiently waited for her to claim it. "Thank you, ma'am!" she exclaimed, cradling the gift.

"I'll be expecting you to send a thank-you note to Natalie. Bring it to me so I can check your spelling."

"Yes, ma'am," Katie responded as her fingers traced the edge of the purple and yellow ribbons that bound the package.

"Aren't you going to open it?" Amelia asked. Katie opened the package slowly as if she were afraid that something would jump out. They waited patiently as, with shaking hands, she carefully saved the ribbons and neatly folded the paper. She drew a length of cloth from the box and held it up. The purple watered-stained silk was marked with swirls of bright color and laced with gold thread. She stared at it in wonder.

"What I do wit dis?" she finally asked. Elizabeth frowned. The piece of cloth was too long for a neck scarf and there certainly was not enough to make a blouse or a dress.

"It's a head wrap." Amelia spoke slowly. She recognized it from the pictures she had seen in Professor Colby's office.

Elizabeth nodded, understanding immediately. "You wear it like a bandanna." Katie did not quite believe her; this piece of cloth was nothing like the head rags she wore.

"Why don't you try it on? I'll help wrap it, " Elizabeth offered. Katie shook her head quickly, peeping at the other packages that were being pulled from the crate.

Miss Genevieve beamed as she accepted a flat box wrapped in pale blue paper and crisscrossed with a piece of Belgian lace. She eagerly tore it open and gently laid aside the layers of tissue paper. "Oh, she has outdone herself this time!" she breathed, pulling an ivory satin bed jacket from the box. Elizabeth glanced over at Miss Evangeline, who ran her hands over the covers of the three books that Natalie had sent her. Miss Evangeline sighed with joy and held one up for Elizabeth to see. "I've so wanted to read her books." Elizabeth saw the author's name on the cover, "Colette."

Elizabeth pulled a small package from the crate with Amelia's name on it, and Amelia was as startled as Katie. She'd had so little contact with Natalie. Her surprise grew when she opened the package and found an elegant black-enamel fountain pen. "I'm afraid to use it!" she finally sputtered.

The next package was for Elizabeth, who opened it unhurriedly. An exquisitely shaped cobalt blue blown-glass perfume bottle lay nestled among the tissue paper. She lifted it carefully for the others to see. Removing the top, she spritzed a small amount on her palm. The others saw the happiness that rippled across her face when she closed her eyes and inhaled deeply of the scent. The sisters exchanged knowing glances while Amelia shivered with memories of a cobalt-blue night and a bright yellow full moon.

"What it smell like?" Katie asked. Elizabeth gestured for Katie to hold out her arm. After a second of hesitation, she thrust her arm out to let Elizabeth spray her. Her eyes widened as she sniffed. "Oh, dat sholl beat flower water!" she exclaimed.

Miss Evangeline peered into the crate. "Oh, here's something else for you, Elizabeth. Seems you got a letter." She pulled an envelope from the box and handed it to Elizabeth, eyeing it with curiosity. Elizabeth took the letter, pretended to show little interest, and put it aside as she turned her attention back to the perfume bottle. Miss Evangeline was a bit put out, until she spied three burlap-wrapped shapes left in the crate. "Gennie, she sent us wine!" she exclaimed, her interest in Elizabeth's letter disappearing immediately.

Now in the privacy of their room, Elizabeth peered inside the envelope and then, reaching in, pulled out several small squares of material. The color of the squares ran the spectrum of blue from sky-blue to deep navy. She handed the squares to Amelia and quickly read the letter.

My dear Elizabeth,
    The charms that you sent were more popular than either of us could have imagined. To my delight and Madame's barely disguised chagrin, they sold very quickly. I attached several of them to plain straw hats. They did not sit in the window long before two young women came in to buy them. One thing led to another, and then they had to buy outfits to go with the hats, quite the opposite way of going about things! We are off to an excellent start!
    We are beginning to work on this year's collection. Madame's designs will use a good deal of blue. I enclose samples from some of the material she has set aside. I will need as many as you can make. I have sent a bank draft. Please use half to buy the things you need. The other half is your portion of what we made from the sales. The ladies do love the tiny flowers! My best to you, Elizabeth. This is only the beginning.
                                                                                      Natalie

Elizabeth held up the bank draft, then handed it to Amelia.
    "One hundred dollars! She sent you one hundred dollars!" Amelia gasped.
    Elizabeth paced the floor in a daze, muttering, "She wants more! She said they were very popular!" Amelia sprang to her feet, waving the draft. Elizabeth giggled and they began clapping their hands together. She grabbed Elizabeth and whirled her around the room. Mischievously, she began to sing

> *Oh, Mary Mack, Mack, Mack*
> *All dressed in black, black, black*
> *With silver buttons, buttons, buttons*
> *All down her back, back, back.*

They were passing the draft between them, waving it above their heads, when they both jumped at a knock on the door. Elizabeth opened it and stepped back as Katie burst in.

"You fix this thing on my head?" Katie pleaded, holding the head wrap. She snatched her bandanna from her head, revealing short hair plaited in tiny neat rows. Elizabeth pointed to the foot of the bed, and Katie obediently sat down.

"What are you going to do with this?" Amelia asked, waving the bank note as Elizabeth began wrapping Katie's head.

"She wants more. That's why she sent the bits of material. I could get those pearl buttons I saw! And that real nice muslin with the blue flowers embroidered on it!'

Amelia was puzzled. "That's a lot of buttons and muslin."

Elizabeth unwrapped Katie's head and started again. "Oh, half of that is what she made selling my charms!"

"Book money!" Amelia announced.

Katie frowned up at Elizabeth. "What so funny?" she asked defensively.

"We're just talking, Katie," Elizabeth admonished her.

"I thought yall was pickin at my hair. I know I aint got dat much."

"You sit still an I'll get you all fixed up," Elizabeth assured her. She tried a couple of different wrap styles, relying on Amelia's nod or shake to guide her.

Finally, Amelia came over to help. "I saw something like this in a picture." She twirled the ends of the cloth and crisscrossed them over the front and tucked them under. Elizabeth nodded with approval, going to get the small hand mirror that sat on the nightstand.

She held it in front of Katie, who studied her image for several seconds and then announced with pride, "Well, looka here! Wait until Potter Early get a load of dis!" She frowned in indignation when Amelia and Elizabeth burst out laughing. Unfazed, she turned back to the mirror and smiled mischievously.

Elizabeth and Amelia strained and struggled as they lifted the old portrait of Burton Devries up the stairs to the attic. "Why are they putting him out after all these years?" Amelia asked when they stopped to catch their breath.

Elizabeth shrugged. "I don't know. Believe me, I ain't gonna miss having that ol man looking down on me!" They hoisted the portrait, turning it at an angle to fit through the door. When they set it against the wall, Amelia stepped back and stared at it. She studied the sharp-edged jaw and the glittering eyes that stared accusingly from the portrait. "Ain't that something?" Elizabeth commented, crossing to get a drop cloth to put over the portrait. "I can't believe how much he and Ol Jackson look alike." Amelia stepped back from the portrait. The likeness was startling. "Both pure evil from what I can tell!" Elizabeth remarked as she draped the cloth over the portrait. "He was long gone before I came to work here, but you could tell that this wasn't a happy house. Miss Genevieve jump at every sound, and Miss Evangeline get up all times of the night, just walking, back and forth."

She looked around the attic at the trunks and crates against the far wall. "I guess we can get to that trunk over there before it's time for us to go. Miss Evangeline say just throw out anything we can't set aside for the church." She crossed to the wall, followed by Amelia, who was plucking the trails of a spiderweb from her hair.

"I hate these things!" Amelia fretted, bending over to help Elizabeth pull the heavy steamer trunk from the wall.

Examining its rusted padlock, Elizabeth remarked abstractedly, "They good for stopping a cut from bleeding." Amelia shuddered with disgust.

Elizabeth stood up and looked around for something to spring the lock. While she searched, Amelia picked up an old rusted iron, walked over to the trunk, and began hitting the lock. "Gal!" Elizabeth swung around to admonish her, but stopped whatever she was going to say when the lock popped open. Amelia exaggeratedly wiped her hands, stepping back to look at her handiwork.

Elizabeth slid the trunk open, and they both admired the usefulness of its design, the side compartment for hanging suits and dresses, and the drawers for underwear and blouses. A single linen dress hung to the side, spotted with age. Elizabeth pulled out the drawers and exclaimed at her find. She lifted a silk peignoir from a pile of lingerie and shook it out, holding it up against her.

"That is beautiful, isn't it?" Amelia said admiringly.

Elizabeth whirled around the dusty space. "Elegant!" She danced gracefully, a grande dame, her head held high, her feet making swirling patterns on the dusty floor.

Even after living with her these past couple of months, Amelia only glimpsed sparks of the vibrant personality that lay behind Elizabeth's quiet, patient manner. Always solemn and purposeful, Elizabeth had Eli's knack for making a pointed comment, inflecting it with a humorous twist. Admiring Elizabeth's dedication to the children in her school, Amelia had taken to stopping by to help with the afternoon lessons. She shared Elizabeth's frustrations with the students who were not interested in their lessons and was delighted with her at the few who could not learn fast enough. They supplemented the meager supplies they received in inventive ways, buying brown paper to cover the cracked slate board and rolls of butcher paper to cut for the students' use. They had managed to find one book of fairy tales to add to the two reading books. She enjoyed the school outings as much as the children, laughing and cheering as Elizabeth led them in footraces along the beach.

Amelia found herself studying this cousin of hers, who seemed so self-contained. There was an air of distraction and restlessness that Amelia sensed as Elizabeth went about her duties. Elizabeth would fall into deep silences, moving quietly around the house and yard as she went about her chores. Uncomfortable with the silence, Amelia sought to draw Elizabeth into conversation. Elizabeth would respond in her own fashion, choosing her words carefully, divulging little beyond what was asked. Amelia noticed that Elizabeth rarely spoke of things in terms of herself and how she felt about things. She understood that it was not Elizabeth's nature to share her wishes or dreams.

Amelia puzzled over this young woman who would disappear for hours in the woods, collecting bits and pieces for her charms. She understood that these trips helped quell the nervous energy that threatened to overwhelm her cousin. Despite her quietness, Elizabeth was not a restive person. Several times Amelia had awakened at night to find Elizabeth gone from her bed. The first time she lay in the dark, waiting for Elizabeth to return. As the time passed, she rose to look for her. Wrapping her quilt around her, she stepped onto the porch and gazed into the darkness, listening for movement. It took her a while before she could see Elizabeth's dark form standing at the edge of the yard, staring out across the water. She had often seen Elizabeth in that spot during the day and wondered where she went as she looked across the water.

While Amelia had no doubts about Elizabeth's love for her family and her dedication to her students, she knew that Elizabeth was finding the return home difficult. She could not help but see the difference between Elizabeth and the other young women on the Island who spoke of little else but their husbands, babies, and church. As far as Amelia could tell, there were few eligible men on the Island, most of them having moved to the mainland for better wages. The rough crowd that hung around Carrie Mae's was out of the question for marriage, and Elizabeth showed little interest in childhood friends who were almost like brothers. Amelia wondered how it would be for her when she returned to New York. Surely she, too, had changed much since coming to the Island.

But Elizabeth had a whimsical, spontaneous side, and Amelia would see it at odd moments, digging for clams and oysters in the shallows for the beach picnic that Elizabeth had decided they would have, clambering up her favorite tree from childhood, or teasing Lucy unmercifully about her intended. It was that light side that now propelled her across the floor of the dusty attic, lifting her heart and loosening her limbs.

Amelia turned back to the trunk and pulled at another drawer. The drawer lurched out halfway before it stopped. "Something's caught in there. I can't see it, but I can hear it." Amelia looked at her broad hands and then at Elizabeth's smaller ones. "You've got little hands. Maybe you can stick your hand back there and pull it out." Elizabeth looked at her skeptically but slipped her hand into the space, seeking whatever it was that remained lodged there. With Amelia shaking the trunk and her reaching for it, the object finally slid down to where she could pull it free. She let it drop into the drawer, and then pulled firmly.

A packet of old photographs held together by a faded ribbon lay in the drawer. Elizabeth turned it over. The envelope that had held the photographs had long since fallen apart; bits of the brittle paper still clung to the photos. Although the pictures had darkened, one could still make them out.

Amelia picked up the kerosene lantern and brought it closer as Elizabeth held one photo under the light. Two women and two men sat at a table on a sidewalk, their glasses raised in a toast. A waiter stood behind them, only the white of his apron and towel visible. Elizabeth smiled. "I bet these are from when the Misses used to go to Paris."

She handed the image to Amelia and held up the next photograph, which showed the women strolling down a broad avenue lined with trees. Amelia had flipped the picture over, trying to read the florid handwriting on the back. It had faded quite a bit, and she held it in front of Elizabeth, who squinted as she tried to read it. "It's Miss Evangeline's handwriting, but . . ." She paused. "We need better light."

She handed it back to Amelia and then exclaimed at the next photograph. Miss Genevieve was dressed in an elaborate ball gown that swirled around her. Her hair was piled on top of her head with a circlet of flowers. Her sparkling necklace was perfectly set off by the décolleté of the gown. An expression of serenity could not hide the twinkle in her eye. "My, my, my, look at our Miss Genevieve." Elizabeth chuckled and handed the photo to Amelia, who shook her head and smiled.

The next photo was even more arresting. In contrast with her sister's bright gown, Miss Evangeline had chosen something dark with simple lines that flowed around her. Her hair was swept up and pinned with a single flower. She wore a black neckband that held a cameo. Unlike Miss Genevieve, she stared directly into the camera, provocatively. "She ain't changed one bit." Elizabeth spoke admiringly. "I bet she was something when she was younger."

They flipped through several photographs; Miss Evangeline wearing a smock and painting at the edge of a field, Miss Genevieve riding sidesaddle with a group of attractive people, the two sisters dressed for a costume party. Elizabeth sighed. "It must have been wonderful."

"When was the last time they went to Paris?" Amelia asked.

"I don't know. They stopped traveling before I came to work here."

Elizabeth's voice trailed off as she stared at the photograph in her hand. She then held it closer to the light and frowned. Amelia, puzzled by her reaction, peered at the photo. It was a group of people having dinner in a large restaurant. Miss Genevieve leaned forward, talking to the older man sitting next to her. Miss Evangeline smiled up at a man who stood behind her.

"One of her many beaus?" Amelia asked.

"I guess so," Elizabeth replied as she went through the other pictures. Her voice faded as she stared at a formal photo of Miss Evangeline and the man. Miss Evangeline glowed as she gazed into the camera. The man's hand rested on her shoulder. "This looks like a wedding picture," Amelia commented. "I thought she'd never married."

Elizabeth spoke slowly as she studied the picture. "Not that I know of."

Suddenly Elizabeth handed the photograph to Amelia. "What's wrong?" Amelia asked her.

Elizabeth walked back quickly and looked at the photograph. "That man," she said, pointing to the photograph.

Amelia studied the ordinary-looking man, stylishly dressed, projecting an air of confidence and possession. She was confused. "Lil Bet, I don't understand. You're going to have to tell me what's wrong!"

Elizabeth started to speak and then stopped herself, pointing to the photograph. "That looks like Ol Trent."

Amelia looked at her as if she'd lost her mind. She looked at the photograph again. "Lil Bet, this is a white man." She spoke calmly. "I mean, it doesn't make any sense. Why would Ol Trent be in Paris?"

Elizabeth spoke quietly. "I swear. This looks like Trent."

Amelia studied the man. He was swarthy in coloring and had thick, dark, wavy hair, but he was no darker than the Italian flower seller that Haagar had argued with for years. For the life of her, she could not see anything in this man in the photograph that reminded her of the shabby but neat figure who made his daily treks back and forth across the Island. "It just can't be."

Elizabeth turned away. "I remember listening to Nana and Miz Emma Julia talk about the Wilkersons. Nana say the boys could all go for white. All the Wilkerson men leave, leave the women to carry on. When I started up the school, I found some things there that had been left from years before, a few pictures of the students. The ladies that ran the school were good about sending pictures back to the folks who sent them money. They had pictures of the children reading, studying, pictures of those who graduated and went on to the mainland high school. I swear, this man is in one of those school pictures. This man is Ol Trent."

Elizabeth slowly extended her hand for the picture. Amelia handed it to her. She turned it over and held it close to the lantern. Miss Evangeline's notation had faded but for a few words. "What does it say?" Amelia asked. Elizabeth strained to read the sprawling French in the dim flickering light. "The happy couple." She sighed as she tried to discern the last few words. "I can't make out the rest of this."

"That was probably part of her trousseau." Amelia pointed to the peignoir that Elizabeth had folded and put back into the trunk. They avoided each other's eyes, both unwilling to continue examining the rest of the trunk's contents.

"It's almost time for us to head back home," Elizabeth said shortly, heading for the door.

Amelia agreed, picking up the lantern. "What do you want to do about these?" She pointed to the photographs sitting on the trunk.

Elizabeth turned impatiently and strode across the room. She hurriedly gathered up the photographs and stuck them in the trunk, closed it roughly, and began pushing the trunk back against the wall.

"We can't leave them up here like this for anybody to come across," Amelia said quietly.

"They been up here for who knows how long! Nobody come across them till now!" The trunk banged into the wall as Elizabeth turned to face Amelia.

Amelia picked up the lock she had sprung open. "I broke the lock. Anybody can get in there. It's nobody's business but hers."

Elizabeth turned and opened the trunk. "I'll give them to her," she said determinedly, reaching in for the photographs.

"What did she say when you gave her the photographs?"

Elizabeth shook her head quickly, never taking her eyes off Willis

George's hands as he rowed toward the Island. It was the first time either had spoken since they left the Bouvier house that afternoon. Elizabeth studied Willis's thick, short hands, noting the many tiny scars from repairing nets and pulling in traps.

"She didn't say a word," Elizabeth said calmly. "She and Miss Genevieve were drinking that wine Natalie had sent. She even offered me a glass when I first came in. It's probably the first time she ever thought of me as someone other than the little girl that worked for her." She was silent for a moment, tilting her head, looking up at the sky. She winced and then turned to Amelia. "Miss Genevieve kept going on about that wine. I was just standing there, waiting for Miss Evangeline to take those pictures." She gave a short laugh. "Amelia, I couldn't look at her. I just held them out to her, and when she finally took them, I walked out."

Amelia nodded sympathetically. She had waited outside for Elizabeth and had been extremely relieved when Elizabeth emerged from the house and climbed into the car. Both knew that this secret would remain in the Bouvier house.

Amelia leaned back in the boat and looked around at the other riders. There were all the regulars that she now knew. She remembered her first trip across, how they'd stared at her and she couldn't understand a word that they were saying. Now, they no longer saw her as a curiosity and greeted her with the familiarity they showed the rest of the Peazants. She smiled at a little boy who eyed the bag of hard candy sitting in her lap and handed him one.

"What you say?" his mother sharply reminded him. He barely got the "Thank you, ma'am" out around the piece of hard candy.

"You're welcome." Amelia responded.

At Willis George's shout, she held on to her seat as they began to move through the rough shallows toward the dock. When they drew closer, she could see a small figure sitting at the end of the pier. Willis George glanced up at the dock as he shouted instructions to J.C. When the figure stood up and waved, Willis George quickened the pace of the rowing. "Lil Bet, who is that?"

"That's Willis George's oldest, Amos. He a long way from home."

Both Elizabeth and Amelia saw the boy's agitation as he waited. Willis George pushed ahead without taking his eyes off his son. The boy wrung his hands and looked behind him at the woods. A large wave broke over the bow, and the passengers in front shrieked. J.C. started to say something to him, his words dying as he saw the expression on Willis George's face. Amelia watched as Willis George deliberately calmed himself and steadily and surely pushed his way to the pier.

As soon as the boat drew up beside the pier, he scrambled onto the dock and grabbed his son by the shoulders. "What wrong, boy?" J.C. and another man tied the boat to the pier and helped the passengers off. The boy turned and waved to the edge of the woods. Sitting in the sand, unnoticed, was his younger brother next to a large cloth-covered basket. The small boy stood up and tried to drag the basket through the sand. Willis George ran down the pier onto the sand, followed by Amos.

J.C. yelled after him, "What wrong, Willis?"

As the others clambered down the pier carrying their packages, Amelia and Elizabeth slipped by them and ran behind Willis George. He tore the cloth from the basket and reached in and pulled out the baby, who began to cry. Turning to his son, he asked, "Where your mama?"

Amelia and Elizabeth both heard his fearful reply as they ran up behind them. "She gone, Daddy."

"It been a long time since we had a baby in de house," Eula remarked as she fed Sugar. Both Eli and Rebecca shot her wary glances. She chuckled when she saw the expressions on their faces. "I didnt say I want another one." Eli visibly relaxed, turning back to his tool catalogue. "I just rememberin how good dey smell. Rebecca, come over look at dis baby. Her not gonna hurt you none."

Rebecca shook her head. "I already got a baby. I dont need no baby."

"Dis a real baby, chile, come over here an see how her smile at you!"

Rebecca dragged over as slowly as she could and was rewarded with a large burp when she arrived.

"Aint her precious?" Eula asked. The baby saw Rebecca and gurgled. "See, her like you, her talkin to you." When the baby blew bubbles, Rebecca looked at her in disgust. She moved close to her mother's side and stroked her arm. "I still your baby, Mama?"

Amelia and Elizabeth exchanged an amused glance as Eula leaned over and kissed Rebecca on the cheek. "Yes, you is. You always Mama baby."

Elizabeth got up and walked over to where Lucy held up Willis George's younger son in the tub as she bathed him. He was falling asleep as she washed him. "He just wore out!" Lucy said sympathetically. "Dat a long way for de two of dem to be draggin dat baby. Dey mama aint got a—" She quieted as Elizabeth hushed her, nodding toward Amos, who sat with Ben, helping him put the finishing touches to a new fishing pole. ". . . crumb of sense!" Lucy whispered, wrapping the little boy in a towel and lifting him from the tub.

"I don't know what's wrong with Sallie Lee," Elizabeth agreed as she helped Lucy dry the child.

Amelia came over. "How's he doing?" She stroked his head.

"He tired! You be tired, too! Comin all over from de other side!" Lucy snapped.

Amelia looked at Elizabeth. Lucy was in one of her moods, but Amelia did not care. "We brought them here!" she reminded Lucy.

Lucy glanced down at the little head that lay against her breast and softened. "Dat was a good thing yall did." She pulled one of Rebecca's old gowns over his head with Elizabeth's help.

Elizabeth said, "Well, with their daddy bout to have a fit, an the children tired and hungry, it was the least we could do."

Lucy shook her head in agreement. "Where you think Sallie gone?" Lucy asked.

"I dont know!" Elizabeth exclaimed. "I hope nothin happen to her in all this darkness."

There was silence, then Amelia spoke. "Maybe she went back to her folks on the mainland."

Lucy looked up at her. "What you know bout dat?"

Amelia explained, "We talked once. She told me about her family."

Lucy snorted, "Mmph! Dat what he get for bringin dat mainlander here! Dey dont—" She started to add more, but was stopped by Elizabeth's warning glance.

"Let me put him to bed." Elizabeth carried him over to the pallet and laid him down gently, pulling the quilt up over him and tucking it around him.

T ry as they might, neither Eula, Elizabeth, nor Amelia could sleep that night. Eula kept an ear out for Sugar, who, once dry and fed, fell soundly asleep. Rebecca had decided to reclaim her spot between Eli and Eula, much to Eli's consternation.

Elizabeth and Amelia lay next to each other in the darkness, both aware of the restless state of the other. While Amelia wondered what had happened to Sallie Lee, Elizabeth could not dispel the image of Trent and Miss Evangeline that had haunted her all day. She closed her eyes tightly, unsuccessful in willing her mind to a quiet place. Amelia also shifted under the covers, and then she stopped as she heard a noise on the front porch. She listened carefully, heard it again, and then nudged Elizabeth. "I think somebody's at the door," she whispered. Elizabeth sat up. The sound came again. Elizabeth got up, wrapped herself in her mother's shawl, and lit a kerosene lantern. She padded to the door with Amelia right behind her.

Slowly opening the door, Elizabeth whispered loudly, "Who out there?"

From the darkness came, "It me. Willis George. Me and Sallie." Holding the light in front of her, Elizabeth stepped out onto the porch. When Amelia followed her, Elizabeth held the light higher and saw Willis George on the bottom step and Sallie standing a few feet away from him, turning from the light as it lit up the yard.

"Everything all right?" Elizabeth asked.

"We come to get de chilren, Lil Bet. I wanna thank yall for taking care of dem." Willis did not look into her eyes. Amelia stepped back out of the light when she saw Willis's discomfort. She glanced over at Sallie Lee, who stood with her arms wrapped around her to ward off the morning cold. Willis stepped onto the porch.

Now Eula appeared in the doorway. "Willis?"

"How do, Eula. Sorry to disturb you. I come to get my babies." Willis spoke humbly.

Eula looked up at him. "Where Sallie Lee?"

He gestured without looking. "She right dere."

Eula peered at her. "She all right?"

"Yes, ma'am," he said too quickly. She looked at him for a long time. Eula had always had a soft spot for this cousin who was raised with her younger sisters and brothers. It was all Willis George could do not to turn away from the sympathy that shone in Eula's eyes.

Finally she spoke. "It real late. Why dont yall go on home an come back an get de chilren when it daytime?" When Willis started to protest, Eula quieted him. "Dey sound asleep. Aint no need to get dem up an be stumblin through de dark wit dem. Let dem stay here, an yall go on home an get your rest."

Willis turned to Sallie, who did not look at him, giving no sign that she had heard a thing Eula said. "I dont want to put you out no more, Miz Eula."

Eli spoke from the darkness at the edge of the porch. "Willis, three more chilren aint gonna make no difference. You got some business you need to take care of."

Willis nodded to Eli and turned to the women on the porch. "I thank

yall, Eula, Lil Bet, an young Miss right dere. Yall done we a good turn."
He nodded to them and went down the porch steps.

Eula stepped forward. "Willis, you aint got to get dem chilren in de
morning. If you an Sallie need a coupla days to work things out, dey
welcome to stay."

He hesitated and shook his head. He walked up to Sallie and spoke
quietly to her. Willis and Sallie stood there for a moment in what appeared to be a war of wills. Abruptly Sallie walked up to the edge of the
porch. They waited for her to speak. Without looking up at them, she
finally spoke tonelessly. "I thank you for looking after the chilren." Eula
nodded sympathetically. As Sallie turned away, she looked at Amelia,
who stood in the dark. Amelia stepped back from the fierce anger that
shone in Sallie's eyes.

They stood there and listened as Willis George and Sallie Lee made
their way toward home. Eula put her arms around Elizabeth and
Amelia. "Yall better get on back to bed." She gently pushed them into
the house. "You coming, Eli?"

Eli stepped onto the porch. "Ima stay out here for a while." He
pulled the door shut after them, then sat in the chair. Standing in the
dark, he had seen everything that could go wrong between a man and a
woman. Knowing the whole of this kind of pain, he would not have
wished it on anyone, especially Willis George.

From the first time he had set eyes on Willis George, a solemn six-
year-old with his name and destination pinned to his rough clothes, Eli
knew this boy for the man he would become. Eli and Eula's brother,
Charles, had gone to the station to pick up this child sent back to his
mother's people after she died by a stepfather eager to move on. Although Willis George must have been starving and frightened by the
long journey he had just completed, he had not complained or cried
when Eli and Charles decided to stop at the juke joint on the way back.
They returned a couple of hours later to find him curled up in the back
of the wagon, shivering in the cold, patiently waiting for them. Eli
would never forget the scolding that Eula's mother put on him and
Charles when they got back. It was a whole week before Eula would let
him come back around. Eula's mother had gotten some fierce satisfaction by sending Willis George with him and Eula wherever they went.
Even now, Eli had to smile at how seriously Willis George took this
chore.

Eula had been the one to reach out to Willis George, who seemed
lost in the swirl of younger sisters and brothers. Early on, she sensed his
need for family and made sure that he was never left out. It had not surprised her at all that Willis George had chosen to stay on the Island

while the others couldn't wait to leave for Savannah and other parts. Eula even understood his choice of a wife, which was something that Eli just couldn't get his mind around.

Eli leaned back in the chair as the essence of his wife settled around him. After all this time, she could still catch him unawares; it was unsettling the way her image could come to him. Eula had always been the constant in his life. Eli did not fool himself for one second. At times, her goodness had tried him, and in turn, he had tried her. But after all they had been through, she had remained true to herself. It had angered Eli, but it had also been his salvation. He knew well the foolish route a man's hurt and anger could take, and Eula had gone every step of that route with him.

Eli still carried a good bit of that sorrow and regret from when he had doubted Eula the most, when she carried Elizabeth, their firstborn. At times, he could still feel the rage and helplessness that had all but consumed him until he first held his Lil Bet in his arms. He took it as his lifelong punishment for having had so little faith.

Eli braced himself as a cold breeze swept across the porch. It wasn't going to do him any good sitting out here in the cold, bringing all that old business back up. It was all a man could do to keep his family safe. As he secured the door behind him, Eli could only hope that Willis George would find a way.

Amelia moaned when Lucy shook her awake. She hoped that Lucy had forgotten her promise from the night before, but she knew better. Sometime during the evening, she had offered to help Lucy plant the bean and corn seeds for the spring. To her surprise and Elizabeth's amusement, Lucy had accepted her offer. All the other times, Lucy had fixed her with a skeptical look and politely, too politely, declined her offer. Lucy shook her shoulder again. "Come on, gal. We can get in a good hour fore Mama have breakfast ready!"

She sat up and glowered at Lucy, who was slipping into her clothes. Although it was almost sunrise, it was still quite dark outside. No matter how used she got to Island life, she did not like getting up in the dark. She slowly began to get dressed. By the time she found her shirt, Lucy was ready and headed out the door to get water to wash up. Elizabeth shifted, pulling the covers over her head. "She better not be laughing," Amelia said to herself as she noticed the covers shaking slightly.

Amelia put the shirt on, then grabbed the old pants that Lucy had

found for her the night before and began to slide into them. Lucy
came in with the bucket. "You aint dressed yet?" she asked, crossing to
the dry sink. Amelia let out a deep sigh, sure that she had heard a snort
or giggle from Elizabeth. Lucy washed quickly, energetically splashing
the water. She thrust the washcloth at Amelia, lit the lantern, and
headed for the door. "I gonna get the seed, the planting sticks, and the
hoes. I be waiting outside for you," she assured Amelia with an unnatu-
ral gleam in her eye.

Amelia hobbled over to the dry sink and washed slowly, delicately. As
Elizabeth burrowed deeper into the covers, Amelia put on her shoes
and socks, hurrying as she heard Lucy returning. She grabbed her
jacket and stumbled for the door.

Lucy stood in the yard, looking up at the morning star. Amelia
came up behind her. "How we go see what we doing?" she asked
indignantly.

Lucy held up the lantern. "We got light, gal! Sun come up real soon.
It be broad daylight in a hour!" Lucy stepped off to the fields with
Amelia skipping to keep up with her.

Several hours later, Amelia staggered to the edge of the field and
wearily leaned against a tree. They had finally planted the last seed for
both fields. She had suspected that Lucy was a taskmaster, but she had
not known that Lucy was merciless. It was not as if she had not gar-
nered her fair share of sympathy and curiosity. Everyone but Elizabeth
had stopped by. Eula had come to call them for a breakfast that Amelia
could not even remember. Eli brought them water. During the short
break, he and Lucy discussed the best type of fertilizer for the beans.
The twins and Amos watched from the edge of the field as Lucy had ordered them and then decided to play in the woods. Rebecca had
brought her dolls for a visit and sat patiently on a tree stump watching
them as they trudged along, Amelia dropping seed and Lucy covering
it with the hoe. At one point, she had heard the sound of the movie
camera and spied Ben diligently recording the occasion.

"It have to do," Lucy announced as she walked up to Amelia after
inspecting their work. She peered from under the brim of her hat
at Amelia's dirt-streaked face. "You look like you could do with some
supper."

Amelia agreed, pulling the bandanna from her head and wiping her
face. "I'm starving."

Lucy began gathering the tools. "A good morning's work will do dat
to you." They slowly walked across the even rows. When they reached
the end of the field, Lucy looked back. "Aint dat pretty?"

Amelia gazed at the neatly cultivated land that had caused her so much pain. Tired, she offered, "If you say so." Lucy looked at her and laughed. They walked back to the house in silence, Lucy waiting for Amelia when she lagged behind.

Elizabeth sat on the front porch feeding the baby. She kept her face blank as they came into view. Willis George's smaller son was playing with Rebecca, but when he saw Lucy come up the road, he took off running to her. She handed the tools to Amelia and swung him up into her arms, laughing that he remembered her from the night before. She waved to Elizabeth and went around to the back to wash up at the pump. Amelia walked up to the porch with a defiant glare, tossed the tools on the ground, and sat down on the bottom step to take her shoes off. Elizabeth fussed over the baby while Amelia dumped dirt from her shoes and shook her socks out. "Becca, could you get me a cool drink of water?" she asked.

"Yall git the field planted?" Elizabeth ventured.

"Mm-huh!" Amelia answered coolly.

"It a good day for plantin," Elizabeth commented.

"How would you know?" Amelia countered. "I didn't see you no-where near that field."

"De all stopped by to see how you were holding up," Elizabeth said as Rebecca returned with the dipper of water.

Amelia drank slowly, then fixed an insincere smile on Elizabeth. "Everybody but you!" Amelia dared her cousin to laugh as Elizabeth's eyes slid from the spikes of hair sticking up to the raw edges on Amelia's foot.

"Yall come on in an help me set up supper," Eula called from the kitchen.

Elizabeth stood up with the baby, but Amelia made it to the door before her. "You could have warned me!" she hissed as she slid into the house.

Amelia's eyes drooped and she yawned through the entire meal. It took her so long to pass a dish that the family quickly devised an alternate route around her. Eli glanced down at Amelia's bare feet. "That some pretty work yall did. Yall got it all done this morning."

Lucy nodded as she ate and fed the little boy. "I figure it take us de whole day, but Amelia work good once you get her going."

Lucy stood up with Willis George's little boy and carried him over to the basin to wash up. She wiped his hands and face and put him down.

He ran over to where his brother and the twins were eating by the fire-place. She stretched and then came back to the table. "We got to get going. You ready?" she asked Amelia.

Amelia slowly opened one eye and looked at her. "What?" Elizabeth started coughing.

"Since we got through so fast, we can get started on plowing dat piece of land I want to use down at the Wilkerson place."

Amelia croaked, "Plowing . . ."

Eula spoke up. "Lucy, I . . ."

"Mama, could you pass me the cornbread?" Elizabeth interrupted.

Eula handed her the bread without missing a beat. "Lucy, I think that Amelia done enough for today. Her looks real worn out." Lucy turned to Amelia, genuinely sympathetic. "You too tired to help me this afternoon? You can stay right here with Mama an get your rest."

Amelia looked up at her, seeing nothing but worry in her eyes. With more determination than she felt, Amelia stood up slowly. "Let's go get that field plowed."

"Gee-up! Move, Homer!" When Lucy shook the reins, the mule moved forward almost eagerly, Amelia sourly observed from her stump by the road. She watched as Lucy expertly guided the mule, straighten-ing the crooked row that Amelia had just completed. Amelia and Homer had regarded each other with mutual suspicion from the very beginning, and despite Lucy's instructions, Amelia had been dragged across the field from the moment she stepped behind the plow. Homer seemed to respond to Lucy's voice alone and had come to a reluctant halt only after Lucy had shouted to him. Amelia quickly handed the reins over to Lucy while Homer stood by, nervously watching Lucy out of the side of his eye. Taking the reins with a firm hand, Lucy checked Amelia for injuries. She seemed to be all right, aside from a few abra-sions and bruises. "Go on over dere an rest a while. I got it." Lucy pointed to the fallen tree by the side of the road.

Amelia thankfully escaped, stumbling across the field. She looked around this piece of land that meant so much to Lucy. The old Wilker-son place was split by the dirt road that ran across most of the Island. Evidently, in its day, it had been a large plantation, worked by many captives. One could still see the fire-scorched foundation stones of the Big House on the far edge of the pasture.

On their way to the meadow Lucy had pointed out the vine- and weed-covered ruins of small shacks. "Dat where the captives live. When we was lil, we play over dere an find all kinds of ol pots an jugs." There were a couple of leaning outbuildings held together by a nail or two.

"The Wilkersons owned all this?" Amelia asked.

"No, dey got deir forty acres. Trinity Wilkerson was de cook for de Sykes family. Dey own de plantation. When de War come, dey run, an Trinity stay an cook for de Yankees. Come de end of de War, dey give her forty acres, an her get de best land she find. Her get de piece where de road run. Her got easy water, creek go cross de back. Her know de land. Her born right here." Lucy spoke with admiration. "Dat meadow, it rich land. Grass grow so thick and green. I know I can get two, three of de yield I get from Daddy's land."

"Any family left other than Ol Trent?" Amelia asked.

Lucy nodded. "Dey scattered all over de place from what I can tell. One of de girls live down in Savannah. It she Charlie and me buyin de land from. Her handle all de family business."

"She ever come back?"

Lucy snorted. "Naw, all dem Wilkersons, dey leave for good. Everybody surprise when Trent come back. But him in a bad way." Lucy stopped and with her arm, swept the land before them. "Aint it beautiful? I clare it de prettiest bit of land roun here!"

Amelia followed her view. The field stretched before them, a brown carpet with clumps of green grass popping up all over. She could see the silvery shimmer of running water from the creek that ran to the north of the field. On the other side of the road, the field was a thicket of swamp grass, saplings, and vines.

Lucy knelt and grabbed a fistful of soil, inspecting it. "Dis here de bit we buyin. I burnt this back last summer fore you got here. Clear out all dem weeds, crazy grass, an young trees. It come long real good." She shook the dirt from her hand and stepped back to straighten the harness on the mule.

Not knowing how else to begin, Amelia blurted, "Lil Bet said the Wilkerson men can go for white."

Lucy shrugged. "Dey was gone when we was comin up." She thought for a second. "Ol Trent, him do look like any other ol cracker, though."

"What about their sister, the one you're going to buy the land from?" Amelia asked.

"I aint never seen she. My Charlie him take de money to she every coupla months an bring de receipt to me, but him dont say nothin bout she." Lucy tightened the belt strap and ran her hand along Homer's spine. "You aint getting nuttin till you put in a full day work!" she fussed.

When Lucy finished the row and turned the plow to start down the next, Amelia could see the pleasure in her face as she admired her handiwork. Lucy had all of the wiry energy of the Peazants and then some. Amelia marveled at how Lucy knew exactly what she wanted and was going after it in her typically determined fashion. Lucy never seemed to have an unsure moment or make a false step. She had heard her mother talk about old folk sense and was sure Lucy had plenty. She had met Lucy's Charlie and could not imagine two people so completely different in personality and so perfectly suited for each other. Whereas everything about Lucy was sharp, from her mind to her tongue to the sharp angles of her body, Charlie was soft, with a voice so low one could hardly hear him speak, a pleasant rounded face, and an easygoing personality that adored Lucy. They were completely at ease with each other, and Charlie could make Lucy blush with pleasure. Amelia had seen the ferocious pride and love in Lucy's eyes when she showed off the piece of land where she and Charlie would build their house.

Amelia looked down at her dirty hands, the chipped nails, and the new callouses. She had no illusions about how hard life on the Island was. Every day but Sunday was filled with chores from morning to night, and the days seemed much longer than up North. Eli and Eula had few amenities, and that was probably more than their neighbors. On her visits to other homes, she had helped the women haul water from the creek, shelled corn for chicken feed, and written down recipes for making candles and soap from tallow. Amelia understood that the prospect of relief from the everyday struggle was what drove people to leave the Island. Those that had stayed behind found comfort in the simplicity of their life, and Amelia truly understood its appeal. As she sat on the log, bruised, dirty, and tired, she lifted her face to the warm sun and took a deep breath of the sweet, clean air.

Reluctantly her mind turned to the thought of her return to New York. She had gathered so much information, and now it was time to put it all together in her thesis. She dreaded going back to that apartment over the funeral home with the three souls in conflict. She missed her mother badly and would always feel great guilt for having left her to deal with Haagar and her father. Desperate to make this up to Myown, she had a half-formed plan, vague thoughts of finding a place for her and her mother to live when she got back. Amelia knew that it would cause an uproar, but she knew how important it was to find a place, that place where one could be oneself, accepted and loved.

Her thoughts were interrupted by Lucy's scream. Alarmed, she stood up as Lucy backed away from the plow and began running. At first,

Amelia thought that Lucy had come across a snake, but as she watched Lucy run in wild patterns, waving and screaming, Amelia knew that no snake would send her haring across the field like that.

"Lucy!" Amelia shouted and took off after her. Lucy slipped on the grass and fell to her knees, sobbing and choking. When Amelia caught up with her, Lucy fought her off, trying to get away.

Amelia grabbed Lucy's wrists and shook her. "Lucy! What is it, Lucy?"

Lucy collapsed against her, unable to hold her head up. Trembling violently, Lucy pointed back to where the mule waited patiently for her to return. "It evil! It evil back dere!" She bent over clutching her stomach.

Amelia stared at her, then got up slowly and walked back to where the mule stood. As she approached, he moved forward to a clump of grass and started chewing. She carefully walked around him to the last spot that had been plowed. She stared at the spot, then kneeled down and looked at an object that the plow had uncovered. She felt her heart begin to pound as she brushed the dirt from a pair of rusted shackles, a chain running from them into the ground. Despite her misgivings, she grabbed a jagged-edged stick that lay in the furrow and began to dig. As she continued burrowing into the earth, her eyes filled with tears as she recognized a human leg bone. Dropping the stick, she jerked away and walked around to the front of the plow and saw, at last, what had sent Lucy spinning. A piece of skull was impaled on the front blade; a jaw-bone with several teeth lay in the scattered earth. She backed away and ran over to Lucy, who was curled on the ground, crying. She pulled Lucy up, slipped her arm around her waist, and half-carried her home.

Amelia sat on the front porch and stared out into the night. She waited for Eli, Ben, and the other men to return. Elizabeth stepped onto the porch, handed her a cup of hot tea, draping a quilt across her shoulders.

"You get all that dust washed out of your hair?" Elizabeth asked.

Amelia nodded.

"Mama say you should eat."

"How's Lucy?"

"She quiet some." Elizabeth sighed. "But she still shakin like a tree. Mama sittin with her." She pulled a stool away from the wall and sat next to Amelia.

Elizabeth looked up at the dark night. The moon lay behind thick clouds, and there was not a star in the sky. Perhaps that rain she had been smelling for two days would finally arrive. In answer to her thoughts, she heard the splatter of the first few drops of rain on the tin roof. Amelia snuggled down into the quilt as the rain blew across the front porch. "They'll be coming home soon if it picks up," Elizabeth commented. As Amelia listened to the sound of the rain, her eyes began to droop. Elizabeth could feel her hand relax as her breathing slowed. Amelia slipped into the sleep of the exhausted, and Elizabeth could only hope that Lucy would soon succumb to the same.

Elizabeth now remembered the time when Lucy had announced that she wanted to buy the meadow on the old Wilkerson place. Elizabeth had come home from school on the mainland to help bring in the crops. A couple of Lucy's friends had joined them to gather up the crop. They had just finished filling the baskets of potatoes and beets and were waiting for Eli to come back with the wagon. The young girls had been teasing each other about the boys who had left to go swimming in the creek. Elizabeth stood apart from them, her seventeen-year-old mind amused at the giggling and the fantasies of the thirteen-year-old girls.

"When I get married, I gonna have a big ol party! Everbody gonna come, an we gonna cook a pig an eat an eat an eat!" Ernestine Palmer proclaimed.

"I gonna do like my sister, an run off to Savannah wit a fancy man." The girls pretended to be shocked at Janie Bowen's declaration, then burst out laughing.

"I going to live wit my cousins in Bofort. Dey live in a big ol house wit lots of people," another girl put forth. One girl expressed the wish for three pair of shoes and two Sunday dresses.

Elizabeth was rapidly losing attention when Ernestine turned to Lucy. "What you gonna do, Lucy?"

Lucy thought for a moment. "I gonna buy dat meadow over dere on de Wilkerson place," she said firmly. The girls hooted, "De Wilkerson place! Why you wanna do dat? Chile, where you gonna get de money to buy dat?"

"I almos gots it worked out." She hesitated as they looked at her skeptically. "I do a bit of croppin for my daddy."

"Gal, you work de land for you daddy for free now! Why him let you crop for he?" Ernestine indignantly pointed out.

"Him got he smithing." Lucy shrugged. "Him like de smithing more dan workin de crops. I tell he dat I do de bean an corn, an iffen he let me, I work de lil strip down by de woods an put in some peppers an onions an he let me keep what I make from dem."

Elizabeth was startled by Lucy's clear thinking. Lucy knew their father well, and that he much preferred his smithing to farming. Lucy and Elizabeth had heard him say many times that he thought he could do better smithing and renting his land out to someone. But everyone on the Island owned their land, and with eight mouths to feed, he could not risk depending only on his smithing.

"How you do dat all by youself? You aint no bigger dan a squito," Janie accused Lucy. "Who gonna help you?"

"I caint do it now, but by de time I finish school, I be ready," Lucy admitted. "I can plow half a field now bout good as Daddy!"

Janie snorted. "What about bringin in de crop? It take all us jus to do dis!"

"Dat right," Lucy agreed. "I think yall be needin money to marry, go over to Bofort, and buy dem shoes, an soda water."

Lucy had been true to her word. Upon returning from the mainland school, she and Eli had argued about her schooling. He had wanted her to follow in Elizabeth's steps, and she would have none of it. It was then that she hit Eli with her proposition, which he rejected immediately. He knew that she was good at garden plots, but had never really worked a field from plowing to harvest. He could not risk the family earnings from the farm. Eula worried that it was too much hard work for her, and Eula could not help much with the twins underfoot and Becca on the way. However, over the next few months, she had worked on him and Eula, and they had all agreed on a compromise. The first year, Eli and Lucy would work the land together, planting and sowing. Lucy would tend the fields through harvest, and if there was enough money from the crops, Eli would buy her seed and let her work the little strip by the woods. Whatever she raised and sold, she could keep, but she still had to work the large crop with Eli. Elizabeth knew that the first year had been disappointing, with too much rain drowning many of the seedlings and the hot sun baking the rest, but the next year had been better. Three years into the agreement, both Eli and Lucy were satisfied. Eli was known to brag about Lucy's farming skills and her ability to get good prices.

Lucy had been set on that meadow for years, and Elizabeth was deeply worried that today's discovery had crushed Lucy's dreams. Elizabeth heard the clop of Homer's hooves as he came up the path leading to the yard. Ben slid wearily from the mule's back and waved to her as he passed to lead it to the stable.

Elizabeth got up and went into the house. Lucy had finally fallen asleep, still shuddering in her dreams. "They on they way back," she said softly.

"Dat potion you make for she put she down," Eula replied. "How Amelia?"

"She sleeping, too," Elizabeth reassured her mother.

They heard a step on the front porch, and Eli entered, soaked through. He took off his hat and shook the water from his clothes. Eula grabbed soft, dry clothes and went over to help him dry while Elizabeth poured him a cup of coffee. He stepped out of his boots and walked over to the fireplace to warm himself. Elizabeth had never seen her father look so gray, so fatigued, so old.

Ben came in and swayed on his feet; Eula quickly handed him the cloths to dry. "Amelia gonna catch cold out dere," he said.

"She was trying to wait up for yall," Elizabeth explained as she went to wake Amelia and bring her in.

Eli turned to Ben. "You get yourself something to eat an get right in that bed."

"Yessir." Ben trudged to the stove, where their dinner waited.

Eula slipped Eli out of his wet jacket and shirt, briskly rubbing him as he sipped the hot coffee. As their eyes met, she gently asked, "Who do you think he was?"

Eli shook his head, dazed. "Was three of dem from what we dug up." He turned from the horror in Eula's eyes and dropped into the chair. "Three of dem, tied together like dogs."

Amelia covered her face with her hands as Elizabeth, fighting tears of her own, put an arm around her.

Eli, his head buried in his hands, spoke tonelessly. "We keep looking tomorrow."

The pilgrimage began at day clean and kept up all day. They came from all over the Island. Amelia had no idea how quickly word could spread until she saw the men, women, and children passing the house on their way to the old Wilkerson place. Walking together in small groups or singly, she saw the quiet purpose in their stride and noticed that even the children were subdued. The older folks made their way, leaning on canes or on the arms of their children and grandchildren. She thought that in her months on the Island, she had met, or at least seen, just about everyone, but there were a few who came that surprised even Eula.

"Lord, have mercy!" Eula exclaimed as a cart drew close to where she and Amelia stood by the road. The man driving the wagon waved to them and pulled over. "Aubrey! I havent seen you since Christmas two years ago."

The man smiled easily. "How do, Eula? It been a while, aint it?" He gestured to the back of the cart. "Muh-dear have to come." Eula ran to the back of the cart.

A feeble hand reached out, and she grabbed it and leaned down, bringing it to her face. "Miz Emma Julia, I think about you all de time! You looking good."

"Dont start dat lying. I old, gal! Look like de ol cooder!" A surprisingly strong voice spoke from the cart. Eula smiled at her, then grew solemn. "Seem like de only time I see Nana's ol friends is at deir funerals."

"Aint dat many lef, gal. Us have de time de good Lord give." Eula nodded. "How Lucy?" Miz Emma Julia asked abruptly.

"Her in a bad way."

Miz Emma Julia spat out, "She come across dat evil buried out dere in dat field!" She looked at Eula ferociously. "It up to we to make it right! Us got to claim our own, take dem back from de buckra!"

Eula agreed. "You sound like my Nana."

"Us all of de same spirit!" Miz Emma Julia snapped.

Amelia peered into the cart at the tiny, wrinkled woman who lay on a pile of quilts. "Amelia, dis Miz Emma Julia, one of Nana's closest friends." Amelia stared at the woman she had assumed was dead, then remembered her manners and reached forward and gently took her hand. "This Haagar grandbaby."

Miz Emma Julia immediately dismissed her with a wave. "Where dat Lil Bet? Dats my gal!"

"She at de school wit the chilren."

Miz Emma Julia nodded with satisfaction. "She always de smart one." Her eyes swept over Amelia, appraised her. "Aubrey, we got to get on over dere!" she ordered. "Yes, maam." Aubrey shook his reins, and the horse started forward. "Yall walkin wit us?" Miz Emma Julia asked.

"We fixin supper for de men. We be along in a bit." Eula waved them on.

Eula and Amelia returned to the house to pack the food. Lucy lay in her bed with her back to the room. Amelia could just barely make out her breathing. When they finished packing the food, Eula asked, "You think you can manage this? I dont want to leave she here an de baby still sleeping." Amelia had forgotten that Willis George's baby was still there. Willis George had arrived at daybreak to get his children, but when he heard what Eli was doing, he had immediately gone to help. Elizabeth had taken Rebecca and the two boys to school with her so Lucy could rest. Amelia picked up the basket and the jug of water and headed to the meadow.

Approaching the area, Amelia could see the crowd of people who watched Ben and another young man dig from a shallow trench. Babies clung to their mothers, who fingered their charms as they stared at the array of bones and shackles displayed on a couple of quilts spread next to the trench. Young men stood by, their usual bravado gone, their faces showing sadness and a hint of fear. A group of people knelt in fervent prayer, while a woman wailed loudly into her apron. Amelia spoke to Carrie Mae and Toady, who had arrived with a group that she recognized from the juke joint. Carrie Mae shook her head and patted her heart as Ben reached down and pulled something from the trench and examined it; Toady looked grim as Ben walked over and gently laid the item on the quilt. Amelia looked for Eli, who was talking quietly with Willis George and another man. Ol Trent made his way through the group to the edge of the trench, squatted down, peering into the furrow. He stood up and walked away, waving and muttering.

There was a low murmur when Miz Emma Julia's cart pulled up as close to the quilts as possible. Eli, Willis George, and another man halted their muted discussion as Aubrey slipped from the cart and hesitantly approached the quilts. There was a collective gasp when he bent down to examine the bones and shackles. At a sharp command from Miz Emma Julia, Aubrey grabbed the shackles, picked up a piece of skull, and took it back to the cart. Miz Emma Julia pulled herself into a sitting position and took the shackles and skull from Aubrey, turning them over in her hands. Shaking the dirt and rust from the shackles, she rubbed them until there appeared a faint imprint in the worn iron. She gestured to Elizabeth. As Elizabeth stepped forward, Miz Emma Julia shoved the piece at her, asking, "What dat say?"

Elizabeth scratched more dirt away with her fingernail and read, "The Sorcerer."

Miz Emma Julia snatched the piece from her and threw it to the ground, spitting. "De Sorcerer!"

A gasp went up from the group. One of the older men cried, "Lord, dont let dat evil come back on we!"

Miz Emma Julia's eyes swept the crowd, taking in the fear on the faces of the older folks and the curiosity in the eyes of the younger ones. She glared at one young girl. "What you know bout de Sorcerer, gal?"

The girl stuttered, then said almost defiantly, "I aint never heard of no Sorcerer!"

Miz Emma Julia took a step toward the girl, who shrank back into the group. "Fools! All yall fools, dont got no kind of sense of who you is an what all went on on dis land fore you got here!" She turned to Elizabeth. "Tell dem, gal! Tell dem bout de Sorcerer!"

Elizabeth spoke quietly, "Caint nobody tell it like you, Miz Emma Julia."

Nodding, Miz Emma Julia stood straight up as she swelled with the importance of the task at hand.

The Sorcerer

as told by Miz Emma Julia

Yes, chilren. Yall always talkin bout how hard things is. Yall tink it bad today cause de buckra snatchin ever lil bit you got. Wont hardly let you have nuttin! Least yall got sometin to snatch! Yall tink it hard workin de fields all day to feed you families. Dey you fields! I hear yall fussing bout how yall aint got dis or dat, dont wanna do dis an dat. Yall dont know what de hard life is! Cant do nuttin but what dey tell you, when dey tell you, an how dey tell you! Belong to dem like a ol cow or some chickens. Dont have no self to call you own! Yall done forgot de ol ways, an dat, chilren, what brung us through de worse! De ol ways help make it better, an I dont care what yall say, it a whole piece better now den it was when I was comin up!

Dem bones dere, dem captives never get to see what you see, never have what you have! Dont know what it like to walk dis land free, drink de sweet water from de creek, eat de wild berry grow in de grass, lay under de sycamore tree an jus lissen to de wind blow! Dey come over on *de Sorcerer* an knew nuttin but misery, pain, an death!

Dis happen before de Big War! Dis de War when de Yankees come down here to let we go! Show folks down here dey wasn't playing! Dere wasnt supposed to be no more sellin of de captives! The Yankees told dese folks so! How I know dat? De word come down from de man dat take care of de Big House in Bofort. I never figger de buckra out. Dey ack like us aint got eyes to see, ears to hear, an a min to put somptin together! Us everwhere, hear everting. De mistress her tell Aunt Rose dat all dat Yankee stuff is just some foolishness. Dese white folk tink dat what dey say, us blieve is! Like us aint got no kinda sense!

Well, dis captive him say de folks in de Big House all worry cause de Yankees say dey got to stop bringin de captives from cross de big water. Now dey was makin good money off dis lan we work, an de Massa Loren want to buy another big place down dere on Edisto. Only ting was him need more captives to work dat place.

Dey was a man, Montgomery Baxter. Him one of de big runners for de captives. I seen dis man, he a big man wit eyes cold as de winter water. Him a greedy man, always want more dan he have. Him like de lil pig push de others away to get he milk. Now, lemme tell you bout de ways of de buckra! Dey mighty particular, dont even like dey own. Call dem crackers, po white trash. De big buckra like Massa Loren, dey call on dem ol crackers to do dat work might bring down de law. Long as dey need de crackers, dey callin on dem. Use de cracker to keep de captive down. But dey dont need dem, dey aint got nuttin to do wit dem ol crackers!

Montgomery Baxter, him a cracker from way back, but dey need him to go get more captives from cross de big water. He a greedy man, an he a smart man. He tell dem dey got to make he a boat dat big enough to carry de captives an fast enough to run if de Yankee come after he. Everbody know de Yankees put boats out dere to stop dem from bringin in de captives an what all else dey try to sneak in. So dey make de boat, an folks say it a big boat, run fas. One of de captives work on dat boat say dey put hidey-holes all over de boat to put de captive in. Him tell de washerwoman dat dem Yankees could go all over dat boat an not know de hidey-holes dere. An fas! De first day dey put it on de water, it run from Charleston down to Bofort in no time. Montgomery Baxter call it *de Sorcerer* cause it run so fast folks not sure dey see it. It come an go jus like dat!

Dey bring de captives out here an off-load dem in de backwaters cause de Yankees watchin de waters roun Bofort an Charleston. I seed dem, an it like to broke my heart. Dey was dat ruint, eyes wild, bit o rag, skin hang from de bones. I born on dis land, an I hear de others talk wit my Mama bout coming over. I knowed it was hard, an de Lord forgive me, I glad I aint come dat way!

Well, dey bring dem in an hold dem here for coupla days, den take dem right to de Massa other place. Far as dey tink, it goin all right! Montgomery Baxter makin he money, de Massa get he captives.

De Yankees sen another man down from up North to keep watch over de water. Him a diffren sort o man, an him change where de Yankees lookin for ol Montgomery Baxter. Name Capin Jame Worthington. Him I come to know when de Big War come. It him gimme dis lan when de War over cause I help he an he men. Lead dem way through de woods from de Rebels waiting to cut dem down like doves in de mornin!

Some folk say captive tole de Capin bout *de Sorcerer*. I dont know. Could have been anybody. Montgomery Baxter was doin all kinds of braggin bout what he do. All I know is dat de Capin start looking roun here. Him catch de lil boats, but him lookin for *de Sorcerer*. It take some time, but him a patient man. Him wait an wait cause him know *de Sorcerer* gonna come. White folks! Oh, dey mad at he! Dey talk bout sinkin dat boat him on, one man say he gonna shoot Capin Worthington when him go to Bofort. Dey dont want to sell he food for he men, but dat all right cause de captives sell he de food dey grow in dey own gardens. He give a fair price.

Well, push come to shove, an *de Sorcerer* come back wit another load of captives. De Capin sit in de lil cove where Nana Peazant house am, an him wait for *de Sorcerer* to come in closer. He wasnt bout to chase *de Sorcerer*. It too fas for dat lil boat him have, but him wait for he like a gopher waitin for de fish. *De Sorcerer* come up an begin to put de captives in de boats to bring dem to de lan. Capin call out to dey an tell dem to stop de loadin off. Baxter an *de Sorcerer* take to runnin. Dey run into de trap de Capin set up, de other boats come round *de Sorcerer*, nowhere to run! Dat Montgomery, Lord, him burn in de hell him made for others! Him brung dem captives on de boat an throw dem over de side. Him know de Capin gonna try to get dem, him get away. Him throw dem ober, de men, de women, lil chilren. De Capin and he men dey try to get to dem, but de chain pull dem to de bottom. Dey jump in de water, but dey can only bring up so few. Dey chains so heavy! Baxter an *de Sorcerer* run, run past Savannah down to Florida. Capin go to ol Massa Loren an tell he what happen. Massa Loren say him dont have nuttin to do wit it, lie through he teeth!

Coupla days go by, an de bodies begin to wash up on de shore. First one, two, den more. De same chains hold dem down now set dem free! Captives see bodies layin on de beach, go tell de Boss Man. Him dont want no part of it, but Capin Worthington say he better take care de bodies an give dem deir propers. De Boss Man call all we together, tell we to pull dem bodies out de water. Him tell de strongest men to dig de place for de bodies. Him say he want it done fore day close. I a lil one, an to dis day, I dont know what came over we. Didnt nobody move to do what de Boss Man say. Everbody go back to dey house, shut de door, an sit in de dark. Didnt nobody want no part of dat dirty work. Wasnt nuttin said. No cook de supper. Even de babies no cry as us sit in de dark waitin for de new day come.

Oh, de Boss Man, him holler, say him gonna beat we, sell we to de first man come through, but it make no nevermind. Didnt nobody come out dem houses! De Boss Man, he got to go down to Bofort, get dem layabout crackers work de wharf to come out here to bury de captives. Dey scared at first, but de Boss Man pay dem double what him say, give dem some of dat ol drink, an den dey work for he. Dem crackers dey hurry to bury dem. Yall see how dey throw dem in de ground wit no care at all.

Dat Capin, him a patient man. Him know Montgomery Baxter gonna come back on up to Charleston, caint stay away no time long. An sholl nough him did, come skulkin back like de dog him was! Thought himself so smart, done change de boat, take off de name, call it *de Liza Marie* after some Mustee woman him stay wit! Him no fool de Capin. Soon as him head into Charleston, de Capin catch him! Take he boat! Put he an all de men on dat boat in de jail! I hear tell Massa Loren have a fit! Threaten dat Capin! Dont you know dat ol judge let dem men go! Capin go on back up North.

Well, de Big War come, an folks goin on bout what dey gonna do to dem Yankees! Ever day somebody goin off to kill dem some Yankees! Montgomery Baxter makin plenty money runnin de cotton cross de big water. Den de Yankees come. Who come back but Capin Worthington, an him bring a whole passel of colored men wit he to run de boat. I tell you it cause some stir down here!

An dey lookin for *de Sorcerer*! Dey get word to ol Baxter, an he dont pay no mind cause he done beat de Capin already. Him go after dem boats bringin stuff for de Yankees. Dat money good! De Capin set de trap. Let word out dat boat comin wit money for de Yankee soldiers! When Baxter hear dat, he come for it an him catch it an run smack into de Capin waitin on de boat for he! Him going to jail agin, but it a Yankee jail up North! Den de Capin have *de Sorcerer* towed into de waters just off Charleston. All de folks see it sittin out dere on de water. Dey tink it Baxter comin in, an dey happy! Standin down dere on de wharf hollerin an all dat such! Oh, dey was happy! Ol Baxter done beat de Yankee agin!

Next ting dey see, dat Yankee boat wit de Capin an all dem colored men come up behind *de Sorcerer*. Dey screaming, "Run!" Dat Yankee boat pull upside *de Sorcerer* an blow dat boat to Kingdom come! *De Sorcerer* gone! Just like dat! Just like de captives dey throw in de water!

Now dey come back to we! Come back to get de proper way from we. It a sign! Us haint been livin right, an de ol ones comes back to tell we. Us got to put dem to right! Us got to move dem from de evil dat brought dem here an live in dis land. Us got to make de journey of de ancestors.

Elizabeth stood at the edge of the yard and felt the wind rise and sweep across the sand. The hair on her arms and neck prickled as she contemplated the long night ahead. She looked up at the sky; it was clearing after having been overcast all day. The last streaks of light faded quickly as the dark approached across the water. She heard Amelia come up behind her and saw the light from the kerosene lamp she carried. "You got de charm I made for you?" she asked when Amelia handed her a jacket. Amelia touched the charm that lay under her blouse.

Elizabeth, Amelia, Eula, and several other women had both worked hard these last two days to get the ancestor ground ready for the ceremony. Iona and Clemmie arrived the second day to help with the preparations, word having reached them back in the swamp. The women worked together easily, clearing the weeds from the place by the old burial ground, sweeping the dirt to level the ground, and constructing the altar according to Miz Emma Julia's instructions. As they went about their work, each woman felt what they had missed when Nana and the others had passed on and this ritual had disappeared from their lives. Clemmie was charged with gathering the items that would dress the altar. Elizabeth tried to get Lucy to join in collecting the waters, the shells, the earth, and other things that were required, but Lucy refused to move from her bed. Amelia had found a large blue cloth with a crackled design among some old burlap sacks that had been sewn together to make sheets, perfect for draping the altar. Eli and Ben built the solid pine coffin that would hold the bones after the ceremony. Ben had inscribed it with the markings as scratched in the sand by Miz Emma Julia. Together they carried it to the old burial ground, setting it behind the altar.

With the help of the other women, Iona and Carrie Mae had set up the cooking place and brought the huge pots for the feast that would follow. Willis George and the men had been up since early morning, casting their nets, pulling in the shrimp, croaker, flounder, and crab that would be prepared. Toady returned from her hunt with two large wild turkeys, a couple of wood hens, and several rabbits. People had begun arriving in the late morning, hauling wagons filled with vegetables taken from their winter storage.

It had been two days of continuous activity since Miz Emma Julia had made the pronouncement. It seemed that almost everyone had put aside their chores to make sure everything was ready for the journey. Everything would be ready when Miz Emma Julia returned.

Ol Trent hung at the edges of the activity, watching every preparation suspiciously, haranguing people about devil worshipping and false gods. It was only when Carrie Mae threatened him with Miz Emma Julia that he backed off, muttering angrily, but no longer interfering. Elizabeth gazed at Ol Trent, trying to summon the confident image of the young man in the photograph.

Sallie Lee had shown up when Willis George had not come back directly that day. She collected her children with barely a "thank you" to Eula. Amelia had felt pity for the little boy who stood by Lucy's bed and patted her on the back to tell her "good-bye." In her one display of emotion, Lucy had turned and hugged him until he squealed and then let him go. He continued to wave to them on the front porch as he followed his mother and big brother down the road.

They arrived at the ancestor ground and found Eula, Iona, and Clemmie checking to make sure everything was in order. Lucy stared at the wooden tablets that marked the graves of the ancients. Amelia immediately crossed to her. "I'm glad you've come, Lucy."

Lucy looked at her with hollow eyes. "Mama an Daddy wouldnt have it no other way."

Rebecca ran up, brimming with excitement. "I been in de cleanin house! Dey dont let no boys in de cleanin house!"

Folks arrived quickly as darkness settled around them. Sitting on the ground around the altar, they remained quiet, awaiting Miz Emma Julia's arrival. A gust of wind blew through the treetops, sending leaves tumbling down on the ceremonial ground. They heard the creak of a cart wheel, and Miz Emma Julia rode into view. Eli and J.C. stepped forward to carry her from the cart. A gasp went through the crowd as she waved them aside and pulled herself up. She stood at the edge of the cart and took in everyone. Nodding with satisfaction, she said, "It good. All de chilren come home!" She gestured for Eli and J.C. to help her down. When her feet reached the ground, she leaned on them to steady herself, then stepped forward tentatively. With each tread, her step became more sure until she was moving slowly but with confidence. She moved through the crowd followed by Aubrey and Eli.

"How many chilren dis make, Mary?" she asked one women as she passed her.

"Leven," came the reply.

She looked at a young man. "You still creepin where you dont belong?"

The man stepped back. "Aw, Miz Emma Julia, why you got to say dat?"

"Cause you dont deserve dat good woman!" she snapped. She stopped in front of Carrie Mae and grinned, showing the one tooth in her mouth. "I caint do nuttin for you! All dat devilment you into!" Miz Emma Julia declared. Despite herself, Carrie Mae blushed. "I just here for de journey!" Miz Emma Julia cackled. "Dem ol ones take anybody wit dem! Dey aint too particular!" She moved on, but then turned back, "You still got dat barley water?"

"Yes, ma'am."

"Send me a lil taste. I aint had none in a long time!"

She peered through the crowd and spotted a middle-aged man with thick salt-and-pepper hair. "Lorda mercy! Leroy, you still de best-lookin coal-black man I ever set dese eyes on!"

The man grinned at her. "How you, Miz Emma Julia?"

"I fine now!"

She reached the altar and inspected the items that had been laid out. She lifted the top from the stew pot and dipped her fingers in the dirt. She pointed to the bottles filled with different types of water. "You get dis water from de river, de swamp, de pond, de creek, de big water like I say?"

Clemmie stepped forward. "Yes, maam."

Recognizing the girl she asked, "Where you mama?"

"She at de cooking place."

"Dat right where her need to be. Tell her no salt. Salt scare de ol spirits, an us need dem tonight!" Clemmie left to give her mother the warning. Miz Emma Julia turned the seashells in the direction of the sea, then moved the herb pot to the middle of the table. She reached into her apron pockets and brought out a box of matches and lit the herb pot. "Lil Bet!" she called. Elizabeth moved quickly to her side. "Start de fires!" Elizabeth drew a twig from the pile that lay on the altar and lit it from the herb pot. She then lit the fires under the water-filled iron pots that sat in front of the altar. Miz Emma Julia reached into her blouse and pulled out a sack. She stood before each hot pot and muttered silently before she dropped a handful of herbs from the sack into the kettles.

Abruptly, she ordered, "Bring me de quilts, bring me de bones of dose dat come afore we!" Eula and Eli brought one quilt forward and laid it at her feet, then brought the other. They stepped back into the group as Miz Emma Julia lifted her arms and began her incantation, throwing her voice to the sky.

> *Chango! Agwe! Mami Wata! Yemaya! Allah!*
> *Gods of de many peoples of Africa, hear my call!*
> *Ogun! Igwe! Dan Bada! Asasc-Yaa! Kamalu!*
> *You chilren callin you from all de places of dis earth!*
> *De chilren stolen from de lands of Ibo, Yoruba, Kissee,*
> *Dahomey, Angola, Gambia, Whydah!*
> *Come! Come! Hear de chilren calling you!*

The night was complete silence, with not even a sound from the woods. Suddenly a large gust of wind swirled through the group, lifting skirts, tugging at jackets, snatching the breath from the babies. The flames from the torches shot up in the air. While some fell to their knees, Eula, Eli, and others looked to the skies as the clouds parted to show the moon. Lucy shrank as the wind seemed to circle her, moving along the edge of the group. Amelia felt the soft caress of the breeze on the back of her neck, her body relaxing. Elizabeth held her arms out and let the wind pass through her body. Miz Emma Julia stood resolutely against the wind as it threatened to bowl her over. Then it stopped as suddenly as it had come up.

Miz Emma Julia looked to Lucy, holding her hand out. "Come, chile, you brought dem to us. You gotta help dem go home." Lucy shook her head, but Miz Emma Julia continued to hold out her hand. Lucy slowly moved toward her as if pulled by a force. "You a lil gal. You gonna need a helper to send dem home." When Lucy turned to her with pleading eyes, Amelia got to her feet to stand beside her.

"Take de quilts an open dem up." Lucy took one end and Amelia the other and gently spread the quilt. They moved to the second quilt and opened it, Lucy turning her head from the bones that lay in the quilt. Miz Emma Julia held out her hand. "Spread out de shackles an de chain as dey lay in de ground." Amelia and Lucy picked up the pieces and strung them out as best they could. Miz Emma Julia spoke, "Now, spread out de bones so we can see de old ones." Lucy looked as if she was about to flee. Caught by Miz Emma Julia's gaze, she began to sob. Eula pressed her hands to her mouth to keep from crying out to her daughter. Eli put his arm around Eula, holding her close.

"Go on, gal. Let dem saltwater tears wash down an cleanse dem. Aint nobody cry for dem for years. Dey lay out in dat field for nobody know how long. Dat why dat field so rich wit de earth. Our elders give it dey life blood. Dey give to we what was took from dem." She gestured for Amelia to spread the bones. Amelia leaned down, hands trembling, and reached for a long piece of bone. When her shaking fingers touched it, she felt a jolt and pulled back. Miz Emma Julia nodded encouragingly. "Dey reachin out to you. Take what dey got to offer." Amelia wanted to refuse, then saw the fear in Lucy's eyes. Heart pounding and breathing heavily, she picked up the bone. She thought it was her imagination, the tingling that started in her fingers and began to spread up her arm. But as it spread over her body, she felt it in every pore as sweat broke out and her skin seemed to flush with blood. She held the bone above her head with both hands and cried out when she felt the waves of fear, pain, and despair wash over her. The others flinched and moaned with her, while Lucy hid her face. Amelia slowly lowered the bone, her arms trembling, her clothes soaking. Miz Emma Julia placed Amelia's coat on her shoulders and stroked her head.

The old woman then reached down and picked up a skull, crossing to Lucy, who cried out and shrank from her. Relentlessly, she grabbed Lucy's hand, struggling with her, and thrust the skull into it. She hissed at her, "Feel deir pain, gal! Feel deir hurt! Only when you feel de pain do de healin begin!"

Lucy shook as she stared at the skull. Just as she was about to let it roll off her palm, her head snapped back as the force hit her. She jerked as if her body were receiving invisible blows, her head lolling and her arms flinging in every direction. Painfully she closed her fingers around the skull and struggled to bring it closer to her. Only when she clasped it to her chest did the force seem to take pity on her. Her head hung low; her body was limp.

Miz Emma Julia stepped in front of the altar, waving the herb pot, the smoke swirling up and disappearing into the night air. "It take a strong people, snatch from de cradle, de wood, de village, put on de boat, an took cross de big water to land dey never know." Miz Emma Julia moved back and forth in front of the altar, acting out the story. Her age fell away as her words rose. "It take a strong people to keep dey all about dem, to hold on de ol ways, to keep de lies true, to know who dey be! It take a strong people to work from day clean to day over to clear de lan, build de house, plow de field, make de indigo, sow de rice, pick de cotton, all to de good of de buckra. Some of we forget how strong dem people was, us look past de old ways, put aside what dey was tellin we bout de right way to live. An now dey come back to we, de ancients who seed dis earth wit deir tears, sweat, an blood!" She leaned over and picked up a skull and a large piece of bone, holding them up for all to see. She began to shake as the forces moved through her, the people in front of her ducking when spikes of electricity flew from her body.

Ogun Iree Ni Tala Conje!
Ogun, God of Iron!
Opah Ne Sole Tu Bayai Se Fue!
Give We You Strength to Carry On!

Yemoja, Ose Bo Kinya To Le!
Yemoja, Mother of Our World!
Bon Me No Candona Kikwala!
Mbata Ke Bi!
Let You Waters Wash We With
De Wisdom of Life!

Elegba, Obebe Ko Nande Be Soma!
Elegba, de Trickster of Man an Woman!
Aru Be Ne Royo Te Ndebe! Pa Li Be Onota!
When de Roads Come Together!
Show We de Right Way!

Oshun, Ori Ye Ye O Tatalu Be Me!
Oshun, She Who Brings Love an Beauty!
Ode Asasu Mbotele So Indo!
Teach We to Treasure Who Us Come From!
Me Ti Lo!
Who Us Are!

The trees behind the altar began to shake with her force. People grabbed onto each other and wailed as the earth began to move. Miz Emma Julia threw her head back and laughed. "Come, chilren, dey telling you to rise up! Free de souls!" she commanded as they slowly got to their feet, holding on to each other as the earth rolled. "We done took de pain an de sadness! All dat lef is de healin!" At her words, there was the sound of drums. Aubrey and two other men took their places behind the altar, alternating the rhythms between them.

Moving to the beat of the drums, Miz Emma Julia picked up the stew pot and began to sprinkle the dirt across the bones, making a full circle around the quilts. She waved for Amelia and Lucy to follow her.

> *Dis de earth dat mark de spot where*
> *de ancients lay for no telling how long!*

She poured water from each bottle onto the bones, changing the direction of the circle. Carrie Mae, Clemmie, and Elizabeth joined the line following her, the tempo of the drums picking up.

> *De water give dem safe passage back to*
> *de old world!*

Rice sprayed from her hands as she flung it to the sky. Eli and Eula moved into the line. Rebecca and several other children ran forward, trying to catch the rice as it rained down upon them. They began to imitate the adults, dancing around the quilt.

> *Dis will provide de sustenance to see you*
> *through de rough journey!*

She laid her hands on the found objects, the oddly shaped piece of wood, the bright tailfeather of the parrot, the stone worn smooth by the waters, and the spiral-shaped seashell.

> *Dis wood will pay de passage to Ogun!*
> *Oshun, her love de colors of de bird!*
> *Elegba use dis stone to mark de place in de road!*
> *Yemaja blow in de shell to let dem know you coming!*

Toady and Ben stepped forward as she raised her hands, exhorting the others to join her in this dance of celebration.

> *Ask the Watchman how long—*
> *How long, Watchman, how long?*

Oh, we dont know how long—
Oh, how long, Watchman, how long?

The wind blew strongly, threatening to extinguish the flames from the torches that surrounded the old burial ground. Amelia looked at the faces of the men, women, and children who solemnly watched Eli and the other men dig the common grave for the bones. Deep sadness had replaced the fear and anxiety that had earlier marked their faces, each one remembering a loved one who lay just beyond the light.

Oh, ask my brother how long—
How long, Watchman, how long?

Slipping her hand into her pocket, Amelia grasped the piece of iron from the shackles. Miz Emma Julia had insisted that everyone take a piece so they would always remember the price the old ones paid for their freedom. Listening to the melancholy dirge that set the rhythm for the shovels as they dug into the soft dirt, Amelia wondered how many more captives lay in secret places, waiting to be uncovered and brought home. She had discovered that folks did not find it easy to talk about slavery. It had not been long ago, and the stories and experiences as drawn from the collective memory and shared from one generation to the next remained fresh. There was still much pain among the elders, and she would never forget how one woman had thrown her apron over her head, crying bitter tears when asked about her family. The young ones knew these stories, having heard them all their lives, and burned with fresh anger at their retelling.

The men stopped digging, and Miz Emma Julia, who lay in the back of her cart, signaled for them to bring the coffin forward. Amelia could see the groundwater that was already seeping through into the grave. Eli and Ben lifted the lid from the coffin. Amelia and Lucy stepped forward with one quilt of bones, Clemmie and Elizabeth with the other. Amelia heard the murmur of many prayers as they gently lowered the quilts into the coffin. All quieted as Miz Emma Julia sat up.

Olodumare, God of All Worlds!
It time for de ancient ones to start de
journey back across de big water!
Back to where de spirits of deir modders
an fadders wait for dem so dey can start de
journey to de land where de moon an de sun play
*   together!*

Olodumare, God of All Worlds!
Help dem cross de way an send down you
blessin on we, you poor chilren who dey leave
behind!

At Miz Emma Julia's nod, the lid was hammered into the coffin. The men stepped forward and lifted the ropes holding the coffin and swung it over the open grave.

Oh, ask my mother, how long!
How long, Watchman, how long?

They sang louder as the coffin was lowered into the grave, swaying to the beat and clapping their hands. Amelia shivered when the first shovel of dirt fell on the coffin. Now, at the end, she was weak with tiredness and could see the exhaustion from the long night in the others' faces. She swayed on her feet and felt Elizabeth's arm go around her and squeeze her encouragingly.

"That was a good thing you did! Standing with Lucy!" Elizabeth whispered in her ear. They both glanced over at Lucy, who stood within the protective shelter of Eli's arms, singing solemnly while the coffin disappeared under the dirt.

Ask the Watchman how long—
How long, Watchman, how long?
Oh, we don't know how long—
Oh, how long, Watchman, how long?

When the coffin was completely covered, folks stepped forward to lay their offerings on the grave; pots of food, a handkerchief, a single earring, a jar of liquor, a wooden carving, a clump of hair, whatever they wanted to leave of themselves. After each person made their offering, they fell in line behind Miz Emma Julia's cart, which led them to the morning feast that awaited them.

The boy slid down on the bench, trying to hide from Elizabeth as she scanned the room for someone to call on. Elizabeth looked past Hanley, Septima, and the few other frantically waving hands and saw him just as he disappeared from view.

"What is the name of this country we live in . . . Clarence?" He jerked upright when he heard his name. Elizabeth hid a smile as she walked to the end of the bench he sat upon. Clarence kept his head low. She questioned him gently, "Do you remember, Clarence? We been talkin bout this for quite a while." Giggles rose from the other side of the room where Amelia worked with the younger children. Elizabeth gazed at them, tapping Clarence lightly on the shoulder.

Amelia had started coming to school with Elizabeth on a regular basis. She called it "seeing that my money is put to good use," but Elizabeth knew how much Amelia enjoyed working with the little ones. Rebecca had started coming with her, evidently to make sure no one else took too much of Amelia's attention. Elizabeth appreciated the help because it allowed her to work with the older ones, whose learning had suffered because of the many teachers they'd had over the past couple of years.

Amelia had started a project with the little ones. They would tell their stories, and she would write them down while they drew the pictures to go with the stories. Granted, the stories did not have that much to them. "Dis is de story bout a baby, a mama, a daddy. Dey live over dere in de house." But the drawings were filled with a wonderful assortment of floating animals with sharp teeth and big grins, and people who leaped, ran, and flew on the paper. They had proudly pasted them in the corner, reminding both Elizabeth and Amelia of Nana's wall at home.

"Clarence?"

He mumbled.

"What did you say?"

He shrugged hopelessly.

"Who wants to help Clarence out? Septima?"

Septima jumped to her feet and confidently announced, "De Newnited Date o Amerca!"

"That's right! Good girl!"

Septima beamed at the praise.

"What is it, Clarence?"

He spoke slowly, carefully. "De Newnet Date o Merca!"

"That's pretty good! Try to remember that!" Elizabeth walked over to the crude map that she had drawn on the butcher paper and pointed to the United States. "We live in the United States. In the state of South Carolina. I hope yall can remember that when the man from the School Board come for his visit."

After six months, Elizabeth had received a notice from the School

Board that they were sending someone out to review her and see how her students were doing. A bit nervous about this test, she had told her father about the upcoming visit.

"You best be careful, Lil Bet," he had warned her. "All dem white teachers dey had out here, dey aint never sent nobody out here to look at dem!"

She had not made as much progress with the students as she had wanted to, but she was pleased that they now knew that school was serious and that work would be done every day. She also could see more of them trying, and that was especially important. She felt good that the children seemed to enjoy the lessons she and Amelia made up from a couple of old textbooks they had discovered in a Charleston bookstore. She just hoped that they wouldn't be too shy to speak out when the School Board person came.

Lucy stepped into the classroom carrying dinner sent by Eula.

"It's time for dinner!" Elizabeth announced. "Yall go on home an be back when your shadow is right there." She pointed. "An Johnny! Dont tell me you were inside an couldnt see that shadow!"

The children jumped to their feet, the older ones gathering their younger sisters and brothers, and headed home for the midday meal. "Hey, Miz Lucy!" they called out.

Lucy stepped to the side as they rushed past her. "Hey, yall!" Lucy smiled at them, her eyes still carrying the wounded look from her find in the field. She crossed over and placed the basket on the benches. "Dey love me when I aint teaching dem! Mama say dis a good day for a picnic."

Elizabeth looked in the basket at the fried chicken, hot corn pone, sweet potato pie, and the jar of bread and butter pickles. "Sweet potato pie!" Amelia and Rebecca sniffed appreciatively.

Lucy sat down on the bench, placing the jar of iced tea on the floor. "Her done killed three chickens dis morning! I dont know what got into she!" She pulled burlap squares from her pocket and tossed them to Amelia. "Gal, did you wash dem hands?" she fussed at Rebecca. Rebecca shook her head. "Get over dere an wash dem hands!"

Rebecca crossed to the cleaning area that Elizabeth had set up for the children. Amelia followed her just as obediently. Elizabeth laid out the food on the benches, offering the chicken to Lucy, who shook her head. "I aint hungry!" Lucy handed Rebecca a chicken leg. She watched indulgently as Amelia and Rebecca dug into the food. Standing up, she walked over to the window and opened it, staring out at the far marsh.

"What you been doing today?" Amelia asked between gulps of food.

Lucy sighed. "Well, I helped Mama pluck an clean dem chickens. Den I worked in de garden, weedin, puttin down some new peas." There was silence as the others ate. Lucy had not returned to the ol' Wilkerson place, and although she seemed more like her old self each day, everyone could see in her the loss of her dream. "Miz Pearlie Jane stopped by an said dey need people to help bring in de cotton over on de south side. I thinkin bout goin over dere an seein what all dey need."

Amelia and Elizabeth exchanged glances. Rebecca eyed the jar of iced tea. Elizabeth reached down and took the top off to give Rebecca a few sips. Lucy turned from the window and flatly stated, "I caint go back on dat land!" Amelia and Elizabeth watched her fingers nervously clutch her apron. "I know dat Miz Emma Julia say it all right, dat de evil been cleared from dat place, but it hurt me jus to think about it!" She blurted out, "I caint go back."

Amelia spoke reassuringly. "Lucy, you need to give yourself some time!"

Lucy shook her head. "Time aint gonna help dis! I tried. I went over dere an stood at de edge of dat fiel, an I was shakin so bad I run home an hid!"

Rebecca piped up, "I go wit you. I not scared!"

Lucy turned back to the window, angrily wiping the tears that threatened to spill. She spoke raggedly, struggling between anger and hurt. "I caint stop cryin! I aint never been one for cryin, an I caint stop!" Elizabeth walked over to her sister and put her arms around her. Lucy shuddered, trying to swallow the tears. Elizabeth held her sister closely.

A cloud moved over the marsh, its shadow rippling across the grass, turning the water from light blue to steel gray. Elizabeth blinked, wishing she could take her sister's pain into her. She lifted her head and saw the figure coming down the path that ran along the marsh. She stared as the figure approached slowly, lumbering along, pigeon-toed, taking his time, sure where he was headed. She began to smile, lifted Lucy's chin, and pointed.

Lucy stared, then shouted, "Charlie! Charlie!"

Charlie stopped and took the hat off his head and waved to the school. Lucy screamed and took off, running as if the devil was after her. Rebecca was about to run after Lucy when Elizabeth scooped her up and brought her back to the window. It seemed to Amelia and Elizabeth that Lucy flew the last few feet, landing safely against Charlie's chest, disappearing into his arms.

"That's why Mama was doing all that cooking!" Elizabeth murmured.

They turned from the window when Charlie held Lucy's face in his hands and kissed her thoroughly.

Love Powder Potion

Mix 2 tablespoons of cornstarch with 15 drops of spearmint, 5 drops of sweet bay, and 10 drops of pine. Sprinkle on the sweetest parts of your body and leave a trail of powder running to your bed.

"**H**ave some more of dat chicken, Charlie," Eula encouraged, pushing a couple of pieces onto Charlie's plate. Amelia glanced over at Eula who had been fluttering nervously around the table since supper had begun.

Charlie swallowed and then spoke in his slow deliberate manner. "Thank you, Miz Eula."

Eli looked at his wife curiously, "You not gonna eat?"

Eula wiped her hands on her apron. "I jus makin sure everbody settled."

Elizabeth spoke up, "Why don't you sit down, Mama?" Eula sank to her chair as Elizabeth turned her attention to Charlie. Her eyes twinkling with mischief, Elizabeth spoke, imitating Charlie's slow speech. "So, Charlie, what you been doin?" She ignored Lucy's bristling as she moved closer to Charlie protectively.

Charlie grinned at her good-naturedly and replied, "Jus workin hard. Tryin to make dat money for me an my Lucy."

Amelia enjoyed watching the teasing between Elizabeth and Charlie. He seemed to be just a simple country man, plain-spoken, easy-going. Charlie was like one of the family, having lived on the Island most of his life, playing and going to school with the Peazant children since he was young. He was the complete opposite of Lucy, heavy-bodied, slow-moving, slow-talking. Whereas Lucy's tongue could cut a strip of skin off a person, Charlie's rumbling voice would most likely lull someone to sleep. Eula had related how Charlie had first been sweet on Elizabeth for a long time, but was too shy to say anything. Elizabeth, unaware of his feelings, had never thought of Charlie as anything other than "ol slow-talking, slow-walking Charlie." Eula had chuckled as she explained that it had taken Lucy to point out to Charlie that he was wasting his time, especially when she, Lucy, was getting tired of waiting for him to come to his senses. Amelia remembered Eula's description. "She took him in hand, and he been there ever since!" Elizabeth leaned forward and passed Charlie a plate of biscuits, imitating him. "How long you stayin, Charlie?"

Charlie leaned back in his chair, tasting his food, and then announced, "Jus long enough to get Mr. Eli's blessin to take my Lucy back so us can get married." Amelia was not sure whose gasp filled the room. She looked at Eula, who fanned herself. Elizabeth blinked in shock. Lucy moved closer to Charlie, trembling with anticipation. Rebecca pouted because she had planned on marrying Charlie when she got older. Ben looked back and forth with relish from Eli, who froze with a chicken wing in his hand, to Charlie, who smiled broadly.

"What you say, boy?" Eli asked ominously.

"Mr. Eli, I come to get my Lucy." Charlie spoke with quiet determination. Eli put the chicken wing down.

"Now, jus a minute here. What happen to all that talk yall been doin bout savin up, taking your time?"

"Dat all good an well, but I miss my Lucy. I go to dat boarding house at night, an all I got to look at is de same men I work in dat pit wit! I work hard everday. I been savin an payin on dat property so we can get married, but I dont want to wait no more."

Eli frowned. "Lucy dont want to live on de mainland—"

Lucy interrupted. "Daddy, I jus want to be wit Charlie. It dont matter where!"

Eli held up his hand. "Gal, I know you been through some hard times, but you jus need to give yourself some time."

Lucy quickly replied, "I dont need no more time! Dem ancients in dat fiel didnt have no time!"

Eli looked at her, baffled. Lucy had never expressed a desire to go to the mainland. She rarely took the boat across to do any of the marketing, and now she was declaring her intention to leave. He looked at Eula for help.

Eula spoke cautiously. "I think it be good if they go on an get married. It aint like us wasnt expectin them to get married!"

Eli shook his head. "Yall was so set on starting dat farm an all fore yall got married. Yall was gonna wait so."

Eula touched his arm. "Eli, dey older dan us was."

Eli demanded, "What yall gonna do bout dat property? Yall gonna give it up?"

Charlie put his arm around Lucy. "Us gonna buy it. Us come back an work it when us ready. I need my wife, Mr. Eli. You know a man need a wife to give him comfort." He squeezed Lucy gently.

"Please, Daddy! I be all right wit Charlie," Lucy pleaded.

Eli was silent for a few seconds. "De preacher dont stop through here till de end of de month, an yall aint even got de license!" Eli finally pointed out.

A look of startled admiration crossed Elizabeth's face as Charlie calmly said, "Us can get de license in Bofort an get married dere an go on down to Tampa."

Eli rose to his feet in indignation. "You know me all my life. You know I wants de best for Lucy. I always do right by Lucy!" Eli glared at him and began to pace back and forth around the table. He looked at the others, who were watching him. "Yall eat!" he commanded, and there was only the sound of spoons scraping the plates.

Eula tore her biscuit to pieces. Eli returned to stand over Charlie. Even though Charlie was sitting, they were eye to eye. "Yall comin back this summer an gonna get married proper in de church! An you better have dat marriage certificate!"

Charlie stood slowly. Towering over Eli, he held out his hand. "Mr. Eli, I put it in your hand."

"To Lucy an Charlie!" Carrie Mae toasted. Elizabeth, Amelia, and Toady raised their glasses. "Yassir, you coulda knock me over. Lucy leavin like this!" They peered suspiciously at the dark, strong-smelling brew that Carrie Mae had poured for them. Amelia smelled it first; Elizabeth stuck the tip of her tongue in it; Toady swirled it around the inside of her mouth before swallowing. Carrie Mae took a drink, tried to stifle the cough, and then croaked, "What yall think? Dawkins got dis real cheap down Savannah way!"

Amelia put her glass aside. "It smells like that stuff you embalm people with!" Carrie Mae frowned at her, then turned to Elizabeth.

"You dont wanta know what I think!" Elizabeth quickly said.

"What you think, baby?" Carrie Mae appealed to Toady. Toady simply shook her head. "Damn! I already bought two boxes!" Carrie Mae complained.

She glanced over at Pidgen. "Pidgen!"

He cut her off as he opened a couple of bottles of beer. "You know I dont drink dat poison!"

Carrie Mae looked around the room. Spying J.C. on the other side, she called, "J.C.! Come over here, boy!"

He trotted over, pleased with the summons. "Yall ladies want me?"

"Dey dont want you, boy! I call you!" Carrie Mae snapped. "I got some new stuff you might like, an cause you such a good customer, I gonna let you an you friends have two for one. Dat mean you pay for one an get de other free!"

J.C. grinned. "Yeah! All right! Dat my woman!" He tried to put his arm around her.

She shrugged him off. "De drink free, I aint! Now, you go over dere an tell your friends de second one on me!"

Sure enough, as soon as J.C. got back to his friends, the group of them trailed over to the bar. Carrie watched in satisfaction and then turned back to Elizabeth and Amelia. "So when yall gonna find yall some good men?" she asked. Elizabeth deliberately looked around the room and then sipped her beer, rolling her eyes.

"Hell, you aint supposed to be lookin in here, no how!" Carrie Mae fussed. "What about you, Cousin?"

Amelia blurted, "I got to finish school!"

"Mm-huh!" Carrie Mae grunted skeptically. "Well, all I got to say is a good woman is as good as a good man any day! Aint dat right, baby?" She reached over and took Toady's hand. Toady stroked her hand in response.

"You wanta dance?" A man leaned over to speak to Elizabeth.

"Thank you, Bo." Elizabeth shot a frisky look at Carrie Mae as she followed the man onto the floor. Elizabeth began to shimmy to the music, tossing away for the moment the slight air of melancholy that had been around her since Lucy left.

Amelia knew how she felt. She missed Lucy, too. Eula had cried tears of happiness and sadness when they saw Lucy and Charlie off at the pier that morning. Eli's throat closed on him when he hugged his second-eldest daughter to him before he turned her over to Charlie with a warning. "Charlie, you been round dem all you life so you know dese Peazant women, dey give you a run for you money! An dat one you taking, Lord have mercy on you, Charlie!"

Charlie laughed. "Yassir, He got to, cause she wont!"

Elizabeth hugged Lucy and then Charlie, kissing him on the cheek, and making him blush with pleasure. When it came time for Amelia to say good-bye, she whispered in Lucy's ear, "When you and Charlie come back, it'll be all right." Lucy nodded in agreement, giving Amelia a fierce hug. Ben recorded all the good-byes, even Eula trying to wave him away, and was still winding the film through the camera as Willis George pulled the boat away from the pier. Lucy and Charlie waved until the boat disappeared in the light morning mist.

Toady stood up. "I got to get on my post." She slipped through the dancers, headed for the front door. When she reached the door, she stopped short as Sallie Lee stepped into the room.

"Aw, hell!" Carrie Mae muttered. Sallie Lee had put her hair up and was wrapped in a tight-fitting dress. She leaned down and slipped a shoe off and dumped the sand at the door. Sliding her foot back into the shoe, she lifted her skirt and showed enough leg for the men to admire. She surveyed the room, looking for someone and not finding him, then switched across to the table where Amelia and Carrie Mae sat. Toady looked after her and then exited, shaking her head.

"How yall?" she drawled.

Carrie Mae responded, "Us fine." She said deliberately, "How Willis George an de chilren?"

"Oh, dey fine! You should see de baby. She gettin so big!" Sallie Lee chattered.

"Yall give she a name yet?" Carrie Mae asked.

"Naw, we gonna wait till she baptised. Maybe the end of dis month." She winked at Carrie Mae. "Maybe we name her 'Carrie Mae.' "

Carrie threw her a sharp glance, "Unh-huh!"

Sallie Lee continued, "Right now, 'Sugar' do just fine. It what yall folks call a basket name." She looked around the room, casually asking, "Aint nobody playin tonight?"

Carrie Mae was blunt. "Sugarnun may stop by after a while." Amelia almost dropped her bottle of grape soda. "But you know how him is. You caint depend on he for nothin!"

Sallie Lee smiled. "Yeah. Well, lemme see if I caint get somebody to buy me a drink." She strolled over to the bar, where J.C. and his friends were still taking advantage of Carrie Mae's two-for-one special.

"I wish Willis George would take care of he business!" Carrie Mae complained.

"How long has she been coming here without Willis George?" Amelia asked cautiously.

"Chile, her done cut loose. Been comin in here ever Saturday, sometimes Friday, for quite a while! You wouldnt think her got three chilren at home!" Carrie Mae shook her head and sipped her drink. She frowned and pushed the drink away. "This some nasty stuff! I bout ready to kill Sugarnun cause him an Willis George use to be dis close. But Toady done tole me to stay out of it!"

Sallie Lee lifted her glass and drained it. She held the empty glass up and stared at the light filtering through. As she lowered it, her eyes met Amelia's, and she smiled defiantly at her.

Elizabeth wrapped the quilt around her and dropped down on the sand where her cousin had rolled herself into a cocoon. She pushed Amelia with her foot. "Hey, gal! We got to get back. Go to church!" Elizabeth looked over at Carrie Mae, who was on her knees, drawing pictures in the sand, and Toady, who lay on her back, her hands crossed on her chest, snoring lightly. "Toady look like she dead."

Carrie Mae sat back and looked at her handiwork. "Her de only person I know dont move when dey sleep!" Elizabeth pushed Amelia again and laughed as Amelia rolled away from her foot. "Come on, gal!" Amelia slowly emerged from the quilt, yawning and stretching.

"Hmm, dat ol New York gal like sleepin out here in dis sand like de ol sand crab!" Carrie Mae teased her. Amelia slowly wiped the sleep from her eyes, shutting them against the rising sun. She did enjoy it, wrapping up in a quilt, burrowing into the warm sand, and waking as the sun came up. Her grandmother would have had a fit, but Amelia vaguely remembered Myown telling her about the pleasures of sleeping on the sand. She now knew what Myown meant. She frowned at Elizabeth, who leaned back, eyes closed, and let the sun wash over her. Elizabeth had that early-morning energy that could be very irritating to a slow riser like Amelia. Amelia knew that Elizabeth could not have gotten more than a couple of hours sleep herself, but she looked like she'd had a full night.

Carrie Mae jumped as a shadow fell over her drawing. She gasped, "Lord have mercy!"

Toady sat up quickly, kicking off the blankets, reaching into her pocket. "Willis George, where you come from sneaking up on somebody? Bout to scare somebody to death."

Willis George stared down at them, his face ashy with exhaustion. "Yall see Sallie Lee?" Amelia looked away, and stood up to shake out the quilt. Elizabeth could not hide the look of pity in her eyes.

Carrie Mae spoke gently. "Why dont you sit down for a minute? You look all wore out."

He shook his head. "I caint! I just got in. Fog blocked us in on de mainland so I couldnt make it back last night." His voice rose with exhaustion and anger. "My babies in dat house, an her aint no place around! Where Sallie Lee?"

Carrie Mae rubbed her temple before answering, "Her was here til we close, an den her left." They all held their breath as he looked from one to the other. They saw the question in his eyes and were terrified that he would ask. He was silent as he struggled with his hurt, his anger, and his pride. Willis George held his head up, summoning all of his sense of himself. "I see yall later," he said briefly and walked away as quietly as he had appeared.

Ben waved to Amelia, signaling her to back up more. She frowned and glanced over her shoulder at Rebecca, whom Ben had placed farther up the road. "It gonna look funny. Becca gonna look like her standin on you shoulder." Amelia backed up until Ben yelled, "That it. Stay right dere! Okay, Becca, now do your dance!"

He laughed, filming Rebecca doing her playful, loose-limbed jig. Curiosity got the better of Amelia and when she turned her head to peep at Rebecca, Ben shouted, "Hold it right dere, Amelia!" He chortled at the image. "It look like you lookin at she!" Pleased with his reaction, Rebecca did the shing-a-ling, imitating the adults she had seen. Ben laughed so hard he could barely hold the camera. "Mama see you do dat, you be in trouble!" Amelia could not help it. Turning to look at Rebecca, she burst out laughing at Rebecca's eye-rolling grin and the way her thin hips shook. Ben stopped filming, "Dat enough, Becca. Dat more dan enough!" Rebecca ran up the road and grabbed Amelia's hand, swinging it.

"You gonna miss all dis when you go back to New York," Ben commented, stopping to film a scattering of wild iris that were just pushing through the dirt at the edge of the road.

"Mm-huh," Amelia said dreamily. There was the honk of geese overhead, and she looked up at the sky. "They're going back, too."

"Dey come dis way ever year. When you comin back?" Ben asked.

"I don't know," she admitted. "I don't know what's going to happen when I get back to New York."

They walked down the road in thoughtful silence. Rebecca ran over to a cluster of spring daisies and picked a handful, scurrying back to present then to Amelia. Amelia stuck one behind her ear and another behind Rebecca's ear, which pleased her very much. Ben resisted any attempt to be adorned with flowers.

A few days earlier, Amelia had told the family that she would have to be heading back to New York soon. She really had to spend the next two months putting together her thesis. Eli wondered why she could not write here on the Island, while Eula fretted that Myown would think she had not enjoyed her stay. Amelia reassured Eula and carefully explained to Eli why she needed the school's resources to finish. While neither were pleased, both understood her reasoning and both knew that she was especially worried about her mother. The latest letter from Haagar had detailed Myown's recent stay in the hospital and the doctor's concerns. Myown had described it as a simple spell of weakness brought on by inhaling the fumes from the preparation room. Amelia knew better.

The hardest person to tell was Elizabeth, Elizabeth who would wrap herself in quiet for hours, Elizabeth whose quick bursts of energy could wear a person out, Elizabeth in whose eyes one could glimpse the wisdom of the ancients. Although Amelia could not claim to know any more about Elizabeth than Elizabeth wanted her to know, she savored the idea that their relationship would be one of continual discovery and surprise. There was more than kinship between them, forged by evenings in front of a fire making charms, reading books, and talking about family. She and Elizabeth had discussed the possibility of a visit in New York when school was over, and they had made plans, both keeping them deliberately vague, for they knew the nature of such things.

"My Lord!" Amelia heard Ben's soft exclamation of wonder. He fumbled with the camera as he tried to capture the picture in front of them. They stood at the edge of the Wilkerson meadow. Amelia could see the ruptured ground where they had removed the bones and hastily replaced the earth. The entire area was covered with flowers, bright, beautiful flowers that swayed gently in the breeze. Rebecca gave a cry of delight and started running across the field with Amelia following her. Ben stood uncertainly at the edge of the field. Amelia turned back to him and yelled, "Come on, Ben. It's a good sign!" Ben followed them hesitantly, then began to run after them.

Rebecca dropped to her knees and reached for the flowers. "No, Becca, let them grow!" Amelia wrapped her arms around her, stopping her. "The ancients, they're sending a sign." She turned to Ben, who arrived breathless. Her eyes were wet with tears. "Aren't they beautiful? Aren't they just beautiful?

Ben nodded in agreement as he held the camera up to capture the red, blue, purple, yellow, and orange flowers that sprang from the rich earth. He walked over to the other side of the grave site and lay down, carefully positioning the camera so that he could see Rebecca and Amelia just over the tops of the flowers. Amelia threw her head back and listened to the lazy call of a bird, breathing deeply of the fresh spring air.

Rebecca quickly tired of sitting quietly and jumped up to explore. "Don't go too far!" Amelia warned. Rebecca nodded as she bent down to examine something in the grass. Amelia scooped a handful of dirt and let it trail through her hands. "She will come back," she said with conviction.

"It good land," Ben agreed. "Lucy aint bout to give up good land."

Amelia looked around. "I want to see where the captives lived." She stood up. "Lucy told me that you used to play there when you were little."

Ben pointed. "That where Becca headed right now."

Amelia turned. Sure enough, Rebecca had managed to cover quite a distance and stood at the bend of the path that led to the outbuildings. "Becca, wait!" Amelia exclaimed, taking off after her. Rebecca laughed and ran down the path. "God bless her!" Amelia grunted as she half-ran, half-stumbled across the meadow.

When she rounded the corner, she saw that Rebecca had stopped in front of one of the shacks that was covered with vines, moss, and leaves. Rebecca was trying to peep through the thicket at the shack. The roof had long since caved in, and the outer walls leaned to one side. Amelia slowed to a walk as she approached. "Becca, you were supposed to wait for me," she chided her.

Rebecca pointed. "Can we go in there?"

"Oh, no, that would fall in on us." Rebecca kicked at the dirt in disappointment. Amelia moved down the path to look at the other shacks. Most seemed to be in the same condition. They were much smaller than the Peazant houses; Amelia could easily imagine the lives of the people crowded inside. She could see them rising early in the morning to begin their chores and work in the fields. At the end of the day, they would trudge home to have their supper, and the families would spend those precious evening hours together, renewing themselves. In that way, it did not seem that much had changed.

She could see the large tree that had at some point begun growing through one of the shacks. As she stepped closer to examine it, she saw through the vines wrapped around the trunk that the bark had been scraped away. She tore at the vines revealing the cross-hatch etchings underneath, similar to the ones that marked the tree on Nana's place.

"What dat writin?" Rebecca asked. It had not occurred to Amelia that it might be some type of writing. She had always thought it was decoration.

She called to Ben, who was slowly coming up behind them, "Ben, take some pictures of this. Becca says it's writing."

He looked at her, slightly puzzled, and stepped back, focusing the camera on the trunk. "Pull some more of dem vines back," he directed her. Rebecca, proud of her discovery, helped her.

"I wonder where Ol Trent lives," Amelia said.

Ben pointed to the thicker woods behind the shacks. "Dem more sturdy ones back dere. He family live in dem. When I was bout Becca's age, dis was all cleared out. You could walk all back dere from here. Dey let dem all go to ruin, though." Amelia could barely see through the thick bushes. Ben, amused by her curiosity, said, "Us go round de other side. Dat how most people get back here."

She looked at him. "I'd heard that this was a popular place for couples to meet."

She laughed when Ben blushingly explained, "Well, most folks live wit dey families, an when yall want to be together, everbody standing dere lookin at you."

He led the way around, finding the well-worn path. Amelia picked up Rebecca as they made their way through the woods. When they stood in the small clearing before the old homestead, Amelia could see that even though the house was barely standing, it had been stoutly built. The walls still showed traces of whitewash, and bits of blue lined the open doorway. There was another smaller house off to the side. "Dat where de ol man live." Ben pointed. "Dey daddy. Nana say him want he peace. De rest of dem stay in dat house."

Rebecca clung to Amelia and asked fearfully, "We goin in dat house?"

"No, Becca," Amelia reassured her. "I just wanted to see it. We can head back now." They turned and began making their way out of the clearing.

"Dere somebody in dere." Rebecca pointed. Amelia and Ben whirled around. There was a movement at one of the windows; a person stood there watching them. Ben said, "It's probably Ol Trent!" Amelia shook her head. They both knew that this person was much shorter than Ol Trent. Ben said quickly, "Folks come back here all de time. Jus like we did." The person moved boldly forward into the light. Both Amelia and Ben gasped as Sallie Lee stared at them across the small clearing.

Rebecca said, "Her no have she clothes on!" Neither one of them could move as Sallie Lee lifted her hand and casually waved to them. Suddenly dark arms slid around Sallie Lee, caressing her breast, pulling her back into the darkness. Amelia, Rebecca, and Ben fled without looking back.

Elizabeth's hands twitched nervously while Hanley frowned at the long division problem that the Board visitor, Mr. Hammond, had written on the butcher paper. Hanley tilted his head and then turned to look at Elizabeth. She could see, when Mr. Hammond leaned back in his chair, that he fully expected Hanley to give up. She nodded encouragingly; Hanley shrugged and began to quickly scribble, working his way through the problem. When he finished, he turned to Mr. Hammond.

"You think it's right, boy?"

"Yassir." Hanley spoke quietly.

"Prove to me that it's right."

Hanley pointed to some scribbling to the right of the problem. "I already done dat." Mr. Hammond sat forward abruptly and got to his feet. He squinted at the scribbling, then came back and sat down, not completely pleased.

Elizabeth rose and crossed to Hanley. Touching him on his shoulder, she praised him. "Hanley, that was real good, Hanley. You did a good job." Hanley shyly held his head down. She gently pushed him toward his seat and patiently waited.

Mr. Hammond looked at the group of brown faces who watched him with much curiosity. He shifted uncomfortably under their steady gaze. He glanced at the young woman waiting for his response. Despite the fact that these were Island coloreds, she had gotten them to clean themselves up, and a few of them even knew their alphabets. He had not expected much. He knew about these Island coloreds, virtually unteachable, but she seemed to have them in hand. At least they sat quietly and were polite in their responses. The room was neat and the walls were covered with the children's schoolwork. He had to admit that she had done an adequate job, and he could not fault her for her cleverness in finding supplies for her students.

He had not wanted to make this trip. It was always hot and sticky out here with every biting insect imaginable. Used to the coloreds in Beaufort, he found these people with their particularly fractured English and watchful demeanor unnerving. He knew they still practiced pagan rites, and he'd heard that their church meetings with all the singing and dancing were nothing more than an occasion to act like heathens. He did not blame the other teachers for leaving. He did not want to be caught out here, the only white man among all these coloreds, at night. If he had not been hoping for that promotion to the County Clerk's Office, he would have put the trip off entirely. After all, no one had been out here since the missionaries left. But Superintendent Gainsborough wanted to know how the colored girl was doing.

Wiping his sweating hands on his handkerchief, he smiled obligingly when she stepped forward. "We put together a little program for you, Mr. Hammond."

"Oh, you did?"

She continued, "Yessir, some of the children are real good at reciting."

He responded expansively, "Well, I caint wait!"

She signaled to two small children in the front to come forward. They stood in front of Mr. Hammond, holding hands. The first child stepped forward, then turned away shyly, mumbling, "In de beginnin, God made de heaven an de earth."

The second child spoke out boldly, "For God so love de earth, him gave he only begotten son." He ended with a bright smile. Elizabeth returned his smile; Mr. Hammond nodded his approval to them.

Septima stepped up and fairly shouted the words of the Twenty-Third Psalm. Elizabeth hid a smile when Mr. Hammond blinked in reaction to Septima's stern interpretation.

Two of the older girls came forward and announced, "We gonna sing for you," then began to sing "Joshua Fit de Battle of Jericho."

Mr. Hammond conducted them with his finger as they sang the first two stanzas. When they finished, he applauded, leaned forward, and asked, "Yall know 'Carolina'?" When they looked at each other, confused, he began to sing the first few lines off-key. When they still did not respond, he turned to Elizabeth and instructed, "I want to hear them sing 'Carolina' the next time I come out here. I expect these children to know at least 'Carolina.'"

Elizabeth nodded and turned to Hanley with pride. "Hanley chose this speech all by himself."

Hanley began, "Four score an seven years ago, our fathers brought fort . . ." Mr. Hammond stiffened and stared at him. ". . . On dis continent, a new nation—"

Mr. Hammond interrupted him, "Wait a minute, boy!" He asked harshly, "Where you get that from?" Hanley, uncertain, looked to Elizabeth. Elizabeth hesitated when Mr. Hammond swung on her. "Where he get that?"

Elizabeth selected a book from several that lay on the bench. "Where you get this book?" Mr. Hammond demanded. "This book is not one of our textbooks!" He flipped through it and then glared at Elizabeth.

"I couldn't get any books from the Depository . . . " she began.

"What do you mean you couldn't get any books from the Depository?"

There was silence in the room. The children stared at the angry white man and their teacher, who had started trembling. He got up and walked over, brushing Hanley back. He looked through the other books, getting angrier by the moment, as Elizabeth took a deep breath. "By the time they let me in, there wasn't much left, an what was left was all tore up. I took my money an what I got from other folks an bought these few books at one of the stores in Charleston."

He held up one of the books and shook it at her. "These books are not authorized! How dare you take it upon yourself to bring this kind of stuff into this class? You're supposed to follow the strict guidelines as set down by the Beaufort School Board!" He yelled at her, "My God, gal, what good is it going to do them to learn this Lincoln? And to hear the words of the Great Traitor come from the mouths of South Carolina schoolchildren!" He glared at her. "You have gone beyond yourself, gal!" He snatched the books from the bench and strode out the door. "You'll be hearing from the School Board on this!"

The children sat quietly, not daring to make a sound. Elizabeth rubbed her temple, then sat down on the bench.

Hanley looked at the others, then back at Elizabeth. "Miz Lil Bet." Elizabeth did not respond. "Miz Lil Bet," he tried again. "Miz Lil Bet, I . . . I . . ."

She stopped him. "Hanley, you did real good."

"But dat buckra mad!" Hanley protested.

She looked at him, hollow-eyed. "You did real good." She gazed at the drawings on the wall. The dancing people and flying animals seemed to mock her. "Yall go on home."

Eli was troubled. Ben had told him of what he and Amelia had seen on the old Wilkerson place, and he was beginning to hear from all kinds of folks about Sallie Lee and Sugarnun. Eli was not the type to get involved in other people's business. Lord knows, he did not believe in preaching to somebody, but he had a lot of respect and affection for Willis George and he knew Sugarnun. Willis George would do anything for his family. No telling how many children Sugarnun had left behind in his travels. A man did not have but so much pride, and he could not stand by and watch a good man come apart behind all this. He had seen Willis George the day before and had turned from the eyes clouded with hurt. He knew the sickness and was at a loss to offer a cure.

He also worried about Elizabeth. Rebecca had come home last week and angrily announced, "Dat man yell at Lil Bet!" When he questioned her, she briefly told him what had taken place. He was not surprised. He had warned her because he knew that the last thing the School Board wanted was to make sure these children got any kind of education other than what they needed to work in white folks' houses. Elizabeth had retreated into that place where she went to put things straight, and neither Eula nor Amelia could bring her any comfort.

One night he awakened for no particular reason and walked out onto the front porch. In the moonlight, he saw someone standing at the edge of the water and recognized his oldest daughter when she lifted her hands to rub her temple. Eula would do the same thing when she was worried or upset. In the old days he would have gone to her, but this was not the old Lil Bet, and he really did not know what to say to his child. He often wondered if he had done the right thing by sending her off to school. He had been so determined to get the most for Lil Bet; he could not bear letting that mind go to seed. He had seen the young colored teachers in Beaufort and knew that Lil Bet could put them to shame. It seemed only right that he would set such store by his firstborn.

There were so many things for which he could never forgive himself. If he had not stayed late that night so many years ago, playing tonk at the joint, Eula would not have grown impatient and started out for home in the dark. He would never forget arriving in the early morning hours and finding out from Nana that she had not come home that night. Nana thought she had stayed at her mother's, and even as Eli strolled through the woods to get her, he had been preparing his lame excuse. Halfway there, he had heard a pitiful cry and, thinking it was some small animal, ignored it. When the cry grew louder and desperate, he had cautiously moved into the brush, prepared to put the animal out of its misery. He had stumbled and fallen to the ground when he saw Eula's dirt-stained shawl lying in the brush. Try as he might, he could not get to his feet and had to crawl to where she lay, bloody and battered. The rage of the women, Eula's mother and sisters, Nana and his sisters, was nothing compared to the madness that filled every part of his body, claiming a permanent place in his soul. He had not made things any easier for Eula, demanding to know who her violator was. She had lived with his foolishness and protected him from himself. And when his mind had taken an evil turn and he had suspected Eula and his best friend, she had withdrawn to the child she carried. He felt the deepest shame when he saw the deep hurt in Eula's eyes at his desperate accusation. Despite it all, she had forgiven him and never spoken of that time. Lord knows, there had been many times when he had expected Eula to fling his failure in his face, but he had never heard it from her, only from the part that would always live in him.

When Lil Bet was a young child, he often caught a certain look in her eyes and wondered if she remembered the rage and helplessness that swirled around her as she lay in her mother's womb. There was no one alive or dead that could convince Eli and Eula that Elizabeth had not come out of her womb to walk among them that last day at the family picnic on the beach before the other Peazants left for parts North. Their Unborn Child had come out of the womb to help Eli accept that she was his child. Although Eli and Eula had never spoken of it afterward, they both knew that it was so. Over the years, each parent had wondered if their Lil Bet remembered that day.

Eli had been frightened for Elizabeth and pulled her back to the Island. Now they were both in pain. "I be back in a bit," Eli called out to Eula and headed off into the woods. He followed the path that led past the old Wilkerson place. Stopping in surprise, he watched Ol Trent work among the flowers that sprung from the earth where the ancients had lain. Ol Trent jumped to his feet when Eli crossed the field and stood over him. Ol Trent stared at him suspiciously, his clothing and hands stained with the dirt.

"Sallie Lee an Sugarnun back dere?" Eli asked.

Ol Trent shook his head. "I run them fornicators off!" When Eli turned away and walked toward the far line of trees, Ol Trent shouted after him, "An that man that committeth adultery with another man's wife, even he that committeth adultery with his neighbor's wife, the adulterer and the adulteress shall surely be put to death!"

Eli pushed his way through the thick briars that led back to where Sugarnun was known to stay when he came to the Island. It was an old hiding place; few people knew about it and fewer had been back there. It was what Lucy would call a "miserable bit of land," dark with only occasional light seeping through, filled with sharp briars, poison oak, sulphorous water, and plenty of snakes. When Eli was younger, he would think nothing of coming through here, tracking a deer or wild pig. But it seemed to be much thicker than it had been in the past and he did not relish the task that he had undertaken.

He did not bother to slip quietly through the area. He wanted Sugarnun to hear his approach. When he reached the clearing, he stared at the crude hut that Sugarnun had built there. Eli had never suspected

Sugarnun of any type of hard work, but sometime over the years, Sugarnun had hauled all this wood back here and put this hut up. Eli now stood in the clearing and called, "Woodrow McKinley Harrison!"

He heard a rustle in the house, and then saw Sugarnun peek out a knothole in the wall. Sugarnun peered at him, then slowly opened the door. "Mr. Eli!" Sugarnun grinned and stepped out into the dim light, wearing just his trousers. "Mr. Eli, aint seen you in a long time."

Eli stared at him, feeling his anger rise. "Boy, you layin up dere! Anybody can walk up on you!"

Sugarnun chuckled. "Aw, Mr. Eli, I heard you comin a while back, but I thought it was Sallie Lee bringin me some supper."

Eli walked right up to him. "Boy, is you crazy?" Sugarnun stepped back from the heat of Eli's anger. He looked uneasy for a moment and then he shrugged. Eli leaned in to him. "Dis aint right, boy! You know dis aint right!"

"Aw, man, her come after me!" Sugarnun protested.

"I dont care what her done, dat man used to be your friend! Dat woman got three chilren! One of em still nursin!" Eli's voice shook with indignation.

Sugarnun rubbed his head and peered at Eli, who persisted, "What you gonna do bout her?" When Sugarnun appeared startled, he said, "Dont be lookin at me like you dont know what I talking bout!"

"Mr. Eli, Sallie know what dis bout," Sugarnun reasoned with Eli. "We was together fore she got wit Willis George."

"What you gonna do, Woodrow?"

"All I wanna do is jus wait out here till Monty Gaines cool off. Den I be outta here, head over to Augusta."

"An what you gonna do bout dat woman?" Eli persisted.

Sugarnun grinned at him. "Sallie dont want me! Us jus havin fun."

Eli demanded, "Why dont you send her back home den? Dont you care what happenin to dat family?"

Sugarnun looked at Eli. "Shoot, soon as I gone, her be done took up wit somebody else. Her dont want nuttin to do wit Willis George!" Eli looked him up and down and shook his head with disgust.

At the sound of someone approaching both men tensed and looked to see who was coming; Sallie Lee pushed her way into the thicket. Her sleeve caught on a low branch, and she pulled it free with a jerk, tearing the dress. Eli winced as she boldly walked across the clearing, swinging the supper pail. She grinned at both of them and then handed the pail to Sugarnun, who immediately opened it and pulled out a piece of meat.

"How you doin, Mr. Eli?" Sallie Lee asked, watching Sugarnun wolf down the food.

Eli waited until she looked directly at him before answering. "You dont have no better place to be . . . like wit your babies!" he scolded her.

"They doin all right. I was jus over there fixin supper. Willis George'll take care of dem." She spoke casually, inspecting the torn sleeve.

"You dont care what you doin to that man? He bout to lose his mind over you!" She smiled as Sugarnun dug into the lunch pail.

Shrugging, she said, "That what happen when you love someone who dont love you."

Eli turned to leave. "Yall fools deserve each other." He started across the clearing and then stopped suddenly, finding Willis George at the edge of the thicket, his shotgun raised.

"Get out de way, Eli!" Willis George shouted. Sugarnun looked up, dropped the pail, and started to duck into the house. Willis George had the gun trained on him. "You run, Sugarnun. I blow you head off!" Sugarnun froze. Sallie Lee watched Willis George, her hands on her hips.

Eli raised his hands. "You dont need to do dis, Willis!"

"Her come to my house. I aint seen she in two days!" Willis George struggled to speak. "Come walkin up dere like her jus come from church. Go in dere an start fixin supper. I glad she home." He glared at Sallie Lee. "Cook de food I work so hard for!" He yelled at Sugarnun, "Come on out here, boy!"

Sugarnun smiled nervously. "Look here, Willis. It aint much of nothing! We can—"

"I said come here . . . an bring my supper pail!" Sugarnun did not move. "Get out de way!" Willis George quickly walked past Eli. "Bring me my supper pail!" Sugarnun slowly bent down and picked up the supper pail.

Eli moved up beside Willis, talking to him urgently. "Dis aint gonna solve nuttin. You caint make her stay wit you if she dont want."

"You better move back, Eli. I dont want to have to shoot you, too." Willis George spoke quietly, then raised his voice to command, "Bring it to me, Sugarnun." Sugarnun scanned the yard, trying to gauge how far and how fast he could get before Willis George could fire the shotgun. He remembered with dismay that he had chosen this place because it was hard to find, protected by the dense brush, the same dense brush that made it hard to escape. Anywhere he ran, he would get caught in the brush like a bird in a trap.

Willis George held out his other hand. "Give it to me. Come on, now. Put dat pail in my hand!" He glanced at Eli. "Aint no need for you to stay. Dis between him an me!" Sugarnun held out the supper pail. "Come closer. I want it in my hand."

Sugarnun cautiously moved forward, letting the pail dangle from his fingertips. He winced and began trembling when Willis George pushed the shotgun up to his chest. Sugarnun began to plead, "Man, I sorry! Her come after me! What I sposed to do?"

Eli appealed to him again, "Yall come up together. Sallie! Sallie, talk to him!"

He desperately turned to Sallie Lee and was stunned by the mixture of contempt and satisfaction in her eyes. She stared at Willis George as if measuring him. She sat down by the door. "Aint nothin I can say! I learned long time, a man's got to do what he got to do."

Willis George reached in the supper pail, pulled out a sweet potato, and took a bite. "Her a good cook. Dat what you want?"

Sugarnun shook his head. "Naw, naw, I dont want she! Her know dat!" Willis George leaned forward, the shotgun pressing into Sugarnun's chest. "What you want me to do, Willis? I leave right now an never come back! I see she on de street, an I dont know she!"

Willis George started to laugh. His shoulders shook, he laughed so hard. The shotgun bobbed from his shaking, making Sugarnun even more nervous. Willis George stopped abruptly, his eyes filled with tears. He began to sob. It was a terrible sound, the cries wrenched from his throat. The sound of this man's agony tore at Eli. Sallie stared up at the sky as if she were looking for rain.

Sugarnun began to whimper, pleading, begging, "I swear on my dead mother's grave, I aint never . . ." He stopped as Willis George stifled his sobs, drew himself up, and stepped back. Sugarnun cried, "Lord, help me!"

Eli spoke quickly. "What gonna happen to dem babies, Willis George? You gonna leave dem here for she to see after!"

Willis George replied calmly, "My sister she take dem in."

Eli argued, "It aint right! Yall brought dem chilren here! Yall aint spose to be pushin dem off on nobody else cause yall got troubles! What you gonna tell dat lil boy, Amos, when dey come to take you off?"

Willis George began to pull back the trigger. "All I wanted was jus a lil bit of dat love her give to he!"

Eli moved as close to him as he dared. "Dem chilren love you! You gonna give up dem chilren love for dese two!"

Sallie Lee got to her feet and walked toward them. It seemed to Eli that she was daring Willis George to fire. She walked up behind Sugarnun and slid her arms around him. Sugarnun desperately pushed at her hands. "Woman, you gonna get us kilt for sure!" She smiled at

Willis George and grabbed at Sugarnun, who slapped her hands away. When she tried to kiss him, he grabbed her and pushed her to the ground. "See dat, man! Dat de way her always be!" Sugarnun pointed to Sallie, who smiled lazily and stretched in the dirt.

Willis George stared at this woman, his Sallie Lee, and felt the helpless love and hunger sweep over him just like it had the first time he saw her. Eli, seeing his hesitation, put his hand on the barrel of the shotgun. Willis George looked at him and slowly removed his finger from the trigger. Sugarnun held his breath until Willis lowered the shotgun and then sobbed with relief. Willis George handed the shotgun to Eli, who laid it against the trunk of a nearby tree. Willis George continued to stare at Sallie, who acted as if she was oblivious to everything that had happened. Sugarnun assured him, "Man, I gettin out of here! I gonna get my clothes an guitar, an you aint never gonna see me again!" He turned and ran into the house.

Willis George knelt down to help Sallie up, and she pushed him away. He tried to grab her and hold her. She fought him, and when Eli came over to pull him away from her, she scampered away toward the woods. "Aint nuttin I do please she!" Willis George said with painful resignation. He turned away from her, his head hung low.

Eli, his mouth dry from anxiety, wandered around the side of the house looking for a water bucket and giving Willis George the time to pull himself together.

Sugarnun appeared in the doorway, guitar in hand. He looked around the yard hesitantly, then began to walk quickly across the clearing to the opening in the thicket. When he reached the space, he looked back at those in the yard. First he saw Willis George standing at the edge of the clearing, gazing into the woods; then he saw Sallie. He only had time to gasp before the wad from the shotgun in her hands blew him back into the thicket.

Amelia looked out over the smooth water, marveling at how unusually calm the ocean was when the world above it was so filled with turmoil and distress. The boat glided smoothly through the water, hurrying Amelia to the mainland so that she could catch the train back to New York. She stuck her hand in her pocket, feeling for the only letter she had ever received from her father. His message had been cruel in its brevity: "Come home. She is back in the hospital. She is not expected to live." Amelia's heart shrank when she read the words, the guilt sweeping over her. Remembering the words of assurance from My-own's last letter, she faulted herself for believing Myown's hopeful tone. She had not even opened Haagar's last letter, sparing herself the continuous demands and complaints. She and Elizabeth cried as she packed to go home. They cried for her mother, they cried for each other, and they cried for Sugarnun.

She listened to J.C. telling a joke as he and the other man guided the boat, and she thought of Willis George, who had spent most of an evening pleading with Eli not to tell the law who had shot Sugarnun. At first, Willis George had intended to claim that he had shot him, and when Eli angrily refused to go along with his plan, he began to plead for Sallie Lee. Amelia and Elizabeth sat in the house with Eula and the others, but they clearly heard the argument that had gone on in the front yard.

Both had been startled the night Ben ran to Nana's house to warn them to keep an eye out for Sallie Lee. She had fled as soon as she shot Sugarnun, and there was no telling what she would do in her state of mind. Ben breathlessly described Eli walking into the house after he and Willis George had carried Sugarnun's body from the thicket. "Him come in de house, an him try to talk to Mama, an him caint say nothin. Her give he water, him still caint talk. Her wipe he face wit de rag an make he sit down. And den him say real quietlike, 'Her kilt he. Her blew he head off!' Mama think him talkin bout Willis George, an her start wailin for dem chilren. Daddy tell she it Sugarnun, Sugarnun dead. I caint hardly believe it!"

Eli and Ben stayed up that night and made the crude coffin for Sugarnun, while Willis George went to get his children for Eula to look after before he searched the Island for Sallie Lee. When he walked into his house, he was startled to find Sallie Lee sitting by the fireplace rocking the baby. She had cleaned herself up, fed the children, and put the boys to bed, waiting for him as if nothing had happened. They sat by the fire for the rest of the night, not saying a word.

Amelia and Elizabeth had helped Eula prepare what was left of Sugarnun for burial. Amelia had assisted many times in the preparing room of her father's business, and she took over when they both faltered at the sight of Sugarnun's shattered head. She gently wrapped his head in a towel and quickly washed his body. Eula brought a clean shirt and a pair of Eli's old work pants for him to be buried in, with Elizabeth quietly commenting that Sugarnun would have had a fit seeing himself laid out in those old farms clothes he hated. They then wrapped his body in a sheet and tucked the old quilt that Eli had found in his shack around him.

Early the next morning, Eli and Ben got up and left to spread the word about Sugarnun's death and his burial that evening. As word spread across the Island, people began to arrive to see what they could do. The men dug a grave for him next to his mother, noting that his stepfather was on the other side and would not be too pleased. The women brought food and spoke in fearful tones about Sallie Lee. No one had seen either Sallie Lee or Willis George.

When they lined up with the torches to make their way to the cemetery, a stir swept through the crowd as Sallie Lee and Willis George appeared with their children. Sallie Lee handed the baby over to Eula while Elizabeth gathered the two boys with her. Then Sallie Lee took her place beside Willis George in the procession. Folks were stunned by her boldness, which would be the talk of the Island for years to come.

Eli had entered the house after that long argument with Willis George and told them that he had agreed not to get the law on Sallie Lee, but that she would have to leave the Island. Willis George would have to take her to the state hospital and sign her in because she was not in her right mind. Eli was insistent; she was never to come back to the Island, even if the doctors at the hospital said that she had gotten better. Willis George had eagerly agreed and promised Eli that he would get her out the next morning. Eli would accompany them to the hospital to make sure everything went as agreed.

They sat on the bench waiting for the train to come in. Elizabeth reached for Amelia's hand, and Amelia clutched her fingers. They had said little to each other on the trip over, and there was much they wanted to say. Each remembered back six months before when Amelia had waited anxiously for Elizabeth at the train station, sure that she had been forgotten. Although neither was sure just how, they had surely changed each other in that short time.

Amelia studied Elizabeth's face. Despite their sadness, when their eyes met, they shared a smile of empathy. No stranger to guilt herself, Amelia realized that she had fled New York to escape a similar burden, the expectations of the next generation, that had been placed on her since birth. She had reveled in this act of rebellion cloaked in scholarly purpose. She had come down here fully expecting to maintain some type of distance between herself and the subjects of her study. Yes, she wanted to learn about her family, and she had really convinced herself that it was all incidental to her gathering the information she needed to support her thesis.

She had arrived with a strange mixture of ideas and attitudes about these people that Myown loved so much and Haagar held in such disdain. Over the years, she had developed an easy way of gliding through the social landscape. When her first efforts to get information from the Island people failed, she had been angry, dismissing them as backward. But she watched how Elizabeth dealt with them, listened more than she spoke, waited patiently through the long pauses and changes in rhythm that marked every conversation, treated superstitions and fears with respect. It had not pleased her at all that her cousin seemed to possess the natural instincts of an anthropologist while she floundered under the weight of her academic training.

It had taken her a while, but somewhere along the way, she realized that what she was learning about her family and herself would be the key to understanding life on the Island. Amelia now chuckled at the notion that she would come down and learn all she needed to know within a short period of time. Her education had just begun, and she knew it would be her life's work. Just like the spiritual they sang at the church meetings, she knew she had a "right to the tree of life."

Elizabeth turned to Amelia, mischief glinting through the sadness in her eyes. "You know what? You been down here gathering everybody else's story. I don't recall you telling yours." Amelia choked back a laugh as her eyes filled with tears at the warm encouragement she saw in Elizabeth's face.

My Story

as told by Amelia Varnes

It was supposed to be so simple. I was going to collect stories for my schoolwork and then go back. I thought I came down here to find out why the people living out here were so different. But now I know I came here because my people left and the others stayed, and I wanted to find out why. I came to find what drove my grandmother's rage and bound my mother's misery. I came to find a truth. Were they leaving cause they wanted to, or were they running cause they had to? I came to find my life story.

I thought I knew, but now I know I don't. They live in these houses that look like they're held together by a string and a prayer. Nana's old house, you can't even cross the room with a candle for the wind will blow it out. But no matter how cold it is outside and how much the wind slips through those cracks, it's warm in that room. I see your mother and father struggling from sunup to sundown to keep their family clothed and fed. And every night they set aside that time to make sure your brothers and sisters do their lessons. You can't tell Becca that she's not the most loved child in the world.

When I first came here and saw how hard folks lived and what little they had, I thought to myself, "Lord, slavery is not that far gone." But now I'm wondering who's living in slavery, folks down here working their own land, or folks up North working to pay that rent and keep the lights on, too. I saw Lucy stop in the middle of her weeding the garden, grab a fistful of dirt, and smell it. You know that look she can get on her face. I wish I could feel that way about something.

I listen to the folks talk, I listen to those old superstitions, stories, and roots and all. I wonder, "How we going to get past all this? We got to be ready when the time comes." But these folks have seen the worst and they just keep on going. While we do all this getting ready, going off to school, learning to talk the right way, they just living like they want to be.

I worry about you, Elizabeth. Every now and then I see something in your eyes that lets me know that you are far away from here. And just when I think it's about to bust out of you, I see you take it, fold it like a handkerchief, and put it away.

My granma has been angry all my life, and I always thought she was mad at me. I thought that if I was good, she'd stop being mad. But no matter how good I was, she was still mad. I'd do what she said. She would be mad. I wouldn't do it. She would be mad. It didn't make any difference. I went to see her daddy, and I think the only way she could have come through all that misery was to be mad and stay mad. It doesn't take much to figure out that she's still running from that old man.

I come to see my mama's sister, and after all these years, she's still weak with love for that man who took her away from my granma and my mama. I'm happy for her, but I'm so sad for my mama cause she should have got that same kind of love from my daddy. She's like a seed that never got any water. I've tried to be to her what he couldn't. But a daughter's love isn't supposed to take the place of a husband's love.

It frightens me, Lil Bet. I expect so little and want so much.

In the distance, they could hear the train's whistle as it drew closer to the station. Amelia and Elizabeth were lost in thought as the porters rushed by, lining up the luggage and cargo for loading. "Yall want I should load dis?" The porter appeared before them. "Yall is gettin on dis train, right?" The young man grinned at both of them, pleased to have the opportunity to talk with these two comely young women. His obvious appreciation drew smiles from both of them.

Amelia pointed to her bags. "It's just me."

The man picked up the bags and spoke to Elizabeth. "An you. You gonna stay right here, huh?" Elizabeth smiled ruefully. "I staying here." He swept his arm before him, pointing the way to Amelia.

Elizabeth and Amelia walked arm in arm to the steps where she would board the train. Amelia whispered fiercely, "You be strong in front of that School Board. You haven't done anything wrong!"

Elizabeth replied, "I'm not so sure they gonna see it that way." She touched Amelia's face. "Give my best to your mama! Write when you get to New York." Amelia nodded and pulled her close for one last hug. Elizabeth whispered, "I'll be all right." The porter cleared his throat, and Amelia hurried up the steps.

Elizabeth walked the length of the platform as Amelia moved through the railroad car. Amelia found a window seat and waved to Elizabeth; the train whistle signaled its departure. Elizabeth waved from the platform until the train disappeared from view.

Elizabeth stared at the large brick building that housed the Beaufort School Board. She had visited the building only once before when she had been hired to teach. On that day she had been filled with such hope and so many plans, but now she felt as if she had let everyone down. Walking to the edge of the building, she started up the narrow path to the colored entrance.

She pushed the door open and stepped into the hallway. A janitor mopped the floor at the far end while she wandered the hallway looking for the meeting room. She heard the sounds of people at work, the papers shuffling, the low voices, several typewriters. She quickly stepped aside as a young man burst from an office. He frowned at her as he turned and hurried up the stairs. As she drew closer, a colored man stepped from the office at the end of the hall and peered at her. She recognized Dr. Buckley from her previous trips to the Book Depository.

He pulled his pocket watch out, studied it with deliberation, then beckoned to Elizabeth to hurry. She quickened her step, and when she stood in front of him, he inspected her from her neatly braided hair to her polished shoes. "You Elizabeth Peazant," he told her. "They called me in to see to you."

She spoke quietly. "The letter said that I was supposed to meet with the Board."

He waved that away impatiently. "They want me to talk to you first, get you straight!" Elizabeth blinked at his scolding tone. He spoke quickly. "Mr. Hammond come back from his visit to your school so upset it was all I could do to keep him from shutting that school down!"

"What did he say had happened?" Elizabeth asked evenly.

"He said you had thrown out all the materials provided by the Board and brought in all this outside stuff and were teaching out of the guidelines. It doesn't matter what you got to say," he interrupted as Elizabeth started to speak. "The Board wants you to know that it will not have you using anything other than the materials provided by the Board. Now I have used these materials for the last twenty years and found nothing that you couldn't use for your classes!"

Elizabeth calmed herself before she spoke. "Dr. Buckley, with all due respect, by the time they let me in to get my supplies, there is so little left that I have no choice but to try to get outside materials!"

Dr. Buckley drew back, startled by the flicker of anger in her eyes. "You've got to learn the system. You think that twenty years ago, when I started, I got everything I needed? I had to learn to work the system just to get the few books I got. You got to wait on things, be patient."

"And while I'm being patient, what's going to happen to my students? How am I supposed to teach them without materials?" she snapped.

"Those children live out there on that island don't need to learn anything other than to read and write their names and figure a little bit! That's all they need for that cropping," he admonished her. "They can't learn much more than that anyhow!" Elizabeth stared at him as he continued to lecture her. "Mr. Hammond say you got them reciting that Lincoln speech. Girl, I don't know what's gotten into you! It's like waving a red flag at a bull!"

Elizabeth trembled with anger and walked away from him. He followed her, leaning over her. "It's real simple. If you want that school to stay open, you gonna teach what they want! It won't hurt those white folks one bit to shut down a colored school, especially one out there on those islands!"

Turning on him, Elizabeth demanded, "I need supplies! I need something more than those torn-up books and that old dried-out paper!"

He looked at her, admiring her temper and willingness to ask for what she needed. "I'll see what I can pull together. Maybe we got a few things you can use!"

He took her by the elbow and led her to the open door. "When we get in there, you let me do all the talking. This isn't just about you, you know." She pulled her elbow from his grasp and stepped into the meeting room.

When Elizabeth arrived at the Bouvier house, Katie had eagerly told her that a package came just for her from the French lady. Now she set it aside as she dropped on the bed, trying to ease the pain that rocked her head. Kicking her shoes off, she lay back, letting the pain and dismay slip over her.

She had said very little during her meeting with the School Board. Indeed, as Dr. Buckley had said, there was no intention of letting her speak or explain what had taken place. She shuddered with humiliation at the way they spoke around her to Dr. Buckley as if she were some child who could not hear, talk, or think for herself. When they lectured her about Lincoln and spoke in exalted tones of the great South Carolinians that she should be teaching her students about, she realized she had gotten more than her share of Eli's temper. She watched Dr. Buckley as he flattered and cajoled the Board Members into overlooking her shortcomings as a new teacher and promised them that he would keep an eye on her. As she recalled her students' eager faces, she agreed with him that this had been the only solution. But it did not lessen her feeling of defeat.

She drifted off to sleep, waking only when Katie knocked on the door to tell her that dinner was ready and that the sisters were expecting her. She washed up and made her way to the dining room. Miss Genevieve greeted her brightly, plunging into French the moment she entered the room. Miss Evangeline had been uncharacteristically quiet, and throughout the mostly silent meal, Elizabeth could feel her glance on her. Elizabeth begged off from joining them in the library afterward, explaining that she was not feeling well. Although Miss Genevieve had been disappointed, she had not been insistent when Miss Evangeline had given her permission to retire.

Elizabeth stared at the small package for several minutes before she reached to open it. The letter from Natalie was filled with descriptions of the new designs they had introduced. She had included a small clipping from a ladies' magazine that praised the style and workmanship of the clothes and made special note of the accessories that were included. Elizabeth could not quite believe that she was reading about something she had made in a French magazine. There was only one passing bit of discord in the letter. Madame's resentment seemed to grow with every success, and Natalie was tiring of the petty bickering that took place over every suggestion. For the first time, she had ended with a wish that Elizabeth come to Paris so they could set up a shop of their own. Natalie was convinced that a little shop that specialized in accessories and was not bound to one house of fashion would do quite well. She knew that between Elizabeth and herself they could produce the charms, the scarves, and the jewelry that these women wanted.

Elizabeth could not believe what she had read, scanning it twice over before the ridiculousness of the situation set in. She shook her head in wonder. She knew nothing about jewelry, and she certainly could not imagine how she would get to Paris. She angrily flung the letter from her, furious that Natalie would even suggest such an impossible thing. It seemed that she had been mocked twice in one day for who she was and what little her future held. She began to cry as she succumbed to the helplessness and loneliness that welled up in her.

At a knock on her door, she stood up quickly, rubbing her eyes. She glared at the door, angry at Katie for disturbing her. Looking around for the letter that she had thrown, she saw it under the bureau and got down on her knees to retrieve it. There was another knock. "Come on in, Katie." She was tucking the letter in her skirt pocket when she looked up to see Miss Evangeline standing in the doorway. Elizabeth did not know what to make of it. Neither of the sisters had come to Elizabeth's room before. Miss Evangeline stepped into the room, shutting the door behind her. She made her way across the room to the chair and sat down.

"How is he?" she asked abruptly.

Elizabeth looked away from her, not wanting to be a part of this conversation. Miss Evangeline waited her out. Finally Elizabeth muttered, "He like he been since he come back out to the Island!"

Miss Evangeline asked, "Still preaching from the Bible?"

Elizabeth spoke bluntly. "Funny how a mind will turn when the heart is broken."

Miss Evangeline mused, "I know I should have thrown those pictures out years ago, but it was all I had of him, of us together."

Amelia stared down at the street below. People scurried along the slippery sidewalks, bundled against the cold spring rain. She heard the rhythmic clang of the medicine cart being pushed along the corridor. Myown sighed, and Amelia turned to her, sympathizing with her mother as she prepared herself for the medicine she would have to take. Like her mother, Amelia was not convinced that the hospital treatment or the medicine was doing her any good. Amelia was determined to wait for the harried young doctor who served the ward.

"Medicine!" The woman's loud voice rang out, prompting groans from the other patients. Amelia moved to stand protectively at the foot of Myown's bed. Amelia reassured her mother with a smile and leaned over the bed to help her sit up.

"It time for you to go home," Myown admonished.

"I'm just waiting to talk to your doctor, Mama."

"Baby, dere aint no tellin when him comin. Him de only doctor down here," Myown explained.

Amelia nodded. "I know, Mama, I can wait." She straightened the blanket and patted Myown's hair. Her mother looked so young and fragile with her hair in the small plaits that Amelia had fashioned. It was Rebecca's favorite hairstyle, and the only thing Amelia had left out was the colored string that Rebecca so loved.

"Dey dont need you down at de parlor?" Myown gently asked.

"I didn't come back to help them, Mama!" Amelia replied shortly. "They can get up off that money and hire somebody to help them. Plenty people looking for work!" She vigorously plumped the pillow behind Myown, trying to stem the rush of anger that swept over her.

It seemed to her that the change that had come over her after her stay on the Island was so palpable that everyone would have noticed it. She felt as if she had sloughed a skin, exposing an Amelia who had a touch of earth about her. This Amelia was ready to challenge, take the risk, and deal with the consequences.

When Haagar had opened the door to Amelia after her long trip from Beaufort, she had flatly declared, "You lookin rough!"

Amelia leaned against the doorway in exhaustion and gazed at her grandmother. A while back, Haagar's harsh comment would have hurt, causing Amelia to reflectively brush her hair or straighten her clothes. But this time, Amelia merely nodded to her as she brushed past and said, "Granma." Haagar watched as Amelia dragged the rest of her bags into the house. She caught Haagar's surprised blink when she straightened and bluntly asked, "Where is my mother?"

After only a moment's hesitation, Haagar replied, "Over at St. Mary's." Turning immediately, Amelia left, closing the door firmly behind her. She saw the parlor curtain move as she went down the front steps, but she did not look back.

It was at the hospital that she received the only welcome she needed. Myown's face lit up when she saw her only child making her way across the room to her bed. She saw the difference in Amelia immediately, from the looseness of her stride to the directness of her gaze to the hair that frizzled around her face.

"You look just like you did when you was a baby!" Myown declared, reaching up for Amelia's kiss. Amelia held Myown close, wincing at the sharp feel of her bones through the cotton nightgown. Myown grasped her hands, "Did you get done what you needed to get done?" Amelia looked into her mother's eyes, beyond the sickness, the tiredness, and the pain to the love that shone within.

She nodded. "I did . . . but I am not finished." Myown looked down at Amelia's roughened hands, turned them over, and gently stroked the callouses. "Those Peazants put me to work!" Amelia teased her.

With a spurt of laughter, Myown countered, "Dey known to do dat!" She squeezed Amelia's hands. "Tell me. Tell me everting."

It formed the pattern for the days to come. Amelia would arrive in the morning right after Myown had breakfast, give her a bath and rubdown, comb her hair, and tell her of everything that had happened during her stay. The stories had brought forth Myown's memories, and the color and insight that Myown brought exhilarated both of them. As Myown slept through the afternoon, Amelia worked on her thesis.

Her first night back, Amelia presented her grandmother with all of the return tickets that Haagar had sent and a hundred dollars she had managed to save. Without preamble, she slapped the money down on the kitchen table. "You should use this to pay for that extra help you need. I came back to take care of my mama!"

While Haagar sputtered, her father commented dryly, "That don't make up for all the time you was gone."

She thought for a moment and then an odd smile crossed her face. In the accent of the Peazants she replied, "Wont nuttin make up for dat!" Amelia noted that in the weeks since she had returned, no one had been hired.

Now, by her mother's side, she turned to face the woman with the cart, who thrust the medicine at her. The woman waited, her hands on her hips. "Doctor say I got to see her take that medicine!" Amelia peered down at the two large pills in the cup. Myown's stillness told her that Myown was holding her breath, willing her daughter not to respond to the woman. Amelia picked up her purse and removed the pestle she had bought at the drugstore. She quickly crushed the pills and added water, swirling the mixture in the cup. She held the cup as Myown drank, encouraging her mother as she strained to empty the cup. When she finished, Myown breathed a sigh of relief.

"When will the doctor be making his rounds?" she asked, handing the cup to the woman.

"I don't know. You the smart one!"

Amelia abruptly turned her back on the woman and sat in the chair by Myown's bed.

Myown's eyes drooped with exhaustion. "You heard from Lil Bet?"

Amelia shook her head. "Not in a while." Despite their promise to each other, neither had proven to be much of a correspondent. She had received an oddly dispirited letter a couple of weeks before that said more by what was left out. From Elizabeth's terse writing, she could tell that the meeting with the School Board had been difficult. She could sense the restlessness in the stiff sentences. Often late at night while she wrote, she wondered if Elizabeth was sitting at the edge of the water staring into the darkness.

"Where your sister?"

Elizabeth glanced up at Ol Trent from the patch of mint she was working. She had noticed him a while back standing at the edge of the yard, but had not spoken to him. Squinting at him in the afternoon sun, she replied, "She gone to Tampa with her husband." It was unusual for Ol Trent to get that close to anyone unless he was preaching. But lately, he seemed to have lost his taste for the long harangues. Eli had mentioned that, every now and then, Trent would show up at the house and stand out front until Eula sent one of the children out with a plate of food.

She crushed a mint leaf between her fingers, sniffing the sweet smell. "She coming back? I done fixed that land for her."

Elizabeth was startled by his declaration. It had been a matter of some speculation across the Island, the way Trent worked that land. Almost everyone had seen him scouring the Island, gathering every type of flower he could find to plant in that field. Miss Pearlie Jane had complained angrily to everyone about his swiping a piece of her running geranium, only to fall silent when she saw the profusion of flowers that now covered the field. It had not occurred to any of them that he might be doing it for Lucy.

"When you coming back to the school?"

Again, she was thrown off by his question. She spoke slowly, masking her frustration. "In a couple of weeks." No one but her family knew why Elizabeth had been teaching over on the mainland for the past two weeks.

As part of her reprimand by the School Board, Dr. Buckley had insisted that she assist at his school under his supervision. He had assured the Board that within a month's time he would have her properly trained. They would not provide a substitute teacher, and despite Elizabeth's protest that the Island school would have to be closed down, the Board had agreed, directing Dr. Buckley to report her progress over the month. Elizabeth could not understand why her students had to suffer for her mistake and despaired the work and time that would be lost. She felt terrible guilt when Hanley had asked if the school was being closed because of him. Despite her reassurances, she could see from his slumped shoulders that her words brought him little comfort. Septima had boldly declared her intention to teach the rest of them until Elizabeth returned.

Her two weeks at Dr. Buckley's school had been bearable. Although she chafed under his heavy-handedness, she did appreciate the opportunity to work with the other teachers. Under any other circumstances, she might even have enjoyed it, but it had only served to reinforce her feeling of restlessness and isolation. Listening to the other young teachers talk about clothes, dances, and special beaus, she realized how far she really was from everything out there on the Island. She could see her life stretching before her; quiet evenings with her family, teaching school, church on Sunday mornings, broken up with the occasional trips to Carrie Mae's. She had always been so dutiful, and it had already begun to wear on her. Try as she might, she could not put Natalie's suggestion out of her mind. Despite her dismissal of such a trip as fanciful, it touched that part of her that wanted to push past the boundaries of her small world. At first she could not see herself in Paris, and then it was all she could see. She knew that these young women found her odd with her quiet, serious ways, and she wondered what they would think if she announced that her dream was to stroll down the broad boulevards of a city thousands of miles away. She yearned to visit the city where the Bouvier sisters had spent so much of their young womanhood and where Miss Evangeline had met her one true love.

Elizabeth had been startled when Miss Evangeline sat on the foot of her bed and spoke of her marriage to Trent. They had met in Paris when the sisters returned to buy Miss Genevieve's trousseau. Trent, a popular concert singer, was about to debut at the Paris Opera House. Her friends had despaired of her finding a man who could bear her outspoken temperament. She and Trent had parried until they both came to the realization that they were only meant for each other. With Miss Genevieve's blessings, they married and settled into an apartment.

One day Miss Evangeline had come home from shopping to find two young colored men waiting for Trent. Although they immediately insisted that they had made a mistake, she knew that something was wrong and had confronted Trent when he came home. He then confessed to her that he was a Wilkerson from Dawtuh Island. She knew that few white people lived on the Islands. He'd been sent off to Fisk University to study farm management, but had joined the Jubilee Singers and toured Europe with them. Reveling in the beauty, the freedom, the acceptance he found in Europe, he decided not to return.

Miss Evangeline fled and took the first boat back to America, leaving Miss Genevieve to deal with Trent. Trent followed, desperate to reconcile with his wife, throwing away his chance to become the toast of Paris. When Miss Evangeline repeatedly refused to see him, he managed to get a job with Burton Devries, her brother-in-law, as chauffeur. It was a source of great pride to Burton Devries that this well-educated young white man would want to work for him.

Of course, Miss Evangeline and Trent could not stay away from each other. It was only a matter of time until Burton Devries caught them. When she flung herself at the gun that Burton pointed at them, it had discharged, striking Trent in the temple. She thought that he was dying and sent for his sister. When the dark-skinned woman arrived Burton had the advantage over her that he had always sought. After Trent began slowly to recover, it was apparent to all that the Trent she knew and loved was gone forever. In his place was an anxious man whose only memories were of the Bible lessons he'd had as a child. Rather than commit him to the state asylum or have him near so that Burton could torture them both, she arranged with Trent's sister to have him return to the Island.

As she listened to the misery and guilt in Miss Evangeline's voice, Elizabeth thought of the many times she had seen Ol Trent pacing the shore, but never seeking to leave. She wondered if this is what came of seeking your dreams; a prison of someone else's making.

Now Elizabeth looked up at Trent, who frowned at her. "What was it like, living in Paris?" she asked. He looked at her and blinked, not understanding what she was asking. "Do you remember any of your time in Paris?" He stepped back, lowering his head, his eyes clouded with confusion.

"Do you remember what Paris was like?" she tried again, in French, and caught her breath as she saw the clear eyes of the young man in the photographs for a quick second. He suddenly waved her away, wheeling about, and with long strides headed for the beach. She started when his words floated back to her: "*Ce n'est plus une mémoire*—It is no longer a memory."

Amelia sat at the editing bench, staring ruefully at the reels of film that awaited her. She had submitted the draft of her thesis for the committee review and now needed to go through the black and white film that had been developed to put together a ten-minute piece that would complement the thesis. She had not seen the film before, for she never had time to review it when she returned. So intent was she upon seeing to her mother and finishing her thesis that she had actually forgotten about it.

Counting the reels now, she realized that Ben had shot quite a bit of film and that her work was cut out for her. She glanced at her watch. She had brought Myown home that morning and wanted to get back as soon as possible to settle her for the night. Over the last couple of weeks Myown had rallied, surprising everyone but Amelia with her will to get better. She had progressed from sitting up to taking a turn around the ward on Amelia's arm. Announcing her intention to leave, Myown had cajoled the doctor into moving up the date of her release. Amelia had worried about her rushing things, but Myown had renewed energy and did not want to waste it by spending an extra day in the hospital.

Amelia looked around for the photo assistant who was to show her how to edit the film. Having set up the projector for her to view the film and shown her how to mark the editing sheet to indicate the footage she wanted, he had disappeared into the darkroom. Amelia inspected the projector warily, picked up a reel of film, and awkwardly threaded it through the projector. Looking for the switch, she flipped the projector on, then pulled the shades to darken the room. She blinked at the shock of light as the overexposed footage flickered on the wall. She could see only the bare outlines of the images, the jerky movements tiring her eyes. Leaning back in the chair, she gazed at the wall.

The sound of the pen falling from her hand awoke her. She had no idea how long she had dozed. Reaching down to pick the pen up from the floor, she glanced up at the wall and met Lucy's suspicious gaze. Placing her hand over her mouth, she stifled her giggle as Lucy angrily waved the camera away. It swung over to Eli, who was cleaning a saddle. Eli blinked in surprise and then stepped back from his work. As he reluctantly returned to his task, the camera moved forward to show his hands buffing the smooth leather. Eula walked between him and the camera and then stepped back to peer into the lens. Amelia laughed out loud at Eula's horrified expression and how she quickly covered her hair with her apron and disappeared into the kitchen.

Amelia sighed, recognizing before her the road through the woods. Her eyes filled with tears when she, Elizabeth, and Rebecca stepped into the frame, waving and heading down the road. Amelia stared back at the camera uncertainly, shading her eyes from the bright sun, clutching her journal to her chest. Elizabeth's gaze was steady and guarded as Ben brought the camera closer to her. It was a test of wills that was broken by Rebecca's small hand frantically reaching up and down in the camera's view. When the camera caught her, Rebecca froze, staring in the lens as if hypnotized. As these images of the Island shone on the wall, Amelia felt her exhaustion fall away and affection and longing sweep over her.

The photo assistant stuck his head around the open door and reminded Amelia, "We close in five minutes." She nodded to him and glanced down at the editing sheet. It had few notations. She had been so fascinated by the images that after the first few minutes, she had forgotten about the editing. At some point, the camera had become unimportant, invisible to the Peazant family, while Ben had somehow caught fragile, revealing moments; Lucy washing up after a long day working the fields, Eli watching Eula comb Rebecca's hair, the twins wrestling, fighting, and then playing with each other as they had always done. Ben had managed to capture a little bit of them all.

She remembered the day that Elizabeth and her class had picnicked among the dunes. Each child proudly held up a treasure from the beach and raced with Elizabeth down the dunes. She felt a chill when the camera followed the fading footsteps along the beach and then moved back to show a solitary figure of a woman at the far end. Now the folks waiting at the dock for Willis George squinted through the morning sun; the women carrying their produce in baskets on top of their heads and the men self-consciously buttoning their waist jackets; Carrie Mae standing wide-legged, with a gap-toothed grin, trying to keep Toady from slipping from the frame; J.C. waving vigorously, grinning as he and a grim Willis George pulled the boatload away from the dock.

There was a marvelous stretch of footage showing the water that surrounded, ran through, and was a part of the Island. It began with a simple dipper drawn from a well, followed the trail of a fast-running creek, disappeared into the thick darkness of the swamp, shot with rays of light that slipped through the trees, and ended with swells that lay offshore. She was riveted at the way Ben had caught the rhythms of Island life, the chickens stirring in the early morning, the people working in the fields, Eli firing up his forge, the fishermen coming in at the end of the day.

And then there were what she could only think of as portraits. A cocky Chance posed for the camera from a tree limb high above. Clemmie disappeared into the shadows when the camera focused on her. Iona's hands skillfully wove a basket with fluted edges, a serene look of contemplation on her face. Elizabeth pulled roots from the ground and frowned at the intrusion. It seemed as if Ben had been everywhere, and she marveled at his insight.

Watching the footage of family, friends, and acquaintances, she realized a reluctance to share the images with strangers, people who would see only the simplicity of the life on the Island, but not realize the richness beyond the view of a casual observer. St. Julien's family were the children of the ancient people, Amelia's people were the children of African captives. Contrary to everything that she had started out to do, she did not want their culture, their ways, how they talked with each other described in academic terms that would leave out the spirit and overlook the common heritage and stories that bound them so closely. She had winced when she reread her thesis proposal with its distant perspective and cold language that attempted to describe people whose lives were filled with wonder, vibrancy, and an uncomplicated honesty. Life for them was hard, a struggle from one moment to the next, but it was filled with the natural pleasures that she was just now beginning to understand and appreciate.

She had pledged to them and to herself that she would try to capture all of this in her thesis. It was an anxious task as she avoided the conventions of the traditional anthropological view and spoke from her heart. At first she had been gratified that Dr. Colby had been so pleased with her draft. He spoke excitedly of using her thesis as a means for raising money for more studies. Now she quailed at the thought of people traipsing across the Island, intruding, prodding, uncovering. Taking her silence for agreement, he did not realize that to her each word signaled the overwhelming change that outsiders would let loose upon the Island. Seven months ago, she would have welcomed the change and found only good in the progress it would naturally bring. But now she feared that same progress, the havoc, the separation that were inevitable.

She quickly gathered her things as the photo assistant entered to put the equipment away. "I haven't quite finished," she apologized when he glanced down at the editing sheet. "We open at ten, so if you want the room, you need to sign up before you leave." He spoke distractedly as he put the projector away. She nodded, stacked the reels on the bookshelf near the wall, and slipped from the room. She signed up on the sheet posted by the door and slowly walked down the corridor. Glancing up at the clock, she gave a cry of dismay and picked up her pace. Caught in the world of the Island, she had lost all sense of present time.

Amelia just made the last trolley and slid into the seat behind the driver. There were only a few passengers at this time of night, shift workers from the bottling plant, busboys from restaurants on West 133rd Street, maids returning from uptown. She closed her eyes, the images from the past few hours playing over and over again through her mind.

As Amelia let herself in, she saw the downstairs lights and knew that her father was putting together the final touches for the next day's funeral. The door to the side parlor flew open, and Haagar frowned at her, tapping her pocket watch. "Do you know what time it is?"

"You know I was at school," Amelia answered patiently.

"At this time of the night?" Haagar questioned her sharply. Amelia waited for her to continue her tirade. "Your Mama been asking about you!" Amelia shot her a glance and headed quickly for the stairs. "She's asleep now!" Haagar snapped. "She tried to wait up for you, but was just plain old tuckered out." Amelia took the steps two at a time. Haagar cried after her, "I don't know why the doctor let her go so soon!"

Amelia said quietly, "Good night, Granma."

Amelia slowly opened the door to the bedroom that she had shared most of her life with her mother. As quietly as possible, she put her things aside and crossed to the bed, where Myown lay with her arms gently folded on her chest. Amelia took her small, dark hand in her own and sat down on the edge of the bed. Myown slowly opened her eyes. She smiled and spoke weakly, "Did you get your schoolwork done?"

Amelia swallowed the lump that came as she thought of how Myown would love to see the people in that film. "I got a little bit done. I'll finish it up this week. How you feeling, Mama?"

Myown nodded with what little energy she could summon. "Jus a lil tired, but I feelin much better now dat I out de hospital." She caressed Amelia's hand. "You eat anything?"

Amelia shook her head. "I'm not hungry."

"Well, your Granma fixed some chicken an dumplings."

Amelia shrugged. "Maybe later. Why don't you try to go back to sleep?"

Myown closed her eyes briefly. "You comin to bed?"

"I got a little bit more work to do, Mama. I'm going to fix up a pallet on the floor so I don't disturb you." She cut Myown off as she began to protest. "Mama, you're not gonna get much rest with me climbing in and out of the bed. Besides, that bed's too soft for me. I got used to sleeping on a pallet, an I like it." She listened to Myown's shallow breathing as she drifted off. Amelia rose from the edge of the bed carefully and crossed to the table and sat down. Turning on the floor lamp, she draped an old scarf over the shade to keep the light from spilling across the room. She pulled papers from her bag and began editing her thesis.

Amelia had been working for a good while before her stomach began to rumble. She tried to ignore it, but the rumblings grew louder, and she knew she could neither continue nor go to sleep without eating something. She tiptoed across the bedroom floor, willing the boards not to creak.

She fixed a plate and quickly ate. When she finished, she washed up the dishes. Stepping into the hallway, she noticed that the light was still on in the parlor. Despite herself, she crept nearer to listen to the low voices. "We got to take care of the bill from hospital," came Haagar's high-pitched reminder. "Just when I think I gettin ahead, something always happens."

She winced at her father's tone. "And she don't look like she getting any better."

Haagar surprised her. "She thinks she getting better, and that's all that matter. The doctor say she need to take her medicine and get some fresh air."

Amelia heard the hesitation in his voice, before he asked the question that she had refused to ask. "How long he say she got?"

As Amelia stepped forward and pushed the door open, her eyes swept from Haagar to her father. And she said simply, "I'm taking Mama home."

Her father looked away from her while Haagar spoke up. "She too sick to go anyplace! How you gonna take her back down there?"

Amelia said with confidence, "She'll be all right once I get her home." Haagar looked to her father for support, but he kept silent.

"That's just plain old foolishness. She's not gonna last two days down there with that wet water air! You gonna kill her, that's what you gonna do." Haagar appealed to him again. "Don't you got nothing to say bout this? She's talking about taking your wife away from here!" He slumped in his chair, his exhaustion showing in his face. She had noticed how much he had aged since she left. For the first time, Amelia felt sympathy for him and the singular, closed life he had chosen. "I got nothin to do with it! Never had nothin to do with it!" he admitted heavily.

Amelia turned from the shard of pain that shot through her. Haagar's face was flushed with anger. Jumping to her feet, she began to shout, her words so garbled with rage that they were unintelligible. She rushed toward Amelia. Without thinking, Amelia threw a com pe sign that she had seen Eli and Ben use. Haagar stepped back, fear in her eyes. "We're going home." Amelia closed the door behind her and climbed the stairs to the bedroom where she and her mother slept.

The children's laughter and chatter drifted through the woods. Elizabeth inspected the flower that Amos and Rebecca presented to her. "This is so pretty. Do you know its name?" she asked. They looked at each other and shrugged.

She had finally been allowed to reopen the school, only two weeks before it was to close for the summer. She had not been surprised when she returned to find that, with the exception of a few students, she might as well have been starting a new school year. She decided that these last few days they would enjoy each other and had taken a note from Amelia's work, spending more time exploring the Island and encouraging her students to tell the stories of their families. It was the only way she knew to make up to them for time and lessons lost.

"Miz Lil Bet! Miz Lil Bet! Look what Septima got!" They ran ahead of her to where Septima had pulled back the tall grass. The rabbit stood protectively in front of her nest, her babies shaking with fear, huddled together as the children pressed forward. As always, Septima took charge, keeping them from getting too close and hushing them.

"How many babies she got?" Elizabeth whispered, admiring her find. "Her got four," Septima confirmed. "Dey only a coupla days old." Elizabeth drew the children away as Septima replaced the grass around the nest.

Elizabeth looked up at the sun and knew it was time to head back to the school. She herded her students down the path. Behind them Hanley and several boys burst from the woods, shouting with laughter as they raced to catch up with the rest of the group. The older girls walked up ahead, stopping every now and then to grab a flower to add to the necklaces they wore. Elizabeth walked with the young ones, who had a thousand questions about everything. Hanley and the others strolled behind, sharing the secret joke that kept them giggling.

As the girls came to where the path split, Elizabeth called to them to take the path that would lead them by the old Wilkerson place. She had passed that way in the morning, searching for early cornflowers, and had been amazed at the variety and abundance of the flowers Trent had planted. Several people had commented that it was always in bloom, and folks had even started to bring him cuttings because they were convinced that this bit of earth was truly blessed. Ol Trent was weeding when she passed and did not acknowledge her bright greeting.

When the meadow came into view, Hanley shouted a challenge and raced toward the garden. The other boys took off after him, and the girls, knowing their advantage, raced ahead, daring the boys to try to catch them. Elizabeth called after the children, urging them not to trample or pick the flowers that Trent had so carefully nurtured. She grabbed the hands of the youngest ones and they ran after the others.

The girls stood at the edge of the garden, quizzing Elizabeth about the different flowers and itching to pick some. The boys quickly became bored and began to race each other, collapsing into a tangle of arms and legs that quickly led to a wrestling match. While the girls lay down in the grass, staring up at the sky and playing "Who I Gonna

Marry?" Elizabeth bent down to examine a patch of tiny, white, feathery flowers. As she touched the plant, bits of pollen clung to her fingers.

"Miz Lil Bet!" So involved was she in her examination that she did not hear Hanley's call at first. A note in his voice finally drew her attention, and she stood up to see that the boys had stopped wrestling. Hanley stood at the edge of the woods and pointed. When she started toward them, one of the boys backed away and ran past. "Miz Lil Bet!" Hanley's call was frantic. She ran to him and followed his pointing finger to where Ol Trent sat against the trunk of the tall elm tree.

Amelia took a deep breath before she opened the door to the room where the Thesis Committee waited. The appointments were running behind, and despite Professor Colby's reassurances, the longer she waited, the more nervous she became.

She had seen two of her classmates exit and watched closely for a sign, a relieved sigh or slumped shoulders. This year's Thesis Committee was notoriously difficult, and the rumor was that they had already decided that regardless of the caliber of the work, they would accept only two of the seven theses submitted. The young man whose appointment was before Amelia's had paced the hall for over an hour, the click from his heels echoing down the corridor. When they called his name, he had jumped and muttered to himself before gathering his courage to enter.

She took the chair before the Committee and measured each of them. She had taken classes from all. With the other students, she had borne the long hours in Professor Rehnquist's class as he had droned on in his thick German accent about cultural patterning, interspersed with anecdotes about the vagaries of fieldwork, particularly the lack of edible food and good company. She had giggled like everyone else when Professor Highman had gotten lost in the Natural History Museum. Aware of the politics in even such a small department at Brooklyn College, she knew well the competitiveness between Professor Anderson and Professor Colby and their students. She had been advised by another student that Professor Anderson seemed to subject Professor Colby's students to the most vigorous review. Professor Colby nodded to her encouragingly as his colleagues flipped through their notes and began to shoot questions at her.

Professor Anderson pushed her thesis forward and frowned. "I've talked to my colleague, Dr. Avery Parks, who has completed the formative work on Negro communities, and he is not familiar with these people that you have studied. What is it about these colored people that make them different from any other colored people?"

"As I have attempted to prove in my thesis, it is the way they live, conduct their daily lives, their beliefs, and their traditions. All of the things that Professor Rehnquist has taught us make up a culture." At the mention of his name, Professor Rehnquist roused himself and nodded in affirmation. He reached over and picked up the thesis, flipping through the pages.

"I'm glad you learned the basics of my anthropology class, Miss Varnes. But also remember my point that a culture must have a distinct history, artifacts, a language, and identifiable values."

"They have all of those!" Amelia said quickly. "They've lived on these islands for years by themselves and have maintained specific traditions that they pass on. They have distinct artifacts, from the charms they wear to the baskets they weave to the way they paint their houses. And their history . . ."

"Ah, yes," Professor Anderson interjected skeptically. "This 'telling the lie.' They are simply stories. There is little there of historic merit. They have long since lost their ties to where they came from!"

Amelia took a deep breath and stated emphatically, "I disagree. It is that telling of the story, that gathering around, that common sharing that is the tie!"

Professor Colby nodded in agreement and said, "It goes back to the first man, sitting around the fire after the hunt, telling the tale. Surely you're not going to dismiss the importance of the oral tradition!"

"Of course not!" Professor Anderson snapped. "I'm just not sure that what these people have to say amounts to a history. Quite frankly, what you have described seems to me to be some kind of crude imitation of the old plantation culture, a patois derived from broken English and the flurried accents of Irish and Huguenot planters, all of which is the obvious product of European influence. Surely you're not suggesting that in the land of secession and large plantations, there can be anything else?"

Amelia was breathless at his arrogance. She felt her temper flare and deliberately calmed herself. She looked to Professor Colby, who watched her steadily.

Professor Rehnquist cleared his throat and weighed in. "Mere vestiges, if anything, Miss Varnes. Not what would be acceptable in a scientific sense. Why, it is an established fact accepted by your own colored sociologists, that the colored people, bereft of a history, culture, and traditions, have long since adopted the ways of the dominant culture, shedding all ties with the African continent."

Amelia spoke with deliberation. "Perhaps for you and others who are not a part of their world, their history begins here, but they have memories and stories from the village, from the slave ships, from the plantations, and you cannot convince them or me that they do not have a history."

Professor Highman waved his hand and struggled to get his question out. "Wh-what about the language? Y-y-you suggest that the language may be more than a d-d-dialect."

It was at this point that Amelia showed her uncertainty. "I don't know. I'm not a linguist, and the language, it has a different sound, different words, a different rhythm."

"A dialect resulting in a simpler structure of English." Professor Anderson shrugged.

Amelia glanced up at him. "You've heard them speak, sir?"

He waved his hand dismissively. "No, not them specifically, but you must remember I studied under Professor Ulrich Bonnell Phillips at Yale and helped gather the information about the Negro people that he included in his brilliant work on slavery. I spoke with Negroes all over the South. All spoke with a dialect of some sort. That did not make it a language."

"How can you say that it's not a language, if it's never been studied?" interjected Professor Colby.

Voice rising, Professor Anderson snapped, "It's never been studied because it is not a language! It has no proper grammatical structure or form! It is an ill-formed manner of communicating developed by people for whom proper English is beyond their intellectual capabilities."

"Is this your latest theory, Professor Anderson?" Professor Colby dryly asked. "That the ability to speak proper English has to do with intellectual capabilities. I wonder how our colleagues in Germany feel about that."

"You know what I mean." Professor Anderson flushed. "I'm simply making a point about Miss Varnes's premise."

Professor Colby cut him off. "It was at my suggestion that she include that theory in her thesis. As I went through the notes Miss Varnes sent back, I noticed certain words that seemed to stand out and sent them over to my colleague at Columbia, Dr. William Payton, the noted linguist. Ten years ago, he spent some time in Africa studying the Bantu languages along the eastern coast. He has a working knowledge, and he was very intrigued by some of the words and their origin. As a matter of fact, he is trying to raise the funds to go down there himself based on what I've shared with him."

The others looked impressed, while Professor Anderson muttered, "Pidgin English at best!"

Watching them scan their notes for more information, Amelia felt a calmness sweep over her. Her worry about her mother, her anxiety about her studies, her fears for their future, and the exhaustion that had dogged her since her return, all fell into place as the strength of the elders slipped over her. Amelia spoke confidently. "It seems to me that what I have done is what you have taught me from the beginning. To go out, observe a group of people in their own setting, and identify the practices and beliefs they have in common."

Dr. Colby nodded. "You're absolutely right. To me, her thesis goes to the heart of our science. Determining without presumption which indicators make up a distinct culture. And I, for one, am very pleased with the work that she has done in a relatively short period of time."

There was silence as the others considered his words. Professor Highman nodded as he flipped through the thesis, searching for some detail. Professor Rehnquist shrugged, tapped his pencil on the desk, considering the point made. Amelia watched Professor Anderson, who flushed when he met her eyes. "Is there anything else before we move on?" Professor Colby inquired.

"The writing . . . ," Professor Anderson insisted. "There seems to be an inordinate amount of adjectives and adverbs. It's not as clean of personal . . . ah . . . feelings as it could be."

"Point noted," Professor Colby responded briskly. "Anything else? Now, Miss Varnes and her research assistant"—she smiled at his reference to Ben—"also took part in an experiment that I needed to have conducted for some colleagues of mine. She'll show you the results of that experiment." He nodded to Amelia, who walked over to the projector and set the film up for viewing.

She had just completed it the night before, carefully, protectively choosing what she wanted to share with them and what she would share with her family when she and her mother returned. From footage of Elizabeth and the children sprinting down the dunes, to the men cleaning the fish on the docks, to the churchgoers shouting in church, there was only the sound of the projector running as the images flashed on the screen. She had put together a pictorial story that ran through the lives of the people, never intruding, but showing their everyday realities and capturing their grace. She had chosen the footprints on the beach as the final sequence.

No one stirred as she turned on the lights and rewound the film.

Professor Colby beamed as she removed the reel. Without either a word to the Committee or a care for what they might have to say, she left the examination room.

Elizabeth looked behind her at Miss Evangeline and Miss Genevieve huddled together in the stern of Willis George's boat. As soon as he learned that Ol Trent was dead, Eli had sent Elizabeth over to get a telegram off to Trent's sister down in Savannah. When Elizabeth got to Beaufort, she asked Willis George to wait for her while she went up to Charleston to let some of Trent's other relatives know. She managed to catch the last bus and went straight to the Bouvier house. When Katie opened the door, she strode past her to the parlor. She entered without knocking, walked over to where the startled sisters sat, and held her hand out to Miss Evangeline. Miss Evangeline slowly held her hand out, and Elizabeth dropped the gold band into her palm.

Miss Evangeline stared at the ring that Elizabeth had given her. She turned it over and ran her finger along the inscription inside the band. Miss Genevieve pulled her robe around her and crossed to the highboy to pour her sister a glass of brandy. Miss Evangeline reached for the glass and drank quickly, as Miss Genevieve put her arm around her, comforting her. Miss Evangeline looked over to Elizabeth with eyes shimmering with tears.

"He looked like he just sat down to rest," Elizabeth responded to her unspoken question. "The ring was in his pocket."

"It never occurred to me that he would have kept the ring," Miss Evangeline said slowly. She looked to Elizabeth desperately. "Do you think he remembered anything?" Elizabeth looked at the old woman, bent with sorrow and regret, and shook her head.

"I really don't know."

Miss Evangeline nodded, closing her fist tightly over the band. "What will happen to him?"

"I sent a telegram to his sister," Elizabeth explained. "They're gonna bury him tomorrow night." She hesitated. "I just thought you'd want to know."

As she turned to leave, Miss Evangeline called after her, looking to Miss Genevieve for support. Not for the first time did Elizabeth wonder which one was the stronger sister. "I want to go back with you." Her voice drifted across the room to where Elizabeth stood. "I need to tell my husband good-bye."

Elizabeth waited patiently as the sisters and Katie scurried around, grabbing what they would need to make the trip out to the Island. She briefly worried about what the night air would do to these older women, but dismissed it when she saw Miss Evangeline's determination. They made the trip to Beaufort and set out with Willis George just as the sun went down. If Willis George was surprised to see Elizabeth with the two older white women, he gave no sign as he helped them into the boat.

"Tell dem to hold on!" Willis George instructed Elizabeth. "We gonna try to get into the pier if the water aint too rough." She warned them and kept an eye out as Willis George and J.C. made their way to the dock.

Eli opened the door when the group walked up onto the porch. If Willis George had been stoic, Eli's surprise left him speechless. He had met the Bouvier sisters years before, but would never have recognized the two shivering old women that Elizabeth ushered into his home that night. Eula heated up coffee and pulled out quilts to warm them.

He took Elizabeth aside as Eula cared for them. "What going on here? I send you to Beaufort, and you come back with these two!"

"They come for Trent's funeral," Elizabeth whispered to her father.

He looked at her disbelieving. "I dont understand. They aint never come out here to see him."

Elizabeth's next words hushed him into silence. "Daddy, Miss Evangeline was his wife." Eli turned and stared at the two women, then retreated to where the rest of his family sat silently watching the visitors.

Amelia had been waiting for half an hour for Professor Colby to show. She looked up at the office clock and then over at his secretary, who apologized, "I'm sorry. He always runs a bit late, but this is unusual." Amelia sighed. "I'll wait a little while, but I've got to get back home."

"Your family must be really excited about your graduation," the secretary ventured. Amelia nodded. Actually she had not thought much about graduation or anything else but the move back to the Island.

She had much to do at home. She and Myown were packing. It had taken so little to get Myown to agree to move back with her. She had resisted at first only because she thought Amelia was doing this for her sake, and she did not want to take Amelia away from the opportunities that the city offered. But Amelia convinced her that this would be the best move for both of them, to return to the Island. Myown had given her a gift by sending her away to learn about her family. Amelia wanted to share with her mother all that she had learned in the place where she had learned it. Eula's response to the letter Myown had sent had been the final assurance Myown needed. "Come home," she wrote. "Come home where you belong."

Just as Amelia stood up to leave, Professor Colby burst into his office, breathless with excitement. "Oh-h! I was afraid you would have left! I have such exciting news!" He waved her into his office. "I was just at a meeting with the Board of the American Anthropological Society, and they want you to present your paper at the yearly conference in the fall!" She blinked and dropped into the chair. "It is a wonderful opportunity," he rushed on. "It guarantees your work will be published in at least two of the most preeminent journals in the country. Why, they may even want to publish it as a monograph! You have no idea of what you have started!" He beamed at her.

Amelia recoiled at his words, her worst fears coming true. He stared at her, puzzled by her pained expression. "When I told them about the film, they could not wait to extend the invitation," he said, but his words died as she began to shake her head.

She trembled and then looked at him. "I can't present it."

"Why can't you? What is this, some kind of stage fright?" She shakily drew in her breath. "What is it?" When she did not respond, he became angry. "I don't understand what's going on here! I got some of the best work that I've ever seen from one of my students and she can't present it?"

Amelia summoned her courage. "I won't present it." She sensed, rather than saw, his body twitch with surprise. They sat in silence for a few seconds until he quietly asked, "Do you want to tell me what's going on? Why you would refuse to present your work?"

"I'm scared . . ." she began slowly, "scared about the kind of change this is going to bring." She struggled to explain. "What's going to happen to my family and my friends when everyone starts flooding in, asking them about details of their lives that are just natural to them? I know it's selfish, but they are a proud people, an independent kind of people. They've survived slavery, crop disasters, hurricanes, and floods, and I don't want them to lose what brought them through.

"The first class I took with you, you taught us about respecting what we were to study . . . but you also taught us about change and how as anthropologists we were not to introduce change. I can't help but worry that I've already brought change, and I'm afraid that if this paper gets published, it will bring about the worst kind of change."

"Miss Varnes, change is going to come to the Island," Professor Colby warned her. "If it's not through you, it will be someone else. You can't stop that. Why, your benefactor is sitting down with planners as we speak, talking about what he's going to build out there in the next few years."

"I know I can't stop change, but Lord knows, I don't have to be an agent of it."

"But what of all your work?" Professor Colby argued. "It's wonderful! You deserve the acclaim it will bring."

Amelia considered this and then smiled slightly. "I didn't write it for that, and I don't need that! I got so much more out of it than that."

"It's a vital piece of work." He pressed her again. "It needs to be shared with others."

Amelia stood up to leave and extended her hand. "I understand what you're saying, but I don't want it published." They gazed at each other until he nodded with respect and understanding, then handed her the thesis.

"You've done excellent work. When you're ready to take it further, you know how to contact me."

She looked around the room and then turned to open the door. Professor Colby stopped her. "Will we have the pleasure of your company at graduation?"

When she turned to him, he was startled at the bright smile that lit her face. "No, I'm going back to the Island. My mother and I, we're going home."

Elizabeth and Katie sat on the back steps, shelling peas. "I aint never heard of nuttin like dat!" Katie frowned at Elizabeth. "Your cousin an her mama movin back down here from New York? Dont dey know everybody down here want to move up dere!"

"When you gonna move up to New York?" Elizabeth teased Katie.

Katie gasped, "O-o-h, chile! I heard bout all dat stuff going on! It too fast for me!"

Elizabeth laughed. For all of her sixteen years, Katie talked like an old woman, most probably like the grandmother who raised her. Elizabeth imagined that Nana would have been like this at the same age. She half-listened as Katie ran on, filling her in on all the gossip about the neighbors that Elizabeth did not know and her friends whom Elizabeth would probably never meet.

School had closed two weeks before, and Elizabeth had come over to meet Amelia and Myown's train, which was due the next morning. The whole family was excited by the homecoming, and Eli was finishing the repairs on Nana's house so that Myown and Amelia could move in with Elizabeth. What had been an uncertain summer took on a different meaning when Elizabeth learned that Amelia was coming back.

She had not seen the Bouviers since she brought them back from Trent's funeral. It had been a quiet affair, with Trent's sister, the Bouviers, the Peazants, and a few others who came to pay their respects to the family. Elizabeth had been surprised when Miss Evangeline had insisted on being taken back to the old Wilkerson place and the shack where Ol Trent had lived. Miss Genevieve decided to stay at the house with Eula, to whom she had taken an immediate liking. They had walked slowly, Miss Evangeline commenting on the wild beauty of the land. When they reached the meadow, she gasped with recognition. Elizabeth helped her to a stump and waited for her to explain. Miss Evangeline shook with tears. "It is the garden we looked down upon from our apartment in Paris. It looked so wild. We thought it was untended until we saw the little man who took such care." Elizabeth walked over to the plot and picked a bouquet from Trent's flowers for Miss Evangeline.

She thought Miss Evangeline would surely collapse when she saw the shack where Trent had spent so much of his time. "His sister said the house would be comfortable, fine for him!" she cried. "That he would want for nothing!"

"He was all right here," Elizabeth reassured her. Stepping ahead, Miss Evangeline made her way to the shack. Running her hands along the rough wood that framed the doorway, she walked into the cool darkness of the room. Elizabeth waited outside, listening to the soft sobs that floated in the air. When she finally appeared in the doorway, Elizabeth saw her exhaustion and hurried to get her back to the Peazant house. The whole family was moved by the depth of her grief, but it took Eli to remind them, "She didn't know him when he was alive!"

Later that night after supper, Elizabeth knocked on the door to the parlor to see if the Bouviers wanted anything before she went upstairs. Miss Genevieve eagerly invited her in. "Elizabeth, what took you so long? We've been waiting for you!"

"I was helping Katie clean up." She noticed the air of excitement about Miss Genevieve. Miss Evangeline sat in her chair, staring into the fire. Her expression softened as she took in Elizabeth. "Come in. Sit down! Would you like a glass of sherry?" Elizabeth, bemused, shook her head. "I just stopped by to see if you needed anything before I went up to my room."

The two sisters exchanged a look, then Miss Evangeline nodded to Miss Genevieve, who blurted out, "We're going to Paris!"

Elizabeth frowned at them in astonishment. "That's wonderful!"

Miss Genevieve went on, "We haven't been back since Sister married, and now we want to go before we're too old!" Her eyes sparkled with excitement. "I can't imagine how it's changed!"

Elizabeth let all of this register and then asked, "When are you leaving?"

Miss Genevieve exclaimed, "At the end of the month, if we can get the house closed up and everything taken care of! We have to get new passports, book passage, buy traveling clothes, so many details." As Elizabeth watched Miss Evangeline, she realized that she had never seen Miss Evangeline just sit; usually she was working on papers, or reading. But now she sat quietly, her hands folded, her mind seemingly memories away.

Elizabeth stood up, "Well, I guess I need to really start clearing out that attic now! If you don't need me for anything, I'll try to finish some of it before I leave tomorrow." Miss Genevieve fluttered her hands at her, then turned frantically to her sister.

Miss Evangeline, sensing her sister's anxiety, said quietly, "We'd like you to come with us, Elizabeth."

Elizabeth's voice shook with shock. "What?"

Miss Evangeline calmly explained, "We'd like you to come with us as our companion. We need someone to help us make the arrangements and see to the details. You'd be perfect. We're not as young as we used to be."

Elizabeth dropped in the chair. "I can't! I don't know how I'd do this! I've got . . ." Her voice trailed off as that old fear swept over her. "My daddy would never let me go over there!"

"You can't say that," Miss Genevieve soothed her. "He and your mother are such nice people."

Miss Evangeline added, "Above all, he seems to be a reasonable man. You could ask."

Elizabeth stared at them as if they had lost their minds. Lord have mercy! They did not know Eli!

"Would you like a glass of sherry, dear?" Miss Genevieve asked with worried eyes.

"No! Thank you! No!" She saw her whole world shift as she considered the possibility of Paris. Her mind reeled with sensations and long abandoned dreams. Just when she had decided that this opportunity mustn't be real, Miss Evangeline turned her head to say, "After all, if we went to Paris without you, Elizabeth, Natalie would never forgive us."

Amelia stood on the station platform and relived the anxiety that she had felt the year before when she first waited for Elizabeth to come for her. She settled Myown on the bench while she went to look for Elizabeth. The trip had taken a lot out of Myown, and she had leaned heavily on Amelia when they got off the train in Beaufort. Amelia had wanted Myown to spend a few days resting at the boarding house, but Myown had insisted on going to the Island as soon as possible. "I wont rest til I get dere nohow," she assured Amelia, who knew that it was the truth for both of them.

The last few days before their departure had been difficult. From the moment of Amelia's announcement, Haagar had subjected them to a cold, angry silence so unlike her usual tirades. Her father had retreated to his business. Amelia felt pity for the two, left only with what they cared about most. She and Myown both longed to leave that house filled with so much anger and pain.

The day before they were to leave, Haagar stepped into their half-empty room, inspecting the boxes that sat sealed on the floor. Myown lay asleep on the bed; Amelia sat at the window staring down on the street activity. "You gonna miss all that!" Haagar announced.

Amelia turned from the window. "I didn't miss it before."

"That was when you knew you was coming back," Haagar said with confidence. "I want you to know that when you get down there and things get rough for you, don't say I didn't tell you the truth of it!" Amelia picked up the shawl that she had kept out for Myown and folded it. Haagar stood at the foot of the bed and looked down on her daughter. "She don't have that long." Amelia started to hush her grandmother, but was stilled by the sadness in Haagar's face. Haagar touched the coverlet at the foot of the bed. "This was the first quilt I ever made, for my gals, Iona and Myown. Lord, they was silly chilren, always gigglin an playin together!" She moved away from the bed and looked at the boxes. "All I wanted was to keep my chilren safe. The only way I knew was to keep them close to me. But it seem they thought it was the worse place they could be. First, Iona run off with that boy. Just look me in the face an walk, no run, from everyting I done for her. And then Ninny Jugs, he couldn't stay put nowhere. Ever time I thought he was gonna stay and take care of his mama, he only come for the money an then he gone, too. I love all my children, but Lord, I love him best. He was the image of he daddy, an everting I didn't give he Daddy, I give to him!" She looked directly at Amelia. "And now you going, too. She sick as a dog, and she willing to die just to get outta here! It don't say much for me, does it?"

Amelia did not know what to say. Her grandma was not an evil woman, but she spared no one in her resolve to get what she wanted. Amelia wondered what Haagar would have been like if she had known love at any point in her life. While she cared for her grandmother, she had to admit that it was from respect and fear, not love.

"Well, I'm gonna be coming down sometime to make sure you doing all right." Haagar watched Amelia closely for her reaction. "It my home, too!" Haagar challenged her. Then she dug in her pocket and pulled out an envelope. "Here!" Amelia hesitated. "It ain't much, but it should ease things until you get settled!"

Amelia took it. "Thank you, Granma!"

"That's right! Whether yall like it or not, I take care of yall!" She moved to the door. "An don't be thinking about trying to get me to stay down there when I come! Cause you can't pay me to stay down there!" She took one last look at the room and swept out.

Later that evening, Amelia helped Myown downstairs to the parlor where she waited for her husband after he completed his work. She had reassured Amelia that after twenty-four years of marriage she had a few things she needed to get off her chest before she left. Amelia, afraid to leave her, had sat on the stairs waiting for her father to appear. He was surprised to see her and he gazed at her suspiciously. "Mama waiting for you," she informed him and saw the look of unease that passed across his face. He entered the parlor and closed the door, while Amelia waited for Myown, who emerged an hour later. She searched her mother's face for a sign of pain or anger and was comforted by the serenity in her eyes.

When they were halfway through the trip south, Myown shared what she had told her husband. "I tol he him got to do right by dat woman got dem chilren for he!" Myown spoke shortly, her soft words edged with anger. "I knowed about she for a long time, livin in dat cold water flat. You an de oldest one de same age! I see dem, an dey living hard, tryin to make do wit de nuttin he give she! He wasnt no kind of daddy to you, he could at least be a daddy to dem chilren!" Her mother patted her hand, comforting her, "It all right! Everything all right!"

Now, Amelia turned as she heard her name. Elizabeth stood at the doorway to the trainyard. They ran to each other and hugged, laughing with excitement. They were both talking so fast that neither of them understood the other. They started, then stopped again. Amelia led Elizabeth to where Myown rested. In no time, they had the car loaded and were headed off to the pier, where Willis George waited for them.

Wiping the sweat from his face, Eli stood at the edge of the roof and looked at the repairs that he had just completed. He nodded with satisfaction and then called out to St. Julien, who worked on the other end of the roof. "Julien, I could do with some water. What about you?" Julien nodded and waved. Eli turned and yelled to one of the many children playing in the yard, "Yall fill up dat bucket down dere, us need some water up here on dis hot roof!" When he could not get anyone's attention, he called to Rebecca, who was playing dolls with Neeny. "Becca! Becca! Get us some water in dat bucket!" She and Neeny jumped up and ran to get the water. Eli mumbled, turning back to his work, "De lil ones always got de most sense."

Julien drained the dipper and then handed it to Eli. From their perch on the roof, they could see all along the shore. At the edge of the dunes, Eula, Elizabeth, Amelia, and Clemmie had set the pots over the fires and were preparing the food for dinner. Farther down the beach, he could see his wife walking with her sister. Myown leaned on the walking stick that Ben had carved for her. Out in the water, Ben and Chance pulled the net filled with fish and shrimp into the boat. Eli followed St. Julien's gaze, then looked down on the horde in the yard. "Whole passel of dem, aint it?" A rare grin spread across St. Julien's face as he watched his children and their cousins wage mock war in the yard below them.

Eli was glad for St. Julien's company. This past week, he had felt himself being surrounded, besieged, by women. His house had not been the same since Amelia and Myown had arrived. They were staying with them until the repairs to Nana's house were completed, and as much as he cared for them, Eli just couldn't relax and be himself with all those women around. He lamented the loss of his Sunday afternoon with Eula. When he saw Clemmie and Iona walk up in the yard with the other children, he had strained to see if St. Julien had come with them and was much relieved to see him bringing up the rear.

What was worse was that they were keeping something from him. He could feel it. When he'd walk up, they would get quiet or start talking about something that did not make any kind of sense. Certain things would be said with a certain tone, and every now and then, he would surprise a furtive glance from one of them. Eula was skittish, running around the house like a mouse, Lil Bet watched him like a hawk, Amelia threw him questioning glances, and every time he looked at My-own, she smiled knowingly at him. He had just about had enough. Something would have to give.

He and St. Julien finished the last bit of work on the roof just as Eula called them to dinner. After making their way down from the roof, they strolled over to where all the food was laid out. For once, the children were fairly orderly, waiting to move through the line and be served. Eula waved Eli and St. Julien to the front of the line and handed them plates piled with red beans, rice, green beans, okra, fresh tomatoes, collard greens, deviled eggs, corn bread, boiled shrimp and crab, and fried brim. They found a place away from the chaos and the chatter among the dunes and ate in silence.

They both looked up as Elizabeth made her way around the side of the dune, carrying two mason jars of lemonade. "Mama sent this to you," she said. Eli and St. Julien thanked her between bites and sips.

"You not eating?" Eli asked.

"I'll get something a little bit later." She stood over them, gazing out to the sea. "Why dont you sit wit us a while?" Eli invited.

Hesitating, she drew a pattern in the sand with her bare foot, then spoke, her voice quivering. "I need to talk with you, Daddy."

There was something in her tone that alarmed Eli. "What's wrong, Lil Bet?" he asked her.

"Ain't nothing wrong. I just need to talk with you, that's all." She stopped St. Julien as he stood up to leave. "No, Cousin Julien, you don't have to go nowhere. This family business." Eli waited patiently for her to find her words.

She started, then stopped, then started again. "Daddy, the . . . the . . . Miss . . ." She stumbled as he began to frown, then it came out in a rush, "Miss Evangeline and Miss Genevieve want me to go to Paris with them!"

So this was what all the whispering had been about. Eli's temper flared at the realization. His response was sharp. "Dey want to take you away from here! Dey must be crazy thinkin I gonna let you go running off with dem!"

"Daddy, it just for the summer," Elizabeth explained. "They need someone to go with them and take care of them!"

"You aint no ladies' maid," Eli snapped. "You a schoolteacher! Dey can find somebody else to do dat!"

Elizabeth looked to Julien, who watched her with steady eyes. She whispered, "I want to go!"

Eli jumped to his feet. "What? Now, you done outdone yourself now! I'd be crazy to let you go haring off like you aint got a lick of sense."

"I want to go!" she said quickly. "If I don't go now, I'll never get a chance like this again! I want to go!"

Eli set his face, frowning at her. "What make you think you got to go anyplace? Dis your home! Right here! Who been tellin you you aint got to be here?" The laughter and the chatter died down as his angry words floated across the sand.

Elizabeth held her head down and then looked up at him. "You."

Eli stepped back from her. "What dis foolishness?" Eula ran around the dune to where they both stood, the rest of the family scampering behind her. "Eula! Eula!" Eli appealed to her. "Talk to dis girl! She tellin me I the one dat tell she her aint got to be here!"

For the first time in her life, Elizabeth raised her voice to her father. "Why you send me away, Daddy, if it not to tell me I ain't got to be here?"

Eli's voice trembled with rage. "I send you for de schoolin so you can come back an help!"

"And I did, Daddy, I done everything you asked me to. I done everything to make you proud! When do I do something for me? When do I do something for me?" Elizabeth cried.

"You aint goin!" Eli shouted. "You get that straight in your head!"

Elizabeth nodded. "Yes, I am."

Eli turned to Eula. "Dis why I send she to school so she can mock me?"

Eula was agitated. "Eli, it aint like dat! She got de chance to do more dan we ever thought, an you gonna stop dat?" Eli stepped back from his wife and looked at all the others waiting and watching him.

He threw a sign of disgust at the ground and quickly walked away. Elizabeth and Eula looked after him, their faces mirroring their pain.

"**D**is gone on long enough." Eula rubbed her back as she straightened from picking the pole beans. She listened to the ring of Eli's hammer against the anvil as he worked the fire and iron. She had always been able to tell Eli's mood by the sounds of his work. She winced as his sadness and anger vibrated through the air. It had been very quiet these past few days, too quiet since Elizabeth had talked to Eli about going with the Bouvier sisters to Paris. Even the twins had been subdued as the silence between Eli and Elizabeth had thickened. It hurt Eula to watch as her husband struggled with his fears and her oldest daughter disappeared into her silence. She had thought to let them work this out together, but they had both withdrawn to that place where they only heard themselves. She sighed with weary understanding. They were that alike.

She looked down at her apron full of pole beans. She still had to snap them and put them on to cook for dinner. It was at times like this that she really missed Lucy. Eula could not remember the last time she had picked beans. It had been Lucy's chore, and she had relished it, saying it relaxed her. Eula shook her head at the thought of picking anything being relaxing.

Making her way to the back porch, she dumped the beans into the basin of cold water. In a little while, Elizabeth would pass by on her way to school, but she would not linger as she normally would have. It had not been lost on Elizabeth and Eula that Eli was up and out much earlier these days, long before Elizabeth would stop by. They both understood that Eli was not being cruel, that he needed time to put it all together. But it had gone on long enough, and now Eula wanted it to end.

She wiped her hands on her apron and struck out for the path that led to Nana's house. She called to Myown, who sat on the front porch, laying out the grass for a new basket, "I be back directly."

Elizabeth had been up before day clean. These days, the sleep would not come, and she would lie in the darkness, trying not to think too hard about Paris or any other possibilities. Mindful of disturbing Amelia, she had gathered her pieces of cloth and flowers and slipped out to the front porch to work on a new charm. But she couldn't make it right and had torn it apart with restless fingers.

As the morning light rose, she built the fire and placed the coffeepot on to boil.

Amelia rolled over and sat up, pulling the covers around her. "You get any sleep?"

Elizabeth shrugged, handing Amelia a cup of coffee. "A bit here an there."

They saw each other from a distance, Elizabeth slowing her steps, Eula rushing forward in anticipation. "What wrong, Mama?" Elizabeth asked cautiously, as it was unusual for Eula to venture out at this time of the morning. "Just missin my oldest. You dont stop through like you used to." Elizabeth blinked rapidly, trying to stop the hurtful tears. Eula reached out and grasped Elizabeth's hands. "He dont want you runnin from him."

Elizabeth nodded. "Then why dont he say something? I come up on him, an he nod an move on."

Eula led her to a fallen tree limb, and they sat down. "He too full. You done hit he wit every hope an fear him have for you all at one time. Him got to lay it out on de ground, throw it up in de air, walk roun it, to see it for what it be."

Elizabeth burst out, "Mama, he wont even look me in the eye!"

"Cause him see all of heself," Eula soothed her. "It fittin dat de one him deny be de one most like he."

"Mama, I done everything he ask, everything! The one thing I want so bad I can feel it burning in me day and night, he deny me!"

Eula slipped her arm around Elizabeth as she rocked with anguish. "Child, your daddy can no more deny you dan he can deny himself."

"Why he hold on to me like that? He let Ben come and go like he please. Lucy gone off with Charlie. Why he hold on to me?"

Eula answered quietly, "Cause dere was a time when he not sure you his."

As a child, Elizabeth had heard the whispers, the bits of conversation, caught the odd glance, but had put it down to the peculiar ways of adults. She half-remembered Nana chasing Miz Lillian out of her yard after a pointed remark about "dat sposed to be image of Eli sitting dere on de steps." She had clapped with delight when Miz Lillian fell in the soft sand and scrambled across the path like an old crab, ducking the crabapples that Nana tossed at her.

It terrified her to ask a question that she sensed had hung over her since her birth. Elizabeth stared into her mother's eyes and saw past the love and honesty she had always seen to a glimmer of remembered anguish. Although she had sensed that there was some trouble between Eli and Eula before she was born, she had never heard Eula speak of her pregnancy in anything other than joyful terms. Elizabeth shivered as Eula's face reflected the memories and emotions of that long-ago pregnancy. Eula saw the fear that shook her daughter and gently squeezed her hand, finally giving Elizabeth the courage to ask, "Why, Mama? Why Daddy think I not his?"

Eula shook her head, heavy with memories. She led Elizabeth over to the old tree stump that sat at the edge of Nana's property. Placing Elizabeth's hands on the markings that scored the trunk, she asked, "Do you member de lie Nana tell bout de coming of de Unborn Chile?"

Elizabeth smiled. The Unborn Chile had been a favorite character of Nana's, always getting into trouble and working her way out. She nodded her head. "I recall lil bits of it. It one of the old stories Nana love to tell."

Eula sat on the edge of the stump and eased Elizabeth down beside her. "De story not dat ol, Lil Bet."

De Unborn Chile

as told by Eula Peazant

When de captives first come to dis lan, dey protect by de ol spirits. Dem ol spirits follow dem cross de big water, an no matter how bad it get, de captives know dat Yemoja, Oshun, Elegba, Ogun, an all de others watch over dey. Dont bring dem no more dan dey can bear, an if it get too much, dey take dem back, sen Aganju to cross dem to de other side.

But time pass, things change from de ol ways, an de captives dey forget to do de things for de ol spirits like dey used to. It a life filled with nothin but hard times, an de captives think de ol spirits dont look after dem no more. Dey dont set out de sweet cake so Oshun will bless de house wit many chilren, dey forget de anger of Shango when lightning rain down on dey heads, dey dont know how Oya can bring life an death to de house at de same time. Now, de ol spirits, dey dont like dis one bit, dis disrespectin de old ways, an some want to make it a bit harder for de captives, but Yemoja stop dem. Her say, "No, time come when dey come back to we."

Come a gal an she a frisky lil thing, pretty lil gal. Her mama, she sisters set such store by she. Dey spoil she, but not too much. Her not think much about nothin, jus being a frisky lil gal, play wit she sisters, work in de field, go to church. Den dere was a boy. Him know she since dey lil. Oh, him an he friends dey use to bother dose gals, chase dem, pull dat hair, all dat kind of boy foolishness. Dey all play together, an one day dat boy see dat lil gal aint so lil no more. Her see he an him no pullin dat hair, him want to walk wit she an hol dat hand. Dey sweethearts, an it not long fore dey marry. An dey happy. Oh, dey scrap every now an den, but dey happy.

One day her go to she mama house and work with she mama an sisters on de quilt for she sister baby. It get real dark, an her wait at she mama house for he to come get her home. But he no come, an her get mad. Her fraid of de dark, but her mad. She mama tell she to stay de night, but no, her gonna go home an give he a piece of she mind! Her strike out in all dat dark wit de lamp she mama give she.

In dat woods dere live de debil, layin out dere in de darkness waitin for somebody to come by. Him gettin weak an him lookin to snatch a soul cause it make he strong. Well, him see dat light comin through de wood, an him see dat lil gal. Him real happy, to snatch de soul of a woman-child make he plenty strong. Woman-child she carry de spirit of life, an de debil always want de spirit of life. Him call on de Big Wind to blow dat light out. An he come on she in de dark an tear at she, come to steal dat soul, take everyting dat woman-child got! But her send dat soul flyin, tell it to fly to de top of de tree. No matter dat debil did to she, tear de clothes from she back, beat she in de ground, dat debil no get she soul! De debil so mad him want she to die, an when him run off in de darkness, him tink she dead. But dat soul come down from dat treetop to find de spirit of life in she. Soul try to get she up, but her too weak.

She man him come looking for she, an when him find she lyin in de brush all broken, him cry like de bear in de woods. Him get her to he grandmother house, but dat girl bout to leave dis worl. Her soul float ober she crying cause her hurt so bad. Dat ol woman her call all de elders together an her tell dem, "Dis gal got a chile coming, an it a special child. Us need dis chile! Cant let dis girl leave here an take dat chile wit she!"

De elders start to callin on de ol spirits, cryin out to Yemoja, Oshun, Elegba, Ogun! Dont let dis gal leave here! Now dem ol spirits, dey been waitin for de call. Just like Yemoja say, dey time come. Dem ol spirits, dey aint tinkin bout helpin so much cause de young folks aint show dem deir propers. Dat ol woman her tell she grandson, "Boy, you gotta call on de spirits. Dey aint lissenin to we!"

Dat man pray to every god him know to bring his woman back to dey worl. Him prayers so pitiful even Ogun feelin bad! Ogun tell he, "We bring she back to dis worl, but it not gonna be easy for you!" Him say him dont care, "Jus bring she back!" Oshun say, "De fault of dis is yourn to bear." Him take de fault. Elegba warn he, "Doubt gonna walk wit you all you days." "Cant be no worse dan it is now!" him say. Den Yemoja tell he, "Dis chile dat comin, her a special chile, dis Unborn Chile, got de ways of de elders. Her come from you seed, an her come from way back. From de first moment she mama feel she move, her know her gonna be a chile wit a way of she own, got she own road to walk. You gonna try to hold dis chile close, but her not belong to you! De more you try to hold dis chile close, de more her got to go! But her always come back if everyting all right wit yall." Yemoja words scare he, but him want he woman back.

First de spirits seek out dat debil, still skulking back dere in dem woods. Dey know dey got to fight de debil to git she soul to come back. An de debil ready cause him like a good fight. But dem some smart spirits. Send Elegba to tell he de joke. Him laugh so hard him can hardly stand up. Meanwhile, Ogun build de iron straps to hold he. Den Oshun walk though de woods, lookin like de pretty woman her is. Him see she. Oh, him caint wait! Him gonna do to she what him done to dat girl. He follow she into de deep woods, an Ogun throw de iron straps round he. Him holler, but dem straps hold he tight for Yemoja. Her come. Him scared cause she plenty powerful. Her call down de fire on he, burn he to a crisp, den her call on de waters to rise an rise an wash he away.

Den de spirits call on she soul who was flutterin all about, tell dat soul to get back in she where she belong! Dey raise up dat woman, an each one give she a bit of dey strength for de days to come. Yemoja warn she, "Chile, you gonna see some trials!" From dat time on she felt dat chile growin inside she. Her was such a restless chile dat her would burst from she mama womb an travel de lan on she own. Causin mischief wherever she traveled, snatch de clothes from de line, steal de pie from de window, scatter de cards when de men was playing. Folks took to callin out to she, "Dere she go, dat Unborn Chile!"

When she daddy forgot what de spirits say an let de doubt turn his mind, de Unborn Chile brought comfort to she mama. An when it time for she to come, her take de longest journey, wore her mama out coming, got she daddy praying to dem ol spirits again. Her come an folks was happy! Cryin an laughin! Didnt know what to do. She daddy hol she in he arms, see he face in she, know how far her come. Him swear dat he gonna do right by she. Dat what him always try to do. Him try to hold she close, but him know dat her gonna leave.

Elizabeth sat in the dark on the porch, waiting for Eli to come home. Everyone else had gone to bed, though Elizabeth suspected that Eula was simply lying down, she too listening for the sound of his return. She had surprised herself in the conflict with her father, had been startled when she felt her temper flare to meet his. She felt shame. She had only to look inside herself to understand her father's fears.

She heard a sound and held her breath. It came again, and she knew that someone was coming through the yard. Drawing back into the chair, she watched Eli make his way to the porch and sit heavily on the steps. He sat, his hands on his knees, gazing out at the dark night. There was hardly a star in the sky and clouds blew past the moon. "Lil Bet?"

She jumped at the sound of his voice. "Yes, sir?"

"First time I lay eyes on you, I knew you was different. I could see in your eyes dat you been here longer dan we ever know. Sometime it scare me, you lookin at me wit de eyes of de elders like you knowed what I was thinkin, feelin. It aint never scared your mama. Her was all right wit you from de first time you move in she. I was de one filled wit doubt and rage. Her was de one wronged, an I carried enough shame for both of we. But when you come, you was mine. An I knew dat, an you knew dat. An I wanted everyting for you, to make up for dat time when I didnt want you." He shook his head. "You was right. I send you away cause I want better for you, an I brung you back cause I fraid of how you become. I so proud of you. I want to bring you back an keep you here cause I fraid you do like all de rest . . . leave an forget about dose dey left behind."

She struggled to speak. "Daddy, I got to go! I got to see what it like out there!"

He raised his hand, stilling her words. He stood and stretched, rubbing his back. He walked onto the porch. "I aint saying you can go. You got to give me time to get my mind around it." He held his hand out to help her out of the chair, "Come on. I know your mama waiting on us."

Peace Bath

Mix five drops of cypress oil with three drops of nutmeg, 2 drops of lavender, and three drops of sweet oil. Fill the tub with hot water and pour the peace bath in. After it has set long enough for the aroma of the spices to fill the room (maybe ten to fifteen minutes), pour cool water in to make a comfortable bath.

It was a killer game of hide and seek. Amelia rubbed her hands together in anticipation as she stalked her prey. She especially like hunting Neeny, who never failed to answer from any hiding place when called. She turned her head and saw the overturned wash tub move an inch. Creeping up to it, she grabbed the sides and lifted it just as Shadda spurted out and headed for the home tree, squealing. Throwing the tub to the side, she dashed after him.

"I ain't never seen my child play like dat." Iona chuckled at Myown's comment. "Come, dinnertime, she gonna be worn out."

Iona looked at the basket that Myown was weaving. "Dat a pretty pattern. Where you learn dat?"

Myown coyly responded, "It sumptin I put together on my own. You aint de only one got a fair hand at dis."

Inside the house, Eula, Elizabeth, and Clemmie struggled to close the trunk. They had packed and repacked the steamer, trying to fit everything in. Even Eli had stopped by and offered unsolicited advice about the best way to pack a trunk. He had also briskly informed Elizabeth that he would be escorting her and the Bouvier sisters to the Charleston train station to see them off. Now that he had gotten his mind around it, he had concerned himself with almost every detail of their trip.

With a final push, they got the trunk closed, only to moan with dismay when Clemmie leaned over and picked up a pair of shoes that they had overlooked. Elizabeth gave up. "Let Daddy and Ben take care of that when they come to get me tomorrow." Eula agreed, collapsing into the chair. Clemmie slid from the top of the trunk and sat down on the floor with a thud. Elizabeth looked around Nana's house, which was now filled with people. She listened to the children playing in the yard and the low conversation from the stoop and it reminded her of the days when Nana ruled from her front porch. With Amelia and Myown in the house, Elizabeth hoped that Nana would not be too displeased with her leaving for Paris.

"Oh-oh! It hot in here!" Eula moaned, pulling her wet blouse away from her back.

"Let's go down to the water," Clemmie suggested.

"The evening breeze should be rollin in right about now." Elizabeth pulled Eula from the chair, and they all walked out onto the front porch. "We going to the water. Yall want to come?" Myown, who loved the water, looked for her walking stick. Iona handed it to her and helped her up. Clemmie supported her as she carefully made her way down the stairs. Amelia came from behind the house to find the procession moving to the edge of the water.

The children ran around them, racing into the water and splashing each other. Amelia's eyes watered as her mother waded into the surf, awkwardly balancing herself, and trying to kick water at Clemmie and Iona. She headed for them, joining in their laughter when Myown lost her balance, and sat down abruptly in the tide. Eula and the kids scrambled around the beach, chasing fiddler crabs back into the water, digging at the air holes with their toes.

Amelia looked for Elizabeth, who had waded farther out into the surf, gazing across the waters as she had done so many times before. Amelia brushed happy tears from her eyes as Elizabeth began a slow, elegant dance, her arms stretched skyward as if she would lift on the gentle breeze and fly.

Joy Cream

Beat 5 drops of geranium with four drops of bergamot, 3 drops of allspice, 3 drops of orange, and 10 drops of lanolin until it thickens. Heat gently over a low flame. Store in a cool place. Deep rub into the parts of the body that need it the most. It will bring joy to the soul.

The typeface used in this book is a version of Baskerville, originally designed by John Baskerville (1706–1775) and considered to be one of the first "transitional" typefaces between the "old style" of the continental humanist printers and the "modern" style of the nineteenth century. With a determination bordering on the eccentric to produce the finest possible printing, Baskerville set out at age forty-five and with no previous experience to become a typefounder and printer (his first fourteen letters took him two years). Besides the letter forms, his innovations included an improved printing press, smoother paper, and better inks, all of which made Baskerville decidedly uncompetitive as a businessman. Franklin, Beaumarchais, and Bodoni were among his admirers, but his typeface had to wait for the twentieth century to achieve its due.